ARKHAM INSTITUTIONS

ARKHAM INSTITUTIONS

WHERE THE MYTHOS MEET THE MUNDANE

Edited by
MICHAEL CIESLAK

Dragon's Roost Press

Arkham Institutions: Examining the Intersection of the Weird and the Mundae is published by Dragon's Roost Press.

All stories in this anthology are original.

Artwork by K.H. Koehler

Printed in the United States of America

Ingram ISBN: 978-1-956824-45-2

Print ISBN: 978-1-956824-36-0

Digital ISBN: 978-1-956824-37-7

Dragon's Roost Press

2470 Hunter Rd.

Brighton, MI 48114

thedragonsroost.biz

CONTENTS

PEOPLE LOVE COSMIC HORROR

Perhaps it is the sense of being something minuscule and unimportant in the universe that readers and authors identify with. Maybe it is the grand scope of the Cthulhu Mythos that draws folks in. Whatever the case, no matter where we go, bookworms and bibliophiles are always asking "When are you going to do another Lovecraft book?"

You hold in your hands the most recent release in what we have come to think of s our **Love The Mythos But Not The Man** series of Lovecraftian anthologies. Our first, *Eldritch Embraces: Putting the Love Back in Lovecraft*, is still a consistent seller almost 10 years in. *LOLcraft: A Compendium of Eldritch Humor* was released two years ago, again to great reception. So naturally we decided to move on to a third.

We don't mean to sound mercenary, it's not just about the sales. People also enjoy *writing* cosmic horror. The sheer number of submissions we receive for these titles reveals how many authors worldwide are dying to play in this particular sandbox.

Unfortunately, this means we had to reject a ton of really well written stories. This is the most difficult portion of putting together an anthology like this. If we could, we would extend the Table of

Contents infinitely into the cosmos, stretching past even the sleeping Elder Gods.

This means that the stories which *do* make the cut are the cream of the cosmic crop.

We hope you enjoy this collection which examines how the mundane institutions of the modern world would be affected by encounters with entities from the Eldritch realm.

We thank the authors for sharing their visions, artist KH Koehler for the amazing cover art, the Kickstarter backers for the financial support, and you wonderful readers for being willing to join us on another Cosmic Exploration.

Michael Cieslak

Dragon's Roost Press

THE OLD GODS' BANKER

S.L. HARRIS

Friends, it all comes down to Money. I mean *all* of it—everything. Cold, hard equations. Cold, hard cash. Yeah, sure, it's an abstraction and a representation, but when you get right down to it, Money's the universal language. The language of the world, the language of the cosmos. All that other stuff—who cares? Let it go off the rails.

So I used to tell 'em, when they'd show up at Arkham Farm, Bank, and Trust with their salt-crusted necklaces smelling of the sea, blubbering about what they were worth; their trapezohedrons, asking about a safe-deposit box; their bags of old Dutch gold, looking around all nervously...I'd always tell 'em: I don't care where it comes from, don't care what you do with it. People do good things with money, people do bad things, and damned if you can tell how it's all going to shake out anyway. Money's just the language, fellas. It's just the wheel the world spins on, and I happen to be quite good at riding that wheel. Doesn't matter which way the world wants to go. Money doesn't care, and neither do I.

This generous attitude had made me very wealthy, a respected man in the ancient and lovely little town of Arkham. It brought me business from the pillars of the community as well as the more marginal elements. Unlike First National or any of my competitors, I didn't require you to have an ancestor on the Mayflower to bank you. In one case at least, I didn't even require confirmation of a physical body. Burghers, housewives, lawyers, Italian workmen, doctors, farmers, goggle-eyed folk up from Innsmouth, college kids, loners from the backwoods. If you got the money, honey, I got the time.

Now, did I worry about fraud, dealing with these unsavory characters? Well. I have a good eye for people, if I do say so myself, I was insured up to my neck, and, when you get right down to it, some fella comes up and says that when he drained his accounts yesterday it wasn't *him*, see, *honest*, it was a crustacean from space in a rubber mask, well. Let's just say no one ever got around to taking me to court.

And theft? The vaults below the Bank & Trust were and are very full, and it was widely known that I kept more—and stranger—capital on hand than most. But you don't do business with the kinds of people I do business with without learning a little about how to keep things safe. I don't just mean my sleepy old security officer, Willy. There were wards down there that even the big fellas would have a bit of trouble getting by. And I was no pugilist, even then in my younger days, but I was no wilting lily either. So no, I didn't worry about theft.

What did worry me? What kept me up at night? Besides the business itself, I mean. Well, confidence, I suppose. The thought that people could start thinking in a different way. That they might give up on the system and that Money wouldn't mean the same thing anymore. Like I always used to say: you doubt the fundamental solidity and sanity of the world, you've got yourself a problem. But there's nice folks up at the asylum will take care of you for that. You start to doubt the fundamental solidity and sanity of the banking system, the world's got a problem. And more to the point, *I* have a problem.

So when the tall man with the unplaceable accent and the bizarre electrical sound and light show arrived in town, I wasn't afraid. But I was cautious, because he was just the sort of man who could make people doubt the reality served up with their apple pie by Ma, Pa, and the Arkham Farm, Bank, and Trust.

It didn't take him too long to find his way to my door. I take it he was interested in personally reaching every man, woman, and child in Arkham, like some two-bit bum running for president. And if you didn't make it to one of his shows, he'd find his way to you.

Old Willy let him into my office, and even sitting the man was awful tall. He had a posture that I can only compare to that of a skeleton hanging up in the medical school. That gaze of his was all sparks and explosions, little lights flaring in a dark so dark you couldn't imagine it. Those eyes could get into you. Convince you do horrible things. Could—if you looked long enough into them—show you something about the universe that you really didn't want to know.

Well, I didn't look too long. I'd heard all about him, about his shows and what happens there, and how people leave. But like I said, business is business.

"How may I help you, sir?" I asked.

His voice was deep and echoing, like it came out of those old colossi that they say have said good morning to the Egyptian dawn all down the millennia. There was *ancient* in that voice. But there was electricity too. There was *tomorrow*. And above all, there was *the end*.

"A new era is upon us," he said, "and I require your participation in the jubilee which I announce. In ancient times, there came a year when all debts were forgiven and the vaults of the king were thrown upon, that there might be festival and feasting, as though there is no tomorrow."

"Is that right?"

"I likewise require that you open your vaults, that in this chaos season, men may be glutted and drunken."

"Oh, you require, do you?" said I. "Listen, Slim. You want my vaults to open, I'll open 'em right up for you, with appropriate collateral and at..." my eyes flicked to the day's numbers, "Eight and a half percent. Just like everyone. Well, everyone I don't know. Now, I hear tell you got some fancy electrical machines you use in your little circus. I'll be glad to hold 'em for you, and you got yourself a loan."

The man's eyes flashed perilously. I saw sparks in them, dying stars, galaxies gasping their last, and streaks flying toward the empty center of the universe.

"I am *not* a peasant begging for a usurious loan. I am a herald. I am *telling* you that a new age is here. There will be a great wild dance of fear and lust and destruction, and if you are not a part of the dance, you will be trampled."

I tell you, I didn't quite get the feeling that even the dancers were getting out of that one without their toes getting a little bit trampled, if you understand me. Slim stood up, and like I said, he was very tall. But I got a little trick—nobody can look down on me. Doesn't matter if it's the Cardiff Giant or J.P. Morgan. It's 'cause I'm on the side of Money, and there ain't a person born who don't look *up* to Money.

Slim left, saying, "You think you know how the world works, but I know the little buzzing minds of men. Your vaults *will* be thrown open, and you *will* be trampled."

I stroked my chin. I could see that this was a man who wouldn't mind telling people how it's going to be. Good.

I t didn't take long for the bank run to start. Like I say, the guy was *electric*. A few well-placed words and it was a panic. All the fine burghers of Arkham were suddenly anxious after their savings, the country people over their few hard-earned dollars, the Miskatonic faculty over the little they had squirreled away, even the Starry Wisdom folks over their tax-sheltered slush fund. I had Willy close us early, but they were pounding on the windows and on the doors.

I'd made my preparations, built up my reserves, put my own lines of credit in place. I've been through a lot of panics. Ninety-three. Ninety-six. Ought-seven. Nineteen-and-ten. But this was different. I've never seen such blind, unreasoning fear. These people had been stirred up by an expert. Damn him.

Nothing for it but to go out and talk to them.

"Friends!" I said. "Friends. You all know me. You know I'm good for it. Are you going to let some stranger, some *foreigner*, tell you I'm not?" A few murmurs and mutterings. "He's telling you all about this new age, and sure, maybe he's right, but the world's always changing, and let me tell you: in the long run, the folks who keep their accounts steady are going to come out ahead. It's the folks who panic who are going to be ruined. "All there is to fear," I said, suddenly inspired, "is fear itself."

I don't know if you'll believe me, but for the first time in my life I could feel Money talking through me, Money working to save itself. Like those Pentecostals speaking in tongues, like the folks out there in the Arkham hills. In the language of Money, I rebuilt the myth for them, rebuilt the necessary story, the confidence to keep the wheel turning.

I stopped the run.

But I knew my opponent. It was not the end.

He returned that night, when the bank was closed in good order, all accounts settled. I told you I'm no pushover, but he was a terror, a nightmare walking into our world from some other that's not like anything we know. I should have kept my doors locked and sealed, but I couldn't say no to that cloaked figure at the door, that voice of command. He swept into my office, and I could feel my hair standing up like in a thunderstorm. Terror and madness were there on his left and right.

But I was on my home turf. Out there in the void he comes from there may be endless chaotic dark and mad piping. But I was sitting in my good chair in the central office of the great temple of Money, and I had my numbers, and my equations, and I clung to those. I hoped it would be enough.

"Let me tell you," he said, "how it will be."

So he began to prophecize. The future he spun out for me felt terribly real. Every detail was seared—is still seared—upon my mind as if I could see it happening in front of me. He tells me of towers falling and trams derailed. Dread machines rising to the sky and falling again horribly to earth. Electricity humming in the wires, bringing death and news of death. He related to me in lurid detail the coming pestilences, the famines, the earthquakes. Winters of great and suffocating snows. Summers scouring the land until not only crops but human hope itself withers and crumbles. Storms of dust rising up to the uncaring sky. Upheaval and uncertainty. Guilt and agony. War and holocausts to shatter the mind. New sciences of destruction, a turn toward entropy, ennui, despair. Every human thing no more than a handful of insignificant ash on a mindless wind. A whole cosmos of dead worlds spinning into blind infinity.

I held fast to what I knew as he tried to carry me with his words toward madness and despair. I held to the ideas of Money, of capital, compound interest, supply and demand, profit and loss. It felt like clinging to a tiny life raft in the cosmic flood he had poured out in my mind. But it *was* a life raft. I kept my mind together, and I think that made him very angry. But when at last he stood to go, he was smiling.

"You see," he said. "The blind idiot god will have his victory at the last. What you do or do not do will not matter. The dance is far, far older than you, and you see the music now, whether you will dance along to it or not."

When he was gone at last, I sat staring into nothing for a long time, replaying all the searing details of his prophecy. There was some magic or power in his voice that keeps every iota in my memory. It was dawn before I found the strength in myself even to move.

I started making some calls.

The weeks and months passed. The terrible man moved on from Arkham, carrying his terrible electric prophecies to far cities, and the terrible future unfurled as he said. But me, I was doing fine. Better than fine.

See, Slim screwed up. He gave me what every banker wants more than anything. What every investor, every stockbroker, every combination, every yokel with a nickel in penny stocks, and yes, every priest and prophet, would have killed for: he gave me perfect information about the future.

And a man with a lot of money to invest and perfect information— well, that man might just as well be God.

I shorted the tram companies before the accidents and played insurance games on those crumbling towers. The arms manufacturers were hurting after the War to End War, so I bought 'em up pennies on the dollar, and when Uncle Sam came knocking, well, I'm a patriot of course, but a man's got to make a profit, sir.

I was into oil before anyone quite understood what oil would mean, and you'd laugh if I told you what uranium mines were going for in 1921. The chemical companies here and over the water, preparing to deal mass death at a healthy profit—one by one, they're mine. Incidentally, I set their top minds to work on some of the essential salts an old fella abandoned in one of the Bank & Trust's safe deposit boxes long ago. With that, it wasn't long before I didn't need to worry about time, or aging, anymore.

Months turned into years. War, famine, pestilence, death, all those pretty little horses trotted in and did their show. It all happened just as that mad prophet said. And it all profited me.

I pride myself on being a pretty cool customer, a logical man, but you'll understand of course if I had a bit of an interest in ol' Slim and how he was doing. Keeping track of a rival, you might say. A fellow like that, well, he could be a stick in the spokes of the big wheel on which the world turns. And I didn't want that.

He came to me again on the eve of the Second War, showed up in the penthouse office of the brand-new skyscraper where I looked down on the gambrel roofs of Arkham and plotted postwar highways and urban renewal, slum clearance and white flight and a nice little central shopping district down the line.

The guy looked terrible. Gaunt and haggard, his skin drawn in on itself, like a walking mummy. But those eyes. Still in those eyes was the same terrible cosmos, the same unspeakable chaotic Thing knocking at the door of our reality. Even with all my money, with all the wards and signs I'd been sure to build into this building, I knew he was dangerous. But it wasn't like last time. This time I had the upper hand.

"I cannot," he said, "find venues any longer for my talks and demonstrations. I find all doors closed to me."

"That a fact," I said.

"And when I look to find the ultimate owner of those shut doors, I trace things up through many hands—to you."

"I see," I said.

"My electrical apparatuses have been taken from me. The materials so critical to my prophetic work have been foreclosed upon. I find that I am unable to access my usual sources even of raw metals, much less the precision equipment on which I rely."

"Well," I said leaning my feet back on the mahogany desk and taking a puff of my cigar. "You know how it is. Times are tough all over."

He leapt up then, and I felt the wind of the hollow nameless void, heard the insane sound of flutes in his voice gone high with rage.

"You think to ruin me," he cried. "You think that you can *touch* me! Surely you can see that I am the faintest flicker of the tip of a finger dipped into this pathetic reality. You are *nothing*. Atoms and void, spinning into the crawling chaos at the heart of reality.

If I'm being honest with you, it was touch and go there. The *force* of that man. He might have drawn me into the place he came from, and that would have been the end of Yours Q. Truly—no, that's not right. I'd only *wish* it would have been the end.

But fortunately for me, I was sitting right there on the world's greatest monument to my very own god. And I had something to say to him. I stood up and jabbed at him with my cigar.

"Listen," I said. "You were kind enough to give me a prophecy once. Now let me prophecy to you. All that stuff you said, it's going to keep happening. And even as it does, the wheels of the world will run on Money. I don't give a flip whether we're running up to Heaven or down to Hell or off to Tinseltown. I don't even care if we're rolling down to your big man in the center of the galaxy. The wheels are going to turn. And anybody that tries to get in their way is going to be crushed. Crushed, you understand, under those big, beautiful greasy wheels. You come around telling me "man is insignificant ashes," like that's supposed to horrify me. No, friend. Let me tell you the real horror. Man is nothing but numbers in a ledger. And then on an electrical screen. And as Money keeps on feeding itself and getting bigger and bigger, they won't even be numbers. They'll be fractions. Rounding errors. People are going to be lost in a great big world, and the only thing they'll have to fumble their way through with is Money. Ships the size of cities are going to sail the dying seas, and they're going to be chock full of the worthless products that a billion human hands have wasted their lives to make for other human hands who have wasted their lives to buy. Every promise, every vow, every church and temple, every home, every parent, every child…every single thing that folks have ever loved or cared for is going to be reduced to transactions in the temple of Money.

"Money will move as quick as light in the aether, and Money will dispose of men and nations alike. Without even thinking about it, pal. There will be no stopping it, no reasoning with it, no comprehending it. There'll be no one, *no one*, not even me, that can get their brain around what's happening. And sure, sure, maybe we're all headed down to your Azathoth. But you know what? When that last human brain goes out, you know what its last thought is going to be? It's not going to be humming your song, pal. It's going to be thinking, worrying, wishing—about Money."

I took a nice long puff at the cigar. I looked at the shrunken, defeated, hollow man before me, and I smiled.

"Mister Nyarlathotep. You are a good and faithful servant of your blind, insane, devouring god. But I serve a blind, insane, devouring god too, and, fella, your Azathoth has nothing on Money."

ELDRITCH EDGE PROMOTIONS 666 RANDOLPH CARTER WAY, INNSMOUTH

K.G. MCABEE

From the Eldritch Edge Promotions' brochure:

We're on the cutting edge! A few of the services we offer:

Branded Necromancy

Mythos Marketing Strategies

Eldritch Event Planning

Dark Design Services

Infernal Influencer Partnerships

Maddening Media Buys

Abyssal Analytics

Come to the Edge for all your eldritch advertising and promotional needs!

You won't be disappointed! We're willing to bet our souls on it!

As soon as I got to the office, I checked with the receptionist to see if I had anything new on the agenda and then got my latte. As I was sipping it, I flipped open the book I'd been carrying around all weekend and reread the description of my new client for the dozenth time…and that was just since I got up this morning. I'd perused it first over coffee and bran cereal with almond milk. Second time, while I was brushing my teeth and deciding what to wear. The third time, I was on the bus to work. Sure I can afford a car. But living and working in the seaside resort—that's gallows humor, in case you wondered—of Innsmouth, I don't really need one. We've got a pretty great infrastructure these days, and the money to keep it up to the council's exacting standards, thanks to the local government finally managing to figure out how to tax the Deep Ones. I'm glad those guys out in the bay now have to pay their fair share, is all I'm saying.

So, as I walked down the hall to my office, I was pretty sure I was letter perfect in the description, but hey, when an extremely powerful client is checking out my agency, I do my homework, believe you me!

So I opened the book again and read:

> *"A vaguely anthropoid outline, an octopus-like head and a face full of feelers, a scaly, rubbery body, claws on hind and fore feet, and long, narrow wings behind, the Great Lord has been described as the combination of an octopus, a dragon, and a human, with human-ish arms and legs and a pair of rudimentary wings on its back. Simply looking upon the creature can drive some viewers insane, a trait shared by more than a few of the Great Old Ones and Outer Gods."*

I shook my head and gave a couple of tsk tsks. Insane? Just by looking at one of these guys? Wimps, is all I can say!

I closed the book, tucked it into my pocket, and finished my latte. My administrative assistant reached out and took my cup as soon as I lowered my hand. I was fighting to keep the delighted grin off my face, and Micah could tell. He knows me that well.

"Well, this is shaping up to be an interesting day, huh, Mikey? I hope you've got everything we need?"

Micah's face turned the same blazing red as his hair. "Hey, boss, have I ever failed you?"

He's too easy to mess with. "Not this week, but how long can you keep it up?" I teased him.

Mikey opened his mouth to argue but, at that exact moment, down at the end of the hall in front of me, the freight elevator went 'dong'. That meant someone was loading below…and it had to be our new client.

People poured out of their cubicles and clustered around me.

"Okay, people, show time!" I said, trying to keep my voice calm and reassuring. "Remember, if we've got all our ducks aligned, this could well be Eldritch Edge's next big client. And the emphasis is definitely on 'big', guys. Now get back to work and remember, look busy!"

They scattered, all except for my crack team gathered around the elevator doorway, which was wide enough for a small vehicle. I only hoped it would be big enough for our new client.

Prospective new client, I reminded myself firmly as I took my place. *Don't let him see how much I need this. Even though I need it bad.* I wiped my suddenly sweaty hands on my designer jacket. Maybe, if this worked out, I could actually afford a new one.

Okay, I admit it, things had been kind of rough since that little snafu with Nyarlathotep. I mean, who knew that a contract transcending space and time and woven in starlight, blood, and madness would be so, well…binding?

Still, I owed it to myself to bright side it, it's not like my mom has *another* soul to lose, am I right? And besides, our company founder is fine—most of the time. Seems a soul isn't necessary in our business and, in fact, could be considered a liability. But Mom did have to step back from the day-to-day and gift me the business, so all in all, I'd say it worked out okay.

And this time will work out too, I reminded myself. *Be positive, girl!* I took another of the deep breaths I'd been taking all weekend.

The *ding!* of the elevator arriving on our floor made me jump, though.

A shudder went through the building, I swear, as the door slid open. But I was proud of my team, not a one of them made a sound.

Our client stepped—slithered? crawled? undulated? pretty much all of the above, actually—out of the elevator. A reek composed of equal parts rotting fish and ancient seaweed rose around him in a miasma, so thick it was almost visible. My eyes started to water. I could hear the air recirculation system struggling to keep up, emitting a distant moan like a dying man.

Hey, this is Innsmouth, after all. The smell of fish is pretty much a given, rotten or otherwise. But mostly rotten. Those darned Deep Ones!

I glanced around at my team. Micah, of course, looked calm and collected. Tiffany, I could tell, was nervous, but Tyler looked fine. Well, Tyler has been with the firm a long time and he's seen a lot. I wasn't worried about him. And I could detect not the faintest expression of distaste or fear or disgust on any of them. Professionals, each and every one. I only hoped my face showed nothing more than innocuous welcome.

I took a deep breath—through my mouth; I'm no fool, and stepped forward with outstretched hand. The things I have to do in this business.

"Welcome, welcome, so great to meet you at last! You would not believe how much we've all been looking forward to this, let me tell you, my team and me," I said, upbeat and cheerful like I'd just won the lottery. And who knows, maybe I had? "I won't introduce them right now, if you're okay with that. I know you've had a long trip getting here. And you'll never know how much I appreciate it. Just sorry we couldn't come to your place."

Silence. I could feel my blood pressure rising.

"Uh, well, okay," I continued desperately. "Let's go straight to my office and have a seat."

My team scattered as I motioned towards my open-plan office. With my particular clientele, I knew better than to have a regular door, but the opening was still a tight fit for him. I followed him as he slithered forward.

Once he was inside, I pushed the sliding door almost closed.

"Oops, did I catch that last tentacle in the door? So sorry, my bad!" I said nervously as I jerked the door back open.

A rumble of, I hoped, laughter bubbled out of one of his mouths; it smelled like an explosion of sewer gas with just a soupcon of skunk.

"Not a problem," my client said, his *basso profundo* rattling the window frames. "I've got plenty more tentacles where that one came from! Just hope the ichor doesn't stain this gorgeous carpet."

I allowed myself to relax a bit. "Ah, a sense of humor! Really good to see you've got such a strong one. It can really pay dividends in our business, sir. Um, I don't want to make any mistakes right here at the get-go. It is 'sir', isn't it?"

Another explosion of sewer gas. I was pretty sure I could detect a faint greenish tinge rising around his octopoid head.

"Sir or ma'am," he said. "I'm flexible, and you can believe me—I'm not just saying that."

I had trouble telling which mouth that comment came from, but that particular problem is par for the course in my line of business. My clients are mostly, well, let's go with non-human, shall we?

I pattered around his bulk and took a chair between him and my floor-to-ceiling windows, offering a view of Innsmouth Bay and the docks below us. I suspect I was grinning like an idiot. "Ha! And there's that snarky humor again! Great! We'll just go with 'sir' for now. With the proviso that your gender is…let's call it fluid, shall we? And let me just say, that's yet another benefit to add to your great sense of humor: the pansexual lifestyle is big, no, *tremendous* these days. Now, Mr….uh, I'm so sorry, but I'm afraid you're going to have to help me out on the pronunciation of your name, sir. I don't want to screw it up!"

His 'head' nodded and several eyes blinked, one after the other. "Do not apologize, please. I'm always having problems with the pronunciation, believe me. Not to mention, the spelling is a real nightmare for everyone. I don't know what the folks were thinking when they named me and the rest of my siblings. In the old language, it's pronounced *Ckkk-sthloohuuu*…but I don't think human tongues or throats can manage that?"

"Well, mine can't for sure!" I bubbled, crossing my legs.

"What I thought. I'll tell you what, let's just be informal, shall we? Call me 'Lu'."

"Thanks so much!" I leaned forward. "Lu it is, then! I'm Amanda Waites, but please call me Mandy. I hope we're going to be working together for a long, long time."

"If we're indeed a good match, you won't believe how long we'll be associated, Mandy," Lu rumbled. "I've been around for a while, you know."

"And plan to be for a good bit longer, I hope!"

I shuffled through some papers Micah had placed on the little table beside me. Of course, I had all the pertinent information on my phone and computer, but our older clients prefer tech they're more familiar with. It can be a logistical nightmare, sometimes, when some of them insist on stone or clay tablets, let me tell you. A good stone carver can cost a fortune, and clay tablets don't do well in our Innsmouth dampness, so we had to invest in special temp-and-humidity controlled safes.

Lu pulled a small golden tank from between his shoulder wings and gave me an enquiring look. "You don't mind if I spritz myself a little, do you? Air conditioning dries me out like you would not believe, so I always carry a canister with me."

"Of course not, Lu!" I said, shocked I hadn't thought of it myself. "I'm sorry! Hold on, I'll get Micah, my PA, to come help with the spots you —oh, never mind. Tentacles!" I giggled. "You can reach everywhere! Can I get you anything else? Something to drink or a snack?"

"Nope, I had a couple of skinned goats before I came, so I'm good." Lu spritzed for a few minutes, upping the fishy smell by about a thousand percent. I was glad for the umpteenth time that I'd had the foresight to install stain-and-waterproof carpeting and a state-of-the-art, heavy duty air conditioning system.

"Ah! Nothing like sea water straight from the old sunken city," Lu sighed. "No pollution at the bottom of the ocean to speak of, you know, though we do get the occasional bits of plastic sinking down, even as deep as R'lyeh. Why, I once had to rescue a minion who'd got one of those six-pack nets caught around his head. You would have loved his expression, Mandy. Funny, let me tell you! We laughed for days!"

"Sounds hilarious, Lu!" I contemplated grinning again but my mouth was getting tired, so I just worked on having my eyes twinkle. I shuffled some more papers. "Okay. All better now, then? Skin moist? Are you sure you got every nook and cranny of those absolutely gorgeous tentacles?"

"I'm good, Mandy, thanks for asking. And you're a bit of a flirt, I see." Lu gave some rumbles that send vibrations throughout his tentacles.

I gave a giggle and shook one finger at him, then continued, all professional, "Okay, now, Lu, I've been reading over your resume— and an impressive one it is, too—and I want to make sure I've got all the information I need to do what I can for you, so to speak. I see you started out your long career as, let me just read this part verbatim, 'the supreme deity in an unspeakable cult dating back to prehistoric times.' Is that correct, Lu?" I looked up and gave him my serious look.

An interesting shade of puce suffused his left eleven tentacles. I can't say he smiled, exactly—he didn't really have lips—but I was sure I could detect a nostalgic look on the left quadrant of his head/body.

"Whoa, just hearing that takes me back to the good old days and the Great Old Ones. Haven't thought about those times in quite a while, not to mention all the rest of the guys in the pantheon. This modern era…well, can we be honest here?" Lu leaned forward and I could hear the big sling chair I'd had specially constructed—cost me a fortune but worth every penny—creak alarmingly. "Let's face it, Mandy, I'm floundering around, trying to catch up."

I laughed, hoping it didn't sound too forced. "Floundering. There's that snarky humor again, Lu."

"It's not snarky, it's real," Lu protested, sending out some eye-watering gusts of fishiness and what sounded like a belch. "Pardon me! But as I was saying, this new world is hard for me to navigate, Mandy, and that's the main reason why I'm here. I want to get some expert help from you and your team."

"And that's exactly what we do, Lu! Expert help is the byword of Eldritch Edge Promotions. We know how it is, and we feel your pain. Heck, some of our other customers have been in your spot."

"Yep, I've studied your prospectus." Now his thirteen right tentacles shifted into a very pretty pea-green streaked with blood-red. "You've got some of my family in your client list, I'm glad to see."

"Yes, we do, Lu!" I winked at him. "And we at EEP understand where you're coming from like no one else can. We get it: You're an ancient and powerful god-like being, and you've been out of the mainstream for a few millennia, taking some well-deserved R & R. But now that you've got all rested up, you're ready jump back into things and wham! What do you find out? Well, might seem to you that you're irrelevant; you could even find yourself on the verge of being forgotten. It's the way of the day, Lu. This modern age is all about the now, the current, the new. We hear it all the time from our other clients, and it all boils down to this: what apocalypse have you caused lately?" I held up both my hands, fingers spread. "In other words, if you haven't been involved in a recent Armageddon or even a minor apocalypse, then what good are you?"

"Exactly how I feel, Mandy."

"Okay, let's get on, shall we, Lu? Now, I see in your bio that you and your dark...cult. Hmm." I looked at him and shook my head slowly. "I'm sorry, but the word 'cult' has some negative connotations these days, Lu. What do you think about having your followers apply for official status as an ancient religion? They can really benefit from the tax breaks. It's not very expensive to get the ball rolling for government recognition and approval. I have some..." I tried to look modest, "... connections on the Innsmouth Council. They'd be glad to help us expedite that."

Three tentacles rippled and emitted a loud pop. I interpreted this as a shrug.

Or possibly a fart, if I was to go by the odor.

"Works for me, Mandy, if you think it's a good idea. Though I understand there are some issues these days about, uh, human sacrifice?"

"We can work around that, no worries. It's all in the wording. You'd be surprised what we can push through here at EEP, Lu. Why, when Dagon signed up with us—"

"Dagon!" he yelped, and his rudimentary wings rose behind his face and spread over his head in a big, quivering, multi-hued fan. "How is that old Fish-Face? Haven't talked to him in centuries!"

"He is doing great and I'll tell him you asked about him. Dagon is one of our greatest success stories, Lu. We've managed to get him inserted into all sorts of things: video games, books, movies. He's loving the attention, plus, it's really raised his profile. From has-been to celebrity, I believe is how he worded it."

Lu's head, almost hidden in the writhing mass of feelers and antennae and beaks and openings, nodded solemnly as waves of unnamable colors flowed through them. "You've put your digit tendril on it. That is exactly why I'm here, Mandy, as I'm sure you realize."

"I have, Lu, and let me just say: I think you've made the right decision." I leaned forward, hitting him with my best 'sincere' look, the one Mom taught me. "Sure, I know it's relaxing, hanging around your sunken city and napping, but you've got to ask yourself: is this really what I was born for? I know you needed some 'me' time to recharge your batteries, but for you undying types, it's important to reinvent yourselves occasionally. I know you can see how necessary that is. Don't you agree?"

"You've hit the nail on the head, Mandy. I can see EEP is all it's cracked up to be."

"We try hard, Lu. We really do," I said in my best, practiced-in-front-of-the-mirror, earnest, straight from the shoulder voice. "We do our research, we study our markets, we plan for optimum outcome. And speaking of research, our library has the best collection of books of ancient power in the entire world, bar none, plus more than a few from several alternate worlds. The classics, of course, Prinn, Abdul A-H, Dee, all those guys. The *Books of Eibon* and *Iod*. The *Cultes de Ghouls*. The *Mysteries of the Worm* in a new translation with updated illustrations. The *Pnakotic Manuscripts* and the ever-popular *Unaussprechlichen Kulten*."

I was glad to see Lu nodding along with my list.

"Of course, we've also managed to get our hands on some new stuff that would curl your, uh, tentacles. And EEP is based in Innsmouth, sure, but we have offices in Arkham, Dunwich and DC. So, we've got all the high and low places covered, not to mention the dark ones."

"You've convinced me, totally. I'm in, Mandy, all the way. Old Azzie was right, I can see. EEP is the company I've been looking for to make all the arrangements for my imminent comeback."

"Lu, you name dropper!" I said, giving him a roguish shake of one finger. "Could 'Azzie' possibly be a 'certain amorphous blight of nethermost confusion...'"

"...which blasphemes and bubbles at the center of all infinity'?" Lu finished the quote with a liquid chuckle. "That's old Azathoth, all right. He's the one who gave me your company's info, though it was kind of hard to make out everything he said, what with that vile beating of drums and whine of accursed flutes that he's so into. Just sounds like noise to me, but then, I live on the bottom of the ocean. Not a lot of music except when I visit the surface."

"So sweet of Mr. Azathoth to recommend us, Lu! I'll be sure to send him a nice thank-you card and a fresh sacrifice soon." I made a note on my pad, flipped over and reread a bit. "Okay, we seem to be on the same page so far. I can see you and EEP going places together. Just one last comment. And please, don't just blurt out the first thing that comes to the top of your, uh, heads. I'd like for you to really think about this, to look at it as a call-to-action on your part."

"I'm ready, Mandy. Hit me with all you've got," Lu said, and I could tell he was taking me seriously: all his tentacles, which had been twining around and through each other the whole time we'd been chatting, got deathly still.

"Here we go, then, and please, like I said, don't rush your answer." I straightened my shoulders and started right into his middle eye, the red one. "Give it some thought. Ready? Okay. You're ancient, you're powerful, you've had worshipers all over this world and countless other realms for millions of years. I know that, you know that, we all know that. Okay, then: what is it, Lu, that you really want Eldritch Edge Promotions to do for you in today's society?"

He settled back a bit and took a few minutes before jumping into an answer. I like that in a client. Shows he's paying attention.

"Actually, I have given this a great deal of thought, a great deal. And while I have an answer that I'm ready to share with you, I'd like to ask you one question first. What do *you*, Mandy Waites, and EEP in general, think my place in this modern world should be and, most importantly, *could* be?"

"Well, that's an easy one," I said in my best no-brainer tone. "Considering who you are and who you've been. Supreme ruler of all, of course, Lu."

"See, I knew I'd come to the right place!" Lu chuckled, making my eyes water from endless waves of fishy stink. We were gonna have to invest heavily in room deodorizers, I could see. "So, Mandy, you think I should go into politics, then?"

"You've nailed it, Lu," I said eagerly. "In fact…well, my team and I have already been throwing some ideas around, working on some bumper stickers. 'Don't Settle for the Lesser Evil' is one of our favorites."

"Ha! That's a good one, all right!" he gurgled.

"And then there's 'Vote for Me…or Die in Agony'."

"Can never go wrong with the classics, Mandy! And it rhymes! You've got some talented folks on your staff, I have to say."

"We hire only the best and brightest," I agreed.

"Okay, what about my campaign platform? Have you given that any thought yet?"

"Well, we thought you'd probably want to bring some of your own crew onboard for that. I know you've got quite a few worshippers, Lu, and there's nothing like absolute loyalty in politics. But don't forget: EEP is here, and we can offer market strategies, event planning, design services, infernal influencers, the whole ball of wax. And we're always ready to provide any and all of the support and backup necessary…for a piece of the action, naturally," I added, just to make sure we were indeed on the same page.

"Naturally. Those who are loyal to me always reap great rewards," Lu said, flapping his wings solemnly.

"See, you're talking like a politician already. You're a natural, Lu!"

"Just one final but very important question, Mandy: can I feast on the blood and bones of my enemies?"

My new client sounded concerned, but I rushed to reassure him.

"Lu, Lu," I said, shaking my head at his silly question, "don't forget this is modern politics. Machiavelli was an infant, Lu. These day, you can feast on the blood and bones of your *friends*! And your ratings will soar!"

ONE MORE BITE

E. N. DAUVIN

Jenna donned her white coat and stepped inside the temperature controlled greenhouse. She breathed in the humid warm air, filled with the scents of moist earth as she checked the notes from Tony's shift on the workbench. The piped in, tinny classical music had been cycling non-stop during the past two weeks of their experiment.

The rented greenhouses were still plastered over with signs reading **"Arkham Greenhouse, Bedding Plants: $5"** leftover from the spring sales.

"Plants leaning towards the speakers. Preferential over light sources."

Jenna measured the angle on several samples. One tomato, smaller than the others had slipped into a crack between two trays.

"Sorry little guy," Jenna murmured, setting it back in a good spot under the lights with the others.

Jenna completed her notes before moving to the next greenhouse. She slipped some ear plugs in before opening the door. The thundering bass shook the floor and rattled the metal tables. The discordant music, created for the experiment by a local musician spewed from the speakers, setting Jenna's teeth on edge.

Tony didn't leave any notes. Jenna flipped through the log sheet. There was plenty of un-updated entries, left blank. "Tony," Jenna muttered, as she dated and carried around the clipboard to make notes.

Tony was a deadbeat lab partner. Always an ideas man, but he rarely came through when it actually came to the day-to-day data collection. Of course, he had made extensive notes on the other conditions, so maybe Tony just didn't like his cousin's music that they had picked for the experimental condition.

The tomatoes, despite the noise that grated Jenna's soul, seemed to be growing better than the classical group, or the control. They reached towards the speakers set up in the corners of the greenhouse, away from the sun and supplementary bulbs. They were at least a foot taller than the other conditions and they also were developing a purple tinge that did not seem to be linked to any nutritional deficiencies.

"Strange." Jenna set the clipboard back on the workbench. This was supposed to be the negative condition—the least likely for the plants to grow well. They were going to have to publish something completely contradictory to what they expected. They would have a time explaining this in their paper.

On the bright side, Tony's cousin could advertise his music as great for growing plants. As long as you could stand the horrible grating guitar riffs. Jenna threw her ear plugs out in the can outside. She could still hear the music outside, as well as another noise, which she could only describe as the straining of the plants as they grew. But that was ridiculous.

"Keep loading the trucks, I'll take this next batch to my grandma!" Tony called as they cleared out the greenhouses. They were in the process of writing the paper on their experiment, and their lease on the greenhouses was nearly expired. The regularly sized plants from the control and classical conditions were already cleared out and distributed, but they were left with the daunting task of removing the jungle from the experimental condition.

The tomatoes were three times the size of the other conditions, all in vibrant shades of burgundy and purple. They hung heavy with fruit, knocking onto the tables and falling off to split on the ground as they tried to dismantle the jungle.

Tony lifted down a pot with purplish fruits hanging down the size of melons. "Oof. Can you believe it? I'm going to give this one to Nanna. She grows tomatoes every year. Nothing like this." He slapped a leaf the size of his face. "I can't wait to see her face when she sees it. This one has to be as big as her head!" He laughed, turning a deep plum fruit to the front. "I'm going get her a whole set up with speakers and a few discs of Trev's music so that she can get her garden going into overdrive!"

Jenna checked the list. There were only ten more plants in the greenhouse, although she couldn't believe it with the foliage hanging down over her head. "Does your cousin want any of them? See what his music created? We are going to have to pawn a few more off on someone."

"Maybe one or two. He's not a big plant guy. But he's gotta see what happened. He might try to market it, the music. Heck, give him two, the kids will like them."

Jenna scratched out two lines on the list. "I only hope that gardeners will be able to bear to listen to listen to his music. It really gives me a headache. I feel kind of woozy when I hear it, like I need to sit down. Especially when I don't have the ear plugs."

"Right? Man, that Trev. He's a character." Tony set his tomato on a dolly to wheel it out.

Jenna watched the tomato leave the green house, unfurling its leaves to the sky as it went through the door.

"What is that?" Brett asked as Jenna struggled with pulling a tomato out of her car at home.

"It's the last one." The pot hit the ground and the plant fluffed its foliage outside of the confines of the car. "We donated the normal ones to the food bank and the community gardens. But we didn't feel right giving them these."

"It's crazy," Brett said as he weighed a tomato in his hands. "Let's get it in the backyard. We can put like a quarter of this tomato in the salad I'm making for dinner." He lifted the plant with Jenna's help and they dragged it to the back yard where it stood by the side of the deck as high as the cedars.

Brett set the plates on the table, complete with purplish tomato diced on top of the garden greens. "This could go a long way towards world hunger, you know? Is that what you said in your experiment? Bigger food, more servings. Although I suppose that might also contribute to food waste," he mused.

Jenna folded her napkin in her lap. "No. We were testing the effects of different music on growth. This was certainly not the expected result. We will have to do more studies next year. Perhaps with more traditional rock compared to what Tony's cousin does. I wanted something really horrible to listen to, that's why we picked this music, but we will have to scale it back a bit, something that doesn't make the gardeners pass out. There must be some overtones, or something that just make my head feel strange."

Brett was already digging into his salad. Jenna forked a piece of tomato.

"How does it taste?"

"Trippy."

Jenna frowned, considering the tomato before popping it in her mouth. "Trippy?"

Jenna awoke on the couch, the dishes still on the table from dinner. Brett was holding his head, curled up in the hall. Scenes of dark, purple space, and some creature, some *thing* rising up from frothing purple seas lingered in her mind as she struggled to get up. It was reaching for her, trying to grab her while she couldn't move away.

She found her phone and looked for her messages from Tony. She slowly typed, frustrated with her numb fingers, "Don't let Nanna eat the tomatoes. And get me your cousin's number."

Jenna sat outside the suburban house on the East side of Arkham, waiting until Tony pulled up to step out of her car.

"This is it," he pointed to the white house with the manicured lawn.

"I expected something... different."

"Like what?"

Jenna shrugged as Tony pressed the doorbell.

Tony turned to her as they waited. "Do you wish you made the music, after all? You had something you wanted to record, right?"

Children cheered inside as heavier footsteps hurried to the door.

"Trev's music was pretty close to what I had in mind. I didn't think it would have that effect though."

A surprisingly normal, slightly more greyed version of Tony answered, surrounded by children and an excited dog.

"Come on outside, I want to keep an eye on the kids with their new playhouse. Even I don't trust my DIY skills."

They followed him through, to the backyard. "So this is about the music, huh? I heard that it went really well."

Tony nodded. "It did. Or certainly I've never seen plants grow like that before!"

Jenna cut in. "However, I have concerns that they aren't entirely, *normal.* At least, after ingesting some of the fruit last night, I have confirmed that something is not normal about it at all."

"What happened?"

"Drug trip, man," Tony chimed in. "She was seeing other worlds. A big monster. Kind of a scary trip, honestly."

"Yes. I am awaiting some toxicology results from the tomatoes, but can you tell me a little about your process, with making the music? Like what instruments were used, any editing software?"

Trev contemplated his kids playing in the yard. "I don't know. Just normal stuff. Guitar, bass, some drums. My usual software. Everyone uses that. But you know, I heard it before. I had dreams, it just flows through you, you know?"

"Can you elaborate on your dreams?"

"Like purple. Lots of purple. And a sea, water. Something was coming out of it, kraken-like. Other planets, man. I had a feeling that it was calling for something. Like it's lonely."

Tony exchanged glances with Jenna. "And did you pass out?"

"Nah, I was already sleeping. But I sure didn't feel good in the morning. I had to write it down. The music was in my head. Just ringing through my ears all day. I thought I'd go mad if I didn't get it down." He leaned in. "I know that the music isn't... nice to listen to. But Tony said you wanted something wild, discordant, and I started having the dreams only a couple days before. I thought it was too perfect, you wanting just the thing I dreamed up."

Jenna rose to leave. "Please, just don't listen to it, or sell it, or do anything at all with it. We can't risk something else happening until we know more."

Tony nodded. "And don't let the kids eat the tomatoes."

"Nah, man. They don't like their veggies."

J enna's phone rang. Tony's face was plastered over it as it buzzed. "Yes, Tony?"

"Jenna, can you meet me down at Arkham food bank?"

Jenna sighed, the tomato plant was still waving in the breeze outside, like some other worldly palm. "What's happening, Tony?"

"I got a call. They've had complaints. They want us to pick up the tomatoes. And there's a gentleman there that wants to speak to us."

Jenna pulled up in front of the food bank. Tony was already there, talking to an older man. He smiled as she walked over.

"Jenna, this is Larry. He frequents the food bank every week, and he ate some of the tomatoes we donated."

"How are you, Larry?" Jenna shook his hand.

"You're the lady from the purple space."

"Pardon?"

"I saw you. In the tomato world. You were trying to tame the octopus man. He's real lonely, you know. All alone up in space. Wants to talk to you. He's been looking for you for a long, long time."

Jenna stared between Tony and Larry.

"There was this music too. Something like," Larry tried to mimic the grating sounds of Trev's music. "Yeah. It was wild. You have any more of those tomatoes? Sheila wouldn't give me any more."

"I'm afraid not, Larry." Tony said, laughing.

"Ah well." Larry wandered down the street, still humming the awful music.

Tony opened the door to the food bank.

Jenna side-stepped him as she walked through the door, avoiding the tables filling the room. "Tony. We only gave the food bank tomatoes from the classical condition."

"I know."

"There was nothing wrong with those tomatoes."

"There had to have been. Or Larry wouldn't have the same dream as you and Trev."

"They must have heard it through the greenhouse glass!"

Tony sniggered as they approached the food-bank counter, in the process of lunch clean up. "Look, Sheila has all our plants lined up for us to take."

Jenna grabbed a pot of tomatoes. "It's no laughing matter, Tony. Any tomatoes that heard that music, however faintly, could be affected."

Tony filled his bear arms with as many pots as he could scoop up. "And so could we."

———

The water was purple. Thick, choking, purple that chilled beneath the skin. Jenna floundered, trying to grip the slippery rocks as she pulled herself from the waters. There was something large behind her, sliding silently through the sea. The tentacles surfaced before the head, feeling, searching for her feet to pull her beneath. The eyes finally poked above the water, shiny, black glass. Peering out from the depths. A beaked mouth, shrieking out the music.

Jenna covered her ears. Her own mouth opened to scream as the horror of the words slithered into her mind.

It swam alone through the purple waters. Calling to her.

She awoke, breathless, clammy. Brett slept peacefully as she left the soaked sheets. She splashed water on her face in the bathroom, only then noticing the red suction cup marks of tentacles encircling her wrists.

———

Jenna waited for Brett to leave for work before she called Tony.

"The dreams are getting worse." she said, considering the tentacle marks she had kept hidden under her sleeve.

Tony still sounded half- asleep on the other end of the line. "Have you been in any music forums?"

"No. Why?'

"There are people all over, having the same dream. Hearing the music. Some people must be more sensitive to it, or something. And some are like Larry. They are saying something is coming. Soon."

"Should we destroy all the plants?"

"Probably. But wait. I'm going to come over."

Tony went straight to the back yard when he arrived. He plucked another tomato from the plant growing ever larger in the backyard and brought it into the house.

He looked around the spotless kitchen, still holding his tomato expectantly. "Knives? Cutting board?"

Jenna pulled some out. "You can't seriously be thinking of eating it, Tony."

"I'm not going to. You are."

"Me?"

He cut off a thick slice. "If you consent. All of these dreamers. They see the same thing. You. With this thing. Now, I'm a scientist. This whole thing is beyond what we believe in. But if this is real, I think someone needs to cut off this line of communication."

"Why me?"

Tony shrugged. "Bears further investigation. Some people pick it up easier? I already tried this with Trev last night, and he didn't find the our tentacle guy again. Just purple soup. So we're going to try with you, if you'll do it."

Jenna considered the slice on the cutting board. "But either way, it involves me going there again."

"If you want. I'll be here. To take notes." He held up his clipboard. "Just like a guided trip. You've done those right?"

"You know I haven't." Jenna picked up the slice. She bit off a chunk. The thrumming of the music pulsed with her heart beat as Tony helped her to the couch.

She reached for the tomato again. "One more bite."

———

"Can you hear me, Jenna?"

The words echoed off the high wall caverns. The purple sea ebbed and flowed up to the cave mouth.

"Do you see anything?"

"Water. And rock."

"The creature. The tentacle guy?"

"Not now. But this is where I left him."

"Do you see anything? Anything to grab?"

"Nothing." Jenna rose from the rock and walked the length of the cave. It was nothing more but an inlet of rock. From the strange barnacles lining the floor, it would be underwater at times. "There is no where to go but out to the water."

"*Don't* go, Jenna. I am wracking my brain here, trying to think of something."

"There are so many stars." High above her, visible through the purple vapour rising above the heaving sea, stars twinkled above. A palette of novel constellations. "This is far from home."

The music was growing louder. The discordant tones that coincided with the entirety of Jenna's being were coming closer. She stepped down onto the rock, her feet in the water.

"The music is growing louder, Tony."

"It's attracted to the music?"

"It makes the music."

There was something slithering in the water. Ripples lapped against her ankles. A light, otherworldly pressure on her wrist made her gasp.

"Jeez, Jenna. Your pulse is crazy. We gotta get you out of there."

Thrumm Thrumm Thrum. White tentacles slithered in the purple water. They were reaching for her, wishing to grasp and embrace her.

"My heart is matching the music. We are connected."

"I'm freaking out here, Jenna. You have to come out."

"I can see him."

The glassy black eyes peered up from the water. The beak was nearly protruding. It lifted from the water, the music coming from the lips with a frenzy.

"You have to change your pulse, get off rhythm."

The tentacles were reaching for her. The white arms, reaching for her limbs to pull her in. Down into that water, that was so warm. Warm and comforting. Would it be so bad, to be dragged within, and never emerge?

The mouth opened again, shrieking with joy as it clasped her ankle. She knew it was joy. It was clear, in the voice. It began to pull, and her toes slipped under the water.

An irritating voice from above woke her. She flicked her ankle, the kraken screaming as it recoiled its tentacle.

"Slow your pulse. You're going to have a heart attack. I'm calling the EMT's. Close your mind to it. Don't let it communicate with you."

It reached again, the tentacles grasping her firmly all along her legs.

Jenna took a deep breath, and slid beneath the water as the tentacles pulled. They cradled her beneath as she went limp. The creature beneath stared at her, pulling her from side to side as it shrieked the music, at her.

Beneath the water it was words. Words that had no meaning. It shook her. She could hardly move, the water was so warm, it flowed thickly around her. The creature shook her again, trying to make her move. Jenna floated limp, she felt the oxygen leaving her as it gave one final shriek. One last word of anguish.

She awoke with a jolt.

Tony's face peered down at hers, drained of all colour. A strange man measured her pulse, the defibrillator set up next to her on the living room floor.

"She's clear."

***

Jenna pulled up in front of Tony's house. A plume of smoke from the back yard rose up to the blue cloudless sky. Tony was poking at his fire pit as she came around the house. The confiscated tomato plants were piled next to the flames. She dragged one more with her over the lush grass.

She still wore long sleeves to hide the fading tentacle marks.

"OK. I've got all the plants," he gestured to the pile languishing on the lawn. And I've debriefed anyone that had dreams. How are you doing?"

"I'm okay."

He pulled a few more tomatoes onto the flames. The fire rose up, rushing and popping, turning a sickly shade of lavender at the base.

He poked at the flames pushing the tomatoes around to crisp evenly. "No one has had any other dreams. And interestingly, anyone who ate the tomatoes after you went in there, has had no ill effects. So it's over? We'll choose some more classic rock for next year's condition."

"I'm not sure I'll be around for next year's experiment." Jenna reached into her purse for the CD of Trev's music, tossing it onto the bonfire. "I might take a sabbatical. Brett thinks I need more time, that I have been waking in the night."

"Shouldn't burn plastic," Tony tutted. He paused staring at the purplish flames. "What do you mean? The creature? Are you still having dreams? I though we cut off the communication. Without the music, the plants... I don't understand what it wanted."

Jenna rubbed at the tentacle marks on her arms. Last night she again felt her skin gripped and ripping beneath their powerful grasp. "How could it be over? He's still alone up there."

Tony handed her a tomato stalk as thick as her neck to toss onto the flames. "You can't feel sorry for it, can you? Who knows what it might have done? What it wanted from you. Why it picked you."

"It was calling for us all. The tomatoes were reaching for it." Jenna let the tomato slip down onto the flames, watching the purple leaves blacken and curl. "I can feel sorry for any who reach out to be heard."

ADJUSTMENTS

ASHER ELLIS

"Have you ever had an adjustment before, Mr. Phillips?"

The oval shaped ring in which my face rested allowed little movement of my jaw to offer an answer. Still, I was able to mutter a barely opened-mouth "no" in response to Dr. Lutch's question.

"Well then," Dr. Lutch said, standing over his patient lying face down on the elevated table. "You're in for a treat."

To this, I did not reply. I was too preoccupied in squeezing my eyes shut—not that it did any good to hide the horrors that followed me wherever I went. Sometimes it wasn't so bad when they existed only as a momentary glimpse from the corner of my eye. I'd turn my head to get a better look and they'd be gone. If only they behaved as such all the time. Just maybe then I'd be able to coexist with these nightmarish images.

But, no. Too often did they make their presence known, stepping out of the shadows to reveal themselves to my eyes alone. No one else could see the deathly black tar that ran from my bathroom sink and tub. Or the eyes that stared back at me when I stood on a subway platform and peered down the dark, endless tunnel.

No one else heard the whispers of a language not found on any continent.

No one else saw the boils of emerald light when they shut their eyes to go sleep.

No one except for me.

But, of course, no one else was involved in the accident that had occurred exactly two months and five days prior. Well, there had been one other person, my coworker, Franklin Lake.

But Lake was dead. And even though my boss, my other coworkers, and the police would all disagree, it was completely my fault. I could've pulled Lake back up after he slipped from the scaffolding, or at least held onto him until the other guys arrived to help. Lake was a large man, sure, but so was I and most of the men who were working on the new Science building at Miskatonic University.

Dangling from the sky-touching platform, all of Lake's two-hundred and fifty pounds pulled on my arm, yanking my shoulder from its socket and tugging my spine from its intended straight line. The pain had been unmerciful and intense, but it was not the knife-life sensation stabbing my back that caused me let go all at once.

It was what I saw—no, what I felt—after my vertebrae finally surrendered to the severe pulling force with an audible pop. Gripping my hand with an unfaltering determination to drag me down was a cluster of constricting tentacles, snaking their way between my fingers with a black, viscous lubricant. My eyes snapped open with fear as they followed the tentacles to their source: a scaly, winged body and a face full of mollusk-like feelers.

Acting solely on basic human reflex, I immediately released my grip and watched Franklin Lake plummet one hundred and twenty feet to his death. There were no scales or tentacles adorning his round, bearded face—only a final expression of absolute terror.

Eventually, when the last of the adrenaline finally dispersed itself from my nervous system, the pain levies broke at last, flooding my entire body with crippling agony. After seeing the bodily sacrifice one man made in effort to save another, no one in their right mind would've accused me of dropping Lake to his demise. Instead, I was met only with sympathy, especially from my employers who rewarded me a fully paid medical leave and accident insurance to cover the expenses. With *Dyer Construction* fitting the bills, my pain quickly faded to a dull ache I could barely notice.

The visions, however, continued to grow in both their frequency and intensity. As did the journals piling up in my bedroom, pages full of detailed descriptions of what I saw and heard. My last completed composition book was the worst of all, containing only one sentence scribbled over and over.

The tar has eyes.

It was this journal that I flipped through when I felt the cool breeze wafting in from my fourteenth floor apartment window. The wind seemed to be calling to me, inviting me to a place far more serene than the nightmare my life had become. "It's so stuffy in there," it seemed to say. "Come out here where you can breathe."

I closed the journal with a precipitous snap and stood up from the bedroom floor. I inhaled a deep breath of the incoming air, its coolness immediately extinguishing the blazing inferno that engulfed my tormented soul. With my eyes closed, I took a step closer to the window. And then another. My feet moved as if on a predestined track, a path leading to a painless plummet and then the sudden stop of salvation.

I would've certainly followed the wind's instructions if not for the mail landing at my feet, blown by the breeze from the pile that had collected on the dining room table.

I opened my eyes and turned them down to my bare toes. Atop the stack of envelopes and brochures splayed across the wooden floor, a simple business card stared up at me. It read:

HERBERT LUTCH, D.C.

ARKHAM CHIROPRATIC CLINIC

While I had failed to notice the card before, its presence now came as no surprise; I hadn't checked the contents of my incoming mail in days. It was simply another item of junk mail, most likely thrown into the mail box of every resident in my building.

Even though the window remained open, I could no longer feel the gentle fingers of atmosphere urging me towards the portal with their determined pull. Nor could I hear still hear the whispers of temptation that had so successfully coaxed me just moments ago. All I could focus on now were the black ink text of the card I flipped over and over in my fingers. I had yet to try chiropractic medicine since my insurance company regarded it as an "alternative practice of medicine," lumped together with acupuncture and reiki healing therapy. Therefore, a chiropractor's fees would've had to come from my own pocket.

But what did that matter now? I'd just been moments away from following Lake's example. Money was the last of my concerns. The only thing I had to lose now was time. Did I really want to endure another day of insanity when the chances were this Dr. Lutch would be as ineffective as the others? Why not just return to the comforting embrace of the evening air and end it all right now?

I didn't have an answer, but I shut the window anyway, sealing it tight with its locking latch. For reasons I could not say, I would keep myself inside for one more night, surrounded by the blackness and the eyes and the oozing pinpricks of strange, green light. Something inside of me, as definite as the oily substance that ran down my bedroom walls like blood, said I *had* to visit Dr. Lutch. But unlike the whispers that never stopping ranting in that indecipherable language, this voice practically screamed.

Doctor Lutch. Doctor Lutch! DOCTOR LUTCH!

The chant did not cease until I found myself sitting in the doctor's waiting room the next day. The back of the business card had revealed the office's location, obscurely tucked away on the sixth floor of the old D.W. Building on Kingsport Ave. There was nothing remarkable about the office—its waiting room awfully typical with its sterile colored walls of off-white and its stacks of horribly uninteresting magazines. A large fern rested in the corner between two perpendicular rows of cheap, thinly padded chairs. Staring up at the wall adorned with a single Courier & Ives reprint, I could not help but wonder what I was doing here. To think I had gone through the trouble of calling the red-headed receptionist sitting behind the counter and convinced her that my situation was a dire emergency. I *had* to see the doctor today. If I needed any more evidence that I'd truly gone insane, insisting to wait in a fluorescently lit room with an outdated issue of *Scientific American* in my hands definitely won the argument for good.

"Must be your first time here."

An extremely thin, older man suddenly appeared in the chair to my left. Or had he been there all along? These days I paid more attention to the dark things creeping in the corners of my eyes than the people sharing my public space.

I cleared my throat and asked, "I beg your pardon?"

The man smiled, his unhealthy gums deep red in their color. A thin carpet of graying stubble covered his sunken cheeks, its color almost matching his faded jeans and flannel shirt.

"I said it must be your first time here. I don't recognize you."

I chuckled. "Are you here so often that you'd recognize anyone?"

"Once a week." The man's answer came without a tinge of shame.

"Once a week?" I echoed the stranger's reply. "And you're still not better?" The urge to walk out the door was increasing with every passing second.

"That's not how this stuff works." The stranger looked around as if he were afraid someone was listening to our conversation. "Chiropractic medicine is a lifelong commitment."

"I don't know about that," I said, looking away from the man's wide, troubled eyes. But I could still feel the man staring straight at him.

"Believe me, you will. But don't worry." The man slapped my knee. "You'll get used to it." He leaned in close enough that I could smell the reek of tobacco on his breath. "You'll adjust."

Before I could offer any kind of reply, the receptionist yelled, "Mr. Phillips!" indicating my turn had finally come. The final puzzled look I gave the thin man received a wink in return before I exited to the long hallway of examination rooms. At room 6 I stopped, opened the door, and was at last greeted by the famous Dr. Lutch.

An image of Bela Lugosi instantly flashed before my eyes upon seeing the doctor. Though clad in a physician's white coat rather than the black cape of Dracula, Lutch shared many traits with the famous horror actor. Handsome but with an edge, the doctor's eyes held the naturally ominous gaze of the most well-known vampire. And even though he offered a welcoming warm smile, there was still an undercurrent of secrecy behind his face, as if he already knew more about me than my own parents.

After a brief period of appropriate greetings and pleasantries, Dr. Lutch went right to business, requesting that I remove my coat and lay face down on the examination table.

"I have to admit, doctor, I come to you with a great deal of skepticism." I struggled to release the words from my mouth, beads of sweat rolling off my brow. I had never been in a room where my visions were more vivid. It was as if instead of them following me, I'd wandered right into their home. Fortunately, while I could feel their presence all around me, the *things* were remaining in the shadows. But I knew they were simply waiting for the right time to strike.

"That's easy to understand," Dr. Lutch said, bending and straightening each of my legs while he looked down my spine. "Many of my patients bring a strong sense of doubt when they first enter my office. It is only natural to be suspicious of something one does not understand."

Another whisper from the far left corner of the room.

Another drip of tar brushing by his ear.

Just concentrate on the doctor's voice.

"Exactly," I replied after a hard swallow. "And I could really use some explanation right about now."

"Well," the doctor said as he ran his fingers up my spine, fingering the muscles around each vertebra. "It all goes back to 1910 when a man named D.D. Palmer theorized that the nervous system controls a person's overall heath."

I opened my eyes to see a black pool forming underneath the table. "Uh huh," I muttered.

"Basically, Palmer noted that nerves are formed of two types of nerve-fibers: afferent and efferent. The afferent take in sensations from the outside world and transmit them to the center your nervous system, while the efferent nerve fibers carry impulses back out. Think of them as one-way streets, each serving a different direction."

"I see," I said, not knowing whether I preferred the horrors of my open eyes to those when they were shut.

Dr. Lutch continued. "So if the center of your nervous system, which is to say, your spine, were to be moved from its natural alignment, it would cause an impingement on these nerve fibers. The result would be either a hindering or amplification of their functionality."

My eyes popped open. With the doctor's last sentence, I momentarily forgot about the horrific world around me. "So what you're saying is that the alignment of my spine is increasing the input of my nervous system?"

"Well, I don't know." Dr. Lutch jotted a few notes on a chart attached to a clipboard. "Do you feel you're feeling more than you're intended to feel?"

And seeing more than anyone was ever intended see.

And hearing more than anyone should ever hear.

"Yes."

Dr. Lutch placed the clipboard on a nearby countertop and returned to my side. "Would you please flip over for me, Mr. Phillips? All the way so that your face is looking up at the ceiling."

I couldn't help but smile. "Gladly," I said, relieved I wouldn't have to see the increasing black puddle of tar that was growing by the second. It had almost reached each corner of the room. But when I was fully turned over and staring up at the room's ceiling, I choked on my own petrified breath.

The creature possessed only one eye, but it was gigantic. It floated in the same black liquid as before, but this dark stain did not obey the physical laws of liquid. Long, coiling tendrils of tar reached out for my face, hovering in front of my eyes in a bizarre slow-dance. The thing's tentacles seemed to be performing their own examination of my body, smelling my flesh and reporting back to that horrendously bulbous eye —the eye that refused to blink, a yellow orb staring straight into my soul and claiming it for its own.

Too frightened to draw even a single breath, I tore my eyes from the viscous creature and looked to Dr. Lutch for help. The doctor, however, who had been standing behind me and gently massaging my neck, was gone. He had been replaced by whatever Lake had transformed into the moment before he fell to his death.

The scaled flesh.

The reptilian wings.

And the face covered in feelers that squirmed in a ravenous frenzy.

What had been Dr. Lutch clutched my throat, reminding me of when the creature squeezed my wrist during my failed attempt to save Lake. Its embrace could mean only one thing: it was about to rip my head right from my neck. It would lick my mind clean of whatever sanity still remained. It would eat my brain whole and then go in search of someone else's consciousness to devour. It would—

CRACK!

The daylight of a perfectly clear afternoon washed into the examination room. The inviting yet cautious eyes of Dr. Lutch peered down over my face.

"How was that?"

I could not answer the question. I turned my head in both directions, rotating my eyes around the room. All I could see was a plastic model skeleton, a couple of posters comparing healthy and unhealthy spines, and a sanitizing station. There was not a single trace of anything that didn't belong in the current place and time.

"What happened?"

The chiropractor smiled. "I just gave your spine a slight adjustment. A little pressure on an isolated vertebra, a quick turn of your neck, and presto. You should be feeling a strong sense of relief, Mr. Phillips. Is this true?"

Relief was the understatement of the century. Not only had the visions and the voices disappeared completely, but I was overcome by the powerful sense that they'd never existed in the first place. Like a nightmare that seems all too real when you're asleep, but the obviousness of its artificiality hits you the moment you wake up.

"I feel great!" I sprang up from the table. "You did it. You cured me!"

Dr. Lutch lowered his head slightly, like a modest actor accepting applause after an award winning performance. "All in a day's work, sir. I'm glad you feel better. But let's not get ahead of ourselves. I'd like to see you back very soon."

I jumped off the table and walked over to a full-length mirror to the left of the door. The only image that stared back at me was my own reflection, not a single shadowy figure looming behind me. And when

I closed my eyes and took a deep, cleansing breath, all I saw was darkness, completely void of eerie green light.

"Do you really think that's necessary, Doc? I'm feeling straight as an arrow."

"That may be true right now, but the human spinal cord is a delicate thing. Daily occurrences such as walking or even sitting for prolonged periods of time can eventually create an impinging misalignment. In time, your symptoms could return."

I reached for the shiny, brass doorknob. "Look, Dr. Lutch. I can't express how grateful I am for what you've done for me, but I'm not sure what my schedule is going to be like in the next few weeks. I plan to return to work."

"I can understand that." Dr. Lutch no longer looked in my direction but flipped through the paperwork of his next client. "But I suggest you speak with my receptionist on the way out and take a slot in my calendar. You can always reschedule or cancel later if you wish. Good day, Mr. Phillips."

"Indeed it is, Doc. Thank you." I swung the door opened and exited without another word.

On my way out, I tried to sneak past the red-headed receptionist, but her trained eye must have seen this tactic before. Despite being occupied with a phone call, she summoned me to her desk and asked if I'd like to make a follow-up appointment. Humoring both her and the doctor down the hall, I looked over the solidly booked calendar and made a date for a Tuesday in two weeks.

"Sorry, there's nothing sooner, Mr. Phillips." The receptionist offered the apology with a genuinely sympathetic smile.

I shrugged. "Don't worry about it. I'm in no rush. I feel great."

I spun to finally leave the clinic once and for all and instantaneously threw my hands up in a reflexive response. There was a person standing right behind me—the thin man in the faded denim pants. He threw his own hands up in an admission of guilt.

"Sorry pal," he said, his voice as raspy as before. "I should watch where I'm going." Before continuing down the hall to his own exam, he leaned in to my ear and whispered:

"See you next time."

I shook my head, knowing the man wouldn't see the gesture.

Don't count on it.

Upon stepping out into the late afternoon warmth, I immediately decided I'd pass on taking a cab and enjoy a nice walk home to my apartment. It felt like years since I'd been able to enjoy a leisurely stroll without looking over my shoulder. But nothing was trailing behind me now, sadistically tormenting me with secret ramblings. And if they were, I could no longer hear a word.

The only problem that remained was my full bladder, the result of buying a twenty-ounce cup of hot coffee on my way home. I practically kicked my own door down when I finally reached my apartment and rushed to the bathroom without even taking off my coat. After relieving myself, I approached the old porcelain sink and proceeded to wash my hands. As I scrubbed between my fingers with a misshapen bar of green soap, I smiled back at my own perfectly sane reflection.

"Walking can bring back your symptoms," I said to myself, laughing with no one else to share the joke. "Sorry, but I've been walking my whole life without a problem." I placed the soap back on its plastic tray. "Chiropractic medicine is a lifelong commitment. Yes, for people who can afford to pay over and over for treatment they don't need."

I laughed once more, shaking my hands dry. But the laughter faded, transforming to a puzzled groan as the last of the water in the sink flowed down the circular, dark drain. A clinging speck of soap rested in the center of the hole like a green pupil in a round, black iris. The drain stared up at me, locking my gaze in a spontaneous staring contest. Naturally, it was I who had to blink first—but had the drain blinked at the exact moment?

After making my way out of the bathroom and throwing my coat in the closest, I collapsed onto my queen-sized bed. Exhaustion claimed my whole body, proving just how much time had passed since I'd been able to do anything at all physical. Staring up at the ceiling above me, I realized I had never before noticed the eye-shaped knots decorating the wooden boards.

Drip. Drip. Drip.

I must have not turned the handle to the bathroom sink tightly enough. I can hear the steady drops falling from the faucet into the sink's drain.

That green unblinking eye…

It was then the thought occurred to me. A follow-up, I realized, never hurt anyone. I was beginning to realize that it was probably the responsible thing to do.

"Right?"

Naturally, no one answered. I had asked the question to an empty room. I was alone.

I looked once again at the many eyes scattered among the boards in the ceiling above me.

Yes, I was alone. Of course, I was.

Still, I decided I would not cancel my upcoming appointment with Dr. Lutch just yet. In fact, perhaps I would call the chiropractic office tomorrow and see if I could move up my date. The receptionist had been very apologetic that Dr. Lutch's calendar was completely full, but it was still worth trying.

From the bathroom, the faucet continued to drip.

Drip. Drip. Drip.

It was just a follow up. Just one more appointment. Just one last adjustment.

Drip. Drip. Drip.

I just needed one more. That was all.

Drip. Drip. Drip.

Just one.

T he woman walked in just like all the others—hands shaking, tired eyes darting from side to side. She gave her name to the receptionist who asked her to take a seat. As always, there were plenty of back-issue magazines to choose from, but she ignored all of them. Instead, she just sat and stared straight ahead, her hands wringing an invisible handcloth.

"Must be your first time here," I said.

She turned but said nothing.

"It's okay," I reassured her. "The first time's always the hardest."

When she did finally speak, her voice came soft and broken. "*First time?*"

I nodded. "It was years ago, but I can remember mine like it was yesterday."

"Years?" She repeated again. The worry intensified behind her eyes.

"But you'll get used to it. I promise." At the risk of overstepping my bounds, I placed a gentle hand on top of hers. The shaking fingers stilled at once.

"Trust me," I said. "You will adjust."

A moment later, the receptionist called my name.

DAMP ENVELOPES

ELIZABETH MCENTEE

September 28th, 1936

Dear Mr. Gilman,

Sir, I will preface this letter by acknowledging that normally reports from me are sent through Mr. Blakeley, but the recent culmination of the circumstances of the past five months have necessitated Mr. Blakeley's immediate retirement and my movement from the role of mailwoman to his former role of Postmaster of Innsmouth. The purpose of this letter is to inform you, with all respect to your authority, of the need to not wait for bureaucracy, as you will hopefully agree that I have acted in the best interest of our town and its essential inhabitants. I request you read my letter in full and act upon it as you see fit at the end of your reading. If I have done right, I will continue this duty faithfully. If I have done wrong, I am prepared to face the proper consequences. I simply request that you consider my serious devotion to my career as a postal worker and the thorough measures I have taken to ensure the continued integrity and intended functionality of the Innsmouth post office while making your final decision.

I began to become aware of the situation during an encounter on April 17th of this year.

Taking a breath of air with notes of sea and dust and something else unknown, I placed my fountain pen on the wide, uneven desk. Left alone for a moment, it rolled defiantly toward me before its brief autonomy was ended by my remorseless stationery. Slowly spinning with a croak of chair, I followed its thwarted trajectory to the window behind me: the only window in the Innsmouth Post Office's back room. The view beckoned to me, and I allowed myself a break. I would ruminate more on the day that interrupted my blissful life in Innsmouth just after a short appreciation of the Manuxet on its unstoppable course. My physical sight gave way to fresh, sentimental memory as I followed its flow past the fading manmade structures and toward the ocean that seemed to mix and blend, through its spray, up into the misty, light rain that often fell in lieu of downpour. Living in Innsmouth meant appreciating water in all of its distinct and indistinct forms. I wondered, as I often have, why it was that more poets did not come here. Then again, Innsmouth was its own little secret, a quiet gem under disregarded old New England brine.

It was no wonder that Mr. Blakeley kept the window so unusually clean and maintained, as the view was truly better than viewing the interior. Like the rest of the post office (and much of the rest of the town), the back room was old, simple, and practical, with the latter being slowly but surely undermined by the creeping rot of the wood that called to mind the other two qualities. At least the wood smelled nice as it rotted. It reminded me of outside, where I would be heading to deliver this letter personally, directly after finishing it.

Prying myself away from the window and sliding back into place at the desk, I thought about how rare of a privilege it was to have a positive outlook in such an admittedly unfortunate town, especially after the blows that the decade prior dealt to the already-declining community. That was not something I took for granted. I knew my good fortune was because of the importance of the mail in a town that had no telephones or telegrams, and I was the face of the mail for a good majority of the town. Thomas was the other, but he was still in training and largely delivered packages to the commercial area and Federal Street. He was only hired a few months prior to the events of this recent spring, and he was only the most recent hire in an unfortunately long string of short-lived carriers-in-training. Meanwhile, I had been on my route for six full years at that point, ever since I permanently moved from Arkham to Innsmouth to take advantage of the job opportunity afforded by the recovery period's post office initiative. It was a pity that more people could not see the beauty of this historic seaport and the rich culture of its residents. The outsiders who caused such commotion in '27 really had no idea.

I sighed at that thought and went back to writing, recalling the events of that day in April.

On that day, I was midway through my usual route, and nothing was out of the ordinary. I picked up outgoing mail from a number of residences and delivered letters to others, with no contact and all doors closed, leaving me in continuous silence with the rain as my only company as I performed my duty. However, when I reached the bleak and shuttered Sturgis household, I was given a start as the old door suddenly opened wide. Standing before me was who I soon understood to be Mrs. Agnes Sturgis, clutching a soaking wet envelope in her outstretched hand.

I nearly wrote "outstretched, wretched, webbed hand," but I knew that was the visceral reaction talking and not my common sense and good taste. The unsteadiness of those of us who could not embark upon that corporeal path to the depths, I knew, was not the fault of those undergoing the metamorphosis, those later stages of what began as merely the "look." I knew it was a tumultuous inner trial period before their reckoning to the depths of the sea or the depths of their despair, and that was not something to fear. It was something to pity, and I was in service to them in their most difficult hour.

But for all of my logical empathy, I simply did not see them in that state very often, and so my senses were not used to their presence even if I fancied my mind being so. And I believed that the influential in the town, like whichever semi-anonymous "Mr. Gilman" would be reading my letter within the shuttered mansion I would soon be visiting but not entering, would prefer me to seem "in my place," and I was happy enough to fill that role for them by including the unfortunately true detail of my startlement. I knew, though, that only a humble nod to my humanness was necessary in such a letter as this, so I decided to be even lighter on recording my own reactions on paper moving forward, to expedite the explanation.

I was able to surmise that she wanted to take this particular letter in all due haste to its recipient, Mrs. Emily Otis, who lived several streets over. However, I had already delivered mail in that area, and on top of that, our policy for outgoing mail has always been, as you know, to hold it overnight, in case it is meant to leave Innsmouth and needs to be checked. I attempted to explain that I could not deliver it sooner than on the morrow, but she croaked out and insisted more, and when I remained reluctant, she went inside and scribbled something down on paper and handed it to me. It said, and I quote, "READ THE LETTER. REMEMBER THE DAMPNESS." I was wary of following the first instruction, and not sure what to make of the second, but I decided to take the most professional route. I accepted the dry note and the wet envelope, nodding with a smile, and went on my way. I heard her slam the door and wail, perhaps to herself. She seemed to be taking the transformation particularly poorly.

Pocketing the note, I considered the wet envelope. It was not sealed well, perhaps on purpose. As a professional with integrity, I would not normally have honored the first request, but it seemed too much like the letter was actually for me in the first place. So after walking a fair bit away, I stood by an abandoned building where nobody could see and opened the envelope carefully.

As its scrawled handwriting began with "Dearest Emily," I had a feeling my initial guess was incorrect, and reading through the erratic and frantic letter confirmed it. This was, indeed, for Mrs. Emily Otis, but as I had gone this far already, I decided to keep reading. I gathered three key pieces of information from the worrisome mail: one, that Mrs. Sturgis was indeed in the final throes of giving in to her own self-horror; two, that Mrs. Otis was in fact Mrs. Sturgis's daughter who had married into a house that kept truths hidden for the sake of respectability; and three, that Mrs. Sturgis wanted to warn Mrs. Otis, with full and detailed written force of terror unknown to most mortals, that she would suffer the same exact fate, and that she should not even try to tough it out for as long as Mrs. Sturgis herself had done. I read it thoroughly, attempted to "remember the dampness" however I could to perhaps fulfill a last wish of a doomed woman, and replaced it into its unevenly-drying envelope, making sure to seal it properly this time.

I did not need to have read the letter to know Mrs. Sturgis was in such a state. I knew those this far along wailed when they were taking it poorly. It seemed the self-acceptance was often much more quiet and contemplative than the self-rejection, which was generally loud and did not last long before it was cut short by some force, whether internal or external. But the letter really drove it home for me. I had generally only heard drips of information about the feelings of people going through this, so this was the first time I had read anything close to an account. I felt for her, and felt haunted by the letter, though I would not admit the latter to even myself at the time. I had always fancied the concept of becoming one of them and I was confident I would not succumb to such emotional limitations, and I thought that it really was a pity that they could not see the wonderful promise of what they'd behold down there.

I completed my route without further incident that day, returning to the post office a little after sundown. Upon hearing my entering, Mr. Blakeley came out to the front desk to receive the outgoing mail. I did not mention to him that I opened Mrs. Sturgis's letter, because I found it hard to explain in that moment why I did so against policy. So I handed him all of the mail, including that letter, and walked the few blocks to my home, all the while idly thinking about the letter.

My hope was that Mr. Gilman would keep reading before passing harsh judgment on my actions here. I was banking on the concept that the town elites who were not arrested during the raids would be wise enough to understand a nuanced situation. Really, the whole of Innsmouth was a nuanced situation. I kept writing, more quickly now as I was fueled by the vivid memory of what came after.

I ate dinner and tried to relax, but I was restless that evening, so I wandered outside and walked along the river, taking in the dim nighttime ambiance. A light rain persisted, causing the water to dance in and out of the shadows in the banks, as if the splashes were lives in a cosmic flow, unknowingly close to being swallowed whole by darkness at every turn. That manner of thought should have prepared me for what I would experience during my slumber, but then again, perhaps nothing could have prepared me enough.

That night, I dreamed heavily, and I knew to take heavy dreams seriously in a town like Innsmouth. Normally, my dreams are rather linear, as my mind prefers a particular order to do things, and my chosen profession has reflected that desire with its routes and methodological procedures. However, this dream was not at all linear, and instead was a panorama of a great undersea battle, or if not a battle, a sustained bout of discord, as Deep Ones lashed out at other Deep Ones in a display of pure mayhem. It did not matter which way I looked. It was chaos all around, and all at once, as if my peripheral vision extended in unnatural ways to the back of my head. The effect was unavoidable pain before my eyes, an image of static, dynamic reckoning soaking into and saturating my psyche, threatening to drown me. It is not possible to relay the true feeling of this dream in words, so I will stop there with my attempt. What was important was that, upon waking, I knew very thoroughly that I was given this dream for a reason, and that I could not treat it as simply fiction. I did not know if what I had seen was the past, present, or future, but I knew I needed to do something about it. And despite the probable inconvenience, I decided to follow through with an honest try to figure this out, for the good of the community.

But since I did not know where to start, I went to work as normal to pick up the day's mail.

Not dwelling on the first dream was difficult, but necessary. The infinite hell of it was paralyzing, even in memory. I needed to not dwell on it both then and at the time of writing this, despite the great difficulty in pulling myself away from that feeling that pulled me down again so readily. Perhaps it was foolish to include it in the letter to Mr. Gilman, but I could not find it within myself to undo what had been written. And, perhaps, the town elites were used to these kinds of dreams in the first place. I took a deep breath, and a few shallow breaths, and looked to the Manuxet for solace. The banks giving definite closure to the inner maelstrom set me back on the right path, and so I turned back and pressed on with my story, like I did every day on my route, to the next door, to the next street.

Mr. Blakeley greeted me at the front desk with a typical stack of letters that I placed in my bag. He was never much for conversation, so I wordlessly gathered myself and left. I was not thinking about pleasantries, as my mind was clouded by the night before. I delivered and collected automatically for a while until I came upon the Otis residence.

It was a relatively-well-kept home, the sort with overwatered flowers surviving in planters outside the front windows, which were not boarded up or shuttered, but instead covered in a more subtle way with fastened inner curtains. It was the sort of house that, as I understood from my daily rounds, was likely to have silence instead of wails. You may correct me if I am wrong, but my assumption here is that this sort of home houses a family who, genealogically, more readily chooses the sea instead of ending things.

Reaching into my bag, I pulled out the envelope addressed from Mrs. Agnes Sturgis to Mrs. Emily Otis, from mother to daughter. "REMEMBER THE DAMPNESS" echoed in my mind as I considered the envelope, which was no longer damp. In fact, it was rather crisp, as I looked it over again. The envelope that I opened and properly resealed the day before would have been at least a little lumpy from how much water had seeped into its paper. The handwriting for the address and return address looked correct enough, but as I looked more and more, this did not seem to be the same paper where it was written. I walked a small distance away from the house to a deserted side street and carefully opened the letter, as I suspected something was amiss.

The paper inside, folded neatly over, contained a pleasant and reasonable message from a mother to a daughter, written in an informal but neat hand and giving no warning but the warning to remember to take what life hands you, no matter how hard it is in the short term, or some equivalent platitude. This was, of course, not what Mrs. Sturgis sent in the slightest bit. There was tampering afoot, and as this letter was meant to stay within Innsmouth, it was not a case for the approved and necessary censorship.

I t was not necessary to go into detail about that censorship, as the Gilmans were those who requested it in the first place, according to Mr. Blakeley. It was not too unusual at all to hand someone mail that had been swapped for a forgery, and Mr. Blakeley made it clear to me when I started that this measure was in place for the protection of the citizens and the town at large after the confusion from the outside world caused such problems. As much as I was not enthusiastic about the tampering, I agreed it was necessary. But that was for mail coming into and out of Innsmouth, and I had never suspected that this was happening for local mail. What also did not need to be said was that Mr. Blakeley was meant to tell me everything necessary to not arouse my own suspicion, which was the purpose of telling me about the known censorship in the first place. Keeping secrets without sharing secrets with the correct people led to the disaster of 1927, at least in part. If Mr. Blakeley was doing something as major as this without my knowledge, it was likely without the Gilmans' knowledge as well. However…

The only person, as you know, who would have been handling the mail before me was Mr. Blakeley himself. But I needed to have more evidence than this, and I would imagine, Mr. Gilman, that you would have needed more evidence if I had submitted this that day instead of waiting. I prefer not to waste people's time, especially a protector of the town such as yourself.

Was that too much brown-nosing? Probably not, I thought. It never hurt. But I resolved to get back on track and push through the rest, as it had started to become a little long-winded and I was not sure how patient the current Mr. Gilman would be with my story.

In the end, I decided against delivering the letter as addressed, due to the revelation I had just uncovered, and instead continued on my route as usual until I reached the Sturgis household, where I intended to show the altered mail to Mrs. Sturgis and field ideas from her as well, if at all possible. I knocked on the door, and received no answer. I knocked a second time, harder, and that was all the poor old door could handle, as it snapped partially from its hinges, darkness spilling out from the cracks to the inside. And yet there was still no answer. I decided against entering, for fear of a number of things, having to answer for trespassing only one of them and perhaps not the most pressing. Instead, I slipped the letter into the mail slot of the broken door, which is why I do not have a copy attached here. However, if you see fit to stop by to check or ask me to do the same, it is likely still sitting just on the other side of that door, as I have not found there to be any activity at the Sturgis residence since then, at least from my observations each day during my route.

So, because I could not collaborate with Mrs. Sturgis like I had briefly hoped to do, I resolved to take matters into my own hands. Since the dampness of Mrs. Sturgis's letter was how I could tell there was a difference, I would look for outgoing letters from wailing houses and soak those in the Manuxet just enough to have lasting water damage before handing them into Mr. Blakeley. Oddly and inconveniently, there were far fewer wailers on my route than usual per day, so it took me three weeks to find only a few with outgoing local mail.

I thought to write about the other thing next, but no, I had to stave it off. It was becoming more and more difficult to do so as the narrative accelerated in time, but I needed to communicate this all clearly and reasonably. That was the most important thing, I told myself, that was the most important thing. I kept writing.

On the other hand, what was convenient was that those who were sending messages similar to Mrs. Sturgis's were not sealing them properly or at all, so it was simple to check their contents briefly to confirm that they were full of the right sort of frightful language, and then to reseal and later dampen.

Mr. Gilman, all of these first few were replaced with falsely-encouraging forgeries. I decided to save these instead of delivering them or returning them to their senders as evidence, and they will be included in this package as examples of the typical replacement letters. They were always general, optimistic, and rather specifically mentioned pushing through doubts. I started to wonder if they had something to do with the decrease in wailing from behind closed doors and shuttered windows.

Mr. Blakeley always accepted the outgoing mail at the end of my route without asking a single question, so I was relatively certain he was not aware of my activities. After all, Innsmouth is a rather damp place, and it was not out of the question that some mail would get wet. Still, I started to wonder if Mr. Blakeley would eventually catch on, so I decided to start soaking more local mail items, not just those that were disturbed correspondence. This served another purpose as a control group, as I suppose I was to be a detective and also a scientist in addition to my duties as postwoman. And as expected, the control group came back water damaged and unchanged while the others were crisp and clean fakes.

At this point, which was very recently, I was ready to confront Mr. Blakeley about the tampering.

I t was not very recently, I had to admit to myself, as I was no longer able to distance myself from what lurked in the depths of my mind. In reality, as far as I could recall, "this point" was approximately two months prior to writing this letter to Mr. Gilman, so perhaps in mid-July. But even though I was ready at the time in terms of ample evidence, I was not ready mentally, and that was not something I would put in writing, as I feared it would cost me my job and potentially more than that. But I could not ignore it within myself any longer. I needed to ruminate upon it and figure out how to move past it without appearing unprofessional in my explanation. After all, solving a problem in the most cordial way and moving on was the postal worker's way, I thought to myself. Thinking in the scope of my work kept me sane this far.

I knew I could not write about the subsequent dreams that plagued my nights with increasing frequency and intensity, and how they affected me so horribly. Though at first I was hesitant to blame anything but the fact I did not know how to solve the problem presented in the initial dream, it became apparent that the dreams grew worse and worse as I collected and read more of the letters I started privately calling "wails." Each night's was the same scene, but it felt that with each "wail" read, the dream would feel more personal, more intimate, even more instinctual, like I was becoming one of the warring-or-tortured creatures. It was a feeling that flooded me such that I felt I would burst, and one of the Deep Ones would burst in turn, bursting with fury such that another would burst in the other sense: alien viscera expanding, sinking, floating, mixing with the thrashing movement of the sickened waters and the depths of myself in turn. Every day I was able to ward away the lingering effects of these dreams by forcing myself to focus on my route, and I became more and more obsessive about intercepting and dampening wails as part of that increased focus. My days turned fully to my route, and my nights to the deep, so much so that by the time I should have done something about the postal situation, I was too locked in this pattern to find the internal means to craft a plan that would stop or expose Mr. Blakeley's disruption of appropriate mail handling. So I continued. Wails seemed to be more and more common, and thus the dreams became more and more immediate and vivid-beyond-vivid at an ever-increasing rate. In addition, Mr. Blakeley's replacement letters became more and more desperate, but I stopped reading those entirely at some point, as I was so very thoroughly focused on the wails.

This continued until last night, when eventuality finally became certainty, and I fully became one of the raging entities of the dreams, full of questions turned to anguish, stripped of language, and sent to war that no longer felt like war. War was organized, war had reason. There was nothing in my mind but blind wrath. I felt the bursting, I followed the bursting, careening around the ruins that I innately knew to be Y'ha-nthei, shapes of terrifying former splendor that felt familiar yet unfamiliar and only fueled my bursting, bursting, into an ancient structure, inward, inward, bursting, bursting, until I grasped a being that felt beyond the imagination of time and space itself: eyes flowing from eyes, limbs flowing from limbs, turning happy void to nightmare. I burst, burst, burst forth and attacked it, with bladed teeth and terrible claws.

And then I awoke, staggered over to the desk, and sat down, damp envelopes scattered in piles all around me. I knew I was in the post office's back room, despite only seeing it as a glimpse before. And Mr. Blakeley was gone. And I knew, somehow I knew for sure, that he would not return. My self-protective mindset kicked in one last time and I sorted out what to do. Due to Mr. Blakeley's absence, I could write the letter I had been formulating in my former waking, walking life. I found a pen and stationery in a drawer, pulled them out, and began a draft.

And now that draft needs a conclusion.

My temporal separation now weakens to an infinitesimal non-point, sending me vulnerable and shivering into the present. The late September weather could be cause for a light shiver, say the remnants of my logical thought, but this shiver is deeper than any caused by a slight chill from the first winds of autumn. The last moments of the dream tumble in my mind's eye incessantly, repeating and repeating as I struggle to find the words for Mr. Gilman. Mr. Gilman, sir. Sir. Your new postmaster, sir. I made the decision, and I am sure. I am sure, and I will stick with it. I will stick with it, and I will finish the letter. I will finish the letter.

I pick up the pen and start writing. I do not know what exactly I am writing anymore. It reads reasonably, even the suppositions and lies. I say that Mr. Blakeley saw the error of his ways and removed himself from his position. I say that Mr. Blakeley found himself near the ocean and was pulled under by bladed teeth and terrible claws. I say that I need to pause the mail a few days to reorganize but will send high priority mail items through Thomas. I write a closing, I sign. I put all I promised in a package. I seal it, and I slightly dampen it with the dampness of the pile at my feet for good measure. I try to stand, and finding that this alone is difficult, I shuffle toward the door out to the front desk, nearly stumbling over something in the process. I get to the counter and wait for Thomas to arrive. He would deliver this. I am too weak.

While I wait for him, I look around at the sparse yet calming lobby, with its pleasing tile floor that creeps up the wall toward the postal boxes. I wonder if it will ever get there and convert the dusty boxes to slick tile. Before they can, Thomas arrives, with his bland-yet-neat outfit and hair and demeanor. I call his name and try to communicate, but I cannot seem to find words. I hold the package out to him, motioning for him to take it, dampness dripping onto the counter and staining it with orderly and sensible purpose. Instead of taking the package, Thomas stops dead in his tracks and blanches, his eyes suddenly aghast. He runs from the post office lobby without uttering more than a squeaking sound. I look after him in slight sadness as my grip falters on the package and on the waking world. The dream calls me in a different way now, and this time I will know what to do next.

LIGHT & POWER

CLANCY NACHT

"**A**rkham Light and Power. How may I help you?"

The words, like a chant, all run together from just outside my office. The cadence is always the same no matter who's speaking but grows discordant with the different tones and inflections. The phrase overlaps. If I pay too much attention to it, I start to feel sick. So, I've learned to tune out the dull roar from the support services crew.

A long shadow appears, strange because I don't usually see such a distinct shadow with the overhead lights. I look up at my doorway.

"Ms. Flay, a word?"

Light glints off his glasses. He's tall and lanky, with tightly curled hair, wearing a classic tweed three piece. Intriguingly old-fashioned, as if he's been brought through time to be excruciatingly formal.

I can't believe I find it so absorbing. Usually, I like bad boys.

A stuffy, older-seeming gentleman isn't normally my thing. That said, I'm hard pressed to estimate his age. He could be my father or my brother. He's timeless like that.

"Sure, Mr. N." I pick up my tablet and carry it with me toward a conference room. With the number of people abandoning the information technology department of Arkham Light and Power, it won't be difficult to find an empty one.

When we leave my office, the chanting has stopped, now broken into a chorus of responses to the calls.

"You don't have to call to transfer your light and power. If your debt has not been cleared, it will follow you wherever you go."

"If you can't pay today, we can find other ways to collect what you owe. How many children do you have?"

"The service tech won't leave until you've satisfied your debt."

The job has its unnerving moments. Should anyone pry open one of the computer cases, there appears to be distinctly non-standard parts inside. I know because I did that once, just out of curiosity.

If I'm being honest, I almost quit that day. Nothing inside the computer's case appeared to be doing anything. It was packed with strange, unmoving gears etched with unnamable designs, all dripping with a viscous red liquid and an odd black polymer the likes of which I'd never seen before.

At first, I thought it had to be a joke, but when I peeked over at the service and support center, the workers tucked in their cubbies, they all just stared at me with their eyes wide and mouths hanging open. Their eternal hubbub quieted until I clicked the case back on. Then they resumed answering calls, and that maddening cadence began again.

I glance in their direction as I follow Mr. N to the nearest empty conference room. They sit chanting their scripts at the callers but suddenly stop, as if they were commanded to be silent and still.

My understanding is that Mr. N powers the servers with them. I've never seen the server room, which isn't completely unusual. I write software; hardware isn't my purview.

But something about how evasive people become when I bring up the server room fuels my urge to see it.

Our conference room has windows to the outside, and before he sits, Mr. N pulls the blinds down over all of them. It casts a pall over the particle board table and cheap rolling chairs.

His glasses glint again as he flashes a smile in the dim light. The gleam of his teeth is almost metallic. Already seated, I'm ready to take notes on the flaws in my code, jotting down whatever changes he wants made.

I still don't understand how the project he has me doing fits with anything else in the business. Not to mention, I'm a little rusty writing this stuff.

But Mr. N appears pleased, so I relax.

Rumor is he's a nightmare to work with. Difficult. Demanding. He's fired so many software developers before me, eliminating them with such coldness that the last took his own life.

I like to think I'm more stable than that, but then, I don't know what Mr. N said to him.

"You are becoming more fluent in machine language." Mr. N states it like a known fact, staring at me with those unnerving golden eyes.

I feel exposed even though it's a compliment.

"Thanks, Mr. N. I appreciated your patience while I got back up to speed. It's something I learned in college but haven't had much cause to use."

I try not to squirm under the weight of his gaze. Something about how he examines me so minutely makes me think he'd like that though, so I do. Just a little.

His smile widens. "You'd be surprised how few are as accommodating as you."

The approval both warms me and terrifies me. He leans in, his smile widening in a way that seems physically impossible.

I blink a few times to clear my vision. A trick of the light. It's so dark in here, and his teeth are so shiny.

"I'm still not sure what my code project has to do with anything. It might help if I were to see the bigger picture. Is it robotics?"

He sits back, and the crummy rolling chair squeals in protest. He always seems to get that reaction out of furniture. I'm not sure why, because he's tall but thin, not of a size to strain office furniture. Just one more odd detail.

"You know, Ms. Flay, I do think you've earned the right to see what it is you're working on. Let's touch base later this week. Make an appointment to visit my office."

My mouth won't move. A sense of foreboding overwhelms me, mingling with excitement. Finally, I nod.

"Now, I do have some changes…."

I make my appointment to visit Mr. N, and the next day, it feels like the rest of the employees are keeping their distance. Not in the usual way, though. Not because they know I'm busy. It's more frantic than that.

A sullen desperation animates them when I enter the break room. They never look me in my eyes. They refuse to use my name. This has never been the friendliest workplace, but even by Arkham Light and Power standards it feels strange.

Then, a couple days later when I come into work, strange symbols adorn my desk. Random twisted, woody dolls. Bits of metal, moon stones, and candles.

There are pitying looks and, even weirder, homemade lunches with my name on them set in the fridge for me to find.

Strange delicacies. Beautiful meats and salads. Exquisite desserts.

It feels a little like being fattened for the slaughter.

What a ridiculous thought.

By the time my appointment arrives, I'm ready.

Mr. N's office—and the servers—are situated in a brutalist office building close to a cave, a short drive through the wild woods toward the coast. It seems impractical, and my Prius struggles over the raw dirt road. Doesn't that bother the execs?

I remain undaunted, determined to see my project through…and to meet with Mr. N once again. This feels big. I wrote exactly what he wanted. It'll move his robot's parts, or whatever he requires it to do. I'm not sure why our public utility even needs an automaton, but if there's one here at the server room, I have ways to speak to it.

I make it on time, my laptop at the ready and I'm dressed professionally. There aren't any other cars in the small lot when I park. Is Mr. N even here?

Of the bosses I assume work out of this building, he's the only one we see on the main campus, so I'm surprised there aren't any other vehicles here. Maybe it's a half day for them?

I'm only halfway out of my car when Mr. N offers me a hand. He must've seen me arrive through the huge dark windows.

"Ms. Flay. I trust you have what I need?"

I nod and pull out my laptop. "It's finished. Do you want me to put it on a thumb drive?"

"No." He grins as he reaches for what I assume is my laptop but instead lays two soft, very cold hands on mine. It's so intimate that I just look up at him, lost.

I've always been drawn to him, but that was just a little workplace fantasy, something to help me through the doldrums of IT work. The way he touches me now makes my pulse race.

When our gazes meet, his smile softens.

He runs his thumb over the back of my hand right there in the open, in the middle of an empty parking lot with a dozen windows looking on like big, dark eyes.

I'm lightheaded. I haven't been so easily aroused since I was a teenager. I crave more touches despite how cold his firm hands are. There's just something about him.

My brain feels so fuzzy that all I want is to follow him. As if reading it in my expression, his grin turns sly. He releases me, turns, and heads for the front doors.

Over his shoulder, he says, "We don't usually let outsiders in here. But you're special."

The compliment dodges my anxious defenses and thrills me to my core. Heedless of what I'm walking into, I follow as if hypnotized by the sound of his voice.

He holds open the door, and I walk right in. Then the door shuts, and for a moment I'm plunged into darkness.

Light leaks between the slats of blinds and from behind curtains in a room that's not only dark but freezing cold. As my eyes adjust, I become aware of crowded areas stacked with the clusters of server racks I expect. Between them, humanoid forms stand powered down, hooked to thick cables. They could be awaiting electricity. Data.

Or the instructions that I've been writing.

I laugh because I don't know how to respond. I'd pictured automating robotic arms, like in a factory. Something rudimentary, intended as an assistant to human workers. The instructions are so basic, not customized to whatever these things are. I wouldn't begin to know how to write for these.

And there are a lot of them.

"Aren't they beautiful?"

Somehow, I'd forgotten Mr. N. He looks like a proud father. Why wouldn't he?

It's as I approach one in the darkness that a chink of light gleams on what is quite clearly flesh. Then I glimpse a human eye in a metal socket. Fingers worn like gloves.

The faces. Faces soldered on with a material I cannot explain or describe.

A scream builds in my throat, but I'm well past fear as I stroke the soft, very cold cheek of one of the unfinished droids. Its eyes sparkle. The veins in the pale sclera are black, as are the irises, very nearly. The pupil contracts, then widens.

It sees.

Another scream burbles up, abortive, but then Mr. N. is beside me. His cold hand rests at the small of my back.

I shiver with more than cold or fright. It isn't revulsion, though I feel that, too.

I can't focus. It's all too much for me to wrap my head around.

So I babble.

"What is this to do with powering Arkham? What is—Do they do the work? Don't they use the power? I don't… Their faces, what are they?"

He chuckles indulgently, pulling me closer as I stiffen. "There are powers far greater than electricity, Ms. Flay. You are truly blessed to be in this time, in this place."

"What kind of powers? What are you talking about?" I turn toward him and realize our faces are kissing close. Closer than I've ever been to him.

I hear him now, not his heartbeat, but a ticking sound, like a clock. His golden eyes aren't set in human flesh. As they move, there is the soft whirr of electronics. His gaze holds a challenge.

"Me. I run this place. I was summoned to keep the lights on, but I am capable of so much more, Ms. Flay."

I try to step back, but he stays with me. The longer I look, the more I realize his face is nothing but a porcelain mask, his glasses painted on. I forget to breathe in the grasp of this…thing, this strange mechanical doll.

This robot that claims to be a god.

"Who are you?"

His lips don't even move anymore as he answers. As he reveals himself to me, the dread builds.

"I have many names and many forms." He gestures to the robots. "Not just these. I am but an aspect of my real form. This is the truest visage you may ever look upon. To accurately perceive me would shatter your mind. Even to utter my name…"

Then he dips his head, and that cold mask touches my mouth. His lips don't move, but I breathe him in. Pain like stinging pins pricks my mouth, a burning on my tongue like electrical wire.

I leap back, slipping free of his arms as I search the room desperately. It's dark, but where can I hide? Can one even hide from such a being?

Beyond rational thought, I find myself already running through the rows of servers, trying to avert my gaze from the robots that grasp at me from between the racks.

"Why me?" I cry as one of the horrifying hands with their flesh gloves grabs hold and rips my shirt.

"Because you can speak to machines in a special way."

The voice comes from above now, and when I look up, Mr. N hovers directly overhead, held up by wires.

"Lots of people can use that language!" I pull my ragged shirt tighter around me and clutch my laptop to my chest.

He floats down in front of me with aching slowness. I steel myself not to run, even when he brings a cold hand to my cheek.

"You are different. These others—" He gestures vaguely toward the other bodies. "They were failures. They had the ambition, but not the empathy."

What could that possibly mean? Machine language isn't empathetic. It just is what it is.

Confused, I stare at the floor until he curls his finger under my chin and tips my face up until our eyes lock. It's his face again. His human face. The face of the man I had wanted to get to know. The genius. The one with the quiet command.

That's when I realize what he means by empathy. He isn't just my boss. I hold further interest for him.

"But that's when I thought you were human."

He leans in, breathes tenderly, fingers warm as he brushes his lips against mine. "I can be human when I choose to be."

That first kiss blazed pain through my mouth, and now I taste the tang of blood.

"What do you want from me?" I close my eyes as I whisper against his lips, or what he manifests as lips.

"Everything," he says as he turns his head and a soft, human tongue gently explores my mouth. A lover's kiss.

I don't kid myself. He isn't offering himself as a lover.

"What will happen to me?"

He presses his hands to my chest, squeezing just enough to be sensual. This is a seduction, and it is heady. Imagine that. Me being seduced by a god.

"Your mind, as you know it, will shatter, but it will also be eternal. A part of me. Carried through time by my recollections. Surviving with me, serving me. Your sacrifice will be remembered, even worshipped when I set this world right."

I open my mouth to him, and at once the stinging resumes. Wires force their way in, shredding my tongue. They exit with wet chunks. The force of the cable entering my mouth breaks my teeth, ejecting some wetly to the floor as others scratch their way down my esophagus when the cable pushes its hard surfaces through inner skin. It tears that tube of flesh apart, spattering my organs with bile that burns me inside.

My gag reflex triggers automatically, starving my lungs of air. The husk of me pointlessly pushes back on the thick cable that's now starting to split, divide itself into myriad clusters of wires.

I bring up my hands, body again reacting without thought. My brain, in its dying moments, fights to save me from myself, but Mr. N grabs my hands tight and hundreds of needles puncture my palms. They break the skin and slither up into veins and arteries, threading through my system.

As my skin splits and peels off, I lack enough air to scream.

But still, I register the pain as Mr. N makes me stronger, fills me with metal, changes my blood to mercury. Despite the chill of the room and my dying flesh, being reforged makes me burn hot as my ribs crack, my vertebra break. He is remaking every cell of my body.

Discarding all my bad parts.

The wires carve a tunnel through my stomach and pull apart my pancreas and spleen. Blood and organs funnel out of the hole, replaced with gears and cables. I feel them as what I am expands past needing a rib cage at all. What remains is pulped into shard and sinew, dribbling to the floor.

When he releases me from our kiss, he stands in the muck of my becoming. I stare dumbly as he absorbs all the gore into him. It rises from the floor into his open palms.

"Are you still in there, Ms. Flay?" His voice is deep. Tender. Conspiratorial. Like we're lovers.

I can't figure out how to move my limbs, so I can't respond other than with my human eyes. I blink twice.

He smiles and picks up the laptop I dropped. Shaking bone fragments from it, he pops it open and puts a jump drive in it.

"Great! Now let's find that promising code you wrote and see if we can salvage your brain. If not, well, you've done very well, Ms. Flay. I'm proud of you."

BOOKS OF THE DEAD

MIA DALIA

I didn't set out to become a librarian. Once upon a time, I longed to be the hero of the adventures that ink the pages of the dusty tomes on these shelves. Time, it seems, makes fools of us all, by tearing out the pages of our stories and crumpling them before our eyes. In the end, you are left standing in the sea of mangled dreams, hoping no one lights a match, for even a crushed illusion is more bearable than the one that goes up in flames.

But one cannot avoid all fires. Life is full of incendiary devices. And sometimes these devices are people.

Arkham Library is an impressive place. I fell in love with it at first sight —that striking, haunted-looking Georgian architecture, that time-worn brick edifice. My feet carried me from the granite sidewalk, past the heavy doors, and there, standing on the polished floors of its vaunted grounds, surrounded by the countless tomes and infinite knowledge, I knew I had found a place where I belonged. Of course, Miskatonic University's Orne Library is the famous one, but I'd like to think the two of them are very different places. And it is my belief that the Arkham Library has more character.

To matriculate at Miskatonic, the most respected institution of higher learning, had been my dream for many years. But the thing about dreams is that eventually one must wake up and face the often-less-palatable reality. I ended up settling for a much smaller school on the outskirts of Arkham, hoping to eventually transfer over.

I arrived there older than most, for as a youth I had neither the funds nor the connections to enroll. Once I had rearranged my expectations to suit my current situation, I came to appreciate the place. So much of my life had been spent waiting to begin my higher education, and now it was within my reach. Anyone who's ever had their dream come true would know how I felt walking the well-manicured lawns, admiring the stately architecture of the collegial grounds. Every cloud above my head, every blade of grass beneath my feet seemed to whisper welcome.

I wanted to study everything, to drink up every bit of knowledge on tap here. Instead, sensibly, I had chosen history, foreseeing a career of one day perhaps becoming a professor myself. Books, I would publish books, I told myself, envisioning my name embossed on leather covers. Well-researched books, the sort one has to travel for.

Before my great and tragic adventure, I had not traveled much. Most destinations I only visited through pages of books. Much to my shame, I'd barely been out of Massachusetts. Arkham born and bred, and seemingly destined to stay put. My parents' humble grocery shop could not support their only son's dreams. For years, I toiled at their store and other menial jobs, saving up money for my studies. Then in a stroke of terrible fortune, my family's business burned down, leaving me an orphan. As I mourned their passing, a letter arrived—its envelope a proverbial silver lining. My parents had at some point taken out insurance of which I was the sole beneficiary. The amount was modest, but it provided me with just enough to finally break free of working life and enter the glittering world of academia.

I arrived with the voracious hunger of one kept away from nourishment for too long. There was nothing I didn't want to try, encounter, study. No one I didn't wish to speak to. In retrospect, I can see how that might have made me unpopular, that uncouth eagerness. Combined with my years, it had likely made me something of an outsider.

It matters greatly at that age, the difference of a mere half a decade. I have long stopped counting my years now that it no longer matters and there is no one to celebrate with. Now I am merely old, like Arkham itself, like the books that surround me. Well, like some of these books anyway, for there is a difference between old and ancient. I have seen ancient, and it stands outside of time itself, humbling all those who behold it.

Back then, I struggled to make friends. Perhaps it was a matter of one's societal standing and class too. My humble origins placed me several tiers below everyone else in the surrounding social stratosphere. I recognized some of their names from the newspapers— the young scions of wealthy families, old money, new ambition. It didn't matter to me then; I was determined to surpass them all. My ambition would be the brightest sun to light that campus, I told myself.

To paraphrase the popular axiom, there's no fool like a young fool. Ambition can only get you so far in a world that turns on the axis of money and power. Still, I tried. When opportunities presented themselves, however challenging or dangerous, I took them. When it threatened to break my back or break my spirit, I persevered. Through the impenetrable ice and blistering sun, I plowed on, telling myself it would all one day be worth it. I was determined to uncover the secrets that would fuel my publication career and put my name on the map alongside the greatest historians of the world.

This is the only thing I learned with any kind of certainty, the only knowledge I can pass on with confidence—the world does not wish to be known. It revels in its secrets. It offers just enough to tantalize and spur you on, then sits back and amuses itself with your failures to uncover its mysteries.

If you disagree with me, you have not looked hard or far enough. Give it some time. In the end, the world will always break your heart.

I love the quietude of the library, but it can weigh on the mind, too, giving one too much time for rumination. Instead, I try to keep myself occupied with various tasks, bustling around as much as my ruined leg will allow, returning books to their rightful places, restoring order.

Being a librarian allows me to get to know the patrons, albeit chiefly through their reading selections and not conversation. I'm afraid I'm too solitary a creature. Even being around people can be draining enough to send me seeking the solace of a written word.

At night, I often stay behind after locking the doors. Sleep hasn't been a friend of mine for a long time; the older I get, the less he visits. My mind whirrs and whirrs around with barely any rest. These days, it takes me to the third floor. Rare collections. I can almost hear them whisper, hushed voices calling my name.

My bad leg protests as I drag it after the good one, one uncomfortable stair at a time. My footsteps echo in the stillness of the afterhours. The alternating duo of janitors who come by most days knows to leave me alone. We pass each other as shadows in the night, silently, with only a hint of a nod. They think me strange, I know. And of course, they are right.

I have stopped putting much effort into hiding my strangeness during the day, and I do nothing of a kind at night. I have come to terms with being the local oddity, the odd, quiet librarian. Let them talk. Arkham has always had its share of the peculiar and peculiarities. There are rumors; I know there are rumors about me. They are passed on in hushed voices from the older to the newer generations of interchangeable youths I see before me.

Rumors are harmless, of course. Words are wicked and barbed things that can do unimaginable harm, but not in the form of rumors. Not in my experience, anyway. Let them whisper, I say, as I go on about my business.

There is no removing me from my position. The library would have to burn down for me to leave. The town feels just enough guilt or pity toward me to keep me around. I am, after all, one of the only survivors of one of the most famous expeditions by its luminaries. A tangential part of a local legend. Whether as a living relic or a macabre souvenir, I am here to stay.

Contrary to my initial plans, I never became a professor nor, sworn to secrecy, have I ever published a book. The library job is my consolation prize. Not the Orne, mind you, that would have been too close for comfort. But this is good enough, the town library. I get to be a part of the community, to be of service. Good enough, I repeat to myself whenever the specters of my youthful dreams come to visit. I am settled here. The Arkham takes care of its own.

When my time comes, I imagine I will simply dissolve into dust, mixing with the particles that already swirl here. Sometimes when the light from the windows catches it just right, it can almost look beautiful. I would love to be a thing of beauty one day, if only for a moment.

I imagine I would always remain here, haunting these aisles, reaching for books I could no longer touch. Sometimes I already feel like a ghost.

The notion gives me comfort, but it frightens me too. Though I may be a failed historian, I retain a strong appreciation of history, and I fear I have done nothing to earn my place in it. No one wishes to be forgotten, no matter what they say. It is why we quest and strive and seek—to find the thing that shall immortalize us.

These days, out of practical considerations, I am taking a more direct approach.

I make my way to the third floor in the sparse illumination of the closed-for-the-day library, casting grotesque shadows all around. A public institution without its public is like a person without a heart. But there are ghosts on every corner.

It was at the University that I met the man who changed my life. A Miskatonic professor with the soul of an adventurer, he sought to find lost civilizations. Failing to secure enough volunteers in his own University, he had come to our smaller one as a last resort with promises of excitement and renown everlasting. His enthusiasm may have put some off but to me it was irresistible. Where others heard danger, I heard the trumpets of glory. Where others imagined privation and struggle, I saw ways to prove my mettle, to go out into the world and live at last, bravely and purposefully. I thought I had finally found a way to live my dreams. It was as if Miskatonic itself had come to me, knocked on my door, and said, "Come, see what you've been missing."

I followed the professor like a dog. Like a shadow. Like a fool. Out of Arkham and into a nightmare.

What came back was a photographic negative of me, leeched of vitality, broken utterly in spirit and partially in body. The latter had healed, limp notwithstanding. I get around with a cane well enough. The former...that's another story altogether.

When sleep does take mercy on me, I still see it as vividly as all those decades ago—the eldritch horror buried beneath the earth; a bloodcurdling visage not meant for human eyes, the terrifying message not meant for human minds.

Back then, we had let the horror lie in its uneasy dormancy. Those of us who could, got away. The rest spilled their blood into the inhospitable earth. I still shudder when I imagine what that blood might have fed.

I tried leaving it all behind, but I couldn't. For better or worse, we drag the backbreaking, heartbreaking weight of our past with us like our shadows. I, who once trained to be a historian, am convinced that we are inseparable from our history.

Back then, nothing I did upon my return mattered. Nothing felt the same. My studies seemed meaningless. The few fragile friendships I had managed didn't comfort me. Our adventure had aged me. Overnight, it seemed, I became someone too afraid to try. My hair had turned as white as the Antarctic snow, and my soul ossified like some of the finds we had unearthed. I was lost to myself and to reason, moving from day to day as thoughtlessly as a windup toy. And this went on for far too long, eventually leading me here, to the Arkham Library.

I'm slightly out of breath by the time I arrive at my destination. Third floor, the last room on the left. The door says *Archive*. A deceptive oversimplification of what the room truly holds.

The keyring in my hand is as heavy and loud as a gaoler's. I find the right one and it turns in the lock, the dense weight of the metal matching my leaden heart. Each time I come here, a part of me screams in protest. Each time that part shrinks. Soon there will be nothing but silence.

I open the door and step inside. There are no windows in this room nor is it wired for electricity. I make do with the portable source of illumination I brought up with me, though by now I know this place by heart. It houses books that are not meant to be.

By the same logic that Medieval Europe locked away in the towers the controversial contenders to the thrones instead of killing them—not wanting royal blood on their hands and moreover never certain when such august personage might become needed—these books are kept here instead of being destroyed.

This is the only room in the library that's off-limits. Few even know it exists. It took me years to find out about it—a secret passed down like an ancient ritual from the retiring head librarian to me. The Arkham Library promotes learning in every possible way, encouraging its patrons to read far and wide. To that end, it offers hundreds of thousands of books, anything from the modern classics to—available by special request only—rare copies of ancient tomes.

Some of these books can be found nowhere else in the world. At least, nowhere people have looked so far. But the volumes in the third floor's last room on the left are the rarest of the rare; the ones that, out of concern for public safety, have been taken out of circulation or have never entered circulation in the first place. These are the tomes of the most dangerous knowledge.

While the Orne has a larger collection, the one at our library is nevertheless impressive, largely fed by the private donations of Arkham's finest and strangest denizens. Some I believe to be copies of the original, but a good copy is still worth its weight in gold. By now, I have perused them all, carefully turning the ancient pages, fingers shaking with forbidden delight. *The Book of Eibon. Dhol Chants. Pnakotic Manuscripts.* A particularly instructive grimoire from the one witch the Salem Trials failed to find.

But there is one book that I keep coming back to again and again. One wouldn't be too surprised to find that it is the famed *Necronomicon*. Of course, Arkham is world famous for being home to the infamous *Book of the Dead*. One wonders if when Alhazred first wrote *Al Azif* back in the eighth century, he knew exactly what he was unleashing upon the world or how long it would survive.

The Orne Library houses several versions of the book. I've heard that one has fallen into terrible disrepair and has been meticulously restored by experts over the past two years, its intricacy slowing the process, though there have been rumors of supernatural intervention.

The copy in the Arkham Library's possession, the one I return to time and again, is the Waite version. It is a little-known fact, but each *Necronomicon* differs. It's not an uncommon thing for a book that has been around for so many centuries, translated over and over again. The Waite version is the one that speaks to me, just as I imagine it had spoken to its last owner years ago.

Though my life has largely been a dreary procession of monotonous days and restless nights bookended by some excitement and adventure on the past end and surely a gravestone in the future, there has been one bright spot in it. Her name was Asenath Waite, and she was radiant.

Some people give off a certain energy; a light, if you will. It doesn't have to be as bright as sunshine to cut through the darkness.

I noticed her right away. A colleague of mine who attended Miskatonic part-time had told me of her, putting a name to the face. A woman amid their venerable and antiquatedly gender-restricted grounds was an unmissable sight. She was a fellow curiosity then, I mused, intrigued by this woman who had succeeded where I once failed.

But I would have noticed her anyway. Anywhere. Asenath Waite was small and slender, with large inquisitive eyes and, as it turned out, an indefatigable appetite for dark knowledge. The Orne alone could not contain all the tomes to satisfy Ms. Waite's blazing curiosity, thus she began to frequent the Arkham Library. She checked out book after book, sometimes staying right here at the library to devour them as if she could not wait to get home. She read, and I watched, quietly, clandestinely, taking care to ensure that she never thought of me as more than a mere piece of library furniture: useful and unobtrusive.

A hereto unknown lightness nestled in my heart upon seeing her. I would step outside and hear the birds sing, notice things I had never paid attention to before.

"Those are whippoorwills," she told me once outside the library, appearing at my side once as quietly as a wraith. "Their song is in their name."

"It's … beautiful," I managed, hoping the color did not come into my pale cheeks to betray my excitement at finally speaking to her. It was beautiful, in a way, and strangely familiar too, as if I had heard it before, a long time ago.

"They foretell a death," she said. "Beware, beautiful things are the deadliest."

With that, she left, and when my heart at last returned to its duties, thrumming within my rib cage, I had observed a near beat in it. Asenath. A-se-nath. I never thought it possible, but I think I had fallen in love.

It came to nothing, of course. I was older, much too timid, and with nothing to offer. Even when shortly after the head librarian died and I received a promotion, there still wasn't much to me. And so, I watched from the sidelines as she met a dashing fellow by the name of Derby, bought a house here in Arkham, and settled down.

Only I did not think a woman like her could ever settle, not truly. And sure enough, there were rumors of unrest in the Derby household. I'd see the darkness in my beloved's eyes become deeper and deeper each time she visited to get new books. We made small talk, and I persuaded myself it was enough.

Then she stopped coming around. I waited and waited, and eventually saw her on the street.

"Oh, it's you," she said, seeing me too.

"It's me." I smiled. "How are you, Mrs. Derby? You've not been at the library in some time."

Her new name tasted bitter on my tongue.

She smiled back. "I have a book of my own now to study. My darling husband has sourced me my own copy of *Necronomicon* for a gift."

"Oh. How generous."

"Indeed." Her smile faded. "Though I'm afraid it is the kind of book that changes its reader to suit its needs."

"How do you mean?" I asked politely, eager to prolong the conversation.

She prevaricated, listening to a trill above our heads. There it was again, the whippoorwill. Death was in the air.

"It seems as though my book might be better suited for a male reader," Asenath said finally, quietly. "Do you believe such a thing is possible? For a book?"

"I have seen enough of this world to believe that anything is possible," I answered her honestly.

"I cannot decide if that is a good or a bad thing," she said, frowning briefly before managing another smile, and excusing herself.

That was the last time we spoke. Asenath Waite was killed shortly after by her husband, Edward Derby. He smashed her head in with a candlestick. That detail never leaves my mind.

The man had likely lost his mind to have done such a thing, though I was not privy to the intimate details of their marriage. All I knew was that he'd been locked away in the Arkham Sanitarium afterward, but not before he burned all of his wife's books. All but one that is. The *Necronomicon* had been saved by one of Asenath's servants, smuggled out, and eventually sold to the Arkham Library, after the University balked at the cost and decided they did not need another copy.

It is my understanding that the version that had been spared the fire varies significantly from the original text. But I do not care about such things. I'm after Asenath's personal annotations in the margins. Her rushed, sloped cursive betrays a restless mind. I trace the words with my fingertips to feel closer to the woman who wrote them. She is the ghost that haunts these pages as she haunts the empty chambers of my heart as I haunt the vast corridors of the library. We are made for each other.

Slowly, I am learning her mysteries. Page by page, the secret knowledge of the book is revealed to me. I have never felt closer to my beloved than I do in these stolen hours. In this darkness.

Perhaps this is my purpose at last. This is the treasure I was always meant to uncover. I did not need to go to the ends of the earth to find it. In the end, it came to me.

After reading for a while, I set the book aside. I lean against the table and close my eyes. Strange new notions are swirling through my mind; the images of eldritch beings begin to take form. It's always the same, but clearer each time.

Soon enough I believe I shall be able to call out to them and receive a reply. I know it's what Asenath would have wanted.

It is a relief to know one's purpose at last. Once, when I was young and sure of the world, I made bold decisions and followed through. But setting fire to a small shop or signing up for an expedition to a faraway land is child's play compared to what I'm doing now.

Sometimes I can still feel the heat of that fire—was that when I first heard the whippoorwills? I can remember the sensation of being so very close to death and things so much worse than death when I was on that fateful adventure with my professor. Certain memories linger with awful persistence.

I try to remember Asenath Waite instead. Her dark beauty, her mesmerizing eyes.

The inner workings of one's mind are a mystery, but the heart is easier to understand. I know just what I would ask for given a choice. Will I be given a choice? I wonder. Because there is nothing I wouldn't do now to obtain what I want. Too much of my life has been wasted. I want—*I need*—the rest of it to matter.

Here, in the darkness, amid all these books, alone with a ghost and a book of hidden knowledge and ancient secrets, I know with unshakable certainty that I would kill, again, if I had to; I'd set the entire world on fire. I'd start right here, in Arkham, my home, my prison, and work my way out. I would set it all to rights.

It's still dark when I leave the library, but I can sense the dawn coming. The whippoorwills sing one last song of the night to me before turning in to rest. The air is crisp, there is no one about, and I think of death as I slowly make my way home.

THE CAT WHISPERER IN DARKNESS

LUCAS FRANKI

The Dunwich Cat Sanctuary stood in a small meadow surrounded by ivy-choked forest, isolated from its namesake village. Danielle Headey shivered as she stepped out of her car; the looming trees towered high enough that their shadows still blanketed the clearing, leaving the night's chill in the air and morning dew upon the unkempt, patchy grass.

After Danielle pulled a jacket out of her car, she turned her attention to the sanctuary itself, a former church built in the late colonial days. It was large and square, save for a sizable antechamber in front, with faded yellow clapboard walls and a ragged, worn-down shingle roof. A sheaf of plastic taped over a wide gap in the second floor waved in the breeze, exposing dark-brown vaulted wooden beams within. When Dr. LeGrasse, her old veterinary sciences professor from Boston University, referred her to the job opportunity in Dunwich, he'd warned her the sanctuary would likely be in rough shape. He hadn't exaggerated.

Naturally, the cats caught her eye next. Some gathered around the building, others wandered the boundary between parking lot and forest, still more gazed down from the roof. At least 20 cats by her rough initial estimate. And who knew how many more were inside, behind the building, or wandering through the woods? Their quality of life could not be great.

At the door, a large black cat approached Danielle, purring loudly as it regarded her with green eyes. She bent over to pet the cat, and it wrapped around her legs, spinning and brushing against her jeans. At the very least, the cat seemed healthy. Good weight, no exposed ribs, well-maintained and lush fur, no visible injuries, bright eyes. But what it did have was an odd, distinct orange pattern on both sides of his body. Three thin lobes swirling around a central point. The pattern seemed vaguely familiar, but for the life of her Danielle couldn't place it.

With a shrug, Danielle stood and reached out for the doorknob, but a soft thump drew her attention; the cat had flopped down, exposing his belly. She couldn't resist going in for another round. "Aw, you're a little cutie, aren't you?" Danielle said, scratching the cat's head as his paws worked and kneaded the air. "I promise you'll have a forever home soon."

As Danielle stepped into the Sanctuary's antechamber, a strong odor washed over her. The smell of cats, naturally, both food and waste, but something else too. She couldn't place it, and frankly she couldn't imagine what was making it. Certainly no cat or person. The room itself was rustic, lined with old, unvarnished and unsanded wooden planks, with natural light filtering through in a variety of colors through stained glass windows. A staircase spiraled up out of sight into a shadowy second floor.

The woman behind the desk looked at Danielle, wrinkling her brow. She was about Danielle's age, late 20s, with pale skin and short black hair. Behind her, perched on a filing cabinet, another black cat sat, glancing at Danielle with a disdain only a cat could manage. Strangely, on the cat's forehead was a similar, if smaller, pattern to the cat Danielle had met outside. "Can I help you?" she asked.

"Hi, I'm the new veterinarian Dr. Armitage hired," Danielle said, reaching out and shaking the receptionist's hand. "I guess this is my first day."

"Oh, right, he did say he'd found someone," the receptionist said. "Sorry, it's just—no offense, but you look awfully ... normal. Not at all the type Dr. Armitage typically gets. You did the research he asked you to do, right? On the history of Dunwich?"

Danielle smiled, trying not to sound too condescending. "Yes, I read all about this town's rather lurid history."

"And you're not put off at all?"

"Frankly, I didn't see anything that couldn't be explained by fear, paranoia, and drugs. Or all three. And while I'm no human disease expert, if Wilbur Whateley didn't have some unfortunate combination of hypertrichosis and Marfan syndrome, I'll turn my degree back in."

The receptionist shrugged. "Well, if you're certain, I'll call Dr. Armitage. He'll be glad to see you."

"Thank you," Danielle said, taking a seat near the front desk. Her heart skipped a beat when she noticed the cat from outside standing a few feet away, tail wrapped around its paws. She hadn't realized she'd been followed. He slunk over and jumped onto Danielle's lap, purring and kneading before settling down in a ball.

"Looks like you've met one of our residents already," the receptionist said after she hung up the ancient corded phone beside her.

Danielle scratched at the cat's chin as he extended his head out, closing his eyes in contentment. "I can't believe no one's adopted him. He's so friendly!"

The receptionist chuckled. "That's one way to put it."

Before Danielle could ask what the receptionist meant, a door opened from the second floor and footsteps clattered down the stairs. An elderly man in a ragged, off-white lab coat over his clothes and with a noticeable stoop revealed himself. Danielle nodded at the man, who she presumed was Dr. Armitage, her new boss.

"Dr. Headey?" The man's voice creaked more than the floor of a cheap haunted house. "I'm so happy you came. Dr. LeGrasse spoke highly of you when he told me he'd found me a candidate for this job."

Danielle shook the doctor's hand. "He made quite an impression on me. I'm glad the feeling was mutual. Especially considering how many students he's met over the years."

He nodded. "He has a knack for remembering true talent and brilliance. Now, if you could come with me, I have so much to show you, and so little time to get you up to speed."

The cat on Danielle's lap let out a whine as she disturbed his rest. "Sorry, little buddy," she said. "I've got people things to do."

Dr. Armitage's office was something out of Danielle's mother's nightmares. Books and papers everywhere, with nary a trace of open floor or shelf space to spare. Luckily, Danielle hadn't inherited her parents' neatness obsession.

Another cat awaited Danielle in the single free chair in front of Dr. Armitage's desk. This one was orange, but centered in the middle of its back was a black version of the pattern she'd seen in the cat behind the receptionist and on her own new friend.

Dr. Armitage snapped his fingers. "Come on, Wilmarth, let our new friend have a turn. Just for a few minutes."

Wilmarth perked up instantly and leapt nimbly over the papers and books strewn across the doctor's desk, positioning himself in prime petting position next to Dr. Armitage's chair. Danielle chuckled. "I don't think I've ever seen a cat listen to a person quite like that."

"Oh, Wilmarth and I have an…understanding," he said. "We've known each other a long time, and I keep my end of our bargain. You will come to understand. In fact, I see you've already attracted someone's attention."

On cue, a paw gently tapped at Danielle's knee. Her friend from outside had snuck in through the closing office door and was standing on hunched back legs, flashing Danielle a pitying glance. "Oh my goodness," she said, scooting the chair back to allow the cat access to her lap. "I'm trying so hard not to adopt this guy right here and now. I know, not a good start, taking the first cat I see, but this boy is just too much."

"Stay close to him," Dr. Armitage said, nodding gravely. "You'll be serving him for a very long time. Keep him happy, and he'll keep you safe."

Danielle registered the odd words, but was too busy petting her new friend to fully comprehend. "Does he have a name?"

"Of course, but since you belong to him now, it's only fitting you give him a name of your own."

"Hmm, how about Mulder? He's tall, dark, and handsome, and this place is giving me some serious *X-Files* vibes," Danielle said, petting Mulder down at the base of his back. His tail rose and he kneaded her leg furiously. "Seriously, what's going on around here, Doc? Your receptionist out there couldn't believe I showed up."

"So, you want to know the history of Dunwich Cat Sanctuary? What the story the books won't tell you?"

Danielle shrugged. "I mean, I guess, but I don't—"

"It all started 100 years ago, with the unfortunate Whateley incident," Dr. Armitage said. "My father helped banish the awful spawn of Yog-Sothoth that Old Whateley birthed into the world, but a power like that does not disappear from the Earth so easily. There were consequences. The barrier between our world and the worlds beyond was stretched thin and torn. It didn't take long for unwelcome interlopers to start crawling through.

"My father and his colleagues at Miskatonic University were well versed in the arcane arts, and for a time they alone were able to stem the tide. But unfathomable beasts kept coming through. They could not handle the threat alone. Then, a stranger appeared at my father's doorstep. Though I was very young still, I can remember him distinctly. A young Egyptian man, beautiful in a strange, unnerving way. I would later learn this to be the embodiment of chaos himself,

Nyarlathotep. He spoke with an authority that made the body rigid, yet compliant. I would have followed him to the ends of the Earth, if he had asked me to. Such is Nyarlathotep's power to command lower beings such as humanity.

"The man referred to the beast of Dunwich as if it were the black sheep of the family, His bastard nephew, he called it. An affront to both our world and his. He offered to clean up the mess. And in effect, he did. However, his method was…unusual, to say the least. Rather than closing the portal, he imbued the area with his dark magic, and all the cats in and around Dunwich were gifted with the ability to combat the evil creatures crawling through the portal. To house these awakened creatures, my father founded Dunwich Cat Sanctuary on the doorstep of the portal the Whateleys left behind. For nearly 80 years now we have cared for the cats, ensuring their well-being and happiness. In exchange, they protect us. If they feel like it, that is. These are cats we're talking about. The Crawling Chaos did not favor these little terrors without reason."

Danielle jerked up, she'd let her mind wander as the old man rambled. "Right, right, very interesting. Good to know. Have you tried selling that story? Could maybe cobble together enough money to fix the roof. And people online love them some juicy ghost stories."

Left unsaid was her sincere doubt over her supposed generous salary. Dr. Armitage claimed she would be receiving $300k a year, thanks to the sanctuary's 'generous benefactors.' Dr. LeGrasse had said something similar when he pitched the job. Considering the sorry state of the building, however, it seemed unlikely she would receive anything close to that. Dunwich Cat Sanctuary was, in all likelihood, flat broke. Danielle would give him the benefit of the doubt for now, since the cats were innocent in all this and she did want to help them. If he couldn't pay up, though, she'd only committed to a month at the long-term hotel back in North Adams. She could easily go back to Boston.

Dr. Armitage's face darkened. "Dr. LeGrasse said you were scientific minded to a fault. Brilliant, but inflexible."

"I believe in science and the scientific method. Not spooky unfathomable gods and monsters. Maybe, if you spent a little less time buried in esoteric nonsense and a little bit more time getting the word out, there wouldn't be so many cats out here without homes."

Dr. Armitage sighed, walking over to the door. "Come. Perhaps a tour will benefit you more than mere words."

They passed through the reception area and into the main hall of the old cathedral, both Wilmarth and Mulder trotting close behind. Danielle suppressed a shiver at the odd scale of the place. The building was the height of a three-story house, and yet she felt as if she had to squint to make out the brooding wooden struts and beams holding up the roof. So she looked elsewhere, and quickly found herself immersed in cat paradise. The church pews had been converted into a gymnasium for cats, with cat trees and platforms and bridges galore. Gentle meows and chirps filled the air, and within a moment a flotilla of cats formed around Dr. Armitage and Danielle. Many more remained aloof, staring down from perches both within the church and along the many additional platforms lining the walls. They all had some variation of the same fur pattern on Mulder, on Wilmarth, and on the receptionist's cat. Perhaps a unique mutation stemming from the founding mother or father of this particular cat colony passed through to their children.

Danielle couldn't pass by without giving the crowd attention. Thankfully, they all appeared to be perfectly healthy and strong. And they were friendly as well, even to her, a complete stranger. At least, they were friendly at first. Each cat stayed for a single perfunctory pet or scratch before retreating. They didn't go far, since she hadn't offended them, and their body language remained warm. But after the fifth or sixth occasion, she noticed Mulder again, sitting inches from her, glaring at each cat that approached. And each new cat gave him deference. Bowing their heads toward him as they moved off.

"Did I make friends with the king of this place?" Danielle asked.

Dr. Armitage shook his head. "I could explain, but it would require an open mind to understand. Now come, before I start introducing you to your duties, there is something I must show you."

Out through the other side of the church and back into the cool morning air. The woods loomed even larger around the back, the trees growing spindly and almost bony at the top. A well-worn dirt path led from the church into the forest, a narrow corridor through dense, spiky shrubs.

It took only a couple minutes to reach another clearing. A small hill stood at the center, its slopes blasted and scarred. At the top was a ruined building, the walls decaying, the roof gone. Fur brushed against Danielle's legs; Mulder was rapidly patrolling around her, growling deeply. His ears were flattened and his tail was lowered and bushy. A few feet away, Wilmarth had taken a similar stance around Dr. Armitage.

"Do you see that building?" he asked.

"Yes?"

"That's the Whateley house. Do not go any closer than this without your companion cat. The geometry of reality has faltered within a roughly 200 foot radius of that house. Mulder will anchor you and defend you from threats so long as you stay close to him, but without his protection...the damage those things and that place could do to your mind and soul is beyond belief." Dr. Armitage shuddered. "It is not worth the risk, Dr. Headey."

Before she could answer, Mulder began to chatter, sinking down into an attack stance, as if he'd spotted a tasty bird just out of reach. His eyes focused on something Danielle couldn't see. For a moment, a cold, almost slimy breeze brushed along her face. Mulder lashed out, and as quickly as it came, the sensation vanished.

"Don't go near the spooky abandoned house," Danielle said, shuddering. "No need to tell me twice."

He pursed his lips, then shrugged. "That will have to do."

"So, got any more ghost stories to tell me, or can we actually do some training? I'm eager to get to work, Dr. Armitage. Get to know all these cats, maybe even find some of them a forever home."

Dr. Armitage frowned. "I had your optimism once. I hope you can hold on to it. Very well, we will head back. I do not anticipate it will take you long to get up to speed, as it were. If you were more open minded, perhaps I would say otherwise, but we can address those issues as they arise."

He turned and plunged back into the woods. With a shrug, Danielle followed, Mulder bounding alongside.

"Oh, we were so close to a good picture," Danielle said as Mulder bounded off the windowsill and into the bottom layer of a nearby cat tree. He'd jumped a fraction of a second before she'd pressed the button. "Don't you want to look good for the Internet? I know I said I wanted you, but my living situation is so weird right now, I just don't know if I can give you the home you deserve."

Dusk had fallen over the woods of northern Massachusetts, and both Dr. Armitage and Francine—the receptionist—had gone home for the day. Danielle wouldn't normally have insisted on staying late on the first day, but guilt gnawed at her. Dr. Armitage had penned her first week's paycheck, and she'd immediately sent it through her bank app. The check cleared; the Sanctuary's money was good. Nearly $6,000 for one week. To make matters worse, her job was almost insultingly easy. Ensure the cats are being fed and watered, play with the cats, clean up after them, give them medicine if needed. Jobs any basic vet tech could do, and would do for a fraction of what she was being paid.

To alleviate the guilt, she'd decided to get a jump on her big plan for Dunwich Cat Sanctuary: a website. Bring the place into the 21st century, show off the residents, and prove to the world that they were innocent cats who deserved good homes. No spooky superstition or far-fetched stories, just hard facts and cute cats. While she couldn't do much from the sanctuary itself, she could get images, and the back corner of the building made a great spot for a photoshoot. Orange light filtered in from a nearby window, providing ideal illumination.

Mulder was her first subject, since Danielle assumed he would be great in front of the camera. He'd followed her the entire day, rarely in the way, the perfect polite little man. But as soon as she'd pointed her phone at him, he'd turned the cat to maximum. Squirming in her hands, leaping from every vantage point she placed him in, refusing to acknowledge her increasingly desperate entreaties.

Danielle crawled down and held her hand out. Mulder gave it a sniff, then backed up further into the box. "Okay, fine, I'm putting the phone away. I'm good on my word, I promise. I'll adopt you. I'll give you a great home."

As soon as the phone disappeared, her cat emerged and curled up next to her head. She smiled and gave Mulder a hearty scratch behind the ears. "Oh, you're such a little ham, you know that?"

No response beyond a satisfied stretch of a front paw.

Danielle remained alongside Mulder for a moment, reveling in his company. Then, he perked up, his little body on full alert. He let out a low rumble, flattening into an attack stance. With a wiggle of his rear, he leapt away, jumping through the nearby open window out into the grass beyond. Danielle moved to the window just in time to watch Mulder vanish into the forest, near the path out to the old ruined house.

Another rumble, this one far louder and deeper, powerful enough to shake the foundation of the sanctuary. The same clammy, viscous breeze Danielle had felt earlier rushed through, much stronger than before. It tore at her face until she squinted and turned away, raising her arm to block the gale. She stumbled away, her gut churning, her skin crawling. The building creaked and groaned, as if the ground beneath it were about to give way.

And then it stopped. The building fell silent. Dead silent. Danielle glanced around. The world stood still. Dozens of cats, every cat in the sanctuary, stood at rapturous attention, eyes pointed at the open window Mulder had vanished through. Straight at the trail and the old house in the distance.

"What the hell?" Danielle asked, waving her hand in front of the nearest cat. "What's going on?"

The cat did not yield to her touch. It was barely breathing, gazing enraptured at the window. Danielle tried to pick it up, grasping it underneath the stomach. Nothing. She pulled, straining her muscles, but the cat remained planted. She checked its paws; the cat hadn't dug in, and its claws were sheathed.

She found another cat nearby and attempted the same thing, with identical results. Something beyond her comprehension was rooting the cats to the spot. "Right," she muttered. "This is a little weird, but there's a logical explanation for this. There always is."

Danielle walked back to the window. The treetops waved wildly, tossed by a storm she could not feel or hear. No birds or insects sang out. The only noise was her heart thundering in her chest. The path beckoned to her, reaching out with silent, unspoken words in a language she could not understand. It was her only lead. And Mulder had sprinted out that way. He'd been the only cat to react, hopefully if she found him she could find an answer to this mystery.

Out into the clearing. Into the woods. The intangible whirlwind beat at the undergrowth, and branches and leaves whipped around. Danielle ducked and wove through the chaos until she emerged into the next clearing. There the Whateley house stood, as placid and unmoving as in the morning. And yet, something had changed. The hill stood a little taller, a little steeper, a little … Danielle couldn't find the word for it. But it made her ill to consider the unnaturally rising slope too closely.

"Mulder!" she cried out. "Where are you, buddy? Are you okay? What were you chasing?"

Danielle grimaced. She was asking a cat for answers. A cat that wasn't even around. "He could be anywhere by now. What are you even—"

The pained yowl of a cat cut through the stagnant world. "Mulder!" she yelled, tearing up the unfathomably steep hill. She knew it was him. She didn't care about Dr. Armitage's warning, she had to protect her cat. She'd only known him for a day, but she would die for him.

The dread in her stomach grew with each step she took. The house did not seem to be getting closer. She stopped to check how far she'd come. The forest was gone. Only the hillside remained. Endless grass, waving in a gale she was not privy to. Her eyes widened, and she stumbled, crawling back on her hands.

"Oh god," she said. "What the hell—"

Danielle's hand fell through the world. Not a hole, she'd hadn't accidentally stumbled onto a woodchuck burrow or a loose bit of earth, her arm had pierced the entirety of reality and dangled… elsewhere. She yanked her hand back; to her immense relief it emerged whole and uninjured.

Danielle scuttled away, curling up into a ball. "Holy shit," she said, struggling to hold back tears. "What the hell is happening? What have I gotten myself into? Mulder, where are you? Please help me."

The world tremored. All at once, an awful, gut-wrenching terror enveloped Danielle, sweeping through her body.

Something had spotted her.

She tried to run, but she barely had time to stand before an enormous tentacle burst through the grass and wrapped itself around her leg. She cried out. The limb pulled. She fell, and for the tiniest instant she could see the hole in reality. Danielle could see her universe, a thin, insubstantial layer in a great void, as easily torn or punctured as wet paper.

While she knew she'd regret it, she had to see what had taken her. In the distance, reeling her in like a great cosmic fisherman, a thing of bloated meat and impossible angles stared back at her with too many eyes and not enough skin. Danielle closed her eyes and tears seeped through. This would be her end.

A small, soft paw swatted at her hand.

Somehow, beyond all logic, Danielle landed hard on grass and rocks. She was back on the hill below the Whateley house, and the world had returned. The forest was back, and the hill was the correct size.

Another smack from a cat paw. Danielle looked down. Mulder had returned, gazing at her with nothing but cat contempt. He delivered another series of soft blows to her leg and meowed harshly. The intent was obvious: He was disciplining her in the same way a mother cat corrected a wayward kitten.

The world shook again. The long, fleshy limb tore through the earth yet again, rising 50 feet into the air. An infinite regression of eyes lined the tendril, and each one glared at them with cosmic malevolence. Mulder swept around, placing himself between the monster and Danielle, butt wiggling, tail sweeping.

The tentacle swept in. Mulder leapt to meet it and swiped out with a paw. The arm recoiled, and Mulder chased after, hopping and striking out, batting and weaving. With each blow, the tentacle retreated and regrouped, only to be beaten back, again and again.

It took Danielle a minute to understand what her guardian angel was doing. He was *playing*. It didn't matter that the monster's arm was as wide as a car and as long as a basketball court, that Mulder was a cat-sized cat, or that the sheer incongruity of the whole thing hurt to look at. The monster was as helpless to him as a feather toy on a string. It was a game, and the unholy terror was losing. Badly.

Finally, the tentacle slithered out of Mulder's patrol route. As quickly as it came, it retreated out of the world and back to whatever nightmare dimension it came from. The silent storm relented, and the comforting sounds of summer swelled. Cicadas buzzed in the distance. Birds called out. A gnat flew close to Danielle's face, and with an impeccable sense of timing, sailed right up her nose.

Despite everything, Danielle laughed. Her thundering heart leveled out. As she relaxed, Mulder wandered over and meowed long and hard, corralling her back toward the sanctuary. He looked back over his shoulder constantly, ensuring he was being followed.

Back through the forest and into the sanctuary. The spell binding the cats inside had passed; as Danielle limped through the door a greeting party swarmed around her. A squadron of cats orbited, all meowing and purring. "I'm okay," she said, flopping down to start petting each and every cat she could lay her hands on. "I'm okay."

"Thank goodness!" Dr. Armitage's age-worn voice called out over the cacophony of meows. He strode through the front entrance toward Danielle with surprising fervor, his cat matching his stride. "When Wilmarth went into his trance, I feared the worst. I'm so, so sorry, Dr. Headey, if I had even the slightest inkling there would be an attack this evening, I would have never—"

"It's all right. I'm…well, I don't know exactly what I'm feeling right now, but surprisingly, I don't think I'm angry at you. You gave me all the warnings in the world. I just assumed…well, you know what they say about assuming."

"If you need some space, I would understand. Or if you want to walk out that door and never return, I wouldn't blame you. You would be far from the first one."

The crowd parted and melted away, and Mulder hopped into Danielle's lap. She stroked the fur on his back, and he purred, slowly blinking back at her. "Just answer one question, and I'll be back tomorrow."

"Yes, you can take Mulder home with you tonight. May he never leave your side again."

Danielle breathed a sigh of relief. "Thank God. Although, if you're in the question-answering mood, I have a few follow-up queries."

He nodded. "Would you like me to explain what happened out there?"

"WHAT IN THE ABSOLUTE HOLY FUCK—"

SOMETHING'S IN THE WATER

JACOB HENRY ORLOFF

"No running!"

The lifeguard didn't so much as bark the order as croak it. Billy stopped dead in his tracks next to the pool, locked under the gaze of a pair of bulging eyes. The shirtless lifeguard's jaundiced flesh fell in flabby folds down his bulbous bulk, liver spots splotching the areas of his body not already rife with skin tags and ulcers. A whistle dangled between a pair of puffy lips, just beneath a squat, deformed nose.

Billy's father had warned him about the Innsmouth look before the family set out from Kingsport for summer vacation, describing the condition as resulting from a mix of bad blood and dysgenics. But seeing it first hand churned Billy's stomach and made him consider waiting an hour before jumping in to swim. He managed to eke out, "Sorry, mister," while not averting his eyes so much as to be insulting.

The Innsmouth Municipal Pool had been built as part of a broader revitalization effort to turn the town into a tourist destination. An investment firm from out West had scooped up properties for pennies on the dollar and immediately began the process of gentrification, starting with the tearing down of the historic Gilman House and replacing it with a Holiday Inn Express. Billy's father had been subcontracted to oversee most of the construction of these various projects, including the pool, and this vacation meant to serve as a victory lap for him, a chance to justify all his long nights and foul moods.

"It's like this, son," Billy's father began one night at dinner, three-fourths through a fifth, his words slurring at that precarious level of drunkenness where the remainder of the bottle would determine whether or not the following hours would be taken up by violence. "And, this isn't something you're really going to understand until you're older, but I've gotta start teaching it to you now. It's like this—" Billy glanced at his mother. She kept her head down, absentmindedly forking the mashed potatoes on her plate, fake blonde bangs covering up a shiner. "—hey! Look at me when I'm speaking to you, boy."

———

Billy stared into the pool, watched the sun dance across the surface of the water, undulating with the currents and eddies formed by the other swimmers making waves. He decided on a cannonball. Pulling a pair of goggles over his eyes, he glanced back at the lifeguard, now distracted, then ran, jumped, tucked.

Splash.

The plunge shocked his body cold, a baptism by ice. He freed his knees from his chest, splaying his arms and legs, and let some of the air escape his lungs. He began to sink, floating with a sense of near weightlessness. The emerald texture that lined the pool shimmered in the distorted sunlight. Swimmers bobbed at the surface, giving the occasional frog kick to stay afloat. Over at the deep end, tucked in a corner and flush with the floor, a large grated drain had been installed.

For some odd reason, Billy had an irrational fear of pool drains. One time, younger, but still old enough to know better, he had stepped on one while playing in the neighbor's pool, felt the hard suction against the bottom of his foot, and got the sudden frightful thought that he'd somehow be sucked through the narrow pipe, and down into the sewers to be flushed out to sea. A silly notion, he ultimately realized, if for no other reason than the dimensions involved. But the municipal pool's drain, however, orders of magnitude larger, could easily swallow a person, and so he resolved to steer clear of it, just in case.

When Billy's feet touched the smooth bottom, a thought occurred to him. His father had recently hooked him on an old movie called *The Matrix*. Obsessed, Billy had seen it at least five times since. Moving his limbs through the water in slow motion, he pretended to be Neo dodging projectiles in bullet time, lunging backwards and returning fire, an imaginary pistol in each hand blasting away at an army of Agent Smiths. With his oxygen depleting, and satisfied with his kill count, Billy dropped his guns, pushed off from the floor, and swam upwards, breaking the surface and inhaling fresh summer air tinged with the scent of chlorine.

"You stupid bitch!" Billy looked over at the digital clock on his bedside dresser, a Marvel-themed novelty flanked by the Hulk and Wolverine. He'd lost track of how long his parents had been fighting. He should've been asleep already, but that was next to impossible with all the yelling. There'd be a lull at some point, when his father got thirsty and searched for the bottle, while his mother went to go pack a suitcase, not really having anywhere to go; his father many years prior having seen to the dissolution of any family ties and friendships she once held. Thus, they'd each retreat to their respective corners, lick their wounds, then come out swinging in round two.

As best as Billy could recollect, his mother had never successfully extricated herself from any of the countless altercations with his father, usually being persuaded by either the threat of violence, or its actualization. During those times, Billy often wondered if she'd remember to take him with her or not. He wouldn't fault her if the thought failed to cross her mind, because within the context of the family dynamic, for all intents and purposes, Billy felt like a ghost. Invisible, unseen, immaterial.

W hen Billy broke the surface of the water, the lifeguard shouted, "Come 'ere, you," and waited for Billy to paddle over to the edge of the pool. "Get out. I told you no running." Billy complied, hauling himself out onto the hot cement. He pulled his goggles up to his forehead, but kept his eyes to his feet, standing in the man's imposing shadow, a fishy odor overpowering the ambient stench of chlorine. "You can come back in an hour."

"Yes, sir." Just as well, Billy thought, he felt like having a snack anyways. Turning from the lifeguard, but still feeling the man's gaze, he meandered over to the front entrance, and went into the boys locker room.

Billy hadn't noticed when he first arrived, but the locker room now had a detectable marine stench, pungent and pervasive, like the time he made the mistake of microwaving a slice of leftover anchovy pizza. He located his locker and opened it, finding his towel, change of clothes, and the leather wallet his father had gifted him for his thirteenth birthday. He felt like such a grown up that day. He pulled out the crisp twenty his parents had given him when they dropped him off earlier, and went to go fill his stomach with artificial sugar and preservatives.

A t night, after the fighting reached its inevitable and ugly conclusion, and his mom wept alone, battered and bruised, and his father poured himself another drink, Billy liked to sit by his bedroom window and look up at the stars. Something about them seemed right, provided a type of order in Billy's otherwise chaotic world. He'd stare into the void, and somehow feel better. He'd even create his own constellations, give them goofy made up names like Yig or Yuggoth. And on occasion, when time and place aligned, he could glimpse Polaris, glowing with uncanny light.

––––––––––––

"Can I sit with you?" The boy appeared to be around Billy's age, his body hallmarked by the Innsmouth taint, skin a kind of gray, too, as if he'd never known the sun before then. He held a tray carrying a soda, a hotdog, and a bag of Cool Ranch Doritos. His yellow eyes never blinked as he stared at Billy, awaiting an answer.

"Sure." Billy's social skills were stunted, never managing to find or keep friends in any meaningful sense, almost exuding awkwardness as a sort of anti-pheromone.

The boy set his tray down and slid into the bench seat across from Billy. "My name's Randolph, but most people call me Randy, but I don't really like either of those names, so I just go by Toad."

"Toad?"

The kid took a slurp of his pop, then bit into his hotdog, talking while he chewed. "Yeah, that's what my friends call me. I have a pet frog. I showed them one day, and they started calling me Toad, even though toads and frogs aren't the same thing, they're totally different, well, not totally different, but you get what I'm saying, but I just went with it, so, now I go by Toad." He swallowed, said, "It's better than Randy," then took a swig from his drink. "Anyway, what's your name?"

Billy for his part had gone to the concession stand thinking he'd load up on sweets, but couldn't resist the tantalizing smell coming off the grill, so instead he opted for a burger and fries, pocketing the change to grab an ice cream on the way out when his parents came to pick him up, whenever that might be. They were supposed to be touring the town, but in all likelihood, they'd wind up in a bar somewhere at the behest of his father, and at that point it'd be anyone's guess as to when they'd return to the pool to retrieve Billy.

"My name's Billy," he replied, dipping a pair of fries in some ketchup.

"Oh, cool. That's short for William, right? Kind of like me with Randy?"

"Yeah."

"Do you have a nickname?"

"No, not really." The kids at school called Billy a variety of names, none of which were meant as a term of endearment.

An uncomfortable silence passed, then Toad asked, "Have you ever played Fortnite?"

As a general rule, Billy's father had placed a strict prohibition on electronics in the home, said all the gadgets and devices did nothing but kill brain cells and encourage bad behavior. They owned a TV in the living room, where they occasionally watched a movie, or the news, sometimes sports, and his father had one in his office, as well as a smartphone and computer for work, but beyond that, the household gave Luddites a run for their money.

Billy had heard of the game, thought maybe he'd watched someone play it once or twice at a neighbor's house. He replied, "A few times, I think. I'm not very good."

"Who's your favorite character?"

Billy took a shot in the dark. "The blue one."

"Human Bill? That makes sense because of your name."

"Yeah, him."

"Yeah, he's cool. I usually play as Peely or one of the Avengers. Hey, have you ever seen those movies?"

Billy relaxed a little at that, loosened up a bit, the common space of superheroes rendering fertile ground for conversation, and providing other avenues of shared interests to explore. Before too long, Billy and Toad had become certifiable friends, laughing and enjoying each other's company while they finished the rest of their food.

Toad wiped his flabby lips with a napkin, tossed it on top of the pile of scraps and refuse now cluttering his tray, then asked, "Do you burn easy or something?"

Billy replied, "What do you mean?"

"Your neck. Looks like it's got a rash on it or a sunburn or something."

Billy touched the areas around his throat, the skin feeling rough and kind of flaky, despite the funny-smelling sunscreen his mother had earlier slathered all over him. "Maybe. I don't know. I don't think so."

"Let's get in the water. That'll help."

"I can't. The lifeguard put me in timeout for running. For like an hour."

"Oh, who? Jack Marsh over there? Forget him. He's an old barnacle. Plus, he works for my dad. He's not going to say anything when he sees you're with me." Toad stood up, brushed crumbs off his chest and lap. "Come on. Let's go."

Billy put on his goggles, and followed Toad, the boy's gait a sort of waddle as if his feet were permanently affixed with diver's flippers. They stopped at the edge of the pool. Billy glanced up at the lifeguard, who registered his displeasure with a scowl, but kept his mouth shut and looked the other way. Toad said, "On three."

"One...

"Two...

"Three!"

Toad dove into the pool and Billy jumped in after him, the plunge not feeling as cold or discomforting as it had the first time. Billy glanced about, turned, and finally located Toad, watching in astonishment as the kid seemed to move through the water with near superhuman speed and grace.

"You gotta make sacrifices, Billy." Billy's father poured himself another drink, topping off a rocks glass with three fingers of whiskey while Billy's mother carefully cleared the table. "Life demands sacrifices." He gulped down a mouthful of booze. "You and your mom don't appreciate me or all the things that I do. All the things that I sacrifice for you. You both take me for granted.

"The food in your stomach? Me. Those clothes on your back? Me. The roof, the lights? Me. All me. Even those stupid comic books you love so damned much. All me. You both don't realize how good you have it, how lucky you are to have me.

"I sacrifice so much for the two of you. I work myself to death to provide for you both. And what do I get in return? Nothing. No respect. Nothing. You're selfish and ungrateful. You both live a comfortable life because of the sacrifices I make—you're welcome." He took another sip, seemed to lose the thread of the conversation, then returned to his thesis statement. "Sacrifice, Billy. I make sacrifices. Someday you'll understand."

Early the next morning, Billy awoke, stirred from one of his recurring nightmares, dreams of winged things he'd come to call night-gaunts, and heard his parents murmuring down the hall. He slid out from under the covers and crept to his bedroom door, the hardwood floor quiet and cool against his bare feet.

His father whispered, "How do you think I got the contract, Suze?" He added, "Nobody works in Innsmouth without going through the Order."

Billy couldn't discern his mother's muffled reply.

"I don't care. We can't back out now. The deal is already done. You had your chance to object. I asked you multiple times if you were OK with this.

"Yeah, well, he's my son, too, you know."

The conversation carried on in a hushed tone, Billy straining, but failing to hear more than an errant word here and there, until finally his father said, "This conversation is over. He's going to swim at the pool. And that's final."

Billy looked pale, sickly even. Staring into the locker room mirror, he noticed his eyes appeared irritated, in spite of the goggles, and small ridges had formed along the sides of his neck. Whether rash or sunburn, the rosacea had spread from around his throat to the rest of his body in ugly splotches. And to top it all off, his acne had decided to flare up again, pimples clustering on his cheeks and forehead. He'd never before shown any sensitivity to pool chemicals. Perhaps the chlorine levels here were off, imbalanced or over-saturated. Even still, in spite of the clear and abundant damage to his skin, all Billy could think about was getting back into the water.

He and Toad hadn't swam for very long, at least that's how it felt, time seeming to suspend in the depths of the pool, while Toad showed Billy ways of moving through the water he'd never before been taught, from his toddling days at Aqua-Tots to the advanced lessons his parents had enrolled him in last summer. So enamored, Billy couldn't even recall coming up for air all that often, even though he must have at some point.

After awhile, the pair decided to take a snack break. Billy retrieved the remainder of his money, and went to meet Toad at the concession stand. Stepping out from the shade of the locker room, Billy winced, the late afternoon sun seeming brighter, harsher, hotter. He shielded his eyes with his hand, surveyed the pool, noticing every one of the swimmers now possessed a bit of the Innsmouth look in varying degrees. Certain there had been normal folk like him interspersed with the locals, he gave the whole scene another once over. Maybe he had been mistaken.

Billy joined Toad in line at the concession stand, behind a woman and two of her adolescent brood, who used her body as an obstacle in a localized game of tag.

Toad asked, "What are you going to get? I'm thinking one of those popsicles over there. The red, white, and blue one maybe. Or the one with gumballs for eyes."

"Fish." The word left Billy's mouth before the thought even registered in his mind. "I'm craving fish."

"I think they have fish 'n chips, but it's not actually chips. It's fries. Chips are what the British call it, I think. At least that's what my uncle told me. He says he's an ain-go-lo-file, or something like that. I think that's the word he used. He likes British stuff." Toad added, "When he texts me, he spells things weird, too, like the British do, with extra u's, and s's instead of z's. He's an odd duck."

The woman in front of them had finished her order, took her tray piled high with confections, and toted her children along to a nearby table. Billy had enough cash left over from lunch to buy two baskets of fish 'n chips, wolfing them both down with ravenous delight before Toad had even gotten half-way through his popsicle.

Billy said, "I need to get back in the water."

Toad's lips were bluish-purple from the frozen treat. "It's pretty hot out, ain't it?" He ate the last of the bomb pop in a single bite, then pitched the stick. "Hey, maybe later you can come over to my house, you know, after we're done swimming, and we can hang out and play Fortnite or something. We live on an island, not far from here. They call it Devil's Reef. I don't know why. That's just what it's always been called. It's actually pretty easy to get to."

"Sure." Billy was preoccupied by his hands, holding them in front of his face, studying his palms. An insidiousness had rooted itself in his body, some kind of hostile takeover, beyond a simple sunburn, rash, or reaction. He could feel it taking hold, changing him bit by bit. He lacked the vocabulary to articulate the sensation, both to himself in his own mind, as well as out loud to Toad, but an implacable compulsion to take to the water consumed his thoughts, a distant call, primordial and abiding. "OK."

Billy stood, in a fugue, and walked over to the pool's edge, discarding his goggles, then diving in.

"You're going to have a good time, Billy, you'll see." Billy's father took a swig from a 7-11 Big Gulp cup full of rum and coke as he navigated the family's SUV down a coastal road leading to Innsmouth. His mother sat quietly in the passenger seat. "We figured you'd be bored touring the town with us, so we decided we're going to drop you off at the pool for the day while we drive around." He added, "Who knows? You might make a friend."

Billy watched the fields and marshlands roll past the car window, turned to look out the side facing the ocean, the foamy surf lapping at the strand of rocky beach, already bored to tears. He knew nothing life changing was going to happen on this vacation, certainly not at a swimming pool of all places. At the end of the day, his father would still be an alcoholic, his mother a battered wife, and he just a boy caught in the middle, navigating an emotional and psychological terrain fraught with the terrors and pitfalls that came with his kind of home life. He hoped he had packed enough comic books for the week.

The water felt sublime, and this time, Billy didn't come up for air, not once. He could see through the water with pristine clarity, becoming mesmerized by the vibrancy of the pool's jade green surface. He turned and saw Toad floating some distance from him, weightless, smiling, then a voice entered Billy's head, startling and alien at first, but gradually becoming familiar, comforting.

"You can hear me, can't you?"

Billy nodded at Toad.

"My dad said you'd be coming. I didn't believe him at first. We don't have a lot of kids on our island, but my dad said that's going to change. Said we're going to have a whole new generation of us Innsmouth folk soon. Come on." Toad swam down to the large drain in the deep end. "You'll get the hang of talking like this. It'll take some practice, but I'll teach you."

Toad removed the grated steel cover. "Oh, and when you meet my dad, he doesn't like being called mister or sir or anything like that, just call him by his name—Dagon."

Billy swam as if he'd spent his entire life underwater, breathed as though he'd never known land, following in Toad's wake through a labyrinth of pipe, then a series of sunless grottoes, until finally they were out to sea, heading towards Devil's Reef with alacrity, where Billy would meet Father Dagon, and be embraced by his new family.

LICENSING

D. MARMARA

The Arkham Department of Motor Vehicles was the type of place where one could expect to encounter profound boredom, or deeply alienating horror, depending on whether one was there to take a driver's test or file a title transfer. The woman behind the counter studied Liam's application in ominous silence, and for slightly less than a human lifetime.

"You're looking to reinstate your license?"

"Yes, please."

"Says here you've got prosthetic eyes."

"That's correct."

"What happened to you?"

"Is that relevant?"

She didn't answer. He knew what she saw. The paths left by his lover were ugly, if necessary. Wounds inflicted in holy practice and long since forgiven. He wondered how many cultists she saw on an average week, how many were less noticeable than he.

"No specifics in Massachusetts law regarding prosthetic eyes," she said. "Can you see out of them?"

"Obviously. I wouldn't be requesting a license if I couldn't use the car."

He didn't mention the scope of his sight. How the eyes, forged for him from starborn metal and circuitry, shaped by the chelipeds of distant travelers, sang a vibrato symphony in his skull. Half otolith and half instrument, they marked his way in deft darkness, a sextant by which he read the language of the spheres.

"The law doesn't mention them," she repeated.

"What's your name?" he said.

A slight pause from her. Was she afraid of him? "Maxine."

"Maxine, if the law doesn't indicate any specific restrictions related to prostheses, then there's nothing to say that I can't hold a license with them. Would you be asking these questions to an amputee?"

"I still don't think I can let you take the test."

"Why not? I've taken it before."

"Almost ten years ago."

"My life has changed since then. If I can pass the visual acuity test, it's no different than if I used corrective lenses."

"Surely you're not serious?"

"Completely. What grounds do you have to deny me?"

"What if you aren't able to drive?"

"Isn't that what the test is for?"

Maxine didn't reply. Did she see? See when she looked into Liam's face? See the sinister forces which marked him? Did she see the dark blood which bubbled up from a fount as old as time and space, an eternal river flowing from a fountainhead of entropy incarnate?

"Look," said Liam. "If I can't pass, don't reinstate my license, but if I do, isn't that evidence that I meet the criteria?"

"I—very well, I guess."

"Thank you."

He sat on a hard plastic chair, next to a teenager, their body marked with the trembling note of the anxious and the very young. He looked at them, saw the intersection of the lines and poles which would shape their fate. Decided to say nothing. He didn't want to make them fail due to nerves.

The chair dug into the back of his thigh and he moved to ease the ache. The department hummed with activity, sparsely populated on a Wednesday morning. And yet the line which passed him seemed always full. The room was cool and conditioned, a barrier against the summer heat and humidity. The air chimed with echoes of a robotic, feminine voice as it called out the numbers. Now serving G-43, at Window Number 5. Now serving B-7, at Window Number 21. An organizational system as esoteric and maddening as if it had been written in the dreaded *Necronomicon*.

"Mr. Horace?"

Liam rose to meet the instructor. He could hear the tap of heels on sticky tile, sense the way the angles of the poles bent around her.

"I'm Tessa Roberts," she said. Her voice was as gentle and even as the artificial announcer's, with a hint of a French accent. "Do you have your paperwork?"

He passed it over to her.

"May I shake your hand?" she said.

A first test, he assumed. He reached unerringly for the ripples, the wake of the path cut through magnetic fields by the movement of her body. They shook.

"Let's go out to the parking lot. Did you bring your own vehicle?"

He shook his head as they walked. "My partner doesn't drive. They never have. Had to take the bus."

"Is that why you're looking to reinstate your license?"

"Mostly." He smiled to himself. "We live a fair way out, in the backcountry."

"Harder to be without a car there."

"Very much so. And I want to take them to the beach."

"Oh, that's lovely."

"This time of year is nice to visit Innsmouth. They've never been."

"Never been to Innsmouth or never been to the ocean?"

"Both."

"I'm sure they'll be excited."

"I hope so." He heard the beep as she unlocked the car, a plain, four-door clunker as old as his previous license, and reached out to accept the key fob.

A strange sensation, to situate himself in the driver's seat again. He felt sweat spring up at the sensation of the seatbelt across his body. An awareness of the fragility of the opportunity presented to him. He ran through a checklist in his mind. Gearshift was adjacent to the wheel. Down one gear for reverse, three for drive. He adjusted his mirrors, a meaningless gesture, but one on which he assumed she'd grade him.

"Are you alright?" said Tessa.

"Fine. I'm fine. Just nerves."

"Understandable. Try to relax. Please put the car in reverse and back out of the parking space."

Liam obeyed. Felt the car roll backwards, the sensation of guiding it sliding into place inside him again. He cranked the wheel, felt the car turn perpendicular to the line of parked ones.

"Pull out of the parking lot and make a right turn, please."

Liam gripped the wheel, and drove.

————

"Make your left turn at the street up ahead, please."

Liam signaled and did so. Rolled to a halt and listened to the inaudible thrum of the electrons as they pulsed through the traffic signals. Heard the shift in the current as it made the switch to green. He let up the brake and drove.

"You're taking us out of Arkham," he said.

"It's a nice day for a drive. I can grade you on the Aylesbury Turnpike as well as Church Street."

"I suppose I should be grateful for that."

He took the next bend in the road with grace. He could feel the car shift in tandem with the curves of the earth. How his body moved with it. Years ago, he'd ridden a motorcycle back into the hill country. Past the deep glens and ancient mountains which hummed with mystery. He wondered if he could ride one again.

"Can I roll down the window?"

"You're the one driving."

He cracked the window, felt the wind rush inside to tousle his hair. This was better. More connected to the thrum of the forest and hills. He wondered how quickly he'd develop the muscle memory for the drive home.

"How did you end up working for the DMV?"

"You want to know?"

"Of course."

"No one wants to know how someone ended up working for the DMV."

"Call me curious."

"I needed work after graduation."

"What was your major?"

"Why don't you guess?"

"Accounting? Communication? Psychology?"

"Fine Art."

"Fascinating. Did you want to be an artist?"

"Photographer. My boyfriend was the one with the knack for painting. I used to model for him. There's a cubist nude that hangs in the student gallery at Miskatonic. That's me."

"What did you like to photograph?"

"People. Their shapes, their expressions. I never ended up with any notable pieces, didn't win any prizes. But I liked doing it. It was Scott who had all the drive, poor bastard."

"Oh?"

She went very quiet for a moment. "You know, don't you? Because you're—like this."

"I can guess, but I try not to assume."

"I wasn't unwilling, if that's what you mean. Just young, naive, and really into a guy."

"I've been there."

She laughed. "Most of the art majors are a little off-center. They'll plan field trips up to Dunwich, light fires, and run naked through the woods. Places where the veil is even thinner than Arkham. They like the idea of reaching out to touch the beyond. What else is art anyway, but a mirror of something bigger? A glimpse of the cosmos turning back onto itself. But most of the students just toy with it. Robes and candles and mummer's chants. They're too scared to venture farther."

"I won't deny it's a profoundly frightening experience."

"Scott wasn't scared. At least he pretended not to be. I think that's why it found us."

"You caught the attention of an entity?"

"I didn't know, not at first. He took me to a performance. Back alley thing, one of those amateur productions in a warehouse. Not advertised, you just have to walk around the streets, half-drunk and close to midnight until you stumble onto it."

"A musical performance?"

"A play."

"I see."

"I hope not. It was, well, it was odd, to say the least. But I didn't think about it so much. Went back to his apartment, had another glass of wine. Crashed."

"After, things began to change?"

"It was Sunday. I thought Scott would have a killer hangover, like me, but I woke up and the bed was empty. I found him in the living room. The light through the curtains illuminated him, all in gold."

"Alive?"

"And painting. Frenetic and focused. Surrounded by his tints and tools. The canvas was splattered like a crime scene."

"What was he painting?"

"Me." She played with the edge of her clipboard. "It was a portrait. But he would paint the face, and then he'd slap more paint on the canvas, covering up my features. He wasn't letting it dry between coats; there were rivulets all the way down to the bottom of the canvas. Like my face was melting. Take the next exit off the turnpike, please."

He hastened to obey. "Was it frightening?"

"It should have been. But when I saw the portrait, suddenly I forgot my hangover, forgot the weirdness, forgot the fucking grocery shopping. He had a bottle of red wine, and he was taking big gulps in between swathes of paint. Drops spilled down his chest like blood. He handed it to me."

"And you joined him?"

"I never went to his little soirées with the other painters. Wasn't my scene. But I took the bottle and tipped it back. And we sang songs that weren't songs, and danced in a dizzying orgy of wine and paint. A naked and terrible bacchanal just for the two of us."

"Ah."

"When I woke up two days later, he was dead. Alcohol poisoning was what the coroner said. That and dehydration. But I knew they were wrong. And they couldn't explain what had happened to me."

"To you?"

"I shouldn't ask you to do anything dangerous—can you pull over to the shoulder?"

Surprised, he did so. The car rolled into the narrow gravel patch, and he tucked it parallel to the barrier, beyond which lay the towering trees. He put the car in gear and turned off the engine.

"Give me your hand."

He offered it and she took him by the wrist. Brought his hand to her face and pressed it flat against her cheek.

"Do you see?"

At first he did not grasp her meaning. Yet as his fingers swept across the soft curves of her face, he realized. Where landmark features should have been encountered, there was only desolate emptiness. Her nose was a scarce bump, her mouth a taut expanse of skin. Her eyes formed a contiguous path from below the ridges of her brows to the curves of her cheekbones.

"Maxine isn't the type of person to notice such things. But I could tell. What you saw, and what everyone else sees, are different. I could tell because of the way you reacted. How you didn't shy away from me."

"It took your face."

"He did. The patron of playwrights, of poets, of painters. That which haunts the long dark of the soul, and transmutes it into burning, golden light. I didn't notice at first, because I could still see. I can still smell. Still taste and breathe and eat. The function of my face isn't lost, but the form is, even to me. When I look in a mirror, I see a mannequin. Or an artist's model."

"A sacrifice to the madness of creation, the artist subsumed into the act of art."

"I keep the painting at home. As a reminder. But nothing else has happened since that day. I started getting noticed, a couple sales, a gallery show, but I still couldn't make rent with the photography. So my cousin suggested I get an office job. Something steady and mindless to pay the bills."

"Hence the DMV."

Tessa laughed. "She said, 'Why don't you apply to the DMV? No one ever remembers their faces.' And I thought, sure, why not? Might as well go where I'm just part of the machinery of civilization."

The car was silent for a moment. Liam felt the frame shake as a car whizzed by in the opposite direction.

"Did you know?" he said. "I used to be a painter."

"Really?"

He nodded. "I've mostly switched to sculpting, after. I enjoy the tactility, though I'll still paint from time to time. Most people assume this is why." He made a brief gesture at his face. "They guess at the story. Make up fantastic tales in their heads. They see it as the ultimate sacrifice. A tragic artist willingly cutting himself off from the touch of the Muse."

"No?"

"I don't see colors in the same way I did when I was ordinarily sighted, true. But you'd be hard-pressed to find two animals among the infinite diversity of life which see the same way, and we don't discount them for it. I see things billions of humans can't see. Wavelengths of cosmic light that were born in the hearts of distant stars, in the blackest depths beyond the rim of space. The patterns of alien chromatophores which form the speech of travelers from dark planets at the edge of the galaxy. The face of my lover. It's no great sacrifice to make to see such wonders."

She sat in silence for a moment. "I noticed they didn't give you any pupils."

"An oversight. My partner negotiated the production of the prosthetics, but they sometimes forget the finer nuances of humanity."

"I have an odd question for you."

"Go on."

"Do they look at you more, or less?"

"Ah, the people around me, you mean? Both."

She let out a shaky laugh. "Yeah. It's a head trip, isn't it? Being both invisible and the elephant in the room?"

"Very much so."

"I wear aviators, when I have to go out somewhere other than work. But I'd look silly wearing them at my desk."

"I hope someday you don't feel the need to wear them at all."

"Me too."

"It's never easy, being touched by forces beyond the ken of mortals. But perhaps your patron tested you, and did not find you wanting. Perhaps your sacrifice will ignite your ascension. No longer a passive Muse, but one with her own songs to sing."

"I never thought of it that way."

"Shall we head back?"

"Please. The office will be closing and we need to print your temporary license. The permanent one will arrive by mail in six to eight weeks."

"That long?"

He could hear the smile in her voice. "Not even a command from the starborn things of old can make the wheels of bureaucracy turn any faster."

———

There was one bus route along the Aylesbury Turnpike out of Arkham which one could take to Dunwich. Liam stood at the Number 9 stop for half an hour, listening to the distant calls of the whip-poor-wills.

The bus approached the stop at 5:09 on the dot. The screech of the brakes cut the air as it rolled to a halt.

"Afternoon, Liam." Santiago, the driver, was a regular on this route, and Liam often his only passenger. "You're coming back early today."

"Wanted to get back home," said Liam, as he tapped his bus card at the fare reader. "Exciting news to report."

Santiago closed the door and the bus lurched into motion. "Oh?"

"Got my license renewed."

"That so? Congratulations."

"Thank you. My partner's going to be so excited. We've been talking about loading up the old pickup and going up to the beach at Innsmouth."

"Lovely spot this time of year. Suppose I won't be seeing you as much then? Since you've got your license?"

"Suppose not. But I'll try to stick with the bus when I can. Good for the planet, isn't it? And I'd miss our talks."

"That's what I like to hear."

The farmhouse was a half mile from the bus stop on the Main Street in Dunwich, insofar as it could be called such. The post office and motel remained, but the old general store had been converted into a Circle K. Between the gas pumps and minor grocery selection it struggled on, though most folks made the trip to the Giant Eagle on the Arkham outskirts. Liam walked and listened to the calls of the whip-poor-wills which heralded the coming dusk. Just as he'd made the walk a decade earlier, young and disillusioned. Heart broken by man and men, the red, pulp meat of it open to the lonely thing which haunted the deep glens which encircled Dunwich.

The farmhouse door was unlocked, and Liam stopped by the kitchen for a glass of water, before circling round to the barn behind the building.

The space inside the barn was cavernous and ill-lit, but Liam needed neither light nor eyes to see. He circumnavigated the pickup truck parked at one end, its bed lined with blankets. An unassuming carriage to cushion a large and precious conveyance. He seated himself on a wooden bench. Reached his hand above his head, palm open in welcome, and waited.

"Sorry I'm late," he said. "The line at the DMV was horrendous."

At first, he heard nothing, then slick, ropey appendages grasped his fingers, enormous annular strands reminiscent of the thick earthworms his grandfather had kept in a bucket for fish bait. The eager touch hummed with familiarity, a rich, tapestried buzz of infrasound.

The appendages wound around his wrist, eerie and insubstantial, now there and now fading into the spaces Between. He squeezed the strands. The hum rose, warm, encouraging, then the grip on his wrist softened, and his flesh vibrated with music from beyond the Gate.

"I did it," he said. "Passed the test. Just like we'd talked about. I've got my temporary license in the house."

His lover hummed its alligator song, a sound out of space, a promise of togetherness. The passage of time meant little to it, for it was intended for the black flow of eternity. Someday, it sang, we will walk the bleak and intestate earth, we will see the frozen city, we will traverse the mountains of the empty seas. We will cleave from our flesh prison and ride the winds as They do. We will open the deep places of the world and all shall be as it was, as it is, as it shall be again.

The song died away, the resonant pipe of the barn ceased its buzzing. A soft, hideous croaking emerged from it. The words were mangled, but filled with trans-dimensional tones. Human emotion projected through an inhuman lens.

"Liam," his lover rasped. "Liam."

Liam smiled. "Likewise, darling. How would you like to go to the beach tomorrow?"

U.S. FISH AND WILDLIFE SERVICE INSPECTION REPORT NO. IF-32651

SARAH HANS

The town of Innsmouth, Massachusetts looks like the image of a town from a Victorian-era postcard, but instead of sepia-toned, everything is gray. The earth is gray, the sky is gray, the buildings are gray, and the people are gray. Like most fishing towns, the place swarms with stray cats and seagulls looking for handouts. Even the cats seem unusually gray, as if they've just accepted that filth is the trade-off for easy meals and stopped bothering to groom themselves. The few cars parked on the curb are models I've only seen in movies set in the 1940s and they're coated in rust and a layer of (gray) mud. As I drive into town in my shiny agency-issued truck, the locals eye me with open suspicion. They're all as pale as fishbelly and watch me with huge, black eyes.

Inbred. They're definitely inbred. Great.

It's not as if I haven't dealt with backwaters before, but I don't enjoy them. Have any of these yokels even seen a Black woman before? There's a good chance they haven't, even on the internet. There's no cell phone signal out here, isolated from the rest of Massachusetts by nearly-impassable marshes, so these people don't even have the benefit of social media to educate them.

I don't have a map of Innsmouth, but fisheries are never that difficult to find, especially in a town this small. I just keep driving toward the beach until I spot the only modern building I've seen since I turned onto the unpaved road that winds through the marshes to Innsmouth. Unlike the rest of the town, the Innsmouth Fisheries building is brand new, built of concrete and aluminum, and painted cornflower blue. A minimal effort has even been made at landscaping the grounds.

There's a gate and a guard station, where I stop and roll down my window to present my badge. "I'm Cherise Brown with the Fish and Wildlife Service," I tell the guard. "I'm here to do an inspection."

Like the other townspeople, the guard is pale, with bulging black eyes. He asks me to wait a moment and goes back into the guard station. He radios someone, explains my credentials, and then nods at me and presses the button to open the gate. I roll through in my shiny company truck and find a parking space.

Before I exit the truck, I get my gun out of the glovebox. I do have a permit for it, but I'm not supposed to carry one while I'm on official duties. I can't risk being caught in the middle of nowhere unarmed, though. I work alone most of the time and sundown towns don't exactly advertise themselves. I check to make sure it's loaded and slide it into my pocket. It's a Glock 26, small enough to conceal easily under my long jacket, and its presence on my person immediately makes me feel safer.

Climbing out of my truck, I'm assaulted by humid air and the reek of rotten fish. This, too, is something to which I've grown accustomed, but the humidity is oppressive and the stench is overpowering, like what I'd expect at a processing plant that's about to be shut down for safety violations rather than in a town a few miles from the shore.

After a few moments of gagging and getting used to the smell—I swear I can taste it—I make my way to the docks instead of the front door. I like to surprise the businesses I inspect. They'll be expecting me at the building, but the docks often give me a lot of information about a fishery, information the managers would often rather keep hidden.

The dock itself is wooden and creaks under my feet. In places the boards even feel spongy. A few old-fashioned wooden fishing boats bob in the water. The fishy odor is even stronger here, as you'd expect. Gulls are everywhere, wheeling overhead and toddling along the docks, their cries a shrill counterpoint to the gentle slosh of water against the hulls of boats. Most of the boats that would be docked here are clearly out in the ocean, catching fish, and I wonder if they're more modern than the ones rocking nearby. Somehow, I doubt it.

The realization makes me feel oddly nauseated, like this place is a relic outside of time and my body hates the wrongness of it.

Finding nothing else odd, I turn and head back to the building. Two people wait at the front door to greet me. One is a slender young woman with long hair so pale it's almost white. She has the look of an Innsmouth native, but somehow on her it works. She's beautiful, with enormous liquid eyes, a tiny button nose, and a perfect rosebud mouth. Her skin is so white she looks like she's never seen the sun, but that seems to be the pallor of everybody here. She looks like she's in her twenties but she wears a brown dress so modest it belongs on someone's grandmother.

Beside her stands an older man, paunchy and fishbelly pale, wearing freshly pressed khaki pants and a polo shirt that matches the color of the building. He has those same unnerving eyes the rest of the town seems to share, but his nose is also flattened and his lips full and rubbery, as if he's had too much plastic surgery. He's also completely bald.

He looks like something out of a Melanie Martinez music video. When he extends a hand, I force myself to shake it. His palm is sweaty and cold.

"I'm Jeremiah Orne, the fishery manager, and this is Miss Danielle Marsh, our community liaison," the man says. He has an accent similar to one you'd expect in Boston, but mixed with an Irish brogue and…something else. His voice is thick and sort of bubbly, like certain words catch at the back of his throat. Like a speech impediment.

"It's so nice to meet you," Danielle Marsh says. Her voice is soft and breathy, making goosebumps rise on my arms. When we shake hands, hers is clammy and limp, the very definition of a dead fish handshake, and I have the urge to wipe my hand on my pants when I let go. "What can we do for you, Miss Brown?"

"*Agent* Brown. I'm here to inspect the fishery."

Her eyes shine like two dollops of black acrylic paint. "Of course. You're very welcome, but please excuse our confusion. We were under the impression a report had already been completed last month."

"And who conducted this inspection?"

Danielle and Jeremiah exchange a look. "Your colleague," he says. "Jason Gonzalez. His report found us in compliance with all federal laws and regulations, even the new one about overfishing."

I remove my sunglasses for dramatic effect. "We didn't receive his report. In fact, nobody has heard from Agent Gonzalez since he came to Innsmouth to complete the report."

Danielle smiles and her teeth are tiny baby teeth, like little corn kernels. I can't suppress the shiver that shakes my body at the sight of them. Fortunately, Danielle doesn't seem to notice. "I can take you to his place. It's not far."

"His place?" I echo stupidly. "Like, his house?" This is the furthest response from what I expected and I can't hide my surprise. A part of me had been certain Gonzalez was dead, probably in some accident, and the locals would be careful to hide it.

Danielle's nod is enthusiastic. Then she frowns. "Have you been worried about him?"

"Not me, per se, but the agency, yes. It's unusual for an agent to disappear on assignment." I watch Danielle closely but she remains guileless. "But it would be great if I could see him in person. And if I could get that report." I'm not really sure I trust Gonzalez's inspection report, but if he's already done one, it'll get me out of here quicker if I just collect it rather than doing my own inspection. And I want to get out of here, especially after meeting Jeremiah Orne. This place has gone from a 2 on my mental creep-o-meter to an 8.

"Probably wise. Why reinvent the boat, right?" Orne grins. His teeth are, at least, not tiny Chiclets. Instead they're huge, white, and perfectly aligned, reminding me of my grandfather's dentures. His giant eyes regard me unblinking and I have to tear myself away from my own distorted reflection in his inky pupils.

I do my best to turn my grimace into a smile before nodding and stepping away with Miss Marsh. She suggests that we walk to Gonzalez's place, but I make her get in the truck instead. It'll be faster, and I can't wait to get out of here.

Though the community liaison appears to have excellent hygiene, she brings the stench of rotten fish with her into the cab of the truck and I regret offering to drive. We make small talk on the short drive, and she insists I call her Danielle. "There are too many Marshes in Innsmouth," she explains. "Half the town will turn around if you call that name!" She laughs and it's exactly the pretty trill I'd expect.

The road to Gonzalez's "place" is unpaved, and once we turn off the main thoroughfare we're bouncing along a muddy backroad. A house appears up ahead, tucked away between the trees so it's practically invisible until we're right up on it. It's a small one-story dwelling, but it looks much newer than the other houses and buildings in Innsmouth, except for the fishery building. It's certainly less covered in vines and mold.

When I park the truck, a man emerges from the house. I've only met Jason Gonzalez a few times in passing, but this is the man I remember. He has golden-brown skin and black hair, with eyes and lips that look small after meeting Jeremiah Orne. I gust out a relieved sigh as he approaches the truck and grins, his teeth perfectly normal: adult-sized, slightly crooked, and a little yellow with coffee stains.

Danielle leaps from the passenger seat and throws herself into the man's arms. "This is Agent Brown. Your bosses are looking for you. I told you they would!"

Gonzalez beams at me and extends the hand that's not clutched around Danielle's slender shoulders. His hand feels normal, warm and firm, and I cling to the handshake for a few extra seconds out of relief.

"It's good to see that you're alive and well, Agent Gonzalez," I confess. "I was prepared for the worst."

"I'm glad you're here. Come talk," he says, gesturing toward the porch.

Danielle unglues herself from Gonzalez and disappears into the house. Gonzalez seats himself on the wide porch swing and I sit in an oversized wicker chair looking out over the marsh. The stink of fish is not so potent out here; instead, Gonzalez's homestead smells like a musty closet.

Taking in my expression, Gonzalez chuckles. "You get used to the smell."

I suck my teeth. "So you're just living here now?"

"Yep. I'll give you my inspection report and you can take it back to the agency. You can even put your name on it, if you like. I'm not going back."

I stare at him, baffled. Before I can think of anything else to say, Danielle emerges from the house with a tray of drinks. She hands me a glass of yellow liquid.

"Lavender lemonade. Danielle's specialty," Gonzalez says, and the expression he turns on her is adoring. Suddenly, I understand why he's chosen to remain out here in this strange place with these strange people.

He's fallen for one of the locals.

It's a tale as old as time, and Danielle is pretty and charming in an offbeat kind of way, but I still find myself disgusted. She's young enough to be his daughter, or at least his much younger sister. I glance at his left hand, where a line of pale skin on his ring finger reveals a missing wedding band. "What about your wife?" I blurt.

His smile shuts off like the flick of a lamp switch. "This is my home now. There's important work to be done here, and I can't let the trappings of my previous life prevent me from fulfilling my calling."

"Your...calling?" I repeat. Sweat starts to bead on the back of my neck.

Danielle seats herself next to Gonzalez with her glass of lemonade in hand. When she looks at him, her eyes seem even bigger and more glossy than before. She offers him a dreamy smile and pats her flat abdomen. "His calling to be the new manager at the fishery and the father of our children."

I swallow a gulp of lemonade past the huge lump of dread that fills my throat. It's very good lemonade, the perfect balance of sweet and tart, with a faint lavender aftertaste. "Well, congratulations. It must be nice to have a calling. If you'll get me that report I'll hurry on back to the agency and let them know you're resigning." I give them both a big, delighted smile that shows my teeth. I try to make my eyes sparkle convincingly.

Gonzalez leans forward and places his elbows on his knees. His glass of lemonade drips condensation onto the porch as he speaks and some kind of animal croaks in the marshes as if trying to harmonize with his voice. "You know, my report didn't find any violations. Innsmouth Fisheries is run by good, honest people. The ocean has chosen to bless them with bounty because they deserve it. There are worse things that a person could do than put down roots here."

"I'm happy for you," I say, my entire body going clammy. My free hand itches to grab my gun, but I tell myself that's ridiculous. No one has threatened me, not outright.

"You should think about settling here, too. Property is cheap and the town is thriving." Gonzalez gestures expansively with one hand and there's something odd about the hand. My eyes flick to his other hand and yes, yes, it's the same as the first. His fingers have a thin layer of flesh between them. They're webbed, like duck feet. Did he always have webbed fingers? I dredge my memories for details but they seem harder to access with the man himself sitting in front of me.

I blink quickly away. I make a show of sipping my lemonade and consider my response. I want to tell him this place is the opposite of thriving; it's dirty, smelly, and rotting. But my intuition tells me that's not an answer he'll like. "I have a home. Thank you, though. Now if you can get me that report—"

"Don't decide so quickly," Gonzalez interrupts. "You've been here what, a few hours? You haven't really seen what Innsmouth has to offer." He grins and leans back, putting his arm around Danielle, who beams at me.

"Again, I have a home, one I'm eager to get back to. About that report…"

Gonzalez waves away my comment like it's an annoying fly circling his head. He turns to Danielle and says something, but the words aren't in English. They're garbled and thick, too many vowels and not enough consonants. Danielle nods, smiles, and replies in that same strange language. They share a kiss.

I put my glass down and stand. "I need to get going." My legs wobble and I catch myself on the chair.

"Stay here," Gonzalez says, and it's not a request, or an offer. It's an order, cold and sharp in the muggy air.

Everything goes fuzzy and I lose control of my limbs. The porch rushes up and suddenly I'm horizontal. I don't pass out completely. I'm fully aware as Gonzalez and Danielle lift me between them and carry me to his truck. I'm unable to move my limbs or talk, and everything has a hazy, unreal quality to it, as if I'm in a dream. Somehow I don't panic, and this must also be a product of whatever they've drugged me with. I'm faintly grateful, because I should be panicking.

They prop me in the backseat of the truck and buckle me in, which I think vaguely is a strange thing to do to a woman they're about to murder and dump in the swamp. We bounce along the muddy roads toward the fishery while Gonzalez and Danielle converse in that unnerving language they used earlier. I wish they'd speak English so I could understand them, but I'm not sure I'd be able to comprehend what they're saying even if they were. Everything is so fuzzy, like my senses are filled with static.

We arrive at the fishery and the guard opens the gate. Jeremiah Orne arrives and exchanges words with Gonzalez while someone retrieves me from the back seat. My vision is starting to clear and my fingers twitch in response to my commands, but I try not to show it, remaining slack in their arms.

Someone props me up on a dolly and fastens the straps so they can easily wheel me around the facility. The interior is spotless as they wheel me past meeting rooms, truck bays, and mechanics working on equipment. Nicely dressed townsfolk passing in the hallway glare at me as if I'm not already strapped helpless to a dolly.

It's like I've stepped into an alternate dimension.

"This is what Innsmouth could be," Gonzalez says, leaning down so he can speak softly in my ear. "They need people to help them modernize, people from outside the town. Not to mention," and now he chortles, "they need some outside additions to the gene pool. Have you seen the troglodytes around town? I couldn't pass up this opportunity to really make a difference for this community."

He wheels me out of the building and down a long ramp to the docks. The boats have returned and I was right: they're all ancient wooden fishing vessels. The fishermen use ropes to tie the boats to the dock cleats. They shout to each other in English and that other language, bragging about their catches and taunting each other.

And the catches are spectacular. I can see why the department sent us to do an inspection. They have to be overfishing. Every ship has nets bulging with slick, silvery bodies. There's no way catching this many fish can be sustainable, especially if they're catching this much daily.

Gonzalez leans down again. "I know what you're thinking, but this isn't overfishing. This is sustainable. Let me show you why."

"I don't know why you're bothering with all this," Danielle says acidly from my right side.

Gonzalez waves her away. "Trust me, baby." He looks down at me. "You're a smart woman. I want to give you a choice, Agent Brown. Or can I call you Cherise?"

I want to scream that no, he absolutely cannot call me by my first name like we're old friends, but I remain motionless.

I'm wheeled back to the building. Gonzalez, Orne, Danielle, and I enter an industrial elevator and it descends for what feels like a long time before we exit. At this point, my legs are feeling more stable, and I can move my tongue and lips. I don't dare make my hands move, but I'm pretty sure they're almost back to normal function. I can feel the sharp edges of my gun pressing into my leg where it still rests in my pocket. I'm going to have to choose my moment carefully, but I can get out of this. I can. I *must*. I will not die at the hands of inbred yokels and some idiot man-child who drank the local Kool-Aid.

The lowest level is almost completely dark, lit only by a few dim lights on the floor. Terror clenches my chest so hard I can barely breathe. My worst fears rush to mind. Is this it? Are they taking me to be processed like I'm just another fish?

We round a corner and I gasp. Hundreds of feet of wall is actually a giant window looking out onto the ocean. We can't be far from the shore, but even so, we're surrounded by the flora and fauna of the sea, brilliantly lit by bright lights. Leagues away, golden shapes shimmer in a mysterious hazy light. If we were on land, I would say the shapes looked like buildings, rather like the adobe houses of the Pueblo. It's a magical undersea kingdom, a fabled place where you'd expect to find mermaids, like the decor in a fancy aquarium but made life-size. I squint, trying to make out more detail in the distant city, but it's too far away. Tiny shapes swim around it, no doubt the inhabitants, and that thought makes me blink. Who lives in this incredible undersea city? Mermaids can't be real, right?

"Isn't it beautiful?" Gonzalez asks. I don't respond.

Fish swim up to the window to inspect us, then swim away again. Some are brilliantly colored and patterned, species that shouldn't exist this far north, or species I've never seen before. Some of them are so large they remind me of dolphins.

"Soon," Orne whispers to my left, gazing at the window like he's homesick. A particularly strange-looking fish swims up to the glass and he places his hand on the transparent surface. The fish twitches and raises its own hand to the glass on the other side. Its eyes shine with intelligence and its flabby lips curve in a smile.

Fish. Hand. Smile.

I swear, I feel the moment my brain shatters with madness. I wriggle my arm out of the straps and snatch the gun from my pocket, pointing it at Gonzalez. "Untie me from this thing. *Now.*"

Gonzalez starts, and then curses and runs a hand down his face in defeat. Danielle quickly works at the straps. Orne shouts, "She has a *gun*? Did you not *check her pockets*?"

"Obviously not," I tell him, stepping away from the dolly. I only wobble a little bit, and my aim at Gonzalez never wavers. "Get me back to my truck and give me that damn report so I can get out of here." I don't really care about the report, but if I come back empty-handed the department will send another inspector. I doubt anyone will believe my wild story about insane fish-people. Without that report, I'll be dooming some other inspector to repeat this wild adventure.

"It's really too bad," Gonzalez says, gesturing to the window casually, as if I'm not pointing a gun at him. "You're about to miss the best part of the day."

"You know what?" I present my free hand, palm up. "Fuck the report. Give me your keys. I'm getting the hell out of here."

Beside me, Danielle sighs dreamily. "Look, he's here."

I don't turn away from Gonzalez, but I'm aware of a huge shadow moving across the glass. My skin prickles with warning. "Keys, now!"

But all three of my kidnappers are too mesmerized by what they see in the window to respond. I lunge for Gonzalez, thrusting the gun against his temple while I dig in his pocket with my free hand. He doesn't struggle and I find the keys quickly. His mouth falls open as he stares at whatever enormous shape moves behind the glass. I see a glimpse of it reflected in his eyes and turn away, keys in hand, and run for the exit.

My escape is all but guaranteed if I can resist the urge to see what glides beyond the glass.

Before I round the corner, I give in to my curiosity. I tell myself I'm turning around to check whether anyone is pursuing me, but I know the truth. All three Innsmouth residents are rooted to the spot; no one is following me.

The thing in the window has the shape of an enormous person–head, arms, legs. I'm reminded of a movie I once saw about a girl who fought giants. This giant, though, has silver skin, webbed hands and feet, the head of a fish, and a long, scaly body that moves sinuously through the water. It's trailed by a slender, snake-like tail. Several of the dolphin-sized fish swim around the giant like backup dancers at a concert, just happy to twirl near him.

Gonzalez turns to look at me and takes a few steps in my direction. "Father Dagon blesses us."

I shake my head. I don't understand what's happening. None of this is possible. That feeling of shattered sanity makes my brain buzz. I raise the gun. "Stay back."

"You see now, don't you?" Gonzalez continues, approaching me slowly. "He is the reason the fish harvest is always so good here despite pollution and climate change and overfishing. He makes sure the people of Innsmouth are fed, and cared for, and wealthy." He gestures toward the undersea city in the distance, now visible again with the leviathan out of the way. I realize with a feeling like a thunderbolt striking my brain that the town looks so dilapidated because the people of Innsmouth have been spending all their money on this golden city.

Suddenly, everything makes sense. This is their retirement plan. I glance between Danielle and Orne, their differences suddenly obvious. Gills flutter at Orne's neck. His transformation is nearly complete. Someday, that will be Danielle, transforming into an undersea creature, eventually joining her people in this sparkling city.

I point the gun back at Gonzalez. He holds his hands up, as if approaching a wild animal. His webbed fingers are obvious. Eventually, Gonzalez also hopes to be a resident of this undersea world, too.

"The surface world is really fucked up, Cherise," Gonzalez says. "But the people of Innsmouth don't have to worry about it. Father Dagon will take care of everything."

I know I should turn and run for the elevator, but the question comes out of my mouth as if punched from my gut. "In exchange for what?"

"Only what any god expects," Gonzalez says, his eyes shining with fanaticism. "Worship. Devotion. Sacrifice."

The water churns as the giant creature moves past the window again. This time, it has something in its mouth. Something fleshy and streaming blood. The thing called Dagon pauses at the window, placing enormous webbed hands tipped with claws on the glass, and stares in to regard us. Danielle and Orne immediately drop to the floor, prostrating themselves.

The sea god's eyes are yellow. Not amber, not gold, but yellow, a color intense and threatening. His pupils are huge and black, reflecting everything he sees. His gaze flicks from his worshippers to me and images blossom in my mind, images of what will be. Climate change and pollution and war are destroying humanity, and soon the oceans will cover the land, and Father Dagon's children will sweep across the world to claim it for their own. He wants to populate the world with his descendants, but the people of Innsmouth have become too inbred, they're becoming sickly and feeble, they're changing into deep ones too quickly. He needs fresh blood, fresh genes, and fresh knowledge of the outside world if he and his followers are to conquer the Earth when humanity inevitably falls. The descent of man has already begun. The only way to preserve anything of the human world is to join the one undersea.

"You see, at last!" Gonzalez chirps happily. "You see!" My vision clears to find him standing with his arms wide, as if to embrace me. "The world is changing. We must adapt. Soon, the world will belong to Dagon's children, and we'll be among them. Our own children will be among them, and we'll live forever in peace and–"

The sound of the gun going off is deafening. I fire once and then run for the elevator, not sticking around to see whether I actually struck Gonzalez. Behind me, Dagon roars his rage and pounds on the glass like a gorilla trapped in a zoo enclosure. If Danielle or Orne are screaming, I can't hear them over the ringing in my ears and Dagon's freight-train howl.

When the elevator door closes, my legs turn to jelly and I sink to the floor. The images that filled my head courtesy of Dagon are still there every time I blink: the world covered with water. Humans forcibly bred by Dagon's amphibious descendants. Cities flooded so they could be transformed into underwater habitats. And finally, his rule over them all, his yellow gaze seeing everything, his mighty fist clenched hard around the remnants of humanity.

The worship. The devotion. The sacrifice. What every god wants.

The elevator doors open and I leap to my feet and run. Wide-eyed Innsmouth residents watch me as I pass but nobody stops me. I take Gonzalez's truck and head for the pitted marsh road that brought me to this cursed place. I force the gun from my cramped fingers, drop it onto the passenger seat, and fish my cell phone from my other pocket.

My mind scrolls through all the options I have now and eventually settles on the one most likely to result in the military nuking the town from existence. When I finally have a flickering bar of cell service, I call a former colleague who now works at the CDC.

"You should know about something alarming in Massachusetts."

WASTED

CHRIS SETTLE

Do you know what the most dangerous job in America is? I'll give you a hint, it's not firefighters or the police. Above them sits the proud garbage collector, the trashman. Now you're thinking, "Oh, Eddie, that makes sense. They do handle a lot of unknown garbage, probably a lot of hazards in there." And in that line of thought, you would be correct, however, neither me nor any of my pals have ever stuck our hands into a bucket of syringes and broken glass.

The leading cause of death and injury is "vehicular accidents." That's how the government labels garbage men getting hit by their own truck. Bad brakes, coworker's not paying attention, or maybe, sometimes the garbage guy sees the truck starting to roll, and stands there for a little longer. I've played chicken with my truck a couple times. It's like when you stand at the lip of a high drop. You stare down into that abyss and you can feel it calling to you. It wants you to jump and be free.

Garbage guys get hit by trucks all the time. I knew this guy, we called him Beef because he had a roast beef sandwich every day for the ten years he worked for Arkham Hygiene Technology Services–or as we called it, FAHTS (it's a lot funnier if you've got the proper accent). Beef had just finished his lunch, and he's working out in the hills to the west. You know where they got that spooky reservoir? That's the one. He was servicing the farms and houses in that area, but on one of 'em, he forgets his parking brake. He jumps down to pick up their trash can and walks right in front of that truck. He lived, the lucky bastard. We called him Ground Beef after that, but he had to retire on account of having no legs. If you ask me, though, I think he did it on purpose. Maybe for a thrill, maybe to end it, but now he's got workers comp. His wife left him too, but ain't that the way of the universe?

Whenever I play chicken with the sixteen-ton wall of garbage, I don't know what I'm looking for. I don't think I want to die, and I don't have a wife to leave me. I don't hate my job either. I didn't grow up thinking I wanted to work for FAHTS, of course. Old Misky had a bad reputation, so it steered me clear of university, but when I found out how much the city was paying for garbage men, I had it made. The job ain't all bad either; I'm up at four with the truck rolling by five. I've got a nifty hydraulic arm that can handle the garbage bins, or carts as we call 'em, but I'll get out to pick up any trash bags. Once a week, I get to take out the recycler, too. It truly is marvelous how much beer New Englanders can drink. You'd think we'd drown in the stuff. Then everything gets taken back to the landfill. The recyclables get hauled to a different facility, but if you ask me, I think they both end up getting sent to the ocean. Ain't that the way of the universe?

It's not easy work, but there are good people. One lady would set out some extra cookies every now and then. Another guy, I think he was an artist, would leave tips when his garbage was overstuffed or too heavy. He even helped me toss out this huge canvas he had, kept it tied down under a blanket, saying the art was trash and not meant for this world. Weird guy, but what artist isn't? Of course, some people turn their nose up at me. They treat me like they wouldn't be buried in their own waste if I wasn't there to take it all away from them.

But they have to pay us high, or else no one would stick around very long. There's already a high turn-over rate, but most of them aren't accidents like Ground Beef. Some people…they just change. I hear it's like that up in Kingsport, too. People quit, or they get fired because they won't quit. They say it's something in the water, but I think it's something in the trash.

Some of my coworkers go out in the morning, but it's like someone new came back in the evening. Their truck is empty and we get long phone calls of angry people saying the trashman didn't come by today. The drivers don't say anything, though. They just turn in their keys and go home, most of the time we never hear from them again. That's if we're lucky.

I think there's something deeply wrong with this city sometimes. I think most of it comes from Miskatonic. They can get awfully high and mighty. One time, I took over a route for a day, and this professor-looking guy waves me over and says, "Make sure to take care of the effluvium generated by the medical building." Crazy, right? Super smart professor and he can't even figure out effluvia is the proper latin plural when he's trying to sound intelligent. That's not the half of it, though, the worst part has to be the dorms.

I don't like to gossip and tell stories about people behind their back, but I knew this garbage woman named Pancake. They called her that on account of her being as flat as…well you get it. She takes a trip around the dorms and gets the usual assortment of condoms and alcohol. But as she's lifting up one of the dumpsters, a few bags fall out, as they often do when they're overfilled. She gets out to throw 'em away properly when she sees one of them is glowing green. And this ain't the "oops I spilled my kid's glow in the dark paint," kinda light either. It's pulsing, she said. Maybe even humming. So she calls hazmat like we're trained to do because she doesn't want to mess with some mad science experiment. Then she tells us that an honest-to-God armored truck shows up, and guys that look dressed for Chernobyl step out. The rest of the day she's worked over by some men in suits that ask her weird questions about whether she heard singing or had seen any dogs around. Then they not-so-subtly implied what would happen if Pancake shared any of the details of that day. Didn't stop us from prying the story out of her over drinks at the bar.

She's not the only one who's found something weird. Everyone here remembers Johnny. That's not his actual name, but for the life of me I never did figure out how he got his nickname. Johnny liked to take things—we all did—things he found in the dump or on his route. We called 'em souvenirs. Technically, it's against company policy to remove anything from the landfill. However, everyone takes at least a little something. Do you know how many perfectly good TVs are just tossed out? That and coffee makers. I'm able to pad my income a little bit by selling them online. We all do it. It's just the way of the universe.

Johnny, though, he took it to the next level. The city was tearing down the old sanitarium, probably to make way for a new shopping mall. Johnny was working with the construction crew, hauling away wreckage and all that. Johnny would regale us with all of the weirdest crap he dug out of that place. I'm talking beds with chains on them, blood drawing machines that looked more like torture devices, and these handcuffs that had long spikes around the cuffs. Johnny swore it was to stop chronic masturbation. Worst of all was the book.

I'm a reasonably intelligent man. I don't fall in with ghost stories and I'm not even a little-stitious. I read those stories ol' Howie wrote about our town, as if he'd ever spent a weekend here. I know they're a crock. But you gotta be some kind of idiot if you're gonna take a book out of a sanitarium that's covered in scribbles and weird drawings.

Johnny didn't see it like that, though. He had these *projects*. Super into film, wanted to make his own movies. I'd seen him working on scripts while we waited in line to dump our trucks. He thought this book would be perfect for his new horror project. Granted, he wasn't wrong, but it's like saying a lit stick of dynamite was perfect for your Fourth of July party. He'd spend his time at the weekly briefing thumbing through that book. He'd even take it out to the bars until we clowned him out of it. After that he stopped going to the bars, then one day he stopped going to work.

I think on some level we all expected something like this to happen. But even when all of the horror movie alarms are going off, that not-so-rational part of your brain says stuff like this doesn't happen. You don't hear from a guy who knows a guy who's sister-in-law is a cop that they found Johnny in his apartment, torn to shreds with his own knife. And those handcuffs with the spikes jammed right through his eyes.

We didn't take a whole lot of souvenirs after that. The demolition of the sanitarium was delayed, too. Apparently one guy snapped and drove over his crew chief with an excavator. I'm not superstitious, but this town stinks sometimes. Like sewage being pumped into the sea. Ain't that the way of the universe, though?

The ugliest case had to be Sucker. Poor guy was too gullible for his own good. You could tell him it was good form to chuck a beer can at the bartender, and your pals could all laugh as he was kicked out of yet another bar. People can be cruel sometimes. I guess I'm people. We told him they threw away gold at the old church. Some kind of Masonic building I guess, the Esoteric Order of Something-or-Other. We told him they pumped that stuff like oil from a well, and they had too much to keep. We told him we had our fill and it was his turn. A little dumpster diving was always a good haze.

We watched from across the street, snickering in the back of Kleenex's Corolla. I cracked open my third—or was it fifth?—beer as he climbed into the rollaway looking for gold. I nearly choked on it when we heard the screaming. Kleenex and Wart thought we should help. I thought we should run. Every light in the neighborhood flicked on, and people were poking their heads out of windows, shouting about how they had to work in a few hours.

I shoved Kleenex out of the way and threw the car in reverse. I don't care what they said about me after that, I know I made the right choice. Those screams didn't stop for a long time. I still hear 'em, less so on nights like this, but they're still there. Of course we never told anyone about that night, and I've stopped playing pranks like that on people. I guess you could say I've grown.

This doesn't matter to you, though. These are ghost-stories that don't touch you. You don't see Ground Beef's car pull up into a handicap spot at the store, and hear how he's living paycheck-to-paycheck in a ground floor apartment by himself. You don't see the empty spot at the bar where Pancake used to sit until some turbo cancer swelled in her brain until it popped like a water balloon. You don't see Truck Number 8 sitting empty because its driver killed himself. You don't see the headlines about the unidentified body found in an alley, and the missing person's poster a widow puts up, looking for the father of her children. To you they're stories. To me, they're the lucky ones.

I guess it's not fair for me to spill the beans on all my coworkers, and not tell my own part in all of this. But in the end, I don't get the easy way out. I still have to work. I have to work and keep this whole world from drowning in its filth. The time is coming. The tide is coming. How long can you hold your breath?

I'm losing you, though. That's alright, soon you'll see. I'll start laying it out. It started with my least favorite route, the restaurants up in Rivertown. A bunch of modern restaurants squatting in historic buildings on the banks of the Miskatonic. These places cut corners wherever they can. Especially with their trash bags. Unholy cocktails of food waste packed to burst. I get more spillage there than anywhere else. By the end of the day, I reek. The worst offender is that new sushi place. Abyssal Sushi or whatever they call it. Their fad is all about fish from the deep parts of the ocean.

Saw this Discovery show about deep sea creatures, you know, before all of this started. Bigfin squid. Terrifying. Looked like those things from War of the Worlds. Can't imagine they'd taste good, or are even legal to catch. That obviously didn't stop the restaurant from serving it, though, because when the bag ripped open and fish guts and burnt rice spilled out, laying on top of that pile was a little Martian tripod. I've got strong nerves, you can't be a garbageman if a little mold makes you retch. But something about that thing, it's spider-like legs and ugly beak. I felt bile rising up in the back of my throat. I didn't realize how weird it was that they'd thrown away the whole fish—or cephalopod, whatever it's called. Fifteen feet of tentacles, unused, stuffed into flimsy plastic, and now it was my job to pick it up.

I wanted to drive away. I should have driven away. You know how much better my life would be if I'd done that? But I guess your life would have been worse. You should thank that squid. I didn't drive away, obviously. I got my gloves, a new bag, and wished I had a shovel. I scooped that mass of tentacles into a bag and heaved it up into the truck. The whole next day my arms felt itchy. Like when you see a spider across the room, and then every little thing feels like a spider crawling over your legs. I felt like that squid was still there. Wrapped around my arms, feeding, suckling off of me.

I didn't remember the rest of the day. I just remember pulling into the parking garage of my apartment building, sprinting up to my place, and finally ripping off my coat to scratch my itch. Dozens of little welts. Small, perfect circles of irritation. They wrapped in spirals up my arm, all the way from my wrist to my elbow. That coat was supposed to be stab-proof. There was no way a stinkin' squid could get through it. I grabbed as much itch-cream as I could from the convenience store. It didn't help.

It started to spread, too. I looked like a leper or something. I was wearing long sleeves and gloves in the middle of April. That wasn't the worst part though. The worst part was the smell. I'd smelled trash day-in and day-out for ten years. Most of my sense of smell had long since withered away. But this was something new. It was rancid, and I could feel it coating the inside of my mouth and throat whenever I took a breath. Air fresheners didn't help, either. I could smell the chemicals in them, the toxic vats in some factory pumping noxious fumes out of one end to push little pods of lavender out the other.

I realized where the smell was coming from. It wasn't around me, it was in front of me. In the future. I was smelling the waste-that-would-be. People stunk. I could smell the gallons of food they threw away each week. The rotting diapers from the kids they produced, that would go on to produce more trash and more children. The apocalypse was coming and only I caught a whiff of it.

In a strange way, the scents gave me sight. It allowed me to see the future of our world. Submerged in vile filth. The landfill already looked like that. A square mile of nothing but trash. Do you want to know a little secret? When they couldn't get rid of the trash fast enough, they had me get in a truck, late at night, and drive a few miles out of town. To a private beach out on the bay. I'd dump that load and go back for another one. I'd do that until dawn, then my manager would slap an envelope into my palm and tell me to keep quiet.

Out into the ocean. That's where we all end up, huh? Underneath the waves, no air, no escape. Pressure building all the time. An ocean of refuse. That's why I still work. That's why I work late into the night, taking out the trash.

The first was the professor. He smelled like moldy books and sticky coffee cups. There was the cookie lady. Her neighbors couldn't eat that many cookies, and neither could her grandkids. They'd get thrown away eventually. I could smell the rotten flour and chocolate on her. New bacteria growing and feeding on chocolate chip cookies. I left the artist. He didn't smell like anything. I think he knew. But he was always ready to tip me when I helped him heave the heavy bags up into the truck.

Now I see you're getting worried. But you must calm down. No one will hear any screaming out in this dump. Too far from the city, do you know why? Residents can't handle the smell. And man, ain't that the way of the universe?

I understand you may be upset, but we all have to accept change. I can smell it on you. All those leftovers in your fridge that you let grow mold? I can smell them. I can smell the milk you got before you went on vacation, bubbling, expanding, waiting to pop and cover your wilting produce in expired milk. That's why I'm helping you. Sure, it might be a little painful, but this is a healing process. I'm giving you a world without trash. We just have to dam the river at its source.

COLOUR OUT OF NOTHING

LIAM HOGAN

W ith two hours to kill, I ducked into Kingsport's surprisingly well-appointed art museum. It was either that or head to the station bar, summoned by a red neon arrow and a sign that promised *cold*, then *beer*, and then *cold beer*. I was under my agent's strict orders to do no such thing.

The building, I guessed, had once been a town hall or something of that ilk. It had that municipal grandeur. The Greek (or was it Roman?) edifice, with its sturdy fluted columns and triangular tympanum, was only marred by the clock that wasn't there, a gaping void, a black and sightless eye. It was a melancholy part of a melancholy town, pretty enough in a quaint, olde-worlde way, but too quiet, especially when compared to the hustle and bustle of New York.

And it wasn't just the clock-eye that watched as I dithered, or so it seemed. Perhaps it was just nerves, the looming appointment that too much rested upon. My exasperated agent, who no doubt considered me a burden if not a lost cause, had wearily suggested, as she handed over the Amtrak ticket she had stumped up for, that I not "fuck this one up."

I'd been the only passenger to get off the underused commuter train that stopped for the briefest possible time, the service so infrequent that as it pulled out again, I half wished I was still on it.

The museum's sturdy doors creaked as I pushed on through. It was an early summer's day, a little too warm to be wearing a suit, even this close to the ocean, but needs must. At least I didn't have to wear a tie; a certain bohemian air was expected of an artist, even a commercial one.

The entrance was gloomy and as empty as the street outside. I thought I'd be glad to be out of the sunlight, but I almost turned around and headed straight back out again, to find somewhere else to watch time tick by. To wind myself up, second guessing my client's eventual reason for not giving me what my agent said was pretty much a last chance opportunity. Things would have gone very different for me, and my client, if I had. It was obvious the museum didn't get many visitors, and, without any staff in sight, I wondered if I'd stumbled somewhere off-limits. An institution that should have had chains and a stout padlock securing its entrance, and a hopelessly optimistic but faded sign that would say it was temporarily closed, "Due to unforeseen circumstances."

From the echoing lobby grand stairs swept up to an upper level, while on the ground floor double doors faced off both left and right, presumably leading to the galleries. Marooned roughly in the middle was a vacant information and ticket desk, coated by a thin layer of dust, the till old fashioned and mechanical. A few leaflets had been abandoned across its surface, promoting the regional amenities, such that they were. I was weighing up whether a trip to historic Innsmouth, or a walking tour of the North End catacombs, was the more appealing entirely hypothetical option (the prices suggested the leaflets were at least a decade out of date, and in all honesty I would have paid *not* to go to either), when I heard hasty footsteps. So I wasn't alone after all.

The man coming down the shallow stairs seemed neither surprised nor alarmed to see me. He was an odd little creature, whose true height was only revealed as he joined me on the lobby marble. He couldn't have been much above five feet tall, and was swaddled in dark, dated attire. I supposed it never really got that warm in this sepulchral interior. His neck vanished into an elaborate cravat in deep plum, the only splash of colour. His features were sallow and fleshy, his forehead glistening and his eyes, what I could see of them behind owlish glasses, were distinctly beady. He reminded me, instantly, of the Nazi agent from *Raiders of the Lost Ark*.

But he was smiling as if he had just met a long lost friend. "Charles Beckford!" he crowed, reaching for and eagerly pumping my hand, which, unlike his filmic counterpart, was unmarred and not the bunch of fat, lifeless worms I'd expected, though nor did it do much to endear. For a moment, I wondered if "Charles Beckford" was who he thought *I* was, someone he had been expecting, but his attentive stance made it clear he was waiting for me to introduce myself in turn.

"MacIntyre", I said, bemused. "Eliot."

"Capital! A *pleasure*, Mr. MacIntyre. And what brings you to our humble art museum on this fine day?"

"Oh..." What indeed? "I happened to be in town, here for a client meeting." I patted the portfolio bag slung over my shoulder. "I'm something of an illustrator," I admitted.

He beamed, the light reflecting from his round spectacles making him look like he had no eyes, making him look like he was about to melt like wax. "An artist! How wonderful! Do you...? Do you mind, if I give you the tour? I'm sure your time is precious, but I *think* I can curate the highlights and perhaps provide you with some inspiration, if you'll only give me an hour?"

I half nodded, half shook my head, and Beckford grasped the response he'd been hoping for.

"The museum has a quite wonderful collection of statuary," my newly self-appointed guide said. "Stone idols and relics taken from all over the county, and from much further afield. But that is perhaps for another visit, hmm? So, the tapestry and paintings, first, and then, if we have time, my own particular area of interest, the illustrated books!"

It sounded dull and dreary, and I immediately regretted my politeness. Still, I could either stew in my own thoughts, or stew in those of Mr. Beckford, whose obsequious attention suggested that my presence had already made his day, and that was rare enough.

We pushed through the left set of double doors to a downstairs gallery. I was waiting for motion sensitive lights to flicker on, but this was more old school than that. My guide lifted a discreet wooden panel by the side of the door, and toggled a half-dozen switches.

The light did not do very much for the paintings that brooded on the walls. Without exception, they were dark to the point of being murky. There was a blasted heath that put me in mind of Macbeth, only less cheery. It had fringes of unsettling colours you would never find in any corporate palette. A seascape, no less sombre, featured a rocky, barren isle crowned by a foreboding tower, or obelisk. A triptych of dank, subterranean places—a cellar, a cave, a crypt—but in each, there was something nameless coming through a well or a crack or a fissure, something more terrifying still.

Where there were people, imprisoned within these overburdened frames, they were small, insignificant, and doomed, warped faces howled out in silent anguish. Outnumbered by other beings; vile, feral things that had crawled from a sick imagination, gothic, and satanic— no, *not* satanic. There was nothing religious, or even anti-religious about these grotesques. They were the antithesis of spirituality, utterly alien, an other-worldly warning that you'd better hope there *wasn't* a soul, if this was where it might end up. Not exactly poster material for the Kingsport tourist board.

"A picture is worth a thousand words, isn't that true, Mr. MacIntyre?"

Perhaps, I thought, but most of these would start with a *D*. Despair. Despondency. Dismal desolation, disturbing depravity, demonic dread... I was envious of Mr. Beckford's warmer clothing. It felt like all the heat, all the vitality, had been sucked from my limbs.

It took a while, standing before one giant, ghastly portrait that commanded the room, to piece together what I was seeing. A cloaked form, but not human, or not quite. Legs and arms too long, too spindly, too insectile, with echoes of writhing tentacles lurking in the background that were somehow still very much part of this haunting figure.

As for the face, it had too many eyes. Eyes that burrowed into me and made me shudder, and, I was sure, would follow me about the room if I could only tear myself away. Though when I tried to count them, those glowering, insatiable eyes, I found I couldn't—it was like they only existed in some nebulous realm just beyond the tortured canvas.

It was made worse by the impression of a sneer on the monstrosity's face, as if it, and the painter of this barbarous assault on all that was kind and good, knew exactly what effect it would have on someone foolish enough to come before it. As if it would continue sneering, even if it were looking out upon the bleak face of hell.

The paint had been layered so thickly—and yet with such a deft hand —that there was a disturbing 3D relief to the work, as if, were I to stand too long in hideous contemplation, the subject might join me, to offer sardonic commentary.

"Astonishing, isn't it?" Mr. Beckford said from too close, making me jump. "*Copp's Hill Ghoul*. We have the largest collection of Pickman in the United States. In the *world*."

"Pickman?"

"Richard Upton Pickman? No? Well, I guess he is only *locally* famous. A Bostonian, whose ancestors hailed from Salem. Much of his work was lost of course, destroyed by the artist himself, and by others, even before his disappearance, nearly a hundred years ago. His reputation was not helped by the Boston Art community taking a distinct and snobbish *dislike* to his chosen subjects. Calling them morbid fantasies, when they were always so much more.

"They say..." There was a pause that drew my gaze from the loathsome painting to this cheerful imp of a guide, who leaned in conspiratorially, though there was no-one there but us.

"They *say* he drew inspiration not from his imagination, but from things he had actually seen, things that haunt the dark chasms of the night, that prey from the edges of unreality."

I grunted, non-committal and faintly embarrassed, but also repulsed by the idea. It was always easier to dismiss the work of a madman, no matter how talented.

Beckford chortled. "It is a strange thing, Mr. MacIntyre. When some of us are exposed to that we can not understand, art can be a way of capturing what cannot be captured, sharing what cannot be shared. More so than mere words, than even poetry. The art of the first and second world wars, for instance. Mankind has always, ever since he lived in caves, depicted both the sacred and the profane on the walls around him. They are, of course, necessarily *imperfect* reproductions. But a true artist, such as Pickman undoubtedly was, can capture the essence of something eldritch, something otherwise unfathomable, do you not agree?"

Under other circumstances I might have laughed in his face. I drew cereal box mascots and redesigned corporate logos to depict their latest, consultant-conjured, mission statements. If I ever had any true artistic leaning, it was beaten out of me by the need to put a roof over my head and food on the table. True artists died penniless and young, that's what three years of fine art taught me. And, if I faintly despised my shallow clients and drank more than I should to compensate, well, that was the American way, wasn't it? You didn't get paid to do a job you loved, so you ended up hating what you did even as you counted the dollars towards retirement.

Not that I'd managed to cobble together anything resembling financial security, for either the present or the future. My already limited client base had been wiped out overnight by the pandemic, by the cost of living crisis, and then, when things *finally* looked like they might be getting a little better, further encroached upon by god-awful AI that responded directly to the client's brief, however inane. It didn't seem to matter that what it produced was a long way from art and light years from *fine* art, from even what Mr. Pickman had created, creepy as hell though that was.

"It's impressive," I had to reluctantly admit. "Though not to my taste. Too dark and old fashioned."

"Indeed," he readily agreed, with a little giggle that suggested some inner, private joke. "But it was worth starting here, before we headed upstairs."

I was expecting more of the same, perhaps brighter lit, but it seemed in whatever past life this building had had, the upper levels, served by such a grand staircase, had been eviscerated, carved inelegantly into drab storerooms and pokey offices. A waste of the space, for all that I was glad there was no more of Mr. Pickman on display.

The only public area appeared to be a study room, stacked chairs and empty tables that would suit a visiting school, assuming the teachers wanted to give their students a case of the heebie-jeebies. Beckford took out a large bunch of keys and unlocked an unlabelled door at the far end, ushering me through. Beyond a labyrinth of piled-high cardboard boxes the room opened out. The walls were lined by oversized books, their leather spines dark and foreboding. There were a few of these on display, in grimy glass cases, open at particularly gruesome images, monstrous beings, monstrous places.

We were, I realised with a start, directly behind the missing clock. The circular void had been filled, temporarily, with a crudely shaped sheet of translucent perspex or something similar, letting in light from beyond, but no view from up high across the street to the railway bar, to the train station, and to the diner where I was due to meet my client. I was surprised, when I took a sneaky peek at my watch, to find that our scheduled meeting was only a half hour away. Had I really been there that long already?

My guide donned a pair of white cotton gloves and led me to the space directly beneath the ghostly, milk-white eye. There was a reading lamp, sickly-green hooded, clamped to the edge of a lectern, church-like in its black-mahogany bulk, but carved with twisted figures that belonged in no church anywhere on earth, not even one belonging to some pagan cult.

On the lectern a thick volume squatted, larger than my portfolio, dark edged, the exposed pages yellowed. A smell rose from the pages, the malodour of ancient decay, the memory of putrefaction, of an unnatural rot.

The text was a meaningless jumble of sinister symbols and disquieting diagrams, drawn, it appeared, by a madman, but Beckford carefully and reverently lifted that sheet, turning it over.

On the page beneath was an insert, as illustrations in early books sometimes were, produced separately from the text, stitched into a space left deliberately blank. No words adorned that solitary sheet, and none, not even a thousand, would have been enough to describe what was there engraved. Each time I tried to focus on just one element of this atrocity, something else ripped my gaze away to it, and then back again. It is peculiar to describe an illustration as *insistent*, as *hungry*, but that was what this image was. The raw fuel of nightmares.

All the while, Beckford hovered at my elbow, expectant, waiting.

"By Pickman?" I quavered, my voice little more than a croak.

"Oh *no*, Mr. MacIntyre. This was etched long before his time. Though there are suggestions he may well have been inspired—set upon the course of his life's work—by such a work as this. Perhaps this very one. Do look closer."

I did not want to. Every fibre of my being told me not to. It felt like I was plummeting into an abyss, an abyss that had no end, no final, fatal impact that I might almost welcome, that might quiet my eternal screams. But it was impossible to tear my gaze away. There was a terrible fascination, in studying lines more boldly slashed than engraved, in necrotic veins of ink that almost throbbed, sickly and sluggishly, pulsing with dark ichor just below the parchment surface, feeding the evil emerging from the parchment. Though this wasn't enough sustenance for it, not nearly enough. If the *Ghoul* had been willing to bide its time, this rapacious image was more impatient.

The unknown artist was no less talented than Mr. Pickman, though the medium was different, rendered in just two colours, black, the black of the deepest, darkest pit, of burnt flesh, of a gash ripped in space through which something stirred, and white, the white of bleached bones, of clouded eyes, of a legion of clamorous things that squirmed and writhed in the darkness...

Something shifted, within my mind. Some wall or barrier crumbled, the ramparts savagely torn away. Suddenly I could see what my guide saw, what he had been so desperate to show me. It was not the image itself, which was ghastly enough, but what the artist was *trying* to do. It was the outline of it, the bare, shivered bones of it, the intent, the something almost hidden behind that shrieked itself alive in awful triumph in my mind as it made its gibbering demands known.

It was horrifying. It was *wonderful*. It was an abomination.

I turned and grasped my guide by the hand, ignoring the slither of his fingers—or were they mine?—and, without a word, perhaps without being capable of a word, stumbled down and out of the museum. My phone burst into chaotic life—I guessed there had been no signal, earlier?—delivering a slew of increasingly irate text messages from my agent, but mostly from the client I was there to see.

I hesitated once again, there in the middle of the Kingsport street. Just behind the sun-scratched sidewalk, the lime-green leaves of the trees, there was a darkness, a sickness, waiting to be revealed. I had much to do. But why *not* start here?

I clutched my portfolio to my side. There was nothing of interest in it, the sketches and ideas I had laboured over in advance of this meeting were entirely worthless, a set of childish doodles. But I always carried a few extra sheets of blank paper, a handful of good pens and coloured pencils. That would be enough.

The tight-clench of a heartbeat later I sat across from him, that client whose name now eludes me, having moved aside the menus, the plastic tubes of ketchup and mayo, and there, inside a drowsy diner to the accompaniment of daytime radio, I tried to *show* him, tried to bring the essence of the image etched forever onto my brain to *life*.

I had not comprehended, before I started, what even a hasty attempt to recreate the images would do. So much more than merely memory, the act of laying it down on the blank page told me this was much more of a challenge than I'd expected. I began again. For a moment, I thought of returning to the museum, to stand once more in awe before that grimoire, that print. But that was my weakness. I knew what I wanted to create, as clearly as I knew anything, and seeing another's version of it would not help me now. I had to forge my own path.

Time froze, hiccuped, and lurched forward again.

Better, but still not *quite* right. I cast the page aside, and started another. The image I was trying to capture was deceptive. Tempting. Treacherous. It could be done, I thought, with no more than about a dozen bold strokes, but they must be *exactly* the right strokes. More precise, more eloquent, than Japanese calligraphy. Nothing else would do. I kept trying, impatient, until my client, who had been watching, immobile and gaping, abruptly stood, grabbed the pages strewn across the Formica table, and stumbled away, the diner doors jangling in farewell.

It was only when my drawing materials were gone that I realised how deathly quiet the diner was. A waitress—I vaguely remembered one coming to the table, to ask if we were ready to order—sobbed, traumatised, in one corner, curled up like a baby. I wondered what calamity had happened while I'd been so distracted. No one offered to explain, so I got up, leaving my portfolio and my wits behind.

Somehow, and I really don't remember how, I ended up back on a train, my finger drawing patterns on the grimy windows, the other passengers shuffling away until I had the whole carriage to myself.

My client was found insensible by the side of the road, his hire car in a ditch, his eyes gouged out, a pile of ash all that remained of the pages he had taken with him. There was no evidence that anyone did anything to him, but then, why would a man do such a thing to himself? The state troopers backtracked, uncovering a trail of witnesses, the waitress, a ticket inspector, a few of the freaked out passengers.

They came knocking on the door of the studio flat I had not left for three days, despite the irate calls from my agent, from my off-on but mostly off girlfriend, from my worried neighbours, kept awake by the animal noises of frustration. Nor had I eaten, or slept, except for a few hours in a brief stupor after I'd drunk the flat dry. When I stiffly awoke, alcoholic fumes clearing from my head, I was inspired into new approaches, new avenues to explore.

In short, I had been busy.

Every surface was covered by scrawled art. When I ran out of paper, by bed sheets and linens, by the blank pages of coffee table art books. I had drawn on the walls, floors, and even the ceilings. With every iteration the lines were clearer, the image more potent.

I was so very, *very* close. So very, very close. I screamed and raged at the interruption, as the knocking became breaking, screamed until I was silenced by a TASER.

The cops who attended the scene, who handcuffed me and dragged me away, who bagged up everything as evidence, they're not doing so well. Haunted by what they saw, driven by the same primal urge that drives me, fixated by that singular design. But they lack the necessary skills to execute it. None of them were artists. None of them could reduce an image, an idea, to a few bold lines. They produced nothing but insipid imitations, and were driven mad, so I am told, by their inability to do better.

The task remained in my hands, and my hands alone.

I was interviewed by a Mr. Danvers, a blind FBI agent. A specialist, he said. It transpired that my client had expired. He reminded me of his name, this Mr. Darby. It still meant nothing.

"Bring me pen and paper, and I will confess everything," I promised. He was too smart for that. He offered instead to transcribe my words, but *I* was too smart for that. He listened to my ramblings anyway, though they were of little help. When they investigated, at my encouragement, for I had nothing to hide and much to share, there was no sign of Mr. Beckford, no mysterious book laid out on a lectern in the room on the upper floor of the Kingsport Art Museum, just lots of the admittedly dire work of Mr. Pickman.

Oddly, there *had* been a Mr. Beckford, once. But he, so Danvers told me, retired decades ago, and is untraceable, even to the prodigious resources of the FBI, and therefore presumed long dead.

That the art museum had indeed been closed for the last six months, and this whole sorry saga may mean it is never opened again, was by the by. I shrugged. I giggled. What was that, to me?

Criminally insane, was the verdict. There was no trial, none of the evidence fit to put before a jury. But the clear assumption was that it was I that had blinded Mr. Darby, I that had frightened him so badly that he refused to eat or sleep, as he wasted away. My blameless giggles did nothing to convince anyone of my innocence. All I did was to open his eyes—it was him, and he alone, that had closed them, the savage beauty of even my earliest renditions too much to handle.

And so I have been committed. To the Dunwich Home for the Incurably Insane, a grand manor no more than twenty miles from Kingsport. An institute that specialises in cases which, though rare, are more common in this part of New England, between Innsmouth and Arkham, than perhaps anywhere else.

It is clean, warm, and I am well looked after. But they won't let me near any of the art materials. No paints, no crayons, no pens or pencils. After I try to show another inmate by carving the lines on his pallid flesh, I am confined to my room. Any attempt to move my food around the plastic plate with its plastic spoon means the food is hastily taken away by nervous guards, and I go hungry. I go hungry a lot.

My padded cell is white and featureless, an entirely blank canvas. I make do. It takes effort, with the restraints, with the soft walls. It's not easy to give yourself a bloody nose when your hands aren't free. But once I do, the ink flows copiously. I work quickly, eager not to waste a drop.

I sit, in the corner of my room, my face a mess. Sit and admire what I have created, the perfect, mad *glory* of it all. More than just a drawing, a symbol, a sigil. More than a warning. This is a message sent out into the infinite void, into the uncaring cosmos. An invitation.

I sit and wait, to see what the world thinks of my art.

I sit and wait, to see who, or what, answers my call.

NO QUESTIONS ASKED

DAVID GONZALEZ

Lieutenant Chavez was in the dining room with the rest when they heard the buzzer. The firefighters all looked up from their plates of spaghetti, puzzled. It wasn't a klaxon, a siren, or any of the normal alarms they were used to hearing daily. Just an intermittent buzzing, barely discernible over the pounding rain. Ward, the kid, a "probie," broke the silence. "Do we even have a doorbell?"

Michaels, the Commander, shook his head slowly, as he spoke through his famous mustache. "No…yeah, but that's not it. Did anybody leave something on? Charging?" The men all glanced at each other as forks and knives were set down. Heads were solemnly shaken.

"Oh, fuck…" Chavez realized, lurching to his feet, "it's the…the box thing." Michaels spread his hands, puzzled. "The baby box!" the Lieutenant blurted as he ran for the stairs.

The men looked at each other for a moment, then all scrambled to their feet, and followed Chavez down the stairs. The "baby box" as the men called it, was a large, clear, plastic drawer mounted to the wall by the front door. It was connected to a small horizontal door, like a wildly oversized mail flap. The sign by this door was quite clear.

Anybody, at any time, could deposit a newborn baby in the box. NO QUESTIONS ASKED.

The box had long been thought of as a waste of precious funds. County Station 19 was a lonely, decrepit, rural facility—grudgingly kept running for the rare farm fire or the slightly more common sight of a pickup drunkenly wrapped around a tree. Everything from the paint to the plumbing was on its last legs, meaning that the station fit in well with the decaying gambrel barns and stoney, untilled fields of the local, perpetually failing farms.

Reaching the foyer, the men could see that the box was, indeed, currently inhabited. A wriggling bundle, wrapped in a brightly patterned afghan, itself wrapped in a plastic trash bag, had been placed in the box.

"Holy shit!" blurted Ward, before the Commander shamed him with a withering glance, and a muttered admonition, as if learning to cuss was an immediate danger to the abandoned infant.

Jackson, huge even without the muscles, boldly strode for the door. Chavez grabbed his friend's arm and shook his head. Jackson impatiently shrugged him off. "She can't have gone far!"

Chavez shook his head. "J, that's not how this works!" The youngish lieutenant, childless himself, was no fan of the anonymous birthing laws, but he was a stickler for the rules, which is why he'd wondered what it might have been, besides his race, that placed him in this dead end.

Jackson, a devoted father of one energetic toddler, turned to Captain Michaels, who nodded sagely. "He's right. Let her go." Jackson sighed, and stepped away from the door.

The captain approached the plastic box. Gently reaching in, he lifted the bundled child. "It's heavy." He looked down, to see a pair of dark brown, almost black, eyes staring intently back at him.

Jackson leaned in and took a look at the large newborn, still sticky with fluids. "I thought babies always had blue eyes."

Chavez chuckled. "That's just you gringos." he said with his Brooklyn accent. "Look at him…" he gestured at the baby's darker skin and surprisingly thick, black hair. "…I think that's one of ours."

Jackson gave a mock sigh. "Oh, Lordy, the invasion continues. Boxes now? Has the river gotten too deep?"

"Probably an illegal." muttered Captain Michaels, matter-of-factly.

Ward looked to Chavez, who didn't seem offended by the term. The young man asked "Even up here? This isn't Arizona."

Jackson chimed in. "Maybe she's getting deported, wanted her kid to live the good life." Nobody disagreed, though Chavez looked, for a moment, like he wanted to respond.

"So now what?" asked the rookie.

Captain Michaels handed the bundle to Ward, who gingerly accepted the responsibility. "Take her upstairs and check her diapers. We'll have to call this in."

Chavez watched Ward trudging upstairs, the baby held away from his chest. He looked at the others and shook his head. "That boy definitely doesn't know how to change a diaper."

"He is here to learn." the captain grinned. "Jackson, go wake up Susie."

The mighty Jackson blanched at the thought of disrupting the slumber of the tiny but temperamental paramedic. "She'll rip my head off, she's been up since…"

A single syllable snuck through the vast mustache. "Go."

As the big man sighed and trod away, Chavez asked the captain "What's policy here? Five-Oh, child services?"

Michaels furrowed his brows for a moment, then admitted "I don't remember. We got a memo when they installed that. I never thought we'd get a customer…let's have Susie assess her, if she's been abused, we'll take her to county and call Arkham county's finest…" He was interrupted by a loud scream from upstairs. With a brief glance at each other, the men bolted up the stairs.

The screaming, though high pitched, wasn't from a woman. Ward kept screaming, again and again, stopping only too refill his lungs. He was scrambling across the floor, on his ass, backwards, looking in horror at the partially open door of the dormitory. His hands left streaks of blood on the linoleum.

Chavez dropped to his knees next to the young firefighter. Looking at the pale, anguished visage and the wide, wide eyes, the lieutenant grabbed Ward's shoulders and shouted into his face. "What happened?" Ward just shook himself free and kept scooting away, screaming, babbling, crying. Chavez looked up to Michaels. "What the fuck?"

The captain looked down at the bloody trail on the floor. "Where's the baby?" He glanced at the dorm door, then walked over and slowly pushed it open. Chavez stood up and walked behind him, but Michaels shook his head. "If it messed up the kid that bad…"

"What could be that bad? I thought…" Chavez stopped, mid thought. The child hadn't seemed to be in any distress. Had they fucked up? Had the baby coded?

"Wait," the captain ordered calmly. "Nobody else comes in here."

Chavez nodded slowly and watched Michaels grimly enter the dorm. Jackson charged up the stairs, followed by a bleary looking Susie, who'd been sleeping in her ambulance. They both looked at the blood, and peered down the hall, where Ward sat with his back against the wall, screaming.

"What the fuck is going on?" yelled Susie.

"I don't know." answered Chavez. He pointed at Ward's pathetic form. "Go…calm his ass down."

Susie, a fairly competent paramedic, was full of questions. "What happened to him? Did he take something? Why is he bleeding?"

"It might be the baby." Jackson volunteered.

"What baby?" screamed Susie, red-faced with the frustration of this insanity.

Just then, the captain stumbled out of the dorm and slammed the door shut behind him. "OhmyGodohmyGodohmyGod…." he babbled as he staggered against a wall.

Shocked, nobody moved. "Captain…?"

"Chavez…give me a minute…" The captain took a few deep, shuddering breaths, then bent over and vomited.

Jackson and Susie both stepped forward but Lieutenant Chavez sternly waved them back. Silently, they waited until the captain's retching stopped. The only sound was Ward, quietly whimpering down the hallway.

Chavez, with an almost painful feeling of dread, asked a question he didn't think he wanted answered. "Sir,…what's the baby's condition?"

Michaels wiped some puke from his famous mustache and took a deep breath. "The…it…it's not in any danger." He held a hand over his eyes, too late to block whatever he'd seen.

Chavez, Jackson and Susie looked at each other, at a loss. "It's not human." muttered the captain.

Chavez struggled to fit that sentence into his understanding of the world. "Somebody…did something really awful to the baby?"

Michaels, still covering his eyes, slowly shook his head. "No. The… baby. It isn't human."

Susie, her typical fury dampened by the situation, slowly approached the captain and put her hand on his shoulder. "Babies are human…all babies…that's why they're babies."

The captain shook his head again. "Don't go in there...I know you're going to go in, but don't...but how could you not?" He barked a short, nasty laugh. "Fuck it." He pulled his hand down from his eyes and reached into the pockets of his coverall. He pulled out a set of jingling keys and handed them to Chavez. "I retire. As of now. It's over. You're the captain now." He shakily walked through the pool of puke and down the stairs. A door opened, and the sound of a car starting was added to the patter of the cold rain. Tires squealed and faded into the distance.

T he three of them stood there for a few long minutes, shaken and awed by the enormity of what had just happened. The rain drummed on the room, and Ward quietly whimpered and mumbled. Chavez held up the keys, and dutifully pushed them into his pocket.

Jackson, with a quaver in his voice, spoke first, addressing Chavez. "Captain...?"

Susie cut him off. "I need to know what baby you guys are talking about."

Chavez answered. "Somebody dropped a baby in the baby box."

Her face softened with concern. "Then what happened?"

Acting Captain Chavez gestured at the blood and puke stained floor, then looked at Ward's pathetic form. "This." They all stood silently for a moment, staring with dread at the door.

"It's not crying." observed Susie, nervously.

"Maybe it died?" suggested Jackson. "Maybe the kid killed it?"

Chavez looked down the hall and shook his head. "I don't think so. We got to respond to this...that's what we do, we Respond. Thats our fucking job...but, whatever is in there, whatever they saw...it was so awful, it broke them. What could be that bad?"

"I seen some shit in Iraq." Susie boldly answered. "I saw a van full of kids got hit by an IED, and I had to untangle that shit, so I know I can handle whatever's in there."

Jackson, with beads of sweat on his forehead, raised a big, beefy finger and pointed accusingly at Susie's face. "Don't you pull that war veteran shit in here. Captain Michaels has seen shit that would turn your hair white. He was at the Kendall fire when his crew burned alive from the phosphorus spill. That man was not soft!" He pointed down the hall at Ward. "Breaking him is no big deal. But Michaels? This is fucking scary."

They both looked to the new (acting) captain, who took a breath, and decided. "Ok, I'm going in. It's my job. I know I'm going to see something awful…but at least I know there's something awful in there. Maybe…if I'm ready for it, it won't get me so bad." He turned and walked to the door. As he grabbed the knob, he felt a small hand on his left shoulder, and a huge hand on his right. He gave a grim little nod as he turned the knob.

Exactly two minutes later, the three of them were sitting at the mess hall table, shakily tossing back shots of (ex)Captain Michaels' secret bottle of whiskey. Some of that prized southern beverage splashed onto their vomit stained coveralls, but nobody cared.

"You guys OK?" asked Chavez. Jackson shook his head and poured another glass.

Susie wiped the tears from her eyes and asked "What the fuck did we just see?"

The (acting) captain focussed his scrambled thoughts. "Tentacles…mouths…what were those things on its waist?"

"Eyes…"muttered Jackson. "Did you see those feet?"

Susie nodded. "Like a lizard…my nephew had a gecko…"

Chavez interrupted. "OK, ok…let's not sweat the details. It's not human."

"The top half was." corrected Susie. "Kind of."

"So, what do we do now? Captain?" Jackson asked shakily.

Chavez, who'd never before hoped not to be a captain, took a deep gulp, and set down his glass with trembling fingers. "I dunno. Part of me just wants to kick that can down the road."

Jackson nodded. "Fuck it. Call the staties. Call the army. Let them deal with this."

Chavez frowned, and reconsidered. "That thing…it already broke two of us…"

"I think…" interrupted Susie "seeing it…broke five of us." She looked at her empty glass, and just took a long pull from the bottle.

"Yeah…" agreed Chavez "we need to know more."

Jackson took the bottle from Susie and regretfully screwed the cap back on. "Do you really want to know more?"

Acting Captain Chavez sighed. "There's a big difference between wanting and needing…You guys go take care of Ward, give him something powerful, knock his ass out…see if that's his blood. Keep that door locked."

Jackson nodded, and asked "What are you going to do?"

"I'm going to find the mother."

"You going to call five-oh for help? What if it's another one of them?"

"I think…" Chavez carefully ordered his thoughts, fuzzy with alcohol. "I think…look at that thing…it doesn't look right, it looks like pieces stuck together…part human…the mother…it wasn't a monster that brought that thing here."

"Then what's the other part?" asked Susie.

"That's what I need to find out."

The security footage showed a small figure, barefoot, wearing muddy pink pajama bottoms and a black hoody, trudging through the dark rainy night, with that nightmarish bundle held tightly against her chest. How far had she walked on this cold and awful storm? Chavez grabbed a radio and took his old jeep, slowly driving down the empty country road.

He almost missed her. He was looking for somebody walking, not floating in a ditch, but that had been her fate. Cursing, he leapt out of the vehicle, angry at having forgotten to bring a medical kit. It wouldn't have helped, he quickly realized. She, apparently human, shockingly pale, was limp and already growing cold. Her eyes were wide, her mouth slack, her expression one of dazed horror.

He couldn't find a pulse, and his brief attempt at mouth to mouth quickly ended when the foul odor coming out of her mouth made him retch. Shaking his head in pity, frustration and disgust, he picked up the sad, limp body and gently sat her in the passenger seat.

Chavez had laid the girl—a skinny dishwater blonde in her late teens—on a gurney in the apparatus bay, when Susie and Jackson came down the stairs.

"How's Ward?"

Susie shrugged and sighed. "Stable? Seriously fucked up... psychologically. Currently unconscious." She stopped as she saw what lay limply on the stretcher.

Chavez nodded. "Good. Keep him down. Where'd that blood come from?"

Susie, normally so quick to answer, stammered a bit as she answered. "His hands...he had...little holes, little holes all over his hands." She looked to the body. "She was already..."

"Yeah, maybe hypothermia…maybe she drowned, I found her in a ditch."

Jackson looked doubtful. "Do we know she's the mother? She's really skinny…I'd have thought…"

Susie pulled on a fresh set of latex gloves and approached the corpse. "Baggy pants, extra large hoody…this is the classic hiding the pregnancy outfit." She unzipped the hoody, revealing a Dunwich Demons high school sports t-shirt.

Jackson shook his head. "Dunwich. Bunch of cousin-fucking hicks. Inbreds."

Chavez frowned. "You could fuck a hundred cousins, and you wouldn't get something like that."

Susie ignored them, as she gently probed the girl's chest, examining the oddly flaccid breasts. Pulling out her scissors, she sliced the shirt up the middle, revealing a pattern of small round sores.

"Looks like a shotgun got her" muttered Jackson.

"Not deep enough." replied Susie, calmed a bit by the work. "This looks like Ward's hands."

Chavez winced. This was only getting weirder. "So…was she the mother?"

Susie sighed, then tugged down the pajama bottoms, and everybody gasped. Deep, black and green bruising with more sores than skin. Bloodless tears. Greenish fluid leaking. Chavez walked away, looking away from that ruined crotch. "Fuck…how did she even make it this far?"

After covering her with a sheet, the three returned to the mess-hall table. They drank in silence, comforted by the numbing alcohol. It was the only medicine that would help them through this.

Chavez eventually broke the silence. "So...a UFO came and... implanted something..."

Jackson shook his head. "No...you're not from here. Dunwich...weird shit happens there, always has...noises coming from the hills, from the ground...there are these pillars...there were never any Indians there."

"So, not a UFO?"

"No, just...bad shit, coming through."

Chavez closed his eyes, wishing he could just turn off his turbulent brain. He wished that sentence had come from somebody far less solid than his huge friend. Madness was for the mad, not for him, not thrust into his lap.

Susie put her hand on Chavez's. "We can call somebody. Call the army or the CIA or NASA..."

Chavez sighed. "I don't know...do we trust them with something like that?"

"They can take care of it." Susie answered, almost desperately.

Chavez looked into the future, and frowned. "They'll let it grow up, to see what it can do...I don't think I want to let that happen."

Susie, who before this evening had been a devout Catholic, suddenly looked alarmed. "It's a baby!"

"That thing" growled Jackson "is not a fucking baby...it's a monster!" He got up and quickly strode to the gear room, shortly afterwards emerging with a fire axe.

Susie stood up, uncertain. "I don't...I don't think...oh, God..."

"Stop talking about God!" yelled the huge man. "That thing in that room proves the Good Book is bullshit, right? Am I right?" He was shaking in fear and fury and drunkeness.

Chavez didn't answer the question. He slowly slid his chair back from the table, then stood, and approached Jackson. He carefully reached for the axe. "I'm the captain now."

"We have to…"

Captain Chavez nodded. "I know. I'll do it."

The thing, the baby…it…had been surprisingly easy to kill. What had broken Chavez's mind and soul had been the clear, oddly accented "NO!" it had yelled, right as the axe descended.

The investigators had never been able to figure out what had happened. The baby-thing, that little horror from Dunwich, had just melted away, leaving nothing more than a stained mattress and a bad smell. Ward and Chavez still saw each other at times in the rec room of the psychiatric facility, where they'd speak to each other in a strange language that neither of them understood, both gibbering and nodding their white haired heads. Neither Jackson or Susie had ever given a coherent explanation of what had happened, or been able to explain how young Heather Whateley's body had ended up at the station. They'd both soon quit, and driven off together in Jackson's pickup, leaving Jackson's beloved wife alone and confused.

In time, this, like all things, was forgotten, the cold case of the oddly dead girl, only briefly a mother, who'd left a pool of greenish afterbirth, complete with two umbilical cords, in the old barn behind her family home.

THE GREEN ACT

KAREN OVÉR

When you sprain your ankle two days before your ballet company summer tour, your options boil down to sitting around your apartment getting fat, or taking any teaching job you can find once you've been cleared to hobble around on crutches.

AJ Valdez was no stranger to sprained ankles. He had a collection of supplies for every grade, from elastic bandages to boots and crutches. As he got older, the sprains grew progressively worse and took longer to recover from.

His summer was shot. He sat on the studio floor, tears squeezing through tightly closed eyelids as his ankle swelled past *grapefruit*, did not pass go, and went directly to *end-of-career* territory.

He called his boyfriend, weeping over his lost summer and the ever-encroaching moment when he would take his final curtain call. Mike carried him out of the studio and off to his orthopedist. He tucked AJ into bed in their loft, beginning the familiar RICE routine. From the midst of ice packs, elastic bandages, and stacks of pillows, AJ made phone calls.

No one wanted to know him.

"Of course they don't," Mike said, when he came home from his poker night. "But Louie da Squid, *he* knows you. So we're gonna spend the summer up in Massachusetts. He's hooked us up with a seaside cottage. Got our own private beach. You always wanna do rehab in the pool, right? Because you can float, work out without putting weight on your ankle. Salt water will be even better."

AJ eyed his lover suspiciously. "Louie da Squid never does favors, especially when he's playing poker. What's the catch?"

"You spend the summer teaching at Arkham School of Ballet. Not exactly a summer intensive. More like ballet summer camp. Seems the kids have no problem taking class hip deep in water, or barefoot on the beach."

"Great. I'm spending the summer teaching ballet to fish," AJ grumbled. "My luck, they will be jellyfish, and I will get stung."

Nevertheless, Mike's old Civic was packed up and they left at midnight, managing to get out of the city in less than an hour. By mid-afternoon, they'd gotten lost once, been turned around at the gates of Miskatonic University, and finally found both Arkham and their summer home.

The beach cottage sat at the end of a lonely road. Along the way, AJ got his first sight of the Arkham School of Ballet. "Is that a Masonic Hall they're using for studio space?"

"Esoteric Order of Dagon," Mike said, peering at the weathered engraving over the front doors. "Gotta love small towns, right?"

AJ punched his shoulder. "Just because I don't play poker with Louie da Squid doesn't mean I don't know about his connections, okay? I was right. I'm gonna be teaching fish."

"Consider it a challenge," Mike told him. "Let's get you tucked up with an ice pack. We've got the rest of the weekend to ourselves."

"Not quite," AJ told him. "If classes start on Monday, there ought to be a placement class on Sunday. Though I can't see too many out-of-town kids coming here."

"You might be surprised," Mike told him.

"If that's supposed to make me feel better, it doesn't." AJ dragged himself into the cottage.

The place was immaculately clean, though the abundance of fresh flowers mingled with the smell of the sea didn't quite cover a faint odor of fish. The kitchen had been fully stocked, including a small chest freezer full of bags of ice and frozen peas.

On Sunday morning they drove into Arkham, touring the town, then settling into a coffee shop for breakfast. Lingering over croissants, they watched a thin, nervous-looking woman rush past the window. Curious, AJ watched her progress as she turned the corner and hurried up the steps of the Esoteric Order of Dagon. "Told you," he said to Mike. "Placement class."

"I'll pay the bill. You get yourself into the car."

"We're less than a block away. I can walk." AJ untangled his crutches and made his determined way toward the Arkham School of Ballet.

Mike quickly caught up with him, holding the door so AJ could maneuver through. "Told you," AJ muttered again. "*Fish*. This is the same smell as at the cottage."

"We've gone right around the town and back towards the beach. For someone who practically lives on sushi, what's your sudden problem with fish?"

AJ shrugged, peering across the foyer toward a side door that stood slightly ajar. Mike was reading a sign posted on a sandwich board. "You're listed as guest artist in residence," he said. "The summer director is a Madame Marsh."

"That would be the woman who unlocked the doors. Let's go introduce ourselves." AJ started swinging his way toward that partially open door.

Madame Marsh scuttled out, slamming the door behind her just as AJ reached it. "Oh good, you showed up. I had my doubts. The office simply cannot be occupied. The drains must have backed up. I'll have it seen to, first thing in the morning. Come along, the students are due any second."

AJ thought he heard faint banging sounds coming from somewhere below the office. Mike seemed to hear them too, for when AJ tipped his head toward the office door, Mike nodded.

Then the students began to arrive, and the usual chaos ensued. AJ's ankle didn't work, but his voice did, and he soon had them putting on their IDs and setting out the barres. Madame Marsh gripped a clipboard as if her life depended on it, but otherwise simply stood in front of the mirror, staring at the students.

A small piano stood in one corner. AJ looked around for an auxiliary sound system, wondering if he'd have to start making a playlist, when a small, stooped figure, swathed in paisley shawls, shuffled into the room and over to the piano.

AJ got a strong whiff of patchouli, and a fainter one of fish. There seemed to be damp spots on the floor in the accompanist's wake. AJ ignored this as best he could, and got the class started.

Something clanged, down below, as the accompanist banged away. Madame Marsh nearly jumped through the ceiling.

"I see that Madame Marsh is warmed up and ready to demonstrate," AJ announced, as a slightly stronger odor of fish passed through the room. "I will be able to do more, once we move to the beach."

AJ saw Madame Marsh's face turn a strange shade of pale. For all of his own uncertainties about this job, Madame Marsh seemed positively terrified.

Does she think the kids are going to turn into monsters, right here in front of us? Yet she hasn't given the accompanist a second glance.

AJ continued the class, quickly sorting the kids into two groups—the younger and less experienced he would leave with Madame Marsh, and the older, more promising students whom he would take out to the beach.

"Very good! Let's take the barres away, then I am going to call you into two groups for the center."

Eventually, Madame Marsh began to settle in, finally relinquishing the clipboard to demonstrate for the junior group. AJ found a couple of the seniors who were quicker on the uptake and more than willing to take the lead. Center quickly sorted out those who'd simply been shy or nervous during barre, as well as those who suddenly lost their nerve without that anchor.

AJ began putting names to faces and numbers, sorting them on the lists and making a few reassessments. He'd already gotten an idea for the final performance. "How many of you have heard of *La Bayadere*?"

To his surprise, every hand in the room shot up.

"And do you know how that translates?" he asked, with a raised eyebrow.

"The Temple Dancer!" the senior group shouted in chorus, with about two thirds of the juniors joining in.

"And how many of you have danced any of it before?"

No one raised a hand. AJ saw Madame Marsh turn that peculiar shade again, and from the corner of his eye, saw the draped figure of the accompanist nodding.

Fear and approval. Interesting combination.

"Okay. Give yourselves a stretch and get some water. Madame Marsh and I will finalize the lists and work out tomorrow's schedule."

AJ steered Madame Marsh out of the studio and toward the office. She stuck her toes in at the door, not wanting to let him in.

Mike opened it behind her. "I've sent the rest of the students down to the beach," he said. "That was very unwise of you, Madame Marsh, locking them out like that."

"But you *can't* - " Madame Marsh gasped, and AJ, seeing the grim look on Mike's face, realized his joke about teaching fish wasn't funny at all.

"But I can," AJ told her. "That's why I was chosen for this particular school. I'm now wondering why *you* were selected."

"I grew up here," she whispered. "But I have cousins in Innsmouth."

"So you know all about it," AJ guessed. "But instead of helping, you want to interfere."

"It isn't *right*," the woman hissed.

"Shall I speak to the school's founder, then?" AJ stood tall on his crutches. "I'm guessing I'll find him with his students. At least I hope I will. I'd like him to take the role of High Priest. I should be well enough, by then, to be the Rajah. Of course we're going to give the story a few twists. Bit of a mash up with *Magic Flute*. Happy endings all round, and everyone will have fun. We'll use the junior group as temple initiates, and use the music from the betrothal celebration scene. Do you think you can stage dances for them?"

"I won't have to—you'll keep *them* away?" she stammered, but looked hopefully at AJ.

"I will take the senior group to the beach, and work with the others there. Yes, they will dance together, but isn't that the point of the summer classes here? *You* must understand that. I would not want to have to tell the founder he made a mistake, bringing you back. I don't think that would work out well, for you."

Once again, that odd shade of pale washed out Madame Marsh's face. She shook her head vigorously. "I can do it," she promised. "Just don't make me go near the water," she added with a shudder.

"Not until the final rehearsals and performance," AJ told her. "You must be there for your students, Madame Marsh. Now let's post the lists and decide upon a schedule."

Peace made with the summer director, Mike and AJ drove back to their cottage. They changed into swim trunks, and discovered someone had laid out a boardwalk down to the beach, all the way into the surf. Off to one side, beneath a large umbrella, were two beach chairs and several coolers.

"You do all this?" AJ asked Mike.

Mike shook his head. "This has all been done since I found the green kids in the cellar of Dagon's hall. Look. There's barres out in the water."

As AJ rid himself of the boot and bandage, he saw an array of ivory-colored barres. There were no mirrors, but AJ wasn't concerned with that.

Mike helped him into the water, helped him turn the barre to an angle, then retreated. Feeling the smooth, cool, definitely *not* metal beneath his hand, AJ suppressed a shudder. He stood behind the barre, where he could work facing both it and the students, with the angle allowing him to demonstrate on his good leg, if needed.

The green kids came in like any other group of students, messing about as they rose from the depths. Staking out favorite spots at the barre, giggling and gossiping in guttural, barking voices.

Hoping he could make himself understood, AJ clapped his hands twice.

The class came immediately to attention, left hands (?) on the barre. AJ gave a standard *plie* exercise, ready to snap or hum along. As he counted off the preparation, a strange, burbling, rather pleasant music came from the depths.

And the class moved with it. AJ put them through a very advanced barre, and found they all rose to the challenge. "Excellent! Clear the barres, please, take a break, then come onto the beach for center."

Mike helped him to a chair, toweled him off, and wrapped his ankle. "How are you gonna teach center?"

"Same as I did in the studio. On crutches. From the boardwalk. I've already picked out a handful who can demonstrate for the others."

"Really? I can't even tell them apart."

"The water is clear enough, but perhaps you'll find it easier, when they come out of it."

Indeed, Mike raised an eyebrow as the students came out of the surf, moving to one side of the boardwalk at AJ's direction. "I'll leave you to it," he murmured, settling back in a beach chair.

AJ clapped his hands, doing a rapid head count as the class came to attention once more. "Right. I don't want anyone pushing over their limits, okay? You can see how easy it is to get hurt, so do your best, but please be careful. And if you need to get back in the water at any point, just do it, okay?"

The class barked in unison.

"Okay. Fifth position, *tendu en croix,* to the front *croise,* to the side *en face,* to the back *ecarte.* Change legs for the reverse."

By the time they got through *grand allegro,* AJ had them sorted out. He gathered them round, and told them his plan for their final performance, including the changes to the story. "I'm hoping your ballet master will agree to be our High Priest."

Something walked out of the surf and onto the boardwalk. AJ shaded his eyes, and looked upon someone who had once been fully human. As the figure approached, it spoke in guttural, barking, but understandable English.

"Seeing that I *am* High Priest of the Esoteric Order of Dagon, as well as director of the Arkham School of Ballet, I would be delighted. And I very much like your adaptation of *La Bayadere.* The Order will assist, of course, as well as the theater students from Miskatonic."

"How are they at building a stage? And ramps? Out there?" AJ pointed to the ocean.

"I am most intrigued," the High Priest replied. "I will send you our best carpenter, this evening."

At the end of the six weeks, AJ was clunking up and down the boardwalk in his protective boot, just to be safe. The green girls were nailing it as the Shades. Instead of coming down ramps out of the stage wings, they would be coming *up* ramps, out of the water.

The stage had been built far enough out to give them the proper depth. The human kids dancing the roles of Solor and Gamzatti would be dancing in aqua-shoes at that point, as would AJ in his character role as the Rajah. Barges were tied up at the back and sides to accommodate dressing rooms and technical equipment. The theater kids from Miskatonic University were scrambling around, making last minute adjustments to lights, running cues, and reveling in the general chaos of putting on a show.

AJ peered through a tiny gap in the front curtains as the dancers warmed up on stage. The beach was packed with picnicking locals. As for the surf between the beach and the stage—

More and more heads were bobbing there. The families of AJ's green kids. The High Priest peered over AJ's shoulder. "Congratulations. A full house."

"Have they ever gotten to see their kids perform before now?"

The High Priest shrugged. "Some of them have come to the hall. Watched from the high balconies. This is so much better, I am kicking myself for not thinking of it."

AJ shrugged in turn. "Maybe that's why I was recommended. Someone from outside the bubble, right?"

The scruffy stage manager, wearing a tee shirt with a screen print of waving tentacles and the phrase *What do you expect? I've only got eight hands!* ran out onto the stage. "Five minutes, please! Five minutes! Opening talent only!"

"Right you lot," AJ gathered all the students, including the junior kids urged forward by Madame Marsh. "Opening talent means our celebration dancers, so the rest of you continue your warmups backstage, and *merde*, everybody. Let's go!"

Madame Marsh had done well with the junior students, giving them choreography that was just difficult enough to challenge, without intimidating. They danced around the High Priest, who mimed his approval and blessing, consecrating them as temple dancers.

Then came the *pas de deux*, Solor the Warrior with Nikiya the Temple Dancer, Gamzatti the Rajah's daughter with The Green Idol of Dagon.

Then it was AJ's turn as the Rajah. After the Green Idol danced his solo, instead of offering Gamzatti to Dagon, in the form of the Green Idol, AJ stormed through the temple, tearing the happy couples apart, and insisting the High Priest marry Gamzatti to Solor.

The High Priest distracted the Rajah, driving him out, allowing the young couples to escape.

End of Act One. The curtain rose on the junior class, and they took their curtain call to a thundering ovation.

"Great job, everyone!" AJ congratulated them. "Now it's time for our green act! Girls, take your places at the ramps, and *merde*!"

Act Two of a classical ballet was usually what was known as a white act, because it consisted of the women of the *corps de ballet*, generally clad in white costumes, performing a series of traditional tableaux. *Bayadere's* Kingdom of the Shades represented the realm between the living and the dead.

Here, it represented the coastal waters at the mouth of the Miskatonic River, the place between Arkham and the deep realm of Dagon.

Solor and Nikiya, Gamzatti and her Green Idol, flee through this realm to escape the Rajah, aided by the Shades.

In the classic series of *arabesques*, the Shades came up from the depths. They gathered the confounded lovers, reuniting them, dancing around them. Guiding them back to the temple.

AJ stood in the wings, waiting for his next cue. After a quick scene change to the temple, he would charge back on stage in a final attempt to thwart the Order of Dagon.

Just hope the Old One doesn't blow his entrance.

AJ needn't have worried. The huge webbed hand came up through the temple "fountain" right on cue, snatching AJ and pulling him, thrashing dramatically, down below.

He was then dumped in a heap on one of the backstage barges.

AJ hurried to the nearest dry wing, to watch the High Priest bless the union of human boy to green girl, and green boy to human girl.

The junior class got a reprise of their celebration dances, along with the Shades.

The curtain came down to thunderous applause, the humans on the beach shouting *bravo,* the shallows churning with underwater applause, accompanied by enthusiastic barks.

The Old One didn't take a curtain call, much to the disappointment of the Miskatonic theater kids.

Madame Marsh came onstage with great reluctance, AJ and the High Priest both having to go to the wings to bring her out.

Lights appeared below the surf, and several of the green kids jumped right from the stage to greet their families. The college kids stripped the stage and packed their gear in record time, and the picnics on the beach turned into a huge party.

The two mixed couples received the greatest attention.

The human kids all quickly changed to swimwear, the phosphorescent glow in the surf now as bright as any pool lights. Even so, several young couples managed to find convenient shadows.

As the night began drawing to a close, several of the younger students wanted to say their good-byes to Madame Marsh. AJ finally tracked her down on one of the barges, behind the stacked ramps.

She was quietly weeping.

"Madame Marsh," AJ said quietly. "Some of your students would like to say goodnight. And you should come join the party. The show was a great success."

She looked up at him, red-eyed, her tear-streaked face an unbecoming shade of pale green. "You have no idea what you've done, do you?" She stood up, pushing her way past him, ordering the student who'd rowed him out to take her to her car at once.

AJ jumped in at the last second. "You must say goodnight to the children. They will miss you," he insisted.

She refused to speak, only shaking her head, her eyes tightly shut. "I never should have come here. I will never come here again. *Never!*"

The moment they reached shore, she jumped out, walking down the beach away from the party. AJ started after her.

"Let her go," the High Priest said, appearing suddenly from the shadows. "She is right. I shouldn't have brought her back. I thought, perhaps, after so much time away, she would *want* to come back. I fear that instead, she felt she *must* come back."

AJ thought back to those horrid days of bed rest, the increasingly desperate phone calls, and the inescapable pull to accept Louie da Squid's offer to teach in Arkham. "It's all but impossible to say no to the Old Ones, isn't it."

"I see you understand the situation. I would've thought the roles would be reversed, you and Madam Marsh."

"Perhaps *because* she is from here, she understands things I'm only just beginning to see. She will *have* to come back, someday, yes? Whether she wants to or not?"

The High Priest nodded. "As I did. I was fortunate that the change did not begin with me until I was more than ready to retire from the stage. I had already begun the Arkham School of Ballet, for the sake of the children who would never fit in at any other ballet school. I hope you will consider returning to stage your marvelous version of *La Bayadere* again. But you should get off your feet. You are not yet fully recovered."

AJ allowed himself to be guided to a chair next to Mike. Both of them were plied with food and drink. The lights slowly faded. The junior dancers were taken home. The seniors continued carousing, indulged by their parents. The four principles, especially, were being feted.

At some point, the party wound down. The two couples were led off by the High Priest, with the last of the revelers falling into procession behind them. Except for the embers of a dying bonfire, Mike and AJ were left in darkness.

"We should hit the sack," Mike said, draining the last of his beer. Looking around for a trash bin, he stood, still holding the bottle.

"Yeah," AJ yawned. "We need to get back to the city." He too, stood, wondering how, but for the dying fire and their two beach chairs, all signs of the party had disappeared.

Faint cheers carried from somewhere in Arkham. Mike dropped his beer bottle in the kitchen trash bin as they shuffled into the cottage. He'd done most of their packing while AJ was occupied with the final tech/dress rehearsal. While AJ showered away the last of the stage makeup, Mike poured them each a glass of wine, turned down the bed, and turned on the TV.

AJ slipped beneath the sheet and took his glass of wine. He was asleep before he finished it, before the opening credits of the film Mike found were barely over.

They drove out of town before dawn the next morning. An ambulance was pulled up outside the B&B where Madame Marsh had been staying, but AJ thought nothing of it, until Mike said something.

"She seemed kinda upset, when she left last night. Think she's okay?"

AJ shuddered, the woman's strange, pale green face with its expression of utter despair fixed in his mind. He shook his head, refusing to answer.

He was still very tired from the previous long day. He dozed off in the car, waking only when Mike pulled into the parking garage of their building. AJ got his crutches out of the back. Mike had wrapped his ankle, but AJ refused to put on the boot. Now he leaned wearily on the crutches as they made their way upstairs.

You have no idea what you've done, do you?

"What the hell did she mean?" he muttered as they walked into their loft.

"Go back to bed," Mike advised. "I think you overdid it, yesterday. But hey, nobody got eaten, right? And you *didn't* get stung by any jellyfish."

"No. No one was eaten," AJ whispered. "But there are other ways to be sacrificed, aren't there? Remember what the ballet master told me, when I asked him to play the part of the High Priest?"

"What?" Mike shrugged. "Something about that Esoteric Order of Dagon, right?"

"Yeah," AJ said with a shudder. "He really *is* a High Priest. And that party after the show, the way all the families reacted to our two mixed couples. Remember that grand procession back into town?"

Mike looked at him, and AJ saw the realization in his eyes. "You think he *actually* married two human kids to two children of Dagon? But those kids, they were so *happy*, AJ. I don't think they sacrificed anything. I think they knew exactly what they were getting into. Or at least they did by the end of the six weeks."

AJ was nodding. "I know. I watched it all unfolding. I was telling myself they were *really* getting into character. But I think they were just really falling in love. And that's what Madame Marsh couldn't bear. That I was putting them together, giving them the opportunity. Encouraging another generation. She's right. I *didn't* know what I was doing."

AJ pulled off his clothes, even removing the bandage from his ankle, and got into bed. "She's one of them, you see," he continued, his voice taking on a dreamlike quality. "A product of crossbreeding. She's starting to feel the call of the deep, and she can't bear it. She wants to remain human, but she can't, because she never was. She's already begun to change, and the call is too strong. I know, because I've already realized I'll be going back there, next summer. No matter if I'm still able to perform, I won't do the summer tour. I will answer that call, and go back to teach at Arkham School of Ballet. You'll come with me, won't you?"

"Of course I will." Mike kissed him. "Can't have you running off with one of those exotic green boys, can I? I quite enjoyed our summer. I love watching you be brilliant. And you were, you know. Brilliant. But you might have to teach *all* the classes next year, unless that cagey high priest ballet master wants to help."

AJ remembered the ambulance outside the B&B as they'd left Arkham, a dark vehicle on the dark street.

Madame Marsh would never make the change. Never go down into the immortality of the deep. Never see her students again.

AJ reached for Mike, pulling him into their bed, huddling against him as if he'd never be warm again. "Why did you say that, about the green boys? You know I would never do that."

"I know," Mike said. "It's the green girls we have to worry about," he said quietly. "They want a bigger gene pool."

AJ recalled the ratio of girls to boys, and another shudder racked him. "Mike? Do you *remember* last night? I don't mean the party. I mean after we went to bed."

"Hush, love. Go back to sleep."

"But what do you think happened to Madame Marsh?"

AJ felt Mike's sigh. He didn't say the ambulance might have been there for someone else. He didn't say it was dark and in no hurry because there was nothing wrong.

AJ drifted into sleep, and Mike said nothing at all.

TAILOR-MADE

PATRICK RUTIGLIANO

Arthur Sullivan knew his business, but few seemed to care he had one. He drummed his slender fingers atop the counter of his tailor shop, wishing the impacts were the footsteps of customers. Instead, he watched passersby walk beneath the elm tree outside and prayed none of his creditors were among them. The inside of the shop was no less depressing. Bolts of fabric sporting herringbone and pinstripe patterns still awaited the first cut where they sat piled on the shelves beside him. The glass cases exhibiting his assortment of buttons, ties, and collars seemed to have accumulated a fine layer of dust no amount of scrubbing could remove. Arthur fancied he smelled it in the air, too—musty as an old attic despite multiple airings and frenzied cleanings. It even drifted into the adjacent apartment to accuse him of failure while he tried to sleep. The frames of his glasses rested neatly on the dark circles beneath his eyes.

Thank goodness Uncle Charles left me a little money in addition to the shop or it would've closed already.

Guilt came at the memory of his uncle's kindly, whiskered face. The old man's sad blue eyes had always brightened at the sight of him, his own son lost somewhere near the Somme. He'd taught Arthur the trade after drink rotted his father's liver in Providence, seeing potential in him, only to die before being able to impart his skill at marketing. Signs, displays, ads in the *Advertiser* and *Gazette,* none of it had helped sales. The well-to-do folks who occupied the homes dotting Miskatonic Avenue, High Street, and Saltonstall Street stopped coming around soon after Uncle Charles passed away. Arthur's fingertips beat a faster tempo.

The old blue bloods probably aren't willing to trust someone my age, regardless of mentorship. They know I was only in the shop a year before Uncle Charles died. I'm still considered new to the trade and new to town, so damn the work I could show them! After all, why take the risk when Boston and its high-end shops are only a train ride away? He cringed at the sound of a familiar engine. *And that's not doing me any favors, either.*

Coughing, laboring, the bus from Innsmouth pulled up in front of the florist shop across the street. Arthur could only see the front half of the vehicle through the window, but he already saw the bystanders on the sidewalks turning their faces away, giving the bus a wide berth. He didn't wonder why. Even from a distance, Arthur caught traces of the "Innsmouth look" in the two men who stepped off the bus. The tweeds and caps were common enough, but the sky was clear enough for sunlight to glare on skin that shone a moist and sickly shade of gray. One man scratched at his temples repeatedly, lifting his cap high enough to reveal uneven shocks of dark brown hair. The eyes were worse, so round and prominent on both men that Arthur had trouble imagining them being capable of blinking. Stooped, one limping with some injury or deformity, the two walked out of sight. The bus driver stepped off a moment later and stretched his back, ugly as his passengers. Pity overpowered instinctive revulsion.

Uncle Charles shunned them like the rest—told me to never let them in the shop. Poor souls. I wonder what causes it. I suppose it can't be contagious as nobody around here seems to catch it even with the odd visit. It must be some hereditary condition.

Arthur watched the driver turn, speaking to someone, before casting a glance his way. To his surprise, the driver pointed toward the shop a moment later. A woman walked into view past the driver's shoulder. Quick steps soon carried her across the street, offering Arthur a clearer look at her. His drumming stopped.

The woman's clothing was of a higher order than her fellow passengers, albeit dated. The high, curved heels had gone out of style with the last decade. A wide-brimmed hat, jacket, and skirt cut just above the ankles were relics of the same period. Still, she wore it all well, her back straight and gait confident in contrast to her fellows on the bus. Her hair—black and bobbed, eyes dark beneath the bangs—was the only sign of modernity. She lingered in front of the window display. Perhaps free of Innsmouth's malady or only barely touched by it, her large eyes didn't bear the same disturbing bulge that usually marked its townsfolk. Taken off guard, Arthur didn't resist when she opened the door and walked down the short flight of steps into his shop.

Prejudice be damned! A paying customer is a paying customer.

He cleared his throat, smiling despite his unease. "Good day, miss. Is there anything I can help you with?"

Her voice was deeper than he expected, tinged with a slight accent he couldn't place. "Possibly. Let me browse a moment longer, if you would."

The woman made a slow, methodical perusal of his wares. Her eyes seemed to settle on each piece in turn, absorbing it for a long moment, before moving to the next. Arthur was relieved to catch the woman mid-blink before she sauntered to the counter. A heavy scent of jasmine perfume traveled with her. A barely detectable odor of the ocean, or something pulled from the ocean, hid beneath it. Arthur chided himself.

Innsmouth is a fishing community. What did you expect?

Still, he struggled to meet the woman's gaze when it found his own. Her warm tone helped set him at ease.

"You have some lovely things here."

"Thank you, Miss...?"

"Chalmers. Clara Chalmers. Thank you for letting me in, by the way. Most of Arkham isn't so accommodating."

He offered a pained smile. "I suppose folks get a bit squeamish. Some of the old wives' tales are bad enough without the odd...uh...malady in Innsmouth giving them more weight."

Clara's eyes narrowed just a sliver. A slight edge crept into her voice, and for a moment, Arthur was sure he'd offended her somehow.

"Yes, 'malady'." The word seemed stuck on her tongue, like a sour candy she wanted to spit out. "It's a progressive condition, you see. And chronic. No one's found a treatment that works."

"That's terrible. I'm sorry."

"Are you now?" She leaned closer over the counter. "If that's true, I was wondering if you might be willing to provide tailoring to some family members of mine. Possibly some others as well. We have no proper tailor in Innsmouth, you see. Your compensation would be more than generous."

Before Arthur could respond, she placed five gold coins on the counter. He didn't see from where she produced them. Arthur picked the stack up. The coins were ancient, whatever markings they'd sported reduced to shallow pits and bumps. A peculiar moisture filmed the lucre. However, the gleam and weight of it felt real. He swallowed his gorge, trying to conceal his excitement.

"I'll need to have these checked to make sure they're genuine, you understand."

Clara sounded bemused at the notion. "Naturally." She extended a rectangular piece of paper between her thumb and index finger. "But when you do, here's my card."

An appraisal of the gold justified Clara's confidence. Lacking a phone number, Charles posted a letter the same day. He got one in return a week later.

Mr. Sullivan,

I'm pleased to find you still receptive to my offer. I would like to bring my father in to be fitted for a new suit on the third. However, as I told you, the ailment he suffers is progressive in nature. My father's condition is severe, and, I would prefer to keep his dignity preserved from the gawking of those less understanding than yourself. I should like to arrive with him after dark—eight o'clock should do. My apologies for requesting you remain open late on our account, but as I've already proven, the reward will be more than worth the inconvenience. What you have in hand now is only half of what I'm offering. I look forward to our meeting.

Cordially,

Clara Chalmers

Another hasty letter back sealed the agreement. A great deal of the weight Arthur was carrying disappeared into the bowels of the postbox with it.

She already paid me enough to catch up on my rent and clear the worst of my debts. Just imagine if I make a repeat customer of her, let alone the rest of them!

Arthur put the remainder of his time before the appointment to good use, expanding his selection of materials and patterns further to meet any possible need. Reservations only crept in with the shadows of the appointed evening. The revulsion to the Innsmouthers he could understand on a visceral level—he'd felt it himself—but there seemed more to the phenomenon than mere physicality. Lately, each time the bus came, and he watched people shy away, he began to detect a fear deeper than mere disgust. There was never a jeer, a shove, or a pebble thrown at the peculiar visitors, merely a desire to keep as wide a berth from them as possible. It reminded him of his Uncle Charles. The old man was normally so gentle, so understanding, but he'd not been willing to give anyone from Innsmouth an inch.

He never explained his view, either. He would just purse his lips or change the subject altogether. Come to think of it, I've never heard more than a handful of people ever mention Innsmouth by name in Arkham. And when they did, it always turned to whispers.

Arthur turned the last of Clara's coins between his fingers, trying to recall what little he'd caught. *There was some kind of epidemic that all but wiped out the town in '46, probably the onset of the illness festering there now. Other than that, it was all so childish. Deals with the devil, the odd human sacrifice by some cult. Absurdist drivel. There was the odd disappearance in the area, sure, but it's not as if that doesn't happen in Arkham, or anywhere else, for that matter. Hell, the* Gazette *just wrote about some college student that went missing here a few weeks ago.*

He returned the coin to his register with a grimace. Even cleaned off and polished, the metal still felt strange to the touch, as if it were sweating minute amounts of saltwater. It even smelled like it. Arthur was still lost in thought when a blue Packard pulled up along the curb outside. He recognized Clara the instant she emerged from the vehicle, still a walking anachronism that stood out against the sleek modern automobile. Her passenger joined her a moment later. The fellow was wide, and a good 5'10" even hunched over. The brim of a slouch hat dipped low enough to touch the turned-up collar of his black overcoat. Arthur couldn't make out anything beneath the hat, but the awkward, limping gait was reminiscent of the man who arrived with Clara during her previous trip.

Even worse, I think. The poor fellow more hops than walks...

Arthur swallowed down any last-minute hesitation and went to open the door for his customers. Clara entered first.

"A pleasure to see you again, Ms. Chalmers."

"And you, Mr. Sullivan." She walked inside far enough for her father to clamber beyond the doorway. The brim of the hat swept slowly, back and forth. "This is my father, Thaddeus Chalmers."

Arthur was about to offer the man a greeting when the scent of rotting fish swam inside his nostrils on a stream of salt air. The smell seemed to envelop his customer in a noxious cloud. Unlike his daughter, Thaddeus hadn't bothered to hide his scent. Given its strength, such an effort would've been pointless, anyway. Arthur discreetly wiped a tear from his eye, fighting back bile.

Keep it together, man. Your future is on the line. You must *get through this, and get used to this.*

Arthur extended his hand on instinct. "Ah, it's a pleasure to meet you, sir."

The brim of the hat rose a hair. Deep in the overcoat's pockets, Thaddeus' right hand lifted into view just high enough to expose mottled gray-white flesh. The skin looked uneven and scabrous, almost scaled. As if its owner had just realized a faux-pas, the hand quickly sank back inside the pocket.

Clara stepped between them. "I'm sorry, but my father's condition has left him rather shy, as you can imagine. His voice was also badly affected by his illness, so I will have to speak for him, I'm afraid."

"Oh—oh, that's fine! Perfectly fine. I understand completely." Arthur swept a hand toward his counter. "In that case, perhaps we should just focus on helping him pick out something that suits him. I have some new things in stock just for the occasion." He pulled several of his recent purchases from the shelves and placed them on the counter.

"So I see. Thank you." Clara slipped her arm around her father's. Her voice became loving, playful. "Come now, Papa. Surely, there must be something nice for you here."

Arthur kept his distance while they searched. It didn't take long. They paused before a herringbone pattern adorning a bolt of blue wool. A horrific grunt belched out from beneath the slouch hat, wet as pond scum. Arthur recoiled in spite of his manners. Clara laughed lightly.

"I believe he's come to a decision." She pointed to the material in front of them. "He would like a full suit in this." She nodded toward another bolt in pinstripes. "And one of the gray there as well. He'll also need dress shirts, a hat, ties, the usual. However, we can address that later."

"Certainly! Excellent choices. Given how generous you've been, I can have them ready for you by the end of the week. I'll just need the gentleman's measurements."

The slouching figure under the overcoat straightened slightly, tensed. Clara glanced at her father with concern. It clung to her features while she spoke. "My father is a sensitive man, Mr. Sullivan. Tread lightly."

That sounded like a threat...

Arthur managed a nervous smile while he retrieved his tape measure from the counter. It died on his lips while he approached his coated customer. Proximity gave the fishy odor renewed strength, roiling his stomach. More of it rode on each guttural, croaking breath.

Arthur gulped. He tried to smile again and failed. "I'll need measurements for your overarm, chest, waist, and inseam, sir. And your head for the hat." He received a nod of assent in turn.

The overarm was easy enough. The tape measure circled around Thaddeus' arms and crossed his chest. Arthur adjusted for the extra fabric in his way. He tried to be gentle with the rest.

"I'll—I need to get under your arms as well, sir."

Slowly, grudgingly, a gray paw of a hand finally escaped the overcoat pocket. The fingers were bizarre, so short and thick they looked as if they were melting into the rest of the hand. Arthur made a desperate effort not to stare at the heavily veined webbing connecting the digits. The stubby but pointed black fingernails were just as difficult to ignore. Arthur's glasses slid partway down his nose.

I'd swear they were claws! God...what kind of illness is this?

The freakish hand cinched the coat's collar closed while its counterpart unbuttoned the coat and let it hang loose. Arthur's stomach roiled at the wave of stench that escaped. He forced himself on, working as quickly as he could. Even with speed, it was an unsettling process. The tape dug into flesh that yielded under it like tallow, though it seemed there should be far more muscle than fat given Thaddeus' sturdy build. Moisture seeped through his customer's shirt at the contact, slicking the tape with a peculiar fluid thicker than sweat. Sweating himself, Arthur wiped it clean with a handkerchief, his hand starting to shake more with each progressive measurement.

That's the chest done...waist done...now, the inseam.

He balked getting the end of the tape to Thaddeus' foot. This close, the shape of the leg seemed off even through the pants, as if it were hanging off the joint at the wrong angle. Arthur hadn't noticed before, but the shoe itself was immense, cobbled together from more than one bit of footwear into a poorly stitched monstrosity that brought Frankenstein's monster to mind. Arthur imagined gargantuan feet to match the freakish hands—gray, scaled, and webbed. The thought of more coins dropping from the latter steadied his nerves.

Don't think about it. Just focus. Focus...

Arthur let out a breath and straightened up. "There...Done...all done, sir. I just need to measure your head."

The paw not holding the coat closed refastened the buttons. The hat's brim slowly turned toward Clara. She smiled reassuringly, nodding at him. With a peculiar, wheezing sigh, Thaddeus dipped his head, pulling the hat off and in front of his face. Only a few strands of silver hair stuck out from the gray-green pate. The ears were miniscule, little more than gnarled knots of flesh hanging off the skull. Arthur's hand trembled while he reached for the hat's brim.

"Sir, I need this a little lower, please. I need to place the tape just a bit above your eyebrows." Slowly, the hat dropped, revealing yet more of the weird, scaly flesh. Arthur took the final measurement, panting after it was done.

"Finished, sir. We're finished."

The hat slid back up. Arthur flinched at the clap of Clara's hands.

"Wonderful!" She strode to Arthur and took his hands in hers. Cold metal slipped onto his sweaty palms. The hat's brim snapped in their direction. "You've been so kind. So patient. Would you mind if I recommend you to the rest of my family? My friends? Similar accommodations would have to be made, naturally."

Arthur's voice came out a rasp. "Naturally." She patted his hand, letting it gently slide off as she pulled away. The sensation was sensual and nauseating at the same time. He returned her wave mechanically while she followed her father to the door. She was halfway through when a question jumped into Arthur's mind. He hadn't even realized he spoke it aloud.

"Why did you take the bus before when you had a car?"

Clara looked at him. A peculiar little half-smile teased her lips. There was more than a hint of cunning in it. "Oh, it's not ours, you see. It belongs to a friend. He was just...passing through and was kind enough to let us borrow it. Goodnight, Mr. Sullivan." She cast a glance toward the bolts of fabric on the counter. "And good luck."

Arthur had little other work to occupy him. He finished the suits early and set up the next meeting, anxious to have the affair done and over with. The day came soon. Evening spread its shroud over the gambrel roofs outside while he paced the shop. He wondered what excuse he could manufacture to keep Clara from singing his praises in Innsmouth, though he knew he shouldn't.

He paused to lift his glasses and massage the bridge of his nose. *Why does the money have to be so good? I could probably coast for nearly a year on what'll be in the register tonight.*

The squeal of brakes interrupted his thoughts. The Packard was back, sapphire blue beneath the nearby streetlight. Arthur walked to the door and held it open, knuckles growing white around the handle while his customers entered. The rank ocean stench followed them inside, swimming onto his palate. He wished he could spit it out.

"Lovely to see you again, Mr. Sullivan. I take it everything is in order?"

Arthur cleared his throat and managed a nod. "Yes. I altered some shirts and collars per your instructions as well. Your father should cut quite a dashing...figure." He led them to the counter, his work ready and waiting for them. Clara's fingers moved over the herringbone pattern.

"Well done, Mr. Sullivan. It's lovely work. Truly lovely." She looked to her father and received the slightest nod of approval in turn. From her purse, she extracted six of the gold coins and placed them beside the suit. "All we owe you, as well as a bonus for your speed. I'm sure we'll have cause to call on you again. Several members of our family have already expressed an interest. Some friends as well."

Arthur's revulsion struggled against his desire for security. It lost the battle, albeit barely. He didn't know why, but he had a terrible fear of both of them besides what he'd gathered of the strange appearance of the elder Chalmers. There was a predatory coolness in Clara's eyes he hadn't been able to escape since asking about the car. Every time he looked into them, the scraps of town legend floated through his brain anew, whispering a warning.

"That's...wonderful. Thank you."

"You're quite welcome. You've earned it." Clara gathered the garments. She'd just turned on her heel to leave when she froze at the sight of a police officer near the car. A sputtering hiss escaped her father's upturned collar. Blond and thick-jawed, the cop strode around the vehicle, moving with the assurance of ready muscle despite being middle-aged. He filled the shop's doorway after completing his examination. The officer took one heavy step inside, gaze flitting from Arthur to Clara and her father. Tension dripped from the cop's voice, though Arthur could tell he was trying to keep it even.

"Whose car is that?"

Clara replied. Her tone took on a juvenile air Arthur had never heard before, disarming and naive. "Oh, ours, Officer. Well, a friend's, actually. There isn't a problem is there? A flat or something?"

The officer stepped closer to them, but only a bit. His hand slipped down toward the butt of his revolver. The strap securing it in its holster already hung loose. "No flat, ma'am. Just missing along with its driver. Do you know a Gerald Garby?"

Clara cupped her hand to her chin. "I can't say that I do."

The officer's gaze moved to Thaddeus, locked there. His nose wrinkled. "There's a rumor he went off to Innsmouth a few weeks ago. Some stupid college dare. He never came back."

"Ah, the friend who loaned it to us does deal in cars. Perhaps he sold it or traded it in?"

The cop's eyes narrowed to slits. "Ma'am, *nobody* in Innsmouth has a car. That's why you all take the bus. Except you two. Seems a little convenient, doesn't it?"

Arthur backed off a step. *I knew something was wrong!*

Clara sighed. "Oh dear, you outsiders think you know everything about Innsmouth. Are you sure it's even his? There is more than one blue Packard, you know."

The cop continued glowering. "Oh, I know it, alright. You might have swapped the plates with some junker's, but only my nephew's Packard has that dent on the fender. And you're going to tell me exactly what you've done with him. You're coming with me. *Now.*"

Neither Clara nor her father made a move when the officer drew his gun. They merely seemed to exchange a glance between them. A chill twisted Arthur's innards at the playful spark in Clara's eyes. She held her hands out in front of her. The officer approached with the gun trained on her chest. He pulled a pair of handcuffs free. The cop managed to get them around her wrists single-handed. He moved on to Thaddeus.

"You next, pal. Let me see your hands. Real slow."

Arthur watched the officer's face contort with his own at the reemergence of the webbed anomalies from the overcoat's pockets. The short, sharp claws gleamed at the ends of the stunted digits. The officer was still fumbling with a second pair of handcuffs when Thaddeus lifted his head.

The grotesque appearance shared by the other Innsmouthers Arthur had seen became a pleasant memory. Eyes nearly as large around as his fist stared, filmy yellow and lidless. The lips were far too thick and wide for the long, narrow face. Short, sharp teeth shone within the open mouth as a fresh blast of fetor was exhaled into the room.

"Christ!" The handcuffs fell from the officer's hand. The other didn't have a chance to pull the trigger before a webbed hand shot out and swallowed the attached forearm with an explosive crack of bone. The officer only got out the first note of a scream before the monstrosity called Thaddeus Chalmers clamped its jaws over his head. Another sickening crack sounded.

The stories... They were true! Wh—what are they? They can't be—what can they possibly be, for God's sake?

Arthur fell to his knees, hyperventilating while he watched the mouth stretch and contort. There seemed to be no bones limiting its actions while Thaddeus' hands grabbed hold of the officer and began shoving the remainder of the cop into his maw. He only paused long enough for Clara to dart forward and snatch the keys hanging from the cop's belt. Her cuffs joined the other pair on the floor.

"There now. All done."

Thaddeus lifted his head, throat stretching like a bullfrog's as the officer's shoes disappeared down his gullet. Stitches gave way, and two buttons popped off the overcoat. Clara clucked her tongue and picked them up along with the handcuffs. Arthur yelped when she placed the buttons in his hand. She leaned down close enough to whisper in his ear.

"Another job for you. Unless you have any objections?"

Arthur caught the bulbous eyes staring at him. The tip of a pink tongue flicked to the obscene lips, near as thick. "No! None at all."

"Good. After all, I would hate for you to disappear. It can happen so easily...so quickly. No one would ever believe such a thing is even possible. Remember that." Clara put a finger to her lips and winked. "Expect to be busy from now on, Mr. Sullivan. We'll be in touch. All of us."

She rose. Her father came near and clapped a hand on Arthur's shoulder. The short claws pinched him. The digits below pressed down a moment, as if testing the firmness of a piece of meat before drawing away. Thaddeus followed Clara out the door, letting it slam shut behind them. Arthur could only stare, trembling while the car started up and pulled out of sight. He fancied his eyes felt a bit like those the Innsmouthers had now: open and unblinking to an awful reality he never knew existed. He removed his glasses and forced his eyelids down with his thumbs. Laughter scraped his throat raw as he tried to find refuge in the darkness there, but it was too late now...far too late.

ONE NIGHT IN ARKHAM

ALEXANDR BOND

S tale coffee, sweat, and cigarette smoke pervaded the police station but the hint of dead fish confused Sean O'Malley. Ever since he joined the force it drifted through the air like a bad tide, particularly near the cells which were usually packed though that hadn't surprised him. All cities as large as Arkham were bound to be swamped by crime. *I didn't expect it to be like this*, he thought as he tried to calm his nerves. *How can anyone deal with this?*

The sound of his fellow officers chatting amongst themselves could just be heard over the rapid clicking of typewriters. It was early in the morning, the sun barely past the horizon. And still his fellow officers sat at their desks typing up their reports. Thinking about it made him twitch. *What am I going to write?*

Sean sat in Captain Hearst's office, his gaze shifting from the scruffy desk to the pictures on the walls. Most were of the captain but some had the other officers as well as the secretary Sue. She was all blond curls and sharp features; definitely the cat's meow though he noticed her attention to the calls lacked a certain urgency. Dedication, as a police officer, was a must. His grandmother instilled that in him, respect for the law and the officer. A police officer had no time for dishonesty. "They exemplified the law," his grandmother told him when he was young and it always stuck with him. Now it weighed on him.

The abrupt creak of the door drew Sean's attention to Captain Hearst. His eyes were chiseled from slate and his body could have been painted by Rubens while a thick cigar hung from his lips. "O'Malley." At the sound of his name, Sean started to stand but the captain waved him back down. "Sit," Captain Hearst ordered then plopped in the leather chair behind his desk, the cigar defying gravity with the motion. Sean obeyed, his stomach roiling. The captain cleared his throat, finally putting his cigar in an ashtray. "Start at the beginning, from the moment you left the station."

S *even hours earlier…*

S ean stared out from the police car's window at the city with its thin alleyways, cramped homes, and gambrel roofs. Streetlights shed long shadows, spilling onto storefronts and stoops. Despite it being well into the evening, numerous people strolled along the streets and yet something about it bothered him. He couldn't put his finger on it but he felt there were less people out than it appeared, It made no sense to him and he bit his lip. It was a strange sensation. He chalked it up to his unfamiliarity with Arkham having only recently arrived in the city.

Turning away, he stole a glance at his new partner. Twenty years his senior, five o'clock shadow, and breath that hinted at a steady diet of tobacco, Kurt Hagen was what the other rookies called an "old timer." He wasn't a detective but his seniority commanded respect even as the others whispered about him behind his back. No one wanted to partner with him. When they were assigned together, Hagen refused to acknowledge Sean for a full minute before finally getting to his feet and pulling on his dark coat. And even then, all he said was "I'm driving."

That was two hours ago and though little had improved, Sean decided it was his job to bridge the gap. "Mr. Hagen..." He started but the older officer grunted in a tone that told Sean the man wasn't interested. *Or maybe it's my imagination.* He supposed it was but before he could try again, the radio crackled and Hagen snatched the receiver.

"Go ahead."

"Got a break in at the cemetery," Sue said.

Hagen glowered. "That crazy doctor again?"

"Don't think so." She sounded bored.

"Fine." Hagen cut across the street, the car jostling along the brick lined roads.

"Crazy doctor?" Sean asked but still only got another grunt in reply. Hagen sped along, easily slipping past the other motorists as they made their way for the cemetery.

Situated on the western base of Hangman's Hill, the cemetery was far larger than Sean would have guessed. Headstones spread out like marble flowers in a darkened meadow, grim and foreboding. A stone wall about three feet high wrapped around the burial ground, its length interrupted by thin wrought iron gates here and there. Hagen parked beside one of the gates, partly on the sidewalk.

"You know how to use that revolver?" Hagen asked as he got out of the automobile.

Sean glanced up, nearly startled. "Yes, sir," he said as he followed suit, looking over the roof of the cab at his partner. He didn't add that he hadn't fired it at a person before. "But surely it's just some vagrant or perhaps a thief." He had heard stories of grave robbers stalking the wealthy dead. The lamplight only made Hagen's grimace more pronounced.

"If we're lucky that's all it is. Come on." He didn't elaborate further instead leading the way into cemetery.

Trailing after him, Sean's flashlight haunted the other officer's steps. He hated graveyards, finding the idea of stepping on top of dead bodies macabre. He suppressed a shiver at the thought, wishing it was November instead of May and he could blame his chills on the weather. Their boots padded the soft grass. They sounded loud in the sudden quiet that descended upon the cemetery like a shroud. The noises of the city fell away, distant like rumbles of thunder from a far off storm. More than once, Sean peered over his shoulder, the hairs on the back of his neck standing erect. *I'm no child. I'm a police officer. Start acting like one.* He refused to add that he was less than a week on the job. As he swept the light back and forth, his attention on anything that might stand out, he discovered with growing dismay that his fellow officer had disappeared.

"Hagen? This isn't funny! Where'd you go?" He wondered if it was some kind of prank, a joke on the new guy. He liked jokes, could roll with them like the next fellow. But he felt being out on patrol was taking it too far. "Hagen—"

A noise drew his flashlight. To his left, something rustled. Mounds of coffee dark earth littered the grass, a ghastly trail leading to an unearthed grave. Sean frowned. He glanced around for any sign of Hagen. Finding none, he stepped carefully toward the grave, the revolver in his hand shaking slightly. The rustling grew louder. Sean tried to picture what was going on in there but the sounds didn't make sense. There were grunts of effort followed by slurping that grew more distinct the closer he got until his heart pounded in rhythm with the dreadful noises. When he was a few feet away, he couldn't take it anymore.

"Come out of there! Right now!" The grunts ceased and dirt cascaded from the side of the open grave as a figure slowly climbed out. Sean's light fell upon a man. He wore tattered clothes, stringy black hair, and a face that pulled a gasp from the young officer's mouth. All that came to mind was the man had been in some kind of fire and yet he saw no scaring, only stretched skin and deformed teeth. He tried to steel his resolve at the grotesque appearance but found himself staring at what the man held. In his grasp was an arm, chunks of flesh missing from it.

"Saint's preserve us." At his words, the deformed man snarled and leapt from the grave, rushing right at Sean. He froze and the man collided with him. They slammed into the ground and it took all of his strength to keep the man from biting him. Rotted breath rolled over him as the man's fangs bit ever closer to Sean's face. A bang shook the world and the man jerked, falling off Sean. Hagen approached, his gun trained on the man. Without hesitation, he fired twice more into the man's chest.

"You alright, kid?" Hagen asked as he helped him get to his feet.

Sean stammered, taking a breath. "He was... he was eating a corpse."

Hagen grunted, a scowl on his face. In the dim light cast by Sean's fallen flashlight, a sinister countenance stole the older officer's features. For some irrational moment, Sean felt unsafe with him and stepped away until he kicked the body of the deformed man. As Sean looked at the dead man, his gorge rose. Not just at the death but at the fact there was something very wrong with the man, something inhuman.

"Damn Pickman's kin. Should have stayed in Boston." Hagen said before stepping over to the open grave. He muttered to himself but Sean wasn't paying attention. The dead man lay on his back, his body still and yet a cold sweat broke out on Sean's brow as an urge to take out his revolver and empty it into the dead man's face almost overwhelmed him. He shut his eyes and breathed. The next moment, Hagen pulled Sean away as the dead man lurched onto his side. The older officer fired three more rounds into the man's face. As silence returned to the cemetery, Hagen looked over the young officer.

"Let's get back to the car."

Sean followed in a daze, only really coming back to himself when they reached their vehicle. He sat down while Hagen took a moment to smoke. Without really thinking about, he grabbed the radio and contacted Sue.

"Go ahead," she said.

"We found the man at the cemetery."

"Oh, is this the rookie, alright." She sounded distracted. "Status?"

"There was something wrong with his face. And he was eating a corpse. Then he didn't die—"

Hagen snatched the radio out of Sean's hand. "Had to deal with a grave robber. Had to defend ourselves. Put him down." He glared at Sean for a moment which confused the younger man.

"Do we need to call the uni boys for this?" Sue asked.

Hagen shook his head as if she could see him. "Nah, just the undertaker." He considered a moment, "better call Alvin. He'll know how to deal with it."

Once that was finished, Hagen got into the car. "That was stupid of you. You don't go mouthing off like that on an open channel. Never know whose listening."

"But I wasn't lying…"

"That's your problem, kid. There's what you saw and what you report. They aren't always the same."

Sean frowned and clenched his fists, mostly to keep his hands from shaking. Hagen sighed and pulled out a bottle of amber liquid from his coat pocket. "Here, drink this. It'll help."

He took the offered bottle and opened the top only to recoil. "This is alcohol… Prohibition—" Hagen's laugh cut Sean off.

"Between them strange folk from Innsmouth peddling their salty hooch and the gangsters profiting on demand, there's more booze here than in Chicago and New Orleans combined. And quite frankly, the city needs it more. No one in this God forsaken place should go for an extended period sober."

"But it's against the law," Sean replied which earned a roll of the eyes from Hagen. Heat scorched his cheeks which helped to calm his nerves. "As police, it's our duty to uphold the law, in ourselves and for the city we protect."

The old timer snickered. "This city isn't like New York, Boston, or even Kingsport, kid. You live here as long as I have, you'll understand that. You see, this town is built on lies. From the university to the historical society to the *Advertiser*. It's like deviled eggs, everyone loves it. The truth only makes you go crazy."

Sean eyed Hagen incredulously. "We're police officers. We stand for truth." Even as he said it, he knew how it sounded, how others would mock him for his ideals.

Hagen leaned back in the seat, grasping his unfinished cigarette. "Let me tell you a story, kid. About twenty years ago, there was an officer. His name was Charles Underhill. Decent man. Fine police officer. Good instincts. He was the kind of man you wished you could be. Sure everyone was jealous of him but couldn't be mad at him over it. It was just how he was.

"Back then the city was just putting itself back together after the typhoid outbreak. And it needed heroes to look up to. Good decent people to set the right example. I think you would've looked up to ole Charlie. Hell, he was only a few years older and I did." He took a long drag off his cigarette before continuing. "So one night in Arkham, this good, decent officer gets a call to a particular house overlooking the Miskatonic. Seemed like a routine call, strange noises, weird lights, and ugly smells. So ole Charlie heads up there but there isn't anything routine about that house.

"Now I'd known Charlie for awhile by then. He was a tough fellow. But after that night, he wasn't the same. A shadow hung over him, and he got jumpy. Not good for an officer to be jumpy. More than once he almost shot someone simply because they startled him."

Sean drummed his fingers on the outside of the car door. "Why are you telling me this?"

"He filled out his report of course," Hagen went on, ignoring the question. "And was called in to speak with the old captain. They went back and forth over that report. He refused to change it, refused to 'hide the truth' as he put it. Captain wouldn't accept it. Warned him. When he wouldn't play ball, he gave him a choice. Resign or he'd send him to the Sanitarium. He resigned."

"So you're saying that they'll do the same to me?"

"I'm saying shut your trap and let me finish." He dumped some ashes on the street. "Everyone felt betrayed by him leaving. Me included. Hell, we've all seen weird shit here and there; that's part of the job. But he couldn't let it go. He went to the papers. Told his story. Said he had proof. You know what he got? Ridiculed. Laughed at. It's scary how fast people can turn on you.

"I caught up with him some time after at Willows Diner. I asked him what happened that night. I heard stories but never saw the reports and though he was vocal about what he had seen, I couldn't help but feel he'd tell me the *real* truth.

"You think you want the truth, until it's something you don't want to hear. He told me what he saw in detail. I won't repeat it. But it wasn't so much what he said that shook me, kid. It was how he said it. This decent, tough man shook as he spoke; there was a mania in his tone, like his mouth was filled with bees. His fingers never stopped tapping the counter and his eyes darted from one part of the diner to the other. And I realized right then he was crazy. What he saw broke him so bad he wasn't human any longer. Just a living reminder of what shattered him. I suggested he get help. He grew angry, belligerent, screaming I was one of the eyeless people. Accused me of not believing him and calling him crazy. The thing is, kid; I did think he was crazy. But I believed everything he said."

Hagen fell silent, his gaze at an arbitrary point in the distance. Sean frowned. "So what happened to him?"

Hagen sighed, finally putting out his cigarette. "About a month later, he murdered his family. Was heard saying they were eyeless people. When confronted by his fellow officers, he shot himself." Silence filled the cab for a few minutes. In that time, an ambulance coach pulled up.

Hagen shifted in his seat, opening his door. Before he got out, he glanced back at Sean. "So, unless you want to end up in the Sanitarium, you write what the captain wants to hear, the public wants to believe. Not what you saw or know."

After Hagen spoke to the undertaker who claimed the body, he suggested they get a bite to eat but as they were pulling away from the cemetery, Sue's voice filled the cab.

"Hagen, you there?"

"Yeah," he said, his tone unpleasant.

"Sorry to do this to you but got another call over near King Street. A neighbor reported screams and sounds of violence. Might be a couple's issue."

He groaned.

"On it."

As Hagen's earlier remarks circled over Sean like vultures, they headed east, past the Carcosa Theater and Blackwood Gentleman's Club. Neither spoke. Hagen wasn't one for idle chitchat and Sean had too much to say even though none of it left his lips. He found it hard to digest the old timer's words. In fact, the more he thought about it, the more certain he became of what was really going on. *He lost his faith. Faith in the job.* He saw it back in Boston. The old police around the neighborhood grew jaded, lax, and corrupt. It explained the alcohol. *Should I report him?* He wouldn't make friends if he did but it was his job. If he slacked, if he dropped his values without so much as a nod, he wouldn't be much of a police officer. He stole a look at Hagen. The man steered the vehicle calmly, weaving between the other cars. His face betrayed nothing of his thoughts save for subdued boredom. Sean bit the side of cheek. *He's given up on it. I can't believe a word he says.*

By the time they reached their destination, Sean had made up his mind to report everything to the captain. It was his duty.

The street oozed history with two-story houses lining both sides. They parked in front of a particularly large home, all dark woods, hunter green painted shutters, and gambrel roof. The streetlamp only served to deepen the shadows clinging to the home and gloomy windows. They strode over an unkempt lawn and onto a sagging porch. A stack of *Advertiser* papers lay haphazardly upon the old doormat while three bottles of milk sat just to the right of the door. Sean frowned at them. *Milk delivery was nearly eighteen hours ago.* He glanced at Hagen as the man rapped on the door which creaked open, the sound like ice sliding down Sean's back.

"Get your revolver out, kid. I don't like this."

Despite his misgivings about the man, Sean complied. Hagen pushed the door open further, revealing a darkened foyer. *I don't want to go in there.* The thought startled Sean for both being cowardly and true. An itch started at the base of his neck and a knot formed in his stomach. He was almost glad they hadn't eaten.

"Come on," Hagen said and stepped inside. Sean almost screamed not to go in but stopped himself as the words touched his lips. *Irrational. Pull yourself together.* Inhaling sharply, he followed him.

Hagen searched for a lamp inside the foyer but gave up quickly, instead relying on their flashlights. Silhouettes of tables and small bookshelves lined the walls while a staircase loomed near the rear of the main hall. Sean bit back a cough as something bitter clawed at his throat. Smoke lingered in the air as well as a few other malodorous scents that reminded him of still waters, dark alleyways, and noises in the middle of the night. The house was still, silent as though it held its breath, hoping they would leave it alone. A large part of him agreed. In the gloom, as he followed Hagen into the kitchen, he could almost understand how that Charlie lost his grip on things. It made his heart thunder and his breath race.

"Take it easy, kid. Steady your breathing."

Sean eyed Hagen. True he wanted to gulp in air but he hadn't showed it that much. Still, he took a beat to get a hold of himself. "I said get it together," Hagen added as they quit the kitchen for a long hallway.

"I'm fine," Sean said after a moment.

"No, you're not. I can hear you practically breathing the Charleston."

Sean paused, perplexed, then a cold sweat slid down his back. "Those breaths aren't mine." *How can they be so loud?*

The two stared at each other, Hagen revealing a dash of concern before his features hardened. "I think it's coming from over here." He gripped his weapon tighter and moved toward a door to his left. Sean trailed behind, his revolver in his hand.

The breathing ceased as they entered the library. Dark wood paneling framed the walls and blended into thick bookcases filled with what Sean could only describe as tomes. Firelight flickered calmly, giving the room a warm glow, the illumination coming from three braziers positioned in the center of the room, each one fueled by thick oil. Chairs, tables, and a long sofa were all moved to the edges of the room. Sean took it all in but his gaze focused on the symbols. Two large rings with smaller script between them were painted on the floor and ceiling. They were unlike anything he had ever seen before. They whispered in eldritch verses and made bizarre visions dance before his eyes.

"Damn, this looks like one for them uni boys," Hagen said, his light tracing the unnatural geometry before them. His words broke Sean out of his silent fit and he shuddered. As he did, his light fell on something behind the sofa.

"Sir, what's that?" As they eyed the object illuminated by the flashlight, it quickly became apparent it was a leg, two to be precise. Sharing an uneasy glance, they circumvented the center of the room, almost kicking a half-filled oil can as they did. The breathing resumed as they reached the sofa. A man in his thirties lay sprawled on the ground. Blood caked his pale face and pooled beneath him. Sitting a few feet away was a woman. She rocked back and forth clutching herself, the source of the strange breathing.

"Check her," Hagen ordered as he stepped closer to the man's body. Sean hurried over to the woman, stowing his weapon. Her brown hair clung to her as sweat slicked down her pallid face.

"Can you walk, miss?" Sean asked as he helped her up. She didn't resist and he guided her away from the body. Her movements were jerky, unsteady, and she leaned on him for support, her fingers tight around his waist.

"There's a weird wound on his back," Hagen said as he stood. "What the hell happened here?"

The woman shook, her grip tightening on Sean. "Miss?" Her head jerked back. Her face contorted then elongated as insect legs as large as pitch fork tines burst from her cheeks.

"Kid!"

Sean shrieked and tried to pull away as the legs bent and grasped him. She held strong until Sean kneed her in the stomach. He pushed her back but she recovered quickly. Without thinking, he drew his weapon and fired, catching her in the shoulder and neck. She stumbled toward Sean before collapsing to the floor. Hagen stepped over and fired another round in her head.

"Just in case." As soon as the words left his mouth, she twitched twice before her chest split open and something crawled out of her body. In the flickering light, Sean wished he could tear out his eyes. A cross between a frog and a centipede, the aberration chittered loudly at them. It was no bigger than a gecko but its unnaturalness more than made up for it. Hagen moved to stomp it but it was quick. It launched itself at the old timer. Sean watched in horror as it skittered up the man's chest and pried its way into his mouth and down his throat.

Hagen gagged then screamed. "It's in me! I can hear it thinking!" He peered around frantically then rushed to the oil can and emptied it over his head.

"What're you doing?" Sean started but Hagen put up a hand.

"Can't let it live, kid." He pulled out his lighter and started to flick it but his hands locked up and it fell to the floor. A second later, Hagen went down to his knees, twitching and hyperventilating loudly as a strange chittering came from his throat. He glanced up at Sean, pleading. In that moment, he understood Hagen's request. A scream bellowed from Hagen as Sean began to move.

———

"O'Malley? Are you listening?" Captain Hearst asked, impatience souring his tone. Sean blinked, his thoughts a cluster of nightmares.

"I'm sorry, sir."

Hearst sighed. "Let's go over what happened one more time. Just the events at the house this time."

Sean bit his lip then nodded. "Like I said. After entering the house, we found the man dead in the library. The woman came up on us from behind and doused Hagen with oil. Before either of us could react, she lit him on fire. I was forced to shoot her to stop her from coming at me. By the time I got to Hagen... he was dead." He had told the story a dozen times already since what happened. It felt less acidic to his taste which bothered him more. *Lies should scald, they should choke.* Yet with every telling, he felt less from it.

Captain Hearst reached for his cigar. "Alright, son. Take a few days off. Not even a week here and you lost a partner. Can't say it will get any easier but that's about as bad as it can get."

Sean disagreed but simply nodded and got to his feet. "Police officers exemplify the law," his grandma's words filled his head. *But whose laws?* He only thought there were two, the almighty's and man's but now he wasn't so sure.

"Just make sure to fill out your report before you go," Hearst said as Sean reached the door.

He glanced over his shoulder. "I will. Reports are easy. Just fill them with the truth." He stepped out of the office, already composing what he'd write.

AQUARMARINE ALERT

JONATHAN LOUIS DUCKWORTH

F rankie pulls into the driveway of 223 Shore Drive, a beachside home that must have been lovely when it was first built nearly a century ago. She knows they're in the right place because of the fishy odor—the same odor her senior partner, Dan Kunkel, exudes. Dan is panting, almost wheezing through his wide, lipless mouth as they climb out of the van. It's a cool autumn evening. Frankie can hear the waves lapping on the shore behind the house.

"Nice place," Dan says. Like all Aquatic Americans negotiating the final steps of metamorphosis, Dan speaks with a raspy croak. His skin is a grayish color, with a slight oily sheen, and there are three little red hairs stubbornly clinging to what used to be a scalp. His unblinking eyes are yellow with perfectly round pupils, and his wide mouth is lined with tiny teeth.

"It's falling apart," Frankie says.

"Only on the surface. The bones are strong."

The house was built in the Colonial Revival-style, probably one of the first houses to go up in the early 30s during Innsmouth's reconstruction. It's hard to tell now what its original color might have been given how all the paint has stripped away, exposing rotting timbers. She shudders to think that there's an eight-year-old child inside of there right now. Only one window lit up as they approach the rickety porch.

They're here on behalf of Essex County Social Services. Most of the time when a divorced father kidnaps his child, it would be a matter for the police or CPS. But when the kidnapping involves an Aquatic American the Amber Alert becomes an Aquamarine Alert, and it then becomes a job for Department of Harmony-certified counselors like Frankie and Dan.

Dan wheezes with every step. Walking even short distances is hard, his legs better suited to kicking through water. Frankie helps steady him as they ascend the porch steps. His shirt collar is damp and grimy with the oily secretions from his gills; she tries not to notice such things more than she needs to.

Now they're on the porch, and Frankie's staring at the door with its peeling coat of whitewash.

"Youth before beauty; you press it," Dan says.

When she presses the doorbell, she receives a small shock. Faulty wiring, probably. Dan can't really laugh, or smile, but he does quiver with gelatinous amusement.

"You knew that would happen."

"Had a feeling. Why don't you use those bony hands of yours to knock?"

But before she can, the lock clunks, and then the door opens inward. A face stares through the wedge in the door, wide, unblinking eyes boring through Frankie. This must be Patrick Olmstead, Angelica West's biological father and current (legally speaking) kidnapper. He must be early in his metamorphosis because he still has most of a head of blond hair, but his nose is flattening out and his ears are shriveling like grapes. Everything in his face seems to be losing its definition except for the eyes which bulge like yellow gems too big for their collets.

"What do you want?" Patrick Olmstead croaks. His eyes don't swivel, so he moves his head to stare between Frankie and Dan. He stares at Dan a lot longer than he does at her.

"Essex County Social Services," Frankie says. "We're here in response to an Aquamarine Alert. Your ex-wife—"

"Wife," Patrick cuts in. "Until the paperwork goes through, we're still married."

"Be that as it may," Dan says, "if your daughter is with you now, you need to let us in. For her sake as well as yours."

Patrick doesn't answer at first. One webbed hand—still mostly human, though on its way to becoming a froglike claw—grasps the inner doorknob. He is thinking of shutting the door on their faces. It happens all the time, much to Frankie's dismay, because it always means that the cops will come, and police never treat Aquatic Americans fairly, in her experience.

But Patrick doesn't shut the door on them. Instead, he opens it wide. "Come in, I guess."

After sharing a thirty minute ride from Arkham with Dan and having smelled Patrick from the door, Frankie thinks she's ready for what the house will smell like. She is not. She almost retches by the time she passes the coatrack in the parlor, feeling horrible for being disgusted by something that Patrick can't help. One of the first things she learned at Miskatonic U's Aquatic American Studies program was that the distinctive "Innsmouther" body odor was primarily a result of human organs (most notably the skin) beginning to rot and slough away—essentially a form of molting.

"Angelica's safe, in case you're wondering," Patrick says. "As if I'd hurt my own daughter."

"No one's accusing you of anything," Dan says. "Aside from the kidnapping, of course. But you'll be fine—provided you cooperate."

"What's it look like I'm doing?"

There's the sound of static, lifeless voices—a television. Floorboards creak and whine under their feet, and somewhere in the house's shadowed innards water drips into an already capacious puddle.

Patrick leads them to what looks like a living room. Peeling wallpaper, dingy, spotted yellow carpet, and an old fat cathode ray television spewing white light onto a little girl currently engaged in doodling on construction paper with a hoard of crayons at her disposal.

"Sweetie, these people are from the government," Patrick says. "They've come to take you back to Mommy."

The little girl looks up from her scribbles with a serene expression. "Hi," she says.

"Hi, Angelica, I'm Miss Rollins, and this is Mr. Kunkel," Frankie says, switching easily to the special, soft voice she first perfected back when she worked in inclusion at Arkham Elementary.

Angelica is wearing jeans and a Hello Kitty T-shirt. Her hair—the same color as her father's, not red like her mother's—is styled in pigtails. Her eyes are bright and blue, and how deep-set they are in her skull is the only niggling clue of what she's going to become in the future. The crinkled remains of a fast food kids meal lies on the carpet beside her, a few limp fries basking in a smear of ketchup. Patrick meanwhile sits down in a dilapidated armchair and takes up an open can of salmon he'd left on one of the arms. Evidently, they've interrupted his meal and he's eager to get back to it.

"I'm sure Debbie's worried, so you can tell her our girl's fine," Patrick says before slurping down a long, floppy gray strip of salmon. His mouth is much smaller than Dan's, and he still has rudimentary lips and probably a full set of human teeth too.

"We watched old cartoons and he showed me all the old maps in the library," Angelica says, kicking up her feet as she returns to drawing.

"She loves maps," Patrick says, his croak managing to convey warm tones of fondness and pride. "She's drawing one now."

"I'm drawing a dinosaur world," Angelica says. "Dad says dinosaurs used to live here millions of years ago, but that our family is even older than that."

"Our blood's older than the dirt," Patrick says, again warm with pride.

"Sweet kid," Dan says. He turns his head toward Frankie. "Why don't you text the mom? Let her know Patrick's cooperating."

He stares past her at a framed portrait on the wall, likely depicting one of Patrick's ancestors.

Frankie digs her phone out of her pocket and searches her contacts for Debbie West.

Debbie seemed like a good mother, but then Frankie had been trained not to let first impressions color how she dealt with her cases or approached complainants. Debbie was thirty-two years old, redhead, average height, with a butterfly tattoo on her left arm. Including Angelica she had three children, the first two from a previous marriage, the eldest a boy of thirteen. When Frankie first sat down with Debbie earlier in the day to take her statement in her living room, she noticed there was still a photo of her with Patrick on the wall—before the changes started to show.

The living room was almost entirely empty, most of the stuff in boxes, ready for the impending move, but that photo still hung on the wall, two very human smiles framed in rosy light.

"I don't think he'd hurt her," Debbie admitted. "I hope he wouldn't. You're going to bring her back, won't you?"

There was alcohol on her breath, not that Frankie could blame her. She was a bit less sympathetic to Debbie's insistence that Dan wait outside on her porch. She claimed she'd feel more comfortable dealing with "another woman," but her disgust at the sight (and smell) of Dan had been palpable and obvious.

"We'll do what we can, and what the situation requires," Frankie told her. "But I have to be honest: if he takes her into the water, there's nothing we can really do to get her back. At that point it becomes a well, *diplomatic* matter."

Despite the brave face she put on, the sinking dread was obvious in Debbie's eyes. "He wouldn't do that. She doesn't know how to swim."

That you know of, Frankie thought but did not say. Aquatic Americans had a natural affinity for the water, even if they'd never tried to swim.

"We'll do what we can," Frankie repeated.

Before leaving, Frankie gave Debbie a pamphlet, a guide on Aquatic American metamorphosis for human parents like her, to help prepare her for the inevitable changes. Debbie thanked her and assured her she'd read it carefully, but as Frankie was standing on the porch she glanced back through the transom window and saw Debbie West in her kitchen, dropping the pamphlet into the trash.

"It's like I said at the arbitration, I never told her what I was, and that's my fault, but she also never warned me I'd married a racist," Patrick says. He has finished his can of salmon, and now a long, flexible black tongue darts from his mouth and flicks around the rim.

Angelica has her headphones on and is watching some kind of weird low budget CGI cartoon on her phone. Dan, tired of standing, has melted onto a ratty couch and now wheezes through his open mouth. Only Frankie remains standing.

"But surely you understand this won't help your case," Frankie says.

"What case? I have no case. The judge all but told me as much. He looked at me, looked at Angelica, said I had no business raising a girl *like that*, that I wasn't fit anymore. Her mother's the same way—you humans love your denial, don't you?"

"It may not always be fair, Mr. Olmstead," Dan says. "But the law is the law."

"I still love her, you know," Patrick says. He holds his face in his webbed hands. "If she'd have me, I'd go back to her. I love Joel and Zoey too, even though they won't so much as look at me now, like I didn't help raise them for ten years. Like I wasn't more of a dad to them than that deadbeat who knocked her up in high school. You know the last time I saw him, Joel threw fish food at me—the kind you feed to goldfish. I taught that boy how to play guitar."

He's trying to cry. But of course, he can't. By this stage of metamorphosis, the tear ducts are completely defunct, so all he can do is make his voice quiver.

"But look at her," Patrick says, sweeping a hand toward Angelica, who's giggling at the screen in her hands. "She's not scared of me. Oh, sure, she was at first. But I think she knows, deep down, even if no one's told her yet. You know her mom was going—is planning to take her away from me, from the ocean. Nebraska, last I heard. Can you imagine? That's no place for her. The ocean is her real home—it always will be."

"For now she belongs on land," Dan says. "You know that."

Frankie thinks back to a paper she read during one of her survey courses at Miskatonic by a researcher, Peta Armitage, who suggested using rather convincing phylogenic and biological proofs that humanity in general was trapped in a "larval" stage and that the "Deep Ones" represented a final adjustment into "adulthood," relating it to the similar process with axolotls and salamanders. That, in effect, Aquatic Americans were the only humans who ever truly matured. The paper disturbed her at the time—it still disturbs her now, for reasons she can't articulate.

Patrick taps his foot and shifts in his chair. "And what if she's happy here? What if I don't want to give her up?"

Frankie can feel her guts knot up. Many times she and Dan have faced recalcitrant parents—a few times they've been threatened with violence, though almost always it's come from the human parent.

"No one wants the police involved, sir," Dan says.

"No," Patrick agrees. "I certainly don't." He looks at Dan, cocking his head. "You're an old-timer, aren't you? Were you in the *camps?*"

Frankie is shocked to see Dan nod. They've worked together for two years now, and she's never asked him about his past, nor has he volunteered.

By "camps," Patrick refers to the internment camps set up in Essex County in the late 20s after the Winter Raid of '27, where the Aquatic American inhabitants of Innsmouth were confined in inhumane conditions, before their submerged kindred retaliated and set off a war that eventually ended with a treaty and Constitutionally-enshrined recognition of Aquatic American rights. Not before hundreds of them perished in the camps. For Dan to have been a survivor, he'd have to be a century old at least.

"I don't like talking about it," Dan says, and this seems at much aimed at Frankie as at Patrick.

"I bet," Patrick replies.

Angelica gets up from where she's lying down and walks across the room to the window, which commands a view of the backyard and the seashore beyond. Frankie follows her. The girl's still watching her colorful video on her phone, but it seems her eyes are staring past the screen at the waves. Frankie unconsciously follows her gaze and finds herself watching the black surf of the Atlantic, like a pane of molasses disrupted by the occasional pale breaker. As they watch the ocean, the men are talking. Dan is giving Patrick one of the pamphlets they carry, if Frankie had to guess it's probably the Know Your Rights handout for Aquatic Americans in legal trouble.

"My dad's not in trouble is he?" Angelica asks.

Frankie hesitates. As a teacher she learned not to overpromise to children, and her current job has only underlined that. "I don't think so," Frankie says at last, kneeling down so that she's at eye level with the girl. From this vantage point, the water outside looks different. Somehow like it's not entirely empty.

"Dad isn't dangerous," Angelica says.

"I know he isn't," Frankie whispers.

"He's not even angry at mom, just sad."

"Grownups are complicated."

"Grownups are silly."

Frankie smiles. "You're a smart girl, aren't you?"

The light from Angelica's phone screen deepens the shadows on her face, emphasizing the furrows under her eyes. There is some part of Frankie that doesn't like that this beautiful little girl will metamorphosize one day. But then she'll live forever, won't she?

"Hey Miss, what's a tumor?" Angelica suddenly asks.

Frankie's caught off guard by the question.

Angelica doesn't wait for an answer. "Dad says we're all living in a tumor."

Patrick clears his throat from the couch. "You put that out of your mind, sweetie, I was in a mood when I said that."

"What did you say?" Dan asks.

Patrick's drooping folds of skin twist with embarrassment. "Well, I think I told her the universe is the discharge that oozed out of a tumor on the skin of reality. Like I said, I was in a mood."

"Are you a practicing Dagonite, Mr. Olmstead?" Frankie asks.

Patrick shrugs. "Sure, I guess. I mean, around Festival time anyway. Any Dagonite who claims to be more observant than that is lying."

"Dagon taketh and Dagon taketh some more," Dan says. He then quivers with mirth while Patrick manages a croaking approximation of a laugh.

A strange thought occurs to Frankie, one that troubles her even though she knows it nonsense—what if Dan and Patrick have been holding another conversation this entire time? She quenches the thought—Deep One telepathy (bioelectric signaling which relies on salt water as a conductor) is a scientifically verified phenomenon, but never has it been established that Aquatic Americans can communicate that way on land. It's latent bigotry talking, she reminds herself.

Frankie's phone starts to ring. Debbie West is calling.

"I better take this," Frankie says.

"If Debbie's calling, you'd be asking for trouble not to," Patrick says.

She steps out of the living room and goes out onto the front porch to answer the call. When she picks up, Debbie sighs.

"Are you on the way?"

"Not quite, Ms. West."

"You're still at the old family house," Debbie says. "I can hear the waves."

Frankie becomes aware of that same rhythmic hiss, the water crashing against the sand. She looks over her shoulder and realizes that from Patrick's front porch one can see a slice of the bay, including the murky shape of the infamous Devil Reef, a rocky shoal visible only because it was somehow blacker than the midnight waters around it.

"Everything's fine," Frankie reports. "We've got it all under control and as I said, Patrick is cooperating."

"You know he took me to that house once," Debbie says. "Before Angelica, before we were even married. He didn't say it belonged to his family, but I should have known, and I should have guessed the truth. God, I was such an idiot. You can't trust them, you just can't. They lie, it's as natural to them as breathing water."

Frankie tries to adopt a diplomatic tack without discounting anything. "What's important is that soon Angelica will be back with you."

And poor Patrick won't see her again, not until the changes start, she thinks.

"You're a really good person, aren't you, Miss Rollins?" Debbie says, turning what should be a compliment into something venomous. "Text me the second you have her in the car."

Debbie hangs up. When Frankie returns through the front door, something is off. It's a subtle change in the air, she feels it the instant she crosses the threshold, the skin of her forearms turning to gooseflesh and her hairs standing on end.

It's a feeling of…what exactly? Emptiness?

As she enters the living room, she finds Dan on his feet, staring into the portrait he'd been gawking at earlier, entirely absorbed in it. But Patrick's chair is empty now, and there's no sign of Angelica.

"Dan," Frankie says. "Where are they?"

Dan doesn't answer, his unblinking eyes fixed vacantly on the flat likeness of the man in the painting.

She rarely ever touches Dan (which she would credit to professionalism and respect but which is probably at least partly rooted in a bone-deep aversion), but now she has no choice but to shake him.

"Ehh?" Dan startles.

"Where are they?"

"Oh, I uhh, I think I zoned out," Dan says, lipless mouth frowning. "Oh dear—I messed up, didn't I?"

"Search the house," Frankie all but screams.

Her entire body becomes a high wattage bulb of incandescent panic and she hurtles through the door, fearing the worst, but she sees Patrick's old Mazda is still where it was before, parked beside their van. That could only leave one other possibility.

Where else would a disgruntled Aquatic American father take his daughter? She races around the side of the house, and she hears the little girl's screams of terror even before she's reached the backyard. There's a low, rotting fence that separates the withered yard from the beach, and Frankie vaults it in a single mighty leap, her legs volcanic with adrenaline.

Out in the black waves, bobbing like a tiny pink fishing lure is little Angelica, her arms thrashing as she struggles to keep her head above the surface. Something is pulling her out further. No, not something —call a spade a spade: it's Patrick. Frankie slips off one shoe and then kicks the other one off, dashing toward the water, plunking through the surf, soon ankle deep, soon down to her knees, ready to plunge in. She's not a great swimmer, and she doesn't have any jurisdiction past the point where the sand gets wet, but that doesn't matter—the only thing that matters is there's a little girl in trouble, and she can't—

Angelica screams louder and flails her hands, and that's when Frankie stops herself, a wave crashing against her chest, soaking her through her jacket and shirt.

Angelica isn't screaming—she's laughing. And those flailing hands are waving to the shore, waving at Frankie.

"Hi, Miss Rollins!" Angelica cheers, lifting higher out of the water as Patrick Olmstead's head breaches the surface, slit gills wide open and a vibrant red. "Look, I'm walking on water!"

Frankie hears herself laugh, weak with relief and battered by the cold wind and the frothing surf. Patrick completes one last circuit in the water and then swims his daughter back to the shore, moving with such speed that it would shame an Olympic medalist. Soon, he emerges from the water, his daughter cheering on his shoulders.

"We did it, we won the race!" she screams.

"We sure did, sweetie," Patrick says, before lifting her off his shoulders and setting her down on the beach.

Frankie holds out her hand. "It's time to go, Angelica."

But Angelica hugs her father's legs—quivering now that he's back on land, out of his natural element—and looks to him for permission.

"Go on," Patrick says. "Go with the nice lady."

She gives her dad one last hug. "I'll call you every day when I'm in Nebraska."

Then she crosses over, to Frankie. Now Patrick Olmstead stands on the sand, the water lapping at his legs, his soaked shirt and slacks ridiculous against his strange, flabby body with its odd, grayish skin.

"I screwed up, didn't I?" Patrick says.

"He's not in trouble, right?" Angelica asks. "He just wanted to take me swimming one time."

There's a wheeze in the air as Dan comes waddling onto the beach. "We'll have to report it, even if no harm was meant," he says, long pauses between words as he catches his breath.

Now that the excitement has died down, Frankie is thinking of tomorrow, when they submit their report to the county, and the county forwards it to local law enforcement and to the county court. They'll report the facts, nothing more or less, and that will be enough for any cop or judge who wants to pursue charges up to reckless endangerment of a minor, and that would be on top of the kidnapping charge.

He must see it in her face before she speaks, because Patrick nods slowly. "I get it," he says. "But if it's all the same to you—I think it was worth it."

He doesn't follow them back into the house. The last time Frankie looks over her shoulder, Patrick Olmstead is still on the beach, looking out at the black water.

———

I nnsmouth is in the rearview mirror now as the sign for Arkham appears off the shoulder. Angelica is quiet, subdued now, not listening to anything or looking at a screen, just staring out the window. There's a small smile in the corner of her mouth.

Dan is quiet also, staring forward as if hypnotized by the strobing yellow lines on Route 1A.

"Dan?" Frankie whispers.

"Yeah?"

"You didn't really zone out back there, did you?"

He can't smile or wink, but somehow his monotone croak conveys a puckish undertone. "I can neither confirm nor deny."

They'll have to think of something to put in the report to explain his lapse of concentration—she'd hate for Dan to get in trouble. It might be unavoidable, though. The law is the law, as Dan himself often says. But it wasn't so bad in the end, what Patrick did. Who could fault a father wanting one last memory with his daughter?

"Did you see the others?" Dan asks after a stretch of silence.

She looks over at him. "Others?"

"In the water. I saw them, and they definitely saw *you*. Must've been the whole family."

"Why were they there?" she asks, suddenly glad that every second puts more distance between them and the coast.

Dan is slow to answer. "Let's just say it's good you didn't dive in."

BILLINGTON'S WOOD BEFOULED

HENRY HERZ

I t rained and it rained and it rained. Eeyore told himself that never in all his dreary life, and he was goodness knows *how* old–six, was it, or seven?–never had he seen so much rain. With each passing day, the gloom deepened and the mud thickened. Blustery winds ripped mouldering leaves off branches. It was as if Billington's Wood State Park were under some form of eldritch assault.

The darkness lingered and lurked, even at mid-day. The unrelenting deluge left Christopher Robin's ensorcelled forest coated with a nasty, venomous verdigris of phosphorescent fungal growths, detestable parodies of toadstools. A stench waxed overpowering, and foreign noises swelled to a bestial babel of croaking, baying, and barking.

Eeyore weathered the storm under the scant shelter of his stick house, chilling raindrops rolling down his protruding muzzle and mildew forming on his tacked-on tail. "Perfect weather for my birthday," he said, conversing often with himself in his loneliness. "The wet discourages visitors, not that I get many anyway."

Over the prior days, a mysterious pond had formed nearby. Though, perhaps pond was too kind a name for a fetid pool of shadowy ichor and tarry stickiness. Unbeknown to the dour donkey, the putrescent juices of Earth's inner horrors formed a gateway to realms of unfathomed terror and inconceivable abnormality.

A newly erupted obelisk towered from the mud at the pond's edge. The nine-foot-tall stone was a soapy, greenish-black hue, with iridescent flecks and striations that made it hard to focus the eyes. Arcane carvings hinted of remote secrets and unimaginable abysses in time and space. Among its reliefs were monsters of abhorrent grotesqueness and malignity—half-batrachian, half-crustacean in suggestion—which one could not dissociate from a certain haunting and uncomfortable sense of pseudo-memory, as if they called up some image from deep cells and tissues whose retentive functions were wholly primal and awesomely ancestral.

When the downpour finally eased, Eeyore decided to stretch his cramped legs and search for edible thistles to stave off his hunger pangs. The oval darkness caught his eye, and he strolled toward the pond, considering it dolefully, as he did all things.

Someone trotted up behind Eeyore, giving him a start. "What's this?"

"Good morning, Eeyore," said Pooh.

"Ah, Pooh Bear. Good morning," said Eeyore gloomily. "If it *is* a good morning, which I doubt."

"Why so sad, Eeyore?"

"Sad? Why should I be sad? It's my birthday. The happiest day of the year."

"Your birthday?" said Pooh with great surprise.

"Of course it is. Can't you see? Look at all the presents I have had." He waved a foot from side to side. "Look at the birthday cake. Candles and pink sugar."

Pooh looked—first to the right and then to the left. "Presents? Birthday cake? Where?"

"Can't you see them?"

"No," said Pooh.

"Neither can I," said Eeyore. "Joke," he explained. "Ha ha."

Pooh scratched his head, being a little puzzled by all this. "But is it *really* your birthday?"

"It is."

"Oh. Well, many happy returns of the day, Eeyore."

"And many happy returns to you, Pooh."

"But it isn't *my* birthday."

"No, it's mine."

"But you said 'Many happy returns'."

"Well, why not? You don't always want to be miserable on my birthday, do you?"

"Oh, I see," said Pooh.

"It's bad enough," said Eeyore, almost breaking down, "being miserable myself, what with no presents and no cake and no candles, and no proper notice taken of me at all, but if everybody else is going to be miserable too…"

This was too much for Pooh. "Stay there," he called, as he hurried off as quick as he could; for he felt that he must get poor Eeyore a present of *some* sort at once.

But first, I must tell Piglet and Rabbit. They will help me throw him a birthday party.

Pooh raced toward Rabbit's home. He leaped over fallen branches and dodged puddles, though noisome mud still splattered his legs.

C hewing on a thistle, Eeyore stood otherwise motionless, contemplating the source and implications of the new obelisk. "This cannot be good. So few things are."

His pulse accelerated for no apparent reason.

With only a slight churning to mark its rise to the surface, a Great Old One slid into view above the dark waters. Vast, Polyphemus-like, and loathsome, the ancient deity spread its two crab-like claws, revealing a thick trunk-like proboscis from which red sucking mouths protruded limply. A score of long greenish-gray tentacles formed an unsettling mockery of a beard. Their arrangement was odd, and seemed to follow the symmetries of some cosmic geometry unknown to Earth or the solar system. A single hideous eye sat unblinking atop a scabrous, multicolored body.

Eeyore's mane stiffened at the malevolent presence. His legs quivered. "Ah, wonderful. A Heffalump here to eat me, I suppose."

"No," replied a voice so deep that Eeyore's chest vibrated. "Not today, at least. We shall arrange for gifts to arrive."

"For my birthday?"

"No." The tone of voice conveyed a negation of all life.

"Well, I'm not surprised," replied Eeyore with a shrug. "No one else remembered, either."

"Silence." Stretching forth its sucker-lined proboscis, the intruder seized Eeyore round the waist and drew him near its Cyclopean eye. "Heed. You will recognize Our presents when they arrive. They are not for you. You must convey them to Christopher Robin to rend asunder his thaumaturgic sway over this realm."

"I don't understand that last part." Eeyore blinked. "But, are you telling me to give presents to someone else on *my* birthday?"

"Yesss. Do as We command, or you shall drown in misery." The creature released the befuddled donkey and submerged into the watery abyss.

Probably no more misery than I already have, thought Eeyore, bobbing like a buoy at the pond's center. *Maybe someone will come rescue me, but I doubt it.*

His enthusiasm squelched by the oppressive landscape, Pooh trudged toward Rabbit's, holding his nose with one paw. There was in the breezes and in the rotting soil, a sinister quality which chilled Pooh to the very core. The area was putrid with the carcasses of decaying frogs, and of other less describable things protruding from the nasty mud.

When will the sun return? he wondered. *I do not very much care for being cold.*

Arriving at Rabbit's home, Pooh put his head into the hole, and called out, "Is anybody at home?"

There was a sudden scuffling noise from inside the hole and then silence.

"What I said was, 'Is anybody at home?'" called out Pooh very loudly.

"No," said a voice; and then added, "You needn't shout so loud. I heard you quite well the first time."

"Bother," said Pooh. "Isn't there anybody here at all?"

"Nobody."

Pooh took his head out of the hole and thought for a little. *There must be somebody there, because somebody must have said 'Nobody.'* So he put his head back in the hole, and said, "Hallo, Rabbit, isn't that you?"

"No," said Rabbit, in a different sort of voice this time.

"But isn't that Rabbit's voice?"

"I don't *think* so," said Rabbit. "It isn't *meant* to be."

"Oh," said Pooh.

He took his head out of the hole, and had another think, and then he put it back, and said, "Well, could you very kindly tell me where Rabbit is?"

"He has gone to see Pooh, who is a great friend of his."

"But this *is* me," said Pooh, very much surprised.

"What sort of me?"

"Pooh Bear."

"Are you sure?" said Rabbit, still more surprised.

"Quite, quite sure."

A head popped up from the hole. "So it is," said Rabbit, looking at him all over. "It *is* you. Glad to see you."

"Who did you think it was?"

"Well, I wasn't sure. You know how it is in the Forest lately. One can't have *anybody* coming into one's house. One has to be *careful.*"

"Quite right, Rabbit. The Wood has become quite Dark and Scary lately. Anyway, I have just seen Eeyore," he began, "and the poor fellow is in a Very Sad Condition, because it's his birthday, and nobody has taken any notice of it, and he's very Gloomy—you know what Eeyore's like."

"Poor Eeyore. Shall we throw him a party?"

"I shouldn't think he'd like anything thrown at him, Rabbit. Just make him a birthday present and meet me at his house."

"You're a good friend, Pooh. I'll shall begin at once." Rabbit withdrew into his hole.

Thinking a snack might be in order before seeking out Piglet, Pooh strode home. He passed a bird's nest, knocked from its high perch by a gust. Empty eggshells lay scattered as if destroyed by something other than the fall. Pooh came upon a slightly phosphorescent squirrel, its corpse undergoing a nauseous liquefaction. His nose wrinkled at the eldritch atmosphere and odor permeating the Wood.

"Oh, dear."

A mighty oak stood devoid of foliage, naked like a prisoner of war. Mounds of rotting acorns piled about the trunk suggested the stacked skulls of an ossuary.

When at last Pooh reached home, his contemplation of the morbid strangeness of Sinister Vegetation was interrupted by a waiting Visitor.

"Hello, Pooh."

"Hello, Piglet. Please come in."

So, in they went. The first thing Pooh did was to go to the cupboard to see if he had quite a small jar of hunny left; and he had, so he took it down.

"It's Eeyore's birthday. I'm giving this to him," he explained, "as a present. What are *you* going to give?"

"Couldn't I give it too?" said Piglet. "From both of us?"

"No," said Pooh. "That would *not* be a good plan."

"All right, then, I'll give him a balloon. I've got one left from my party. I'll go and get it now, shall I?"

"That, Piglet, is a *very* good idea. It is just what Eeyore needs to cheer him up. Nobody can be uncheered with a balloon. Meet me and Rabbit at Eeyore's."

So off Piglet trotted, buoyed by the prospect of cheering up his friend. But his good mood dissipated quickly.

Dead, overhanging branches formed a wooden tunnel through which he scurried. Fungal yellow slime hung like putrid congealed jelly with suggestions of translucency.

"Oh, dear." Quivering, Piglet scurried faster.

Upon reaching home and retrieving the balloon, Piglet headed for Eeyore's. He held it very tightly against himself, so that it shouldn't blow away, and he ran as fast as he could, thinking how pleased Eeyore would be.

BANG!

Piglet lay there, wondering what had happened. At first he thought that the whole world had blown up; and then he thought that perhaps only *he* had. And then he thought, *Well, even so, I needn't be face-downward*, so he got cautiously up and looked about him.

Well, that's odd. I wonder what that bang was. And where's my balloon? And what's that small piece of damp rag?

It was the balloon.

"Oh, dear!" said Piglet "Oh, dear, oh, dearie, dearie, dear! Well, it's too late now. I can't go back, and I haven't another balloon, and perhaps Eeyore doesn't *like* balloons so *very* much."

A Putrid Maelstrom of vapors drifted downward from a broad, overhanging branch, where the Great Old One had lurked in ambush. It withdrew the sharp claw with which it had pierced Piglet's balloon.

Piglet shook, his hooves rooted to the ground. "Are, are, are you a W...W...Woozle?"

"You could say that," it prevaricated. "It would seem your gift is destroyed. You may replace it with this one."

The creature's beard of hideous tentacles extended, setting on the ground before Piglet a damnable eldritch tome with the glowing title, *Daemonium Convocatio*.

"Th...Th...Thank you. What does it say?"

The creature's malevolent eye flicked to the cover. "Happy birthday."

Piglet shook with a nameless alarm. "I *think* that I have just remembered something. I have just remembered something that I forgot to do yesterday and shan't be able to do tomorrow. So, I suppose I really ought to go and do it. Now."

Off sprinted the petrified porker toward Eeyore's, bearing both the book and the burst balloon.

A s Rabbit considered what to get Eeyore, he recalled that nobody had ever picked Eeyore a Bunch of Violets, and the more he thought of this, the more he thought how sad it was to be an Animal who had never had a Bunch of Violets picked for him. So with that in mind, out he ventured.

I took a while to locate blooming violets amid the storm's wrack, but eventually, he gathered a large bunch.

"Now, it's off to Eeyore's." He trotted through the Forest, smelling the flowers, and feeling very happy.

His contentment waned when he encountered a fallen tree, its rotting wood ravaged by repulsive, wriggling worms. Shutting his eyes, he rushed past.

Rabbit entered a mouldering, baneful clearing. A wave of Abnormal Horror swept over him as something colossal pushed through the undergrowth with creaking joints and nitrous wheezing.

An abyssal voice croaked and jabbered in a hateful, guttural patois. "*K'yarnak phlegethor l'ebumna syha'h n'ghft. Ya hai kadishtu ep r'luh-eeh.*" The eldritch invocation wilted Rabbit's violets.

The Great Old One lurched into the clearing, wreathed in a pestilent miasma.

Rabbit shivered uncontrollably. "Are… Are you a Jagular?"

"You could say that," it prevaricated. "It would seem your gift is destroyed. You may replace it with this one." Its beard of slimy tentacles writhed, setting on the ground before Rabbit a needle-sharp knife, its point coated with a viscous black substance.

"What is it?" said Rabbit, with a jump. And then, to show that he wasn't frightened, which he most certainly was, he jumped up and down once or twice more in an exercising sort of way.

"A letter opener."

"Many thanks, but if you'll excuse me, I must be going." The terrified Rabbit bounded toward Eeyore's as fast as his legs could carry him, bearing both the wilted violets and the knife.

C lasping a small jar of hunny in one paw, Pooh left his snug home. Through the oppressive muck he trudged, determined to brighten Eeyore's day. He held his nose against a pervasive, detestably fishy odor.

Pooh's tummy rumbled, for it hadn't been all *that* long since he'd had a Snack. *No*, he told himself. *This hunny is for Eeyore.* He followed a winding path through sickly pines. Rotting cones lay scattered on the ground. He halted in his tracks upon reaching a Tenebrous Glade, feeling an overpowering unease.

The Great Old One approached, its crouching, shambling gait abominably repellent.

The change in menace from vague premonition to immediate reality delivered a Profound Shock, and fell upon Pooh with the force of a genuine blow. He stood paralyzed in terror as the creature extended its serpentine proboscis, pierced the lid of the jar, and sucked out the contents.

"Are, are, are you a Heffalump?" asked Pooh, his heart pounding.

"You could say that," it prevaricated.

"Why… why did you eat my hunny? That was for Eeyore's party."

The creature unfurled its tentacles, setting a cake on the ground. A dark mucilaginous frosting, black as a Stygian night, enveloped the pastry. It smelled of decay and seemed to absorb light. "A cake is far more suitable for a birthday party than a pathetic jar of honey. Give your friend this instead."

Pooh's last vestige of courage evaporated. "Well, I must be going." He fled frantically, clutching both the empty jar and the cake.

The monster's laughter, devoid of humor, reverberated through the Benighted Woods like pestilential tempests from the gulfs of hell.

P uffing for breath, Pooh reached Eeyore's at the same time as Piglet and Rabbit. His gaze fell upon the dark waters. "Eeyore!"

Looking very calm, very dignified, with his legs in the air, floated Eeyore in the center of the pond.

"It's Eeyore," cried Piglet, terribly excited.

"Is that so?" said Eeyore, turning slowly round three times. "I wondered."

"Eeyore, what are you doing there?" said Rabbit.

"I'll give you three guesses. Digging holes in the ground? Wrong. Leaping from branch to branch of a young oak tree? Wrong. Waiting for somebody to help me out of the pond? Right. Give Rabbit time, and he'll always get the answer."

"But, Eeyore," said Pooh in distress, "what can we—I mean, how shall we—do you think if we—"

"Yes," said Eeyore. "One of those would be just the thing. Thank you, Pooh."

There was a moment's silence while everybody thought.

"I've got a sort of idea," said Pooh at last, "but I don't suppose it's a very good one."

"I don't suppose it is either," said Eeyore.

"Go on, Pooh," said Rabbit. "Let's have it."

"Well, we all seem to have two presents. If we all threw the heavier, scary ones into the pond toward Eeyore, they would make waves and wash him to the far shore."

"That's a very good idea," said Rabbit, and Pooh looked happy again.

"Very," said Eeyore.

"Supposing we hit him by mistake?" said Piglet anxiously.

"Or supposing you missed him by mistake," said Eeyore. "Think of all the possibilities, Piglet, before you settle down to enjoy yourselves."

Rabbit felt it was time he took command. "Right. When I say 'Now,' we will toss into the pond the creepy letter opener, the spooky book, and the nasty-looking cake."

The others nodded.

"Now," said Rabbit.

The friends heaved the malignant gifts. Splash. Splash. Splash.

With a shout, they rushed 'round to the other side of the pond, and pulled at Eeyore; and soon he was standing among them again on dry land.

"Oh, Eeyore, you are wet," said Piglet, feeling him.

Eeyore shook himself, and asked somebody to explain to Piglet what happened when you had been inside a pond for quite a long time.

The accursed items sunk into the bottomless murk, inflicting their three-part curse on the Great Old One's portal instead of Christopher Robin. The obelisk crumbled to sepulchral dust. There was a bursting as of an exploding bladder, a slushy nastiness as of a cloven octopus, and a stench as of a thousand opened graves.

The four gagged until a sudden breeze blew away the odor. The pond water cleared. The sun broke from behind heavy cloud cover to smile upon the friends.

"Well done, Pooh," said Rabbit kindly.

"Many happy returns of the day," said Piglet.

"Meaning me?"

"Of course, Eeyore."

"My birthday?"

"Yes."

"Me having a real birthday?"

"Yes, Eeyore, and we've brought you presents."

"Meaning me again?"

"Yes."

"My birthday still?"

"Of course, Eeyore."

"Me going on having a real birthday?"

"Yes, Eeyore. I brought you a balloon."

"*Balloon*?" said Eeyore. "You did say balloon? One of those big colored things you blow up? Gaiety and song-and-dance?"

"Yes, but I'm afraid—I'm very sorry, Eeyore—but when I was running along to bring it you, I fell down."

"Dear, dear, how unlucky. You ran too fast, I expect. You didn't hurt yourself, Little Piglet?"

"No, but I—I, oh, Eeyore, I burst the balloon!"

There was a very long silence.

"My balloon?" said Eeyore at last.

Piglet nodded.

"My birthday balloon?"

"Yes, Eeyore," said Piglet sniffing a little. "Here it is. With—with many happy returns of the day." And he gave Eeyore the small piece of limp rubber.

"Is this it?" said Eeyore, a little surprised.

Piglet nodded.

"My present?"

Piglet nodded again.

"The balloon?"

"Yes."

"Thank you, Piglet," said Eeyore. "You don't mind my asking," he went on, "but what color was this balloon when it—when it *was* a balloon?"

"Red."

"I just wondered... Red," he murmured to himself. "My favorite color... How big was it?"

"About as big as me."

"I just wondered... About as big as Piglet," he said to himself sadly. "My favorite size. Well, well."

Piglet felt very miserable and didn't know what to say.

"Many happy returns of the day," called out Rabbit. "I've brought you a Bunch of Violets. They weren't so wilty when I gathered them, but there you are."

"Here I am, indeed. No question about it. Thank you, Rabbit."

"And I've brought you a present, too," said Pooh excitedly. He raised the empty honey jar. "It's a, er, Useful Pot. And it's for putting things in. There."

When Eeyore saw the pot, he became quite excited. With the burst balloon, he bound together the wilted violet stems. He gently placed the flowers in the Useful Pot.

"Why," he said. "Together, your gifts form a Lovely Centerpiece. It will be perfect in my home."

"I'm very glad," said Pooh happily, "that I thought of giving you a Useful Pot to put things in."

"And I'm very glad," said Piglet happily, "that Rabbit and I thought of giving you Something to put in a Useful Pot."

But Eeyore wasn't listening. He stood staring at his new centerpiece, as happy as could be.

A s the friends sat and exchanged stories of the day's strange events, up strode Christopher Robin.

"Has everyone noticed? The sun shines, the birds sing, and the flowers bloom. Your kindness has saved from a Great Menace the Wood I love so much."

He smiled and sat down beside them. "What do you love best in the world, Pooh?"

"Well," said Pooh, "what I love best?" and then he had to stop and think. Because although Eating Hunny was a very good thing to do, there was a moment just before you began to eat it which was better than when you were, but he didn't know what it was called. And then he thought that being with Christopher Robin and the others was a very good thing to do: and so, when he had thought it all out, he said, "What I like best in the whole world is being with my friends."

"I like that, too," said Christopher Robin, "but what I also like doing is Nothing."

"How do you do Nothing?" asked Pooh, after he had wondered for a long time.

"Well, it's when people call out at you just as you're going off, 'What are you going to do, Christopher Robin?' and you say 'Oh, nothing,' and then you go and do it."

"Oh, I see," said Pooh.

"This is a nothing sort of thing that we're doing now."

"Oh, I see," said Pooh again.

The pit of Christopher Robin's stomach ached with longing. He wished the visits to his wondrous realm could continue forever. But his friends had now proven themselves capable of protecting Billington's Wood, and he had growing up to do. "Pooh," he whispered.

"Yes?" said Pooh.

"When I'm—when—I'm—gone…" His throat tightened. "Pooh?" He put out a hand for Pooh's paw.

"Yes, Christopher Robin?"

Christopher Robin's shoulders fell. "I'm not going to do Nothing any more."

"Never again?"

"Well, not so much. They don't let you. They're sending me off to school and telling me to forget about Childish Ways."

Pooh waited for him to go on, but Christopher Robin was silent again.

"Yes?" said Pooh, helpfully.

"Pooh, when I'm—you know—when I'm not doing Nothing, will you come here sometimes to think about us?"

"Yes." Tears formed in Pooh's eyes.

"Pooh, promise you won't forget about me, ever. Not even when I'm a hundred."

Pooh thought for a little. "How old shall I be then?"

"Ninety-nine."

Pooh nodded. "I promise."

Author's Note

Billington's Wood is a fictitious forest mentioned in August Derleth's story, *The Lurker at the Threshold*.

ARKHAM MUSIC HALL

EMILY LOWERY

To whoever finds this testament, I must implore you to understand that I used to like music. There was a time when music gave me such immense joy that it would be unfathomable for me to deny playing it for the simple reason of my love of the craft. Melodies flowed through my veins and my heart's beat kept time with the ripple of my fingers across the keys. In my youth, I wondered if I was born a husk, a puppet, only brought to life with the power of music. With the likes of Chopin and Mozart manning my cross-brace, I was able to harness that power. There was a mesmerizing, manipulative nature to it. Pick the right notes, in the right order, with the right instrument, and you could do incredible things. I have seen music pull tears from their ducts, burst chests open with joy, calm the masses, and start revolutions.

Music became the great love of my life. There was a euphoria that washed through me when performing, the audience in the palm of my hand. What would I make them feel today? Should they be in awe of the beauty of nature or should I leave them with a sense of melancholy that will follow them into their dreams? It was exhilarating.

A prodigy from childhood, I never had issues getting selected to perform. My parents were all too eager to drag my sister and me across every state to enable my addiction. Their son was going to be someone someday. So it came as no surprise when they congratulated me on landing my first professional soloist engagement out of college. Even if it meant I'd have to move from the sunny city of Los Angeles to the small town of Arkham across the country.

I have to admit, part of me was apprehensive about the move. I was quite fond of the city. Its bright warm days and exciting nightlife were filled with opportunities for an aspiring musician like me. The dark and rainy rolling hills of Arkham seemed like a steep trade for one contract. However, everywhere else I had sent audition tapes to had either declined or offered an understudy role. I found it frustratingly odd but blamed my relative youth compared to those I was competing with. Twenty-four was practically an infant in most classical music circles and these were no longer children's competitions or recitals. Arkham Music Hall was the only institution to offer to make me their featured pianist for the season. There wasn't much debate after that.

The last time I saw my mother was on the doorstep of my childhood home. The sun warmed the back of my neck and the smell of sprinklers on freshly cut grass filled my nose. She had stood on that stoop, lips pulled up along with her silver-streaked auburn hair, and she told me to stay safe. I promised I would because at the time neither of us knew what I do now. What you must be surmising due to the state of this testament. That stepping out of the taxi from Boston Logan International Airport and onto the cobblestone road of Arkham would make her request an impossible task.

Walking down those roads, I lamented at how different the town was from my home. The dreary weather only accentuated the decay of the area. The faded brick and rotted wood on most buildings might have simply shown age but the overgrown plant life and scattered trash suggested complete neglect from whoever ran this town. The only similarity I could draw was from the people. No one paid any mind to the strange man in a suit walking down the street with two large rolling bags of luggage. The few people I saw spared a glance and then returned to their tasks. Like the performer walking down the streets of LA in full costume makeup, people avoided me like the plague lest I ask them for money.

I turned my nose up at the area, a smug smile forming as I trudged forward towards my living quarters. I wouldn't be forced to find a rundown room for rent. I would be staying in the city center at Arkham Music Hall. The downtown of Arkham was much more lively in the sense that there were more people and the streets were better maintained. However, there was a constant heaviness that never shook from my shoulders. It was as if the air itself in Arkham was pushing back on my being there. I just brushed it off as homesickness mixed with the oppressive lack of color. There was a gray tint to everything, even the people seemed to take on a pallor that made me uneasy.

There were only a few buildings in Arkham that I would commend for their architectural genius and beauty; the capitol building, the library, the university, and the music hall. The hall stood as a monolith on the west end of downtown. The pointed gables of its roof scraped the heavy clouds above while the lancet windows plunged to the earth in an incredible yawn. Bricks so red they seemed to glow in the dusky air; with others so black around the windows that they pulled whatever light they could in. I studied what I was sure to be a statue sat at the top of the tallest gable between the spires of two towers. I could not make out exactly what the statue was of from my vantage point but my mind filled in the simple example of a common angel, sitting chin in hand and looking down thoughtfully at the townsfolk below.

I tucked away the rolling handles of my suitcases and picked them up from the grip on the sides of each, making my way up the steps to my future. Internally—and perhaps once or twice externally as well—I cursed the amount that I had packed, sure that I looked like a fool struggling up the concrete steps. I was gearing up to throw my left arm, using the momentum to follow through with the next step up, when an older gentleman placed his hand on my bag. The big city instinct to shove the would-be robber away was cut off by the man's words.

"Mr. Herod, the Arkham Music Hall welcomes you and your talent." His voice was so deep and smooth that I immediately imagined him as the baritone soloist who pulled women under his hypnotic spell with ease. Astonishingly tall, the man stood a complete head above my six-foot-three stature. His skin was so deeply tanned that, compared to the other inhabitants of the town, he was practically golden. He was muscular and the cut of his jaw was not at all hidden under the nicely trimmed beard. With his silver hair pulled back into a classically messy bun, I had a clear view of his eyes. Those eyes locked onto mine and demanded so much attention that I am surprised I can recall any other aspect of him. There was a preternatural quality to them that even with the naïveté that I so cluelessly took for granted, I still noticed it. They were black, though black is not even a good enough descriptor for just how dark the irises pooling within those sockets were. Maintaining eye contact was like trying to stare into the obsidian void of a black hole, painfully impossible.

I tore my gaze from the edge of the abyss and refocused on his hand, putting down my suitcase and reaching a hand out to shake. "I'm happy to be here, Mr…"

"Nyar, I am the manager of the music hall." He took my hand in a firm grip. "I'm happy to have found someone at such short notice. Musical talent is sparse in this town. With my usual pianist taking leave for a while, I began to worry I wouldn't be able to find a suitable replacement."

I returned his grasp, the large gold ring on his pinky finger digging into my hand. "Well, Mr. Nyar, I am eager to get started." I flashed my best stage smile and earned my release from his grip.

"Wonderful!" He said with a clap. "Let's get you settled in."

There was a strange dichotomy born inside my being when I walked into Arkham Music Hall for the first time. Like an unstoppable force meeting an immovable object, my soul moved to soar with excitement; all while an indescribable dread anchored it to the pit of my stomach. Stepping over that threshold, I knew my life had been transformed and would never be recognizable to my past again.

The expansive lobby was ready and waiting for large crowds to fill in over the checkered laminate floor. There was a stench that surprised me, a dense mustiness that one would associate with an old rain-bogged attic rather than a high-class establishment. The only light being produced in the large room was emanating from two industrial lanterns attached to each side of the ticket booth. The windows let in little gloomy light from the overcast sky and the room was intertwined with shadows. Marble columns lined each side of the walls leading to the ticket booth. The swirling bases at the top of each column bore down on me like eyes as I struggled to keep pace with Mr. Nyar.

I nearly fell forward when he came to an abrupt stop just to the right of the booth. "You can place your things in the apartment upstairs." He gestured to the single door on the far right wall. "I expect you to be on stage and ready for a preview performance by seven o'clock sharp."

"Oh, I-" I started, but he was through the double doors to the auditorium behind him before my voice could catch up with my confusion. The door's echo reverberated through the empty space of the lobby behind me. I was alone. However, the unmistakable pressure of being watched on the back of my neck told me I wasn't. Turning, only the shadows and the columns' eyes greeted me. I was thoroughly unsettled at that point and took my bags quickly to the door leading to my home for the next five months.

Thankfully the staircase, though narrow and winding, was not too long. I shuffled up with effort but was standing in front of an old wooden door before too much sweat broke free. Looking out the window just before the door I could see the street, bustling with people all too busy to look up at the tower attached to the hall. All except for one. She caught my wandering eye as she captured my gaze with her own. Staring directly at me. I leaned back from the pane and examined it. The window was about the size of my shoulder width and the glass was dingy with caked on dirt. It must have been ages since anyone had bothered to clean it. Leaning back in, I saw the woman was still staring.

I concluded she must have been looking at the building as I had. She could not have possibly been able to see me. Yet, I keep thinking back to that moment. To the way her lips dipped downward and her arms crossed tightly around her body as if ashamed. Everyone else on the street that day did not spare a single glance at the building. They all walked by with eyes averted as I was led up those steps and part of me can't help but think that they knew the fate that was to befall me that night. Or perhaps I just wish they did. There is some comfort in the thought that there was a chance for help, even if it never came.

To say I was disappointed when I opened that small door to my room would be a laughable understatement. The claustrophobic wooden box had only an old mattress on the floor in the far left corner and a wardrobe on the right. Far from the luxurious one-bedroom apartment I had been picturing. It resembled a prison cell more than a respected musician's living quarters. The floorboards screeched with every step, their brittle fibers cracking. I dropped my bags onto the mattress only to be met with a cloud of dust. The musty smell from the lobby had grown tenfold. I pressed my hand to my nose, teeth grinding.

What sort of establishment let this happen? I thought I was signing on for a professional venue and yet all I had seen seemed to be abandoned. It was as if the music hall was simply an old relic left to rot, ignored by everyone except its single caretaker. With heat rising in my chest, I began to march back toward the door. Mr. Nyar would hear a word or two from me.

Stomping down the stairs, uneasiness quickly began to eat at my anger. Once I was again alone in the dim lobby light, it had all but been completely replaced. I chewed at the inside of my bottom lip while shifting from foot to foot in the doorway. With a deep breath, I pushed forward the thoughts of how ridiculous the whole thing was and attempted to bury any disquietude. I straightened my spine and raised my chin as I strode towards the auditorium door that Mr. Nyar disappeared behind. All while making a point to ignore the sinister eyes bearing down on me from above.

I yanked on the handle, eager to leave the lobby. The door did not move. I pushed and again it did not move. I could not stop myself from looking around me at that point. Shadows flowed down from the ceiling like drapes, wrapping around the columns and pooling on the floor. I was searching them, for what I am not entirely sure; maybe answers or a more vivid warning of danger. Unfortunately, every warning I had received seemed at the time as tangible as those shadows and slipped from my mind's grasp. It left only an unintelligible dread that I was keen to ignore.

Amongst the darkness, there was a slight flicker of light that caught my directionless vision. I waded through the waves of shadow and rushed to the lighthouse in the far left corner across from me. There was a single door with a small window. A light faintly glowed through it. My heart racing from the quick adrenaline-fueled jog across the lobby, I clung to the handle of the door but did not move to open it right away. I dreaded the possibility that this door would be locked and I would have to make the pilgrimage back to my room with nothing. A pointless journey that only served to frighten me rather than get answers about the state of the hall.

I sucked in a steadying breath before pulling on the handle. It swung open with such ease that I stumbled back a bit. Once I gained my footing again, I peered inside. The light had been coming from a lantern hung on a hook on the wall to the left. Turning, I saw another winding stairway. It could have been Mr. Nyar's office or another bedroom. Nevertheless, it was a chance to talk to the man. The stairway looked to have considerably fewer windows than my side as the darkness formed a wall past the glow of the lantern. I sighed and took the lantern from the wall, knowing this would not be a pleasant climb.

I was never particularly afraid of the dark when I was a child. The uneasiness darkness can give a person in a new place is one thing but real fear of the dark, I never had. My parents at no time felt the need to plug a night light into my wall nor did I ask them to. Sleeping in total darkness was the only way I would feel truly rested. Although walking up that twisting stairwell, I undoubtedly felt that kind of fear for the first time. Surrounded by darkness closing in and a feeling in the air that I could only describe as malice, I pushed onward, thinking it was silly. Air could not be malicious or evil. However, this stairway was much longer than its counterpart and with each step, I felt my rationality begin to wane. Scared of nothing solid but of the darkness itself as if it would reach out and pluck me from the safety of my light.

The relief I felt when I finally reached the door was immense. There was also a small window, similar to the one in my tower, on the wall by the door. It was getting late, the sun only peeking out from the horizon, so the light was even fainter than earlier. I pressed my forehead to the glass, trying to get a good look. This window faced the roof with a clear view of the statue at the top. My brow furrowed, trying to understand what I was looking at. It was not a crouched angel like I had assumed from the street. Instead, it was some sort of amalgamation of things. At the center of the statue was an eye surrounded by carved vines, intertwining randomly. Poking out of those vines were eight sharp points, almost like they were encased in a star.

Whispers broke my transfixed stare, snapping my neck back towards the door. I placed my lantern down by my feet and pressed my ear to the wood. There were multiple voices, all indecipherable. Only breathy mumbled nonsense came to my ears, almost hissing. Who was in there with him? He did say that there was to be a preview performance that night. I thought that maybe they could be patrons or donors who would need to approve of my performance. As soon as the thought formed in my head, I began to be able to decipher the jumbled whispers.

"*Are you sure he is capable?*"

"*This place has been a mess.*"

"*We want to make sure it is taken care of.*"

Finally, Mr. Nyar's familiar baritone broke through the medley. "You will all see at the performance, he is exactly what we need. I dare to say his love for music rivals that of my father. Once he is playing, you will be sure there is nothing to worry about. The music hall is in good hands."

I pulled back, surprisingly satisfied with the conversation. The music hall was re-establishing itself after a long sabbatical. Mr. Nyar's mention of his father made me think that the hall might not have been in use since he was a child. That explained the current state of things. I was to bring this cathedral back into the light, open its doors, and convert new followers with my music. The first man they had chosen could not fulfill his obligations and now it rested on me. Mr. Nyar was putting his faith in me to bring this place back to life and I was sulking around in the dark, trying to find someone to complain to. I felt ashamed. I could have been using that time to practice.

Picking up my lantern I hurried down the steps, no longer paying any mind to the darkness. I put the lantern back on its hook and made my way back to my room. All of the running around had made me sweaty and my clothes rumpled so as soon as I got to my room I changed into a fresh suit. I looked through my music for a piece to showcase, wanting to impress Mr. Nyar and his possible investors, eventually deciding on a Beethoven medley with original work mixed in to show my traditional and innovative talents. I played through the whole thing in my head once before my watch showed a fifteen-minute warning. I cursed myself again for wasting time before heading downstairs to the auditorium.

I half expected the door to still be locked as Mr. Nyar was nowhere in sight. However, when I tried to pull on the handle it creaked open ever so slightly. The large oak was heavy and took more effort to open than the rickety planks that led to the towers. Light and color blinded my dulled vision as I entered. Blinking, I took in the magnificence of the room. The vast auditorium could sit hundreds. Rows of ostentatious red velvet seats with gold trim glittered in the light of the tremendous chandelier hanging in the middle of the room. Also a shining gold, the chandelier dripped with rock crystals among multiple rows of flickering candles. At the top was a large crystal star with eight points. It reminded me of the statue on the roof. My heartbeat quickened and my mouth dried. I couldn't look away, even as the light began to burn in my eyes. I did not blink. I did not move. Just that star and I locked in together.

"Are you ready, Mr. Herod?" Mr. Nyar's hand clamped down on my shoulder and I jumped, finally breaking contact with the view. Blinking away tears, I nodded. How long had I been staring at that star? Looking down at my watch it showed that it was two minutes to showtime. Confusion swarmed in my chest as I made my way to the stage. It hadn't felt like ten minutes had passed and yet they had. I climbed the stairs on stage left. It was time to begin.

The moment I made contact with the bench in front of the exquisite grand piano, the lights went out. The next second a spotlight hit me. I squinted, adjusting to the harsh white light. When I was able to see my music I turned from the now black seating area. I always hated that I could not see the audience when the stage lights were on. I wanted to absorb their experience with my music, see the way I play them as I do my piano. Looking out, I could only see outlines of three people standing in the back. The only person I could make out was Mr. Nyar in the front row.

I unfolded my sheet music and placed it on the music desk. My fingers faintly brushed on the ivory keys. This was the beginning of the career I always dreamed of. I let that feeling drown out all others. I would not let my paranoia and curiosity steal from that moment. With a single deep breath, I came to life.

Beethoven's "Appassionata" cascaded out of my soul down my arms and out my fingertips. I swayed with the rhythm as it built, ebbing and flowing like waves in the Pacific. When it ebbed at just the right moment, I switched to "Für Elise." For the first time since leaving home, I felt my mind clear. I was composed within the stream of notes. I moved on again to an original piece, splicing it in seamlessly with the build of such a well-known classic. The performance continued as such, ecstasy and serenity emanated from the sound, rippling through me.

When I hit the final note, I was breathless and lightheaded with a beaming smile. As the vibrations of the music settled in my skull I noticed the silence. There was no applause nor cheers not even shouts of disdain. Just silence. My smile faded, glancing down to where I had caught Mr. Nyar sitting before I began. The chair sat empty. I searched the room for the three outlines who I assumed to be the people I had overheard but found nothing. I grimaced in an odd mixture of confusion and embarrassment.

A loud smack on the rim of the piano jolted my attention from the lack of audience back to the stage. Mr. Nyar stood with a smile and his hand gripping the piano. The gold ring on his finger caught my eye in the spotlight. I hadn't seen what that large ring had on it when shaking hands earlier. The image of an eye within a star. I put my hands into my lap, rubbing them on my thighs, and suddenly felt very cold.

"Well done," Mr. Nyar said. He then turned to the seemingly nonexistent audience. "Well done!" A roar of applause erupted from the darkness. I jolted in my seat and Mr. Nyar grabbed my arm, forcefully pulling me up.

"What's happening?" I asked, shaky and unsure of what else to say. My eyes told me there was no one there but my ears were almost ringing with the noise of a crowd.

"Your faith is never misplaced when in me, children!" He bellowed over the commotion. His head lolled back and to the side, black eyes drilling into mine before snapping back and looking to whoever was out there. "They are not much at all, however, everything has its talents, its purpose. We may have found one of *humanity's* only redeeming qualities."

I backed up while he spoke, shaking as the icy grip of fear took hold of my spine. The way he spat the word *humanity* out like rotten infested meat. The way the crowd had begun to whisper in that hissing gibberish. It all made my chest tight. I was beginning to hyperventilate through gritted teeth, tensed and ready to run from an unknown danger I was now sure surrounded me.

"It has been an eternity," he said with a heavy sigh. "I believe we have all earned a break." He brought his hand up and pulled at the tie holding his hair. Only it wasn't hair. Suddenly I wasn't sure if it had ever been hair as the silver tentacle-like appendages swarmed around his head and slithered down his back. He turned with a foul, closed lipped smile. Those all too dark irises bled out into the little white his eyes held until it was nothing but black, as if he possessed no eyes at all. His suit melted into smoke. He was now wearing a cloak of shadows intertwining with the writhing parts of him.

I was paralyzed with incomprehension and terror. The sight before me was too mystifyingly horrible to be able to fight, run, or even look away. All the while, those hissing whispers began to hum. The melody was a song long forgotten but ever-present throughout the universe. It was the frequency of the stars and the tempo of the ocean's waves. It was the percussion of tectonic plates slamming together, the shift of the Earth's crust. I was consumed by the sound of the birth of the universe and the inevitable death of everything. I could do nothing more than stand, shaking with the tension of every muscle fiber in my body threatening to snap from the strain of such an intense hysteria.

At that moment, I watched as his eyes stretched out from their sockets and consumed me in darkness. I was enveloped by those onyx pupils as if moving down an esophagus, pulsing and tight. I struggled and screamed with a panic I had never thought possible. A scream so loud and long that I felt my throat strain to the point of tearing. I kept screaming, even when I could no longer hear it. His voice rang out in my mind instead—a gong producing sounds that could not be perceived as words but bore knowledge into my very soul all the same. With that horrible knowledge, my fear born of confusion became a dreadful terror that only understanding can bring.

Azathoth is sleeping. Azathoth must never awaken.

Only once the information had settled into every molecule of my being, did the pressure around me release. Though I still could not see anything, I felt Him instantly. A being so great and powerful that He would end all of existence with just a blink of His tremendous eye. I fell to my knees in that void and sobbed over the humming that had returned. Curling in on myself, I shook with each cry because while I now understood my fate, I could not begin to comprehend the mental pain and sorrow that had blossomed from it.

The spotlight came on. A piano, alone in a void of nothing. My strings were tied and my cross brace pulled toward the bench. No longer was I in control of my movements, all I could do was play. I sat and looked out into the vast expanse of darkness where a blind god slept for eternity. A god who had been sung to sleep by His children so the universe could continue its existence. His children, who now wanted a break. My fingers numbly pressed on the keys. Debussy's "Clair de Lune" erupted from the strings and pedals. The humming stopped and there was only me.

How long is a break to one that is eternal? I can't begin to say. I have no clue how long I have been playing. It already feels like an eternity and yet I have not slept, eaten, or died. I could be dead, I suppose. Perhaps I died that night in the music hall. Perhaps I had a heart attack the second my performance ended and this is hell. My eternal punishment for my arrogance. Either way, I have begun to play my story in a code of all the notes that the piano will allow on repeat. If you can hear me out there in the physical world, whether it be Earth or some far-off planet, I hope you can decode this message. Please, I beg of you, please find me. Give me respite from this hell.

I really did love music once.

WHAT OUR FATHERS WROUGHT

WILLARD BRANNEN

Harry sat in the back of the cab, rain assaulting the car all around him. Lightning flashed, briefly illuminating the darkened Arkham streets. Another severe rainstorm, another power outage. *You'd think by 1912 they'd have figured out this whole electricity thing*, Harry thought to himself.

"Sure is a strange time to be out and about mister," the cabby remarked. For the third time. Harry looked at the man in the rear-view mirror but said nothing.

"What'd you say you were headed into town for?" the cabby asked, again.

"Work."

"At this hour?"

Harry nodded, "The dead don't sleep, so neither should we."

"What was that mister?"

"Nothing. How much farther?"

The driver looked down at the map he had open in the seat next to him, "Just about 5 more minutes, mister."

Harry looked at the man's hands, briefly illuminated by a flash of lightning. Were those tattoos? The next flash gave him an even better view. Those were definitely tattoos across the back of his hand and fingers. Harry had of course seen many a man with tattoos in his time as the county coroner, sailors and fishermen often had such markings. But these were like nothing he'd ever seen. The lines were jagged, as if carved with the tip of a knife. Harry pointedly looked back out the window.

The next flash gave him a brief reflection of himself. His brown hair, flecked with gray, was a mess from the rain he'd been soaked with from his front door to the cab. He pushed it back to keep it out of his face at least.

The car came to an abrupt stop, "We're here mister."

Harry looked out the window and could see the Sherrif approaching the vehicle. His door opened a moment later, "Evening Harry, sorry for the late call."

Sherrif Arnold North was a hefty man. In his mid-50s, his grey mustache was stark under the shadow of his policeman's cap.

He offered a hand to Harry, "Thank you Arnie." Harry took the man's hand, rough and meaty and allowed Arnie to help him from the cab. Harry grabbed his cane from the seat and shut the door. Arnie had brought an umbrella, bless him. He held it mostly over Harry's head as they marched up the stone steps.

"What, may I ask Arnie, would necessitate a call at this hour?" Harry had little patience for strange calls at, he checked his pocket watch, now 3 AM.

"You'll have to see for yourself Harry, won't make much sense elsewise."

Harry furrowed his brow. In the time they'd both served as public servants, Harry had never known Arnie to be at a loss for words. On much of anything.

Arnie grabbed his elbow as they cleared the last step, stabilizing him. Under the cover of the entryway Arnie collapsed the umbrella, shaking the water from it. He retrieved his keys from the pocket of his sopping trench coat and unlocked the door. The sign on the window, *Arkham Police Headquarters & Coroners Office* swung inward, and Harry stepped inside.

He'd had late nights before, but this was an entirely different matter. No power meant no lights. No people meant no sound. The white stone walls and floors seemed oppressive in the dark, even the flashes of lightning couldn't fully alleviate it.

Arnie locked the door behind them. "Spooky," he remarked.

Harry turned with a raised eyebrow. Arnie shrugged, "It is."

Arnie's torch illuminated the darkened hallway as they approached the great stairs that would take them down to the coroner's office. To Harry's office. Harry leaned heavily on the stone siding on the interior of the staircase for balance. Arnie offered a hand, but Harry shook his head. He could handle this.

As they turned to head down the second flight, Harry saw light, movement. He froze.

"One of my guys, don't sweat it." Arnie assured him, "Deputy Haskins, that you?" he called down.

"Yeah Sherriff. Though I think you just shortened my life expectancy. My wife will be on you for that one."

Arnie chuckled, "I've got the good doctor with me, come and give us a hand, would ya?"

Deputy Haskins appeared at the bottom of the stairs, briefly blinding Harry with his torch. "For God's sake Deputy, point that thing somewhere else."

"Right, sorry Sherriff." Haskins was a young man, around 25 by Harry's estimation. He was clean shaven, his uniform neat and tidy despite the weather. His boyish grin greeted them at the bottom of the stairs. "Evening Doc, hope you weren't sleeping too well."

Harry forced a smile in return, "No rest for the wicked, Deputy."

The three of them walked down the hall toward the morgue in silence. Their boots echoed off the stone walls. Harry caught light up ahead, more movement. *More* people? As they turned into the doorway of the morgue Harry caught sight of at least half a dozen more officers loitering around the slab in the center of the room.

"Alright, break it up, doctor coming through," Arnie said.

The men shuffled about, moving away from the sheet covered body on the slab. The familiar mix of chemical scents washed over him, and Harry relaxed a bit. This was his territory now. But there was something else, something floral. He could smell it over the chemicals, which only further confused him. He strode up to the table, reaching for the sheet, but Arnie's large hand stopped him.

"Let me tell you what you're in for first." Arnie looked at him grimly. "This is something I've never seen before, Harry. And I don't like it, not one bit. So, if you've got a reasonable explanation for this, I'd be over the moon to hear it."

Harry nodded, reaching for the sheet again. As his hand drew near, he had the strangest feeling. Warm static washed over him, the hairs on his arms standing tall in response. It was like getting too close to a powerline. He hesitated, pausing to wait for the feeling to go away. It didn't.

Breathe Harry, don't let Arnie spook you. He tried to reassure himself. *Just another body, another autopsy.* He lifted the sheet, pulling it down to reveal the corpse's head, neck, and upper chest. He heard Arnie turn away, the other men mumbling amongst themselves, one man even gagged.

Bursting from the eye sockets were what looked to be some kind of yellow plant. Harry didn't recognize it. It seemed to have grown through the man's eyes and out the front. Blood had stained the area around the eyelids, running down his face as though the man had been weeping blood. A wide toothy smile adorned the face as well. *Too wide.* Harry thought. The corners of the mouth had torn nearly all the way to the outer corners of the eyes. *Torn, not cut.* He thought. How could someone smile so wide and hard that they tore their own flesh?

The teeth were odd as well, mangled as though the man had been chewing on gravel for some time before expiring. Harry could see the nerves in some of them, exposed to the air as they were.

One of the officers vomited into the sink. Harry looked at Arnie sternly, "Clear the room please."

Arnie nodded, "Alright lads, out ya go. You've all done enough for the night, go home. We'll call in the morning if something comes up."

Most of the men began to shuffle out immediately, but a few remained. Haskins spoke up, "We need some answers here Sherriff. This is seriously messed up, we need to know what the hell is going on."

Arnie clapped him on the shoulder, "You'll know as soon as we do Haskins, but for now the doctor needs to work and I assume you don't want to hold the light for him." Haskins shook his head before shuffling out with the rest of the men.

"Hold your light up high Arnie, I need to see better. There are some candles in that cabinet over there, I'm going to need as much light as we can give me."

Arnie retrieved the candles. Pulling a lighter from his pocket, he began lighting them one by one. "What could do something like this to a man Harry? Tear his face up like that. Why's his face stuck like that anyway?"

Harry waited for Arnie to finish, "I think he did that himself." Arnie turned, pallid.

The candles gave much needed light to the room. Harry wheeled the cart with his tools over and gave the body another look. There was something about the tears in his cheeks. He retrieved a magnifying glass from the tray and bent over to inspect closer. There seemed to be, and he couldn't quite believe it himself, gold in the man's wounds. Harry grabbed the tweezers from the cart without needing to look up, and tapped at what looked to him like a gold vein running through the wound and continuing under the man's skin.

"Metal?" Arnie was leaning over now too.

"I wasn't sure through the blood, but I believe so. Gold, specifically."

"So what, this guy got gold put in under his skin and decided to get it out?"

Harry shook his head, "No, the way it's interwoven with the tissue it looks like it," he paused, considering his next words carefully, "grew there all on its own."

Arnie straightened, "How is that even possible?"

"I don't know Arnie. But one thing at a time. There's a book on botany on that shelf," he gestured across the room, "Grab it please, I need to identify these plants."

Harry grabbed a small set of scissors from the tray, snipping off one of the pinnate leaves from the plant. Crimson blood began to run out of it. He stood straight, "Arnie?"

"Yeah, I got it. Here's—" he stopped short, "Is that plant *bleeding*?"

Harry nodded, "Like it's tied into his vascular system, yes." He held the leaf under the magnifying glass. The small veins across the leaf were tinged slightly red, like blood ran through them. He set the magnifying glass and leaf down, taking the book from Arnie.

"Should we, I don't know, do something about the bleeding plant?"

Harry didn't look up before he answered, "He's quite dead Arnie, I don't think it's going to bother him much." He flipped through the book quickly, looking for the telltale yellow leaves. It took him a minute, but there it was, "*Ferulago galbanifera.*"

"Never heard of it. Never seen it either." Arnie muttered.

"That's because it isn't native here. Nor anywhere on this continent, in fact." He turned the book, handing it to Arnie, "It's native to eastern Europe, Russia, and Turkey."

"How the hell did it get here if—" Arnie stopped when they heard the distinct sound of metal on stone from the hall. "Stay here Harry." Arnie's hand went to his service revolver, but he didn't draw it, not yet.

But now, Harry was alone. He'd been alone with bodies before, many times in fact. But this felt different. Something felt wrong.

Harry. A whisper, but that was definitely his name. He whipped around, scanning the room. Nothing. Not a scrap of paper out of place.

Harry. There it was again. Chills ran down his spine, like cold water on a hot summer day.

"Who's there?" he tried to say, but his voice sounded choked. He cleared his throat, "Who's there?"

Harry. The book, Harry.

Book? What book? The botany tome he'd just been looking through? He looked for the book and saw that Arnie had set it down on the tray. But nothing seemed different about it.

Why had he expected it to be different?

A soft golden glow came from a side table closest to the window observers would watch him operate from.

The book, Harry. This voice, this whisper, it seemed almost familiar. He wasn't unsettled by it, not really.

But why not? Shouldn't he be?

Rolling the cart out of the way, Harry stepped toward the table. He could see it now, a book that seemed to be completely bound in gold, symbols etched into it's front. Familiar and unfamiliar at once. He reached for it.

Harry. He looked up. There, in the reflection of the theatre window he could see that the body on the slab had sat up, its head turned 180 degrees to stare at him through those lifeless, sprouted eyes. He whipped around, just as Arnie darkened the doorway.

"Harry? You alright?"

The body was as it had been. Nothing out of place.

"Looking through our vics stuff? What do you hope to find there?"

Harry turned back to the table, there was no book bound in gold, only a leather satchel. Simple, and worn.

"I uh," he cleared his throat, "I was hoping to find something about these plants, maybe something to explain why our man was in eastern Europe."

Arnie nodded. "Makes sense."

"Find anything out there?" Harry looked at his reflection in the theatre window. His hair was mussed again.

"Nah, could have just been a rat."

"A rat, right." Harry knew neither of them really believed that.

He reached for the satchel, warm static again overtaking his body. More intense than before, it felt like thousands of tiny needles pricking his skin all over his body. He opened the satchel quickly, and there it was.

Bound in gold leafing, was a book that seemed to hardly fit in the satchel.

"The hell is that?" Arnie looked over his should.

"I don't rightly know."

Harry. The book.

His hand moved of its own accord, picking up the book. It was heavy, heavier than any book he'd every held. He knew it was, but his arm didn't seem to notice. It felt…

Right.

A creak like an old door that had long since rusted shut came from the book as he lifted the front cover. Arnie reached past him, slamming it shut again.

"Are you out of your god damned mind, Harry? Creepy book bound in gold, found on the body of a dead man with plants growing out his eyes and you want to *open it*?"

Harry looked back at the book, at Arnie's hand as the gold of the cover grew to overtake his skin.

Arnie screamed. The flesh of his hand sizzled as the molten gold crawled up and over his thumb and pinkie. Harry pulled the book, trying to tear it free of Arnie's hand.

"Ah God, Harry, stop. You'll take my damn hand off!"

Better that than the gold continue to spread, he knew. He roared as he pulled with all his might, as the gold hardened in place and degloved Arnie's hand up to the wrist. Blood slopped onto the floor as Arnie recoiled in shock, clutching at his now bloody hand.

"Shit, Arnie." Harry dropped the book on the table with a terrifying thud as he ushered Arnie over to the sink. He grabbed the chlorhexidine.

"This is going to hurt, but the antiseptic will—"

"Just do it man!" Arnie bellowed.

Harry poured. The hand was still fairly clean, as minimal bubbling came from the meat of Arnie's hand. Arnie didn't scream, shock had fully overtaken him. Harry grabbed clean bandages, wrapping Arnie's fingers individually before binding the whole hand together as tightly as he dared.

Arnie was pale. Harry hurried over and wheeled a chair to him, "Sit down Arnie, you have to sit." He did so, collapsing onto the seat.

"Harry. What, what happened to me?"

Harry shook his head, "I don't know Arnie. I don't know."

Harry. The book. The voice was more insistent now.

"No! He needs help." He shouted back.

"Who's there, Harry?"

"No one, you just rest here. I'll phone for help."

"No!" Arnie shouted, reaching for Harry's shirt, "No. Don't leave me down here alone. Something is here Harry; can't you feel it? Following us. No, no. Stalking us. Like we're prey and it's the predator. Maybe that's what happened to that guy, maybe he got caught by—" Arnie cut off.

"Arnie?" Harry turned to look at what Arnie was looking at, eyes wide and mouth agape.

There was no body on the slab.

Harry. Take up the book.

He turned fully around now, and standing by the table, grinning wickedly from ear to ear, was their body. It had retrieved the book and was proffering it to him.

Take up the book, Harry.

He knew that voice.

Take it. It was coming from the corpse now standing opposite him.

Why did he know that voice?

It is time.

It couldn't be.

Son.

Harry saw the resemblance now. The shape of the nose, relatively undisturbed by the splitting smile below it. His nose.

His father stood on the other side of the room, arm extended, book in hand.

"You're dead."

"Yes." It responded. It, for Harry could not accept that this thing was his father.

"How are you doing this?" Harry took a step toward it.

Arnie grabbed his sleeve, "Harry, don't. We need to call the mayor, the chief, we need backup."

"Can't, the power's out, the phones won't—" Harry turned to look at Arnie, "The phone's won't work."

Arnie's face began to split, a horrifying smile tearing his cheeks open as the corners of his mouth reached for his eyes. Gold shined from the bloody tissue under Arnie's skin, reflecting the candlelight back at him.

"There's no time, Harry." It was still Arnie's voice, the gaping maw of his mouth moving to match the words. He still sounded concerned, but what Harry saw didn't match that. He couldn't wrap his mind around it. A hand on his shoulder.

"Son. It is time to call him."

"You're *not* my father." Harry pushed with all his might against this thing that pretended to be his father. It didn't budge.

"You were always weak. Always a disappointment. You can't even walk on your own."

Rage began to bubble inside Harry's chest. "I'll kill you."

"You don't have the spine to do any such thing, Harry."

Harry swung as hard as he could, a right hook to the jaw. He heard his hand make contact, a hollow thud against metal before his hand pounded in pain. The thing reached for him, grabbing the front of his shirt and vest.

"I told them you didn't have the nerve, Harry. They insisted it *had* to be you. But I see now, they were wrong. You're too weak. You can't even—"

The gun in Harry's hand went off. A hole punched through the front of the things skull, blasting brain matter and skull fragments across the room. When had he retrieved Arnie's service weapon? The smile fell from his father's face, skin now loose. The body crumpled to the floor, book still held firmly in hand.

You are strong, Harry. Show them your strength.

A different voice this time, deep but gentle. He felt a strange sense of calm wash over him. He knelt carefully, taking the book from his father's dead hand. It was warm, washing him with that same pin prick feeling all over his body. But this time it wasn't painful, it was reassuring. Like coming home after a long day at work, the house warm from the fire.

He lifted the cover again, ignoring the great creaking as he did. There were words written here *ecce rex aureus*. Latin?

Read it, Harry.

"Behold, the Golden King."

The world around him shook, like an earthquake never felt by mankind. The ceiling cracked, and through those cracks he saw a soft golden light shine. Not like the light of the sun, he didn't feel he needed to shield his eyes. A chunk of the stone ceiling fell, crushing the slab in the center of the room. Through the hole in the ceiling he saw... stars. But they were wrong, their positions unfamiliar. And they swam in a swathe of reddish orange fog.

The observation theatre window shattered, glass shards exploding into the room. The shards stopped less than a foot from him, holding in the air.

Come and see. Behold your Golden King.

Harry stepped over the body of his not father, book still open in one hand, gun in the other. As he neared where the glass had been he saw now that he was the one looking through a window. The vastness of space expanded infinitely before him. And there, in the center of what he could see was a flat stone dais, a throne of golden stone in the center.

Come and see.

Harry climbed carefully through the window, he felt no pain in his leg, no difficulty using it at all. As his feet touched the floor on the other side of the window frame, the tiles fell away around him, moving to form a stone staircase down to the dais. Harry descended, marveling briefly at his ability to walk. He realized that he was looking at the back of the throne, it's towering back to him. He felt calm, more at peace with his place than he ever had been before.

When he stepped onto the dais he looked down at his feet. It was made entirely of glass; he could see stars below him. Normally his vertigo would have caused him to waver, but not here. Not when he was so close. The throne began to rotate silently, spinning around to face him.

Until he saw it, him. A robe of shinning golden thread, empty inside where there should have been a person holding its form. His mind reeled as the being stood from the throne, raising up to the height of a skyscraper. He dropped to his knees.

You have come. That voice again, soft, like the whisper of a parent to a frightened child. But Harry wasn't frightened. He knew he should be, but the enormity of what he beheld overtook his fears.

Release me, Harry. Unbind what has been done here.

"Why me?" Harry asked it, "I'm nobody, just a man."

All men are just men, Harry. Until they are needed. Now you can succeed where your father failed. Release me, and power beyond your imagining shall be yours.

His whole life had been pain. The abandonment of his father, the blame of his mother, his broken body. But none of that mattered now. He could hardly feel it at all, all he felt was…

Peace.

I have prepared the sacrifice. The robed figure gestured as Arnie floated down, horrific smile gone from his pained face.

"Why him? He has been good to me."

This is why. It is not a sacrifice if you hate them. That is justice.

He understood. It had to be someone who mattered, someone who cared about him. Which was why his father didn't count.

Turn the page. Harry did so, and there, cut into the pages of the book was a golden dagger, shining and deadly sharp. Arnie's body landed lightly on top of a stone table. Where had that come from?

The robe gestured to Arnie again. *Go now my son. Claim your place at my side.*

Harry got to his feet, walking slowly toward Arnie, who seemed to be sleeping. But he was in pain, that much was clear. Harry could take that pain away, like his had been taken. He could give Arnie peace. He raised the dagger up, positioned it over Arnie's heart.

A gunshot.

"Doc!"

Harry turned, "Haskins? What the hell are you doing here? You're supposed to be at home."

The room was as it had been, but Arnie was now on the slab in the center of the room. No collapsing ceiling, no shattered window. His leg began to give out.

Another man caught Harry under his arm. The cabby?

"You don't need to do this doctor. It's a lie, it's all a lie. Let me help you."

How did he know what was happening here? His tattoos. Harry saw them with renewed vision. They *had* been carved with a knife, a knife he had been holding. But it was gone now, only Arnie's revolver was in his hand.

Kill them all, Harry. Then you can have peace.

The voice was calm still, but he saw things now. Shooting the cabby, his head rocking back as he collapsed to the floor. Shooting Haskins, gun falling from his hand. A shining knife plunging into Arnie's heart.

You can be free, *Harry. Take what is yours.*

"Okay." He said aloud. The cabby helped him to right himself, taking the book from his hand.

"You're making the right choice, doc." He said, clapping Harry on the shoulder.

Take what is yours. Release me.

"I know." Harry said flatly.

Then he put Arnie's gun in his mouth and pulled the trigger.

THE PUPILS OF DR VOGT

JAKE MATTHEWS

I 've murdered the children. God forgive me, I've killed them all.

It is my opinion that the matters described in this letter, the destruction of the Honeycomb Clinic for Troubled Children, the death of its proprietor, Dr. Vogt, and the disappearances of a score of children under the age of five, ought to be a matter of public record. I will be called mad by most and be made no less a killer by my confessions, but I will not die a liar. But as to the true end of it—what I witnessed that day on Pickman street, and its hideous implications…

The Honeycomb Clinic was a grand old manor house in Upper-West Arkham. There was nothing about the building to suggest malevolence. Its walls were clean and painted warm yellow-brown, its lawns trim and green. If there was any sign this was not simply the home of some well-to-do gentleman, it was that there could sometimes be seen an unusual number of small children at play in the yard.

Honeycomb had an excellent reputation for the care and teaching of children with abnormal needs. It was due to this reputation that I had personally referred eight small children to the doctor's care and arranged for financial assistance for six.

I was a family advisor with the Brighter Dawn Foundation, Arkham branch. To put it briefly, we work to secure private and government assistance for children from at-risk families. Although I am not a social worker, I had some of the same training, and would, at times, make recommendations for the needs of some of the more troubled children.

Some were simply victims of bad chance; the Bonpensieros, for example. Mr. Bonpensiero runs a perfectly respectable bakery here in Arkham. He is a decent man and, in my opinion, a good one. After the death of his wife, however, his four-year-old boy Jack fell completely mute. Jack needed more attention, and more specialized care, than his father could provide, so I referred the family to Honeycomb. Other families had more challenging circumstances, and it was on behalf of one of those that I visited the Clinic.

I knocked and introduced myself to the young nurse who answered the door. She led me inside. I asked to speak with Ezekiel Wilkins, and I was led to a gaunt, dark-featured boy of about five.

"Ezekiel?" the nurse said. "Mr. Thatcher would like to say hello." She told me she would inform Dr. Vogt of my visit and left. I knelt down next to the boy.

Truth be told, most advisors with the foundation would have dismissed the parents' concerns. Dr. Vogt was a respected man, and a scientist, and we had seen nothing but results from his work with the children. I trusted Vogt. I fully expected to find everything was well but, working with families, I had found value in digging beyond the obvious.

"Hello, Ezekiel. How are you feeling today?

"I'm well, Mr. Thatcher. How are you?" Ezekiel sat cross-legged on the floor, book spread across his lap. There were no other children sitting near him. Looking around, I noticed none of the children were sitting near one another

"I'm fine, thank you. What book do you have there?"

"Carlton and Chetney's *Theory of Natural Selection.*"

"My! That's quite a mouthful. Does the book have nice pictures?"

"They're alright. They're no Darwin, although I like some of their points."

I blinked.

"Who introduced you to Charles Darwin, Ezekiel?"

'Thomas read *On the Origin of Species* last week."

"And have you read it as well?"

Ezekiel paused.

"No. Thomas explained it to me."

"These are very advanced books for boys your age."

When I referred Ezekiel to Honeycomb two months ago, he could not write his own name. Truthfully, I had been worried Ezekiel would prove unteachable, his apparent brightness overshadowed by a lack of focus and proclivity to tantrums that had already led to two different caregivers asking him not to return.

"Could you read this line for me here?" I pointed towards a random spot on the page.

"So as was observed with the mighty thunder lizards being supplanted by the smaller, though more cunning, mammalian creatures, we see the brutish proto-man replaced by homo sapiens, with his greater development in both cognitive capacities and communication organs. We see, therefore, that two adaptations can and will, inevitably, elevate any species to the apex of their ecosystem: intelligence and language. Humanity, therefore—"

"That's fine, that's fine, thank you. I'm very impressed, Ezekiel—you must have been working hard. Are you proud of all the work you've done?"

Ezekiel shrugged.

"Your mother certainly is. I was talking to her earlier today. She mentioned you've been having dreams."

The boy stared blankly back at me with his huge dark eyes.

"Dr. Vogt says my mother is a degenerate."

"What? You heard him say this?"

"No," Ezekiel said. Then "Yes. It's okay. It's true—her family are all bootleggers. I've seen her stills."

I was lost for words, real shock amplified by the discomfort of hearing something cruel you've thought yourself in confidence spoken suddenly by another. It's a dreadful feeling, like being caught at a crime. Before I could recover myself, I felt a tap on my shoulder and turned to see the nurse.

"Dr. Vogt would like to see you in his office," she said. "Take the last door on the right. Ezekiel, it's time for your vitamins." She handed him a small glass filled with a clear, sweet-smelling liquid.

I thanked her and told Ezekiel I would like to speak with him again before I left. Two things of note caught my attention as I walked down the hallway. First, every single child was occupied with a book, just as Ezekiel had been, and all sipped the same clear drink. No child played, or ran, or even spoke. The second was a strong smell of fresh paint coming from the kitchen.

To my surprise, the last door on the right was locked. I tapped on it.

"Hello? Dr. Vogt?"

"That's the wrong door."

I turned and saw little Susan Bellows standing behind me.

"What was that, sweetheart?"

"She misspoke—that's the door to the cellar. Mr. Vogt's office is upstairs, the door on the left.

I opened the door on the left and, sure enough, revealed a flight of stairs.

"Thank you, Susan. Are you doing well today?"

"Fine, thank you, Mr. Thatcher."

"Good, Susan, good." I had worked with the Bellows family for years, so I reached out to give Susan a pat on the head. She ducked away from my hand and left. Strange, I thought. Strange that an affectionate little girl would suddenly shy away from a friendly gesture—I could hardly keep her from holding my hand six months ago. Children changed, I reasoned, and not always in ways one can predict or understand.

Dr. Vogt's office was as orderly as the rest of the Clinic. A converted attic, the room was small and bright, lit by electric lights strung along the steepled ceilings. The room was a long vault, beginning at the stairs by me and terminating at the single round window behind Vogt's mammoth desk. As he stood up from his desk to greet me, haloed by the daylight behind him, the room felt more like a church than an office. Then, my eyes adjusted to the light, and the doctor's broad smile welcomed me.

We shook hands and sat.

"And to what do I owe the honor of your company, Phillip?" he asked.

I cleared my throat.

"This is a little awkward, Hyram, but I've been speaking with one of the parents—"

"Ms. Wilkins?"

I didn't answer him. A cagey look flashed across his face.

"Did she ever spill the beans on who Ezekiel's father is, by the way?"

"No, Hyram. She still insists she doesn't know."

"Pity." Vogt's smile died past the corners of his mouth. "Ezekiel is a fine young man. He's doing remarkably well here with us. What is his mother is doing for work nowadays?"

"She's found a job with a cleaning service. Spends most of her time up at Miskatonic now."

"Excellent! She's doing quite well for herself, given her disadvantages. Child out of wedlock, no education. Best for her and Ezekiel that she left Dunwich and joined civilization."

I had my own reservations about Ruth Wilkins, former rumrunner and lately of Dunwich, but overt hostility from the normally cheerful doctor troubled me.

"I take it she's called you too, Hyram?"

"She calls incessantly. Completely fails to understand what it is we're doing here."

"She's worried for her son."

The smile vanished entirely.

"How about you, Phillip? Are you worried about Ezekiel?"

The more I looked at the doctor and his office, the more I realized something was off. His shirt was wrinkled. His hair was disheveled, the circles under his eyes dark. I chose my next words carefully.

"Ms. Wilkins is not the only parent who has called me, Hyram. There have been complaints. Bad dreams. Moodiness. Changes in appetite. You have to admit the growth these children have made intellectually is absolutely staggering."

"What are you asking, Mr. Thatcher?"

What was I asking? Are you abusing these children, bullying them, frightening them? The questions had all seemed ridiculous a few minutes ago. But Vogt's demeanor...

"I need you to explain what goes on here, Doctor. In detail. How are children who were writing on the walls in their own filth eight months ago suddenly reading foundational science? What is your process?"

"I don't think I'm obligated to tell you, Mr. Thatcher. I wasn't under the impression you were a social worker?"

There was something wild behind the man's glare.

"You're right—I'm not a social worker. But if a social worker *were* to visit Honeycomb, be assured they would have the full weight of the law behind them." Panic flashed across his face.

"But you and I are colleagues," I placated. "Friends. I think you do good work here, doctor. If the parents are worried about *how* their children are being helped, I may be able to calm them, so long as I understand what I'm a party to."

Dr. Vogt slumped in his chair and rubbed his eyes.

"An ally," he murmured. "Maybe it is time for one."

"You seem stressed, Hyram. Have there been any…problems? Here? At home?"

Vogt laughed, hollow and bitter as breaking deadfall.

"Home? This *is* home for me. I do not own a second property. I never remarried after Helen died. My son—" his voice hitched. "This is the best way I can help Nathaniel now. To honor his memory. But problems here? No, only small ones. They're only children, after all, it's to be expected. Little things go missing here and there, of course, but they always find their way back. Good as gold, most of the time, perfect little ladies and gentlemen."

"What sorts of things go missing?"

Vogt waved the question away. I remembered the fresh coat of paint in the kitchen and asked him if one of the children had made a mess of the walls.

"A mess!" The laugh returned. "Oh, somebody made a mess alright!" When Vogt tried to regain his composure, giggles forced their way through his lips. My heart sank. He seemed positively manic.

"Doctor Vogt, something is clearly wrong. For God's sake, you seem like you're on the verge of a nervous breakdown. Please, tell me what's wrong so I can help. What happened in the kitchen?"

Vogt grabbed my wrist and glared at me. The laughter was gone and for a moment I thought Vogt might be a danger to *me*, let alone the children. I was going to have to go to the police. He must have seen the worry on my face, however, because he released my hand and fell back into his chair.

"I'm sorry, Phillip. I'm sorry—I realize how this must seem. I will tell you what's been happening here, why the children may be…upset. But first let me tell you about my work, what we're accomplishing. Let me explain the stakes."

The house was dead silent, waiting for him to begin. Not one child could be heard.

"It started with Nathaniel. My son. He died six years ago, you may have even known he was sick for a long time before that. Nathaniel had a rare neural-degenerative disorder, Hoffman-Campbell syndrome. A sort of childhood dementia. He was so smart. So bright, my boy. He knew his alphabet and numbers at age four; he was reading small books and poems by five. We would go on walks along the Miskatonic and he'd point to the different plants and animals. He'd ask 'Daddy, what's his name? What does he eat? Where does he live?' And he'd always remember. His little hand in mine…God. Oh God help me.

"Nathaniel didn't begin to show symptoms until he was eight. It started with short term memory loss, irritability, and a lack of focus. Over time, he started regressing. At eight, he wrote a theme on *Peter Pan*, his favorite book. By the time he was fourteen, he could no longer clean himself, Mr. Thatcher. My son forgot his own name…and mine.

"I saw what was happening to him. I spared no expense. I took him to the best doctors, used my contacts through the University and my father's fortune to take him to experts in London, Edinburgh, Paris.

But there is no cure for Hoffman-Campbell. So, I became determined to find one.

"My research started out mundane, working with the neuro-chemistry lab at Miskatonic. As the years waxed and my poor little boy's mind waned, I became desperate. I started looking at folk cures for memory loss, anti-aging, anything. I wanted to test these cures, see if they had any basis in scientific fact. I powdered white rhinoceros horn and grew mandrake in the University greenhouses. My correspondence grew until I was in touch with the occult heads of North America and Europe. And still nothing worked.

"Eventually, one of my contacts put me in touch with a Captain McComas, lately of the British royal navy and now resident of Flintlock Island. Flintlock is in the south pacific—who knows what it was called by its original inhabitants. The community there was almost entirely white sailors and their descendants. Rumor had it that the inhabitants were all uncommonly old, yet still retained their mental capacity. I wrote the captain. When he wrote back, he explained how sympathetic he was to my son's condition and shared the local cure for an aging mind.

"McComas said there was a species of sea sponge that lived in the deep waters near the island, down in the old volcanic vents. The islanders would harvest this sponge and eat it to stave off the mental ravages of age. The captain was even kind enough to ship me several dried specimens for study.

"Sponges are remarkable animals. Yes—animals, not plants. Profoundly ancient, you know, so much so they may be a sister species to every living creature. They can regenerate practically any tissue loss. And they may be responsible for our brains, you know. The earliest proto-neurons we've discovered are in sponges, clustered around their stomach. At least, that's most sponges."

Dr. Vogt leaned forward and grinned. Any sign of grief had vanished from his face, replaced with an almost manic glee.

"Phillip, do you know what was so remarkable about this Flintlock sponge?"

"I'm sure I don't, doctor."

"These proto-neurons, the ones usually centered around the stomach, are distributed *throughout the entire animal!* Do you understand what that means—a creature, a direct ancestor of our own, *whose entire body functions as a brain!* I was sure, I was *sure* this would be the breakthrough I needed. McComas' islanders ate the sponge. I wanted something stronger. I analyzed the tissue, broke it down, rendered it into a concentrated serum."

"But it didn't work."

"What?"

"It didn't work. Your son passed away."

"It was too late to save Nathaniel. These diseases, they ravage the body as well as the mind. Nathaniel…was lost. But! There was *some change!* Mr. Thatcher, in the final days there was *change* in my son. When he looked at me he *knew* me, my boy *knew* me, sir, for the first time in over a year. It was too late for him. But I knew I could help others."

"Did you tell McComas? About your success with his sponge."

"Oh, I tried. But Flintlock Island woke up not long after his package arrived. The volcano wiped out the whole population, the poor devils. I never did get to thank him."

Something about this bothered me, introduced some missing piece to the puzzle. Unable to put my finger on it, though, I asked him to continue.

"I moved to the next stage of testing. Rats, monkeys. I discovered the serum had an efficacy inversely related to the development of the subject's brain. The young and elderly are more affected than healthy adults, for example."

"You're administering this drug," I said. "To the children. Has it been approved? Why haven't I heard of it before?"

"It hasn't been approved—we're still in testing." Vogt waved off the question like a gnat. "The parents know their children are being given nutritional supplements, they signed wavers. They knew what they were getting into."

I thought of Ms. Wilkins, lately of a Dunwich hovel. I somehow doubted she understood.

"I realize you might have hesitations, Mr. Thatcher, but it's *working!* And not just on Hoffman-Campbell. It has had a positive effect on every disorder, every disease of the brain. My God, Thatcher, it's doing more than healing them, it's *improving* them! Every student here shows intelligence and maturity far, far beyond what would normally be possible for a child their age. You spoke with Ezekiel. Can you imagine what he'll be like as an adult?"

I was appalled. Vogt was playing with these children's lives. But if the children had not suffered any adverse effects? I was having trouble wishing more than a slap on the wrist on him. Isn't that what any teacher in the world would want for their students? Calmer, sharper minds, freed of the pains of disease? Were the changes in these children so bad? Something was still wrong, though, that I couldn't put my finger on.

Vogt, not realizing my mind had wandered, continued.

"…than that. As soon as one learns something, the others all seem to know it."

"I beg your pardon?"

"Shared memories, Thatcher. Shared intelligence. Connected *consciousness.* The implications are staggering, not just for these children, but for our entire species."

The mania had returned to his eyes. I stared at his strained grin and the sweat across his brow. He was raving, imagining impossible results in his experiments to cope with his grief. Sadness settled in my heart. I would have to try to find Vogt help. I would have to find other accommodations for the children, speak with their parents…

I pushed further.

"These results sound incredible, Dr. Vogt. Why do you seem distressed?"

He grew maudlin again.

"There was an incident last week. One of the nurses. She was preparing lunch in the kitchen and...there was a grease fire. Caught her arm, her hair, her face...spread to the walls.'

"My God!"

"She was hideously burned, but she survived. Her screams had every adult in the kitchen within seconds; we were able to extinguish her."

"How awful. How are the children coping?"

He scoffed.

"Better than her. *They* all agreed it was better to keep the accident a secret. *She* on the other hand...I'm paying her and her family well for their discretion, but they keep threatening to talk."

"Talk about what?"

Another dismissive wave.

"She says it wasn't an accident. Clumsy idiot keeps saying someone tampered with the stove, and that she was pushed. It's nonsense. None of the other nurses were anywhere near her."

I don't need to explain the darker implications of what was left unsaid, of who else the nurse might have said sabotaged her.

"You said some things had gone missing, Dr. Vogt. What sorts of things?"

"Damnit, Thatcher, you're missing the point! None of this matters next to what I'm accomplishing here. This isn't some confession of guilt. I need an *ally!* Someone to help keep the parents calm while I finish my work. Once I've refined the formula, I can increase production of the drug. I can save—I can change the world. *We* could change the world, Thatcher."

I should have humored him, told him I would put minds at ease. Then, when I had left the house, I should have gone straight to the Foundation, the University, even the police for help stopping this man's experiments. Vogt had already revealed more than enough to shut down Honeycomb for good.

I put my hand on his arm. "If I'm going to be a part of this, I need to know everything. Could I see where you're manufacturing the serum?"

He looked as though he would object, but I kept my face firm.

"Yes, yes, very well. Follow me."

"Where are we going?"

"I told you. I have no office or home outside of this building. My laboratory is in the cellar."

The cellar. Where my life ended.

Vogt unlocked the door with a key as antique as the house and led me down into a dry, cool room lit with Edison lamps. Two tables of chemical equipment occupied the floor. The floor was stone, and the walls were stone, and one corner was blocked off by a sort of curtain.

"Well," he said. "Feel free to look around."

The cellar stank of antiseptic and standing water. Walking over to the tables, I was surprised at how simple the equipment on the tables was.

"It's not really such a complicated process," Vogt explained. "Not unlike distilling, although it's a bit faster."

There was not much to see, although the longer I stayed down there, the more I became aware of another smell, foul in a way I could not place.

"Any questions?" Vogt asked. Smiling again.

"What's behind that curtain?" I asked.

"Junk," he said. "Old tools and antiques from the house's previous owner. I just ran out of room."

Ran out? I thought. That was it.

"With Flintlock Island gone, how are you replenishing your supply of the sponge?"

"What?"

"Surely, your stores must be running low."

Vogt said nothing. The ceiling creaked as someone walked above us. I stared at that curtain in the corner.

"Doctor, I need to see behind that curtain."

"No."

"Why not?"

We argued. Vogt started shouting at me, and I, now convinced he was hiding something, dug in my heels. Then, I was shocked as things became violent. Vogt tackled me. We crashed, upturning one of the tables, and glass shattered on the floor around us. He grabbed at my throat as he screamed about strange things.

About books he had read while searching for a cure.

How the world was never really ours, that we were less than ants to the planet's true rulers.

And how ants still thrived beneath our feet.

Then my hand found a heavy steel funnel and I brought it against his temple, knocking him cold. I was slow to stand, slower to catch my breath, and all the while I stared at that damned curtain. What could be so important as to murder over, after everything else he had told me? I walked closer. That evil stink got worse. I paused within arm's reach and wondered if I really wanted to know. Then, I threw away my last chance at sanity and threw the curtain back.

The figure behind the curtain was seated in a crude tub of salt water, submerged for so long that the parts of it which were still human were swollen and soft as hot taffy. Its body was still mostly mannish; it might have been a boy of about eighteen. But its head…

Out of the thing's shoulders grew what I, at first, mistook for a titanic tumor, so vast it rendered the host immobile, pressing him down into the tub even as it leaned against the wall. As I stared, my eyes found the pattern of regular hexagonal pores that bore through the entire mass. A sponge, meat-pink and dripping with dark orange pus.

The real horror of it was there were still…*pieces* lodged into the sponge. A cluster of teeth here. A patch of skin, still white and healthy. Two ears pressed together by tectonic motion and a lidless, bloodshot eye stared forever in the distance. Fragments of Nathaniel Vogt's identity, worn like a broken mask by the thing that had burst through his skull and consumed him.

There were sections missing from the sponge as well, clean and obvious excisions. This, I surmised, was where Vogt was replenishing his supply. What a terrible way to die, I thought. A monstrous, agonizing death. And then *it moved*, turning that bloodshot eye on me. I screamed.

"I'm not so cruel as you think." Vogt was climbing back to consciousness. "I love my son. I speak to him while I work. I read to him. My boy was always so bright, my boy, my precious son."

The Nathaniel-thing reached one puffy, sodden hand towards me. I ran from the basement. Little did I know the penultimate horror was waiting at the top of the stairs.

The hallway was crammed with tiny figures as every one of doctor Vogt's pupils waited for me. Twenty pairs of eyes fixed on me.

"It's okay," I told them. "Everything is okay. I'm going to go get help."

"You hurt Doctor Vogt," said Jack Bonpensiero, mute no longer.

"He'll be fine, he just—how do you know that?"

"Nathaniel saw," Ezekiel said.

"We know you know," Susan continued. Other voices chimed in.

"You want to hurt us!"

"I would never!" I screamed.

"You want to stop us."

"I want to help you!"

"It's too important. We have to finish it."

"Finish what?" I asked.

Then it hit me. With cold, demoniacal clarity. Shared memories. Group intelligence. Nathaniel down there with his father, watching him distill the serum, comprehending with fantastical intelligence. In understanding, ensuring the rest of the children understood as well. Little things go missing...like equipment. Keys. Incisions in the sponge. Sabotaged stove, all the nurses distracted...

Just like distilling. And Ezekiel's poor bootlegger mother beside herself with worry and terror.

"Why," I asked. "Why go to the trouble to distill it yourselves? Why not just let Dr. Vogt make you more?"

The children didn't answer. Ezekiel took a knife from behind his back and lunged.

Despite his advanced intelligence, he still had the body of a four-year-old. I was able to catch him easily, but when I grabbed his wrist, my fingers sank *into* him. His flesh was soft, pliable as though he had lost his bones. It squelched and buckled and dark orange welled between my fingers. I jerked my hand away. Deep grooves remained in his arm. Where the flesh was distorted, I could make out tiny, hexagonal pores.

Ezekiel, poor, troubled little Ezekiel Wilkins. Still human in appearance, but no more humanity left than the thing in the basement. A fate to which I had condemned him.

My mind broke. I screamed, I shoved, I ran over and through and past them. I tore out of the house, and I didn't stop running until I had put ten blocks between myself and the inhuman spawn of that thing in the cellar.

I went to the police. They might not have believed me, but I was friends with a few officers through the foundation and they raided the house. They found Nathaniel, mute and immobile in the cellar. Vogt was dead—evidently, he had taken his own life rather than be caught. The nurses had managed to corral a few of the children before they scattered, but nine of Dr. Vogt's pupils had vanished.

The other eleven were taken into custody and, eventually, government men took them away. An asylum, maybe. But maybe not.

The police accused me of no crime, but the parents hold me responsible. As do I. I quit my job at the foundation. In recent days, my time has been spent wandering the streets of Arkham.

Now comes the final horror, the part I was not sure I could bear to write. I have come this far but, God help me—

I was on one of my wanderings. I found myself across the street from a familiar storefront. Bonpensiero's bakery. A small crowd had gathered there. A sign explained they were giving away free sweets.

Bonpensiero, whose youngest son Jack was one of Vogt's longest running experiments. Who had no time to look after his son when he was home. Jack, classmate of Ezekiel Wilkins, who access to his mother's defunct distillery. Children swarmed the place, fell on buns and cookies and cake and devoured them. One of them turned and seeing me, smiled and waved.

I don't know what to do, but I know I can't live with myself. I've killed the children I sent to Honeycomb for care. Innocent, vulnerable children whose families came to me for help. And in so doing, I may have killed untold children. All of them. The noose is tied beside me and waiting.

Because I can't live with myself, and I can't live with them. Vogt raved that this world was not meant for us. Maybe it will be theirs, now. Surely, it is not mine.

I will not be an ant in a world of men.

THE SEWAGE TREATMENT POND

JASON P. BURNHAM

Heading eastward along the Miskatonic River, one passes a dreadful and ill-regarded island, shadowed with grey standing stones overgrown by moss that cast shadows even on pitch black moonless nights. If a traveler can pass this island with their faculties intact, on the eastern side of Arkham and the southern bank of the river, they will come to find a large pool of dark green, stagnant, and stinking water. The poorly lit three room building and electrical shack adjacent this pond functions as Arkham's sewage treatment center and the medical office of one Dr. Robert King. Savvy new referrals to Dr. King's practice would find verification of his medical credentials nigh impossible to confirm, but returning patients would see no other doctor in the world given the chance.

It was on a rainy grey day when the Miskatonic threatened to subsume the sewage treatment pond into its member that one Amelia Danvers brought in her son Alabaster for a second opinion on a most troublesome and enduring rash that her little five year old simply couldn't shake.

"We're just at our wits end, Dr. King," Amelia said, finishing with a flourish. She'd wrinkled her nose at the sewage pond when she'd arrived, concerned about what she was getting herself into, but Dr. King had an excellent and disarming bedside manner. Amelia was confident now that this man could help her son.

"May I see your rash, Alabaster?" Dr. King asked in his slow baritone.

"My friends call me Al," said Alabaster.

"Very well Al," Dr. King smiled, "show me where the spots are."

Al pulled off his turtleneck, leaned forward, and showed Dr. King the back of his neck. Amelia grimaced, waiting for the awful reaction she usually got from doctors.

But King gave her none. He pulled on a latex glove and rubbed his finger gingerly over one of the meaty, punched out sores that ringed little Alabaster's neck and went up into his hairline. Where his finger touched, a line of thick, black fluid slowly oozed from the sores. He removed the glove and threw it into a bin marked "Incinerate" on the side.

Unable to hold herself back any longer, Amelia blurted out her questions. "What is it doctor? What can we do?"

Dr. King washed his hands, dried them, and pushed his small circular spectacles up his nose so he could look her square in the eye.

"Now Miss Danvers, the field of Medicine has advanced by leaps and bounds in the last couple decades, and I think most people agree on that." He put his hands on his knees, stood, and adjusted his white coat, which was more of an off-white coat, though Amelia Danvers couldn't tell if that was a trick of the wan light or from lack of laundering. "So when I tell you that things in Arkham don't always follow the rules of Medicine, you must believe I know what I'm talking about."

Miss Danvers nodded eagerly. She'd do anything if it helped Alabaster.

"Best I can put it, there's a miasma of the blood got your boy. It's curable, but it won't be no easy task. The only thing I've seen work for this requires a mercury patch coupled with direct bloodletting." He pulled off his glasses and cleaned them with a handkerchief. "I'd be happy to do both if you're willing. Done it quite a few times to good success."

Amelia Danvers bit her lip. Alabaster had no idea what any of Dr. King's speech had meant, especially with the itching, clawing sensation that always throbbed in his neck.

"How much will it cost?" she asked. "You see, the boy's father isn't in the picture and I—"

Dr. King chuckled. Laughter didn't match his long face and thus was very unsettling to most people. Amelia Danvers hardly noticed.

"I don't charge for this service," Dr. King said.

Amelia frowned, not wanting to get her hopes too high. "That's so kind of you, but... why?"

"Well, my dear, the cure to your son's dermatologic miasma infiltration is part of how I maintain the operation of the sewage treatment plant."

After a tearful parting of a thousand thank yous, Dr. Robert King collected the residual cinnabar and blood drippings from Alabaster's recently cured neck rash. He carried these elements to a crucible filled with copper pellets and a tincture of wild garlic that he always had on hand for cases of miasmic infestation. He knew if he looked at Alabaster's blood under a microscope, he could see things no human should look upon more than once on purpose.

When the crucible was full, he fanned the flames beneath it and let the components come to a simmer. In three to five weeks, the concoction would be ready to present as a delicacy to his most prized and loathed business partner. Dr. King was fairly certain the entity that lived somewhere beneath the murky pool of water outside the building had no idea they were in business together. Fortunately, Dr. King didn't need the creature's permission to harvest the saponifying chemicals its carapace excreted when it surfaced to collect its blood and cinnabar meals.

Dr. King was going about fixing up a crucible of material that was properly cured and fermented when there was a loud knock at the door. He frowned and checked the clock on the wall—half past five, too late to be one of his patients, which meant he could ignore it and go about his business. All his patients knew to send him a telegram if something urgent came up—they didn't need to try to haul themselves from Arkham or beyond in a morbid state when a telegram could alert him that a house call was imminently needed.

Dr. King resumed his proceedings at the crucible and there came another, more urgent knocking. He squinted at the door, remembering the time Johnny Prior brought his son to that very threshold after he'd fallen into a mucinous puddle on Hangman's Hill and come out without skin on his hand. He shuddered, left the crucible and shuffled toward the door. Perhaps whoever was knocking was in such a bad way that they'd forgotten all about telegrams.

As he made his way to the door, an unfamiliar man's voice angrily shouted. "Open up! Water Inspector!"

"Come back during business hours," King grumbled. He turned back to his concoctions.

The knocking came again, loud enough that he thought it might splinter the door. "If you don't open up right this minute, I'm going to shut this whole operation down!"

Dr. King harrumphed and took his time to rearrange the look on his face into something approaching civility. He took a deep breath and threw the door open wide and quickly.

It had the desired effect—the man on the other side jumped back in alarm. The look on his face progressed from anger, to surprise, to a measure of fear as he took in Dr. King's appearance. At six-foot-seven, Dr. King had to duck under most doorframes, including the ones in his own office. He had thick, sausage-shaped fingers from years of hard use and his hands were greying from mercury exposure. He only used cinnabar when absolutely necessary, but in Arkham, it was often necessary.

The supposed water inspector fumbled with his words. "I… I'm here to inspect your facility."

"You're not from around here, are you?" Dr. King studied the man.

Sweat formed on the man's brow. "H-how did you know?"

"For one thing, Arkham don't have no Water Inspector," Dr. King began. "And for another, nobody from Arkham wears an all brown jump suit with their name stitched on it." He studied the badge and read it. "*Matthew.*"

Matthew the water inspector did his best to swallow the unanticipated fear he felt of this man. "I… yes. I'm from the Massachusetts State Board of Health. I've been sent here to inspect your facility because of high levels of downstream mercury contamination which we suspect to originate from somewhere in this town. I must know your process so that I may assist you in fixing it."

King chuckled and turned to retrieve the mixture he'd been working on when Matthew had interrupted him.

"What am I waiting for?" Matthew said into the door as it closed in his face. He didn't have the constitution to follow Dr. King uninvited.

Dr. King walked past Matthew with the crucible in his gloved hands.

"What's that?" Matthew called out.

"My process," Dr. King said as he strode toward the pond. "The one you intend to fix."

Matthew stared after him, unsure what to do. He hadn't been invited to follow, but the flickering yellow lamp above the front door was rubbing him the wrong way and at least he knew he wouldn't be alone if he followed. Matthew hurried to catch up with Dr. King rather than face the unknowns of standing on his front step by himself.

When Matthew caught up, Dr. King was attaching the crucible to a long, thick metal apparatus on the bank of the stinking, dark green pond. A fog was rolling in and visibility across the pond and river was quickly decreasing in the fading sunset.

"What's that?" Matthew asked pointing to the apparatus. He felt a sudden itching in his neck. Had something bitten him? He rubbed furiously at a spot on the back of his neck.

"Iron," replied Dr. King tersely.

"What is it's function?" Matthew asked with increasing annoyance.

"Iron's the best metal for this. Heavy, sturdy. Sometimes rusts, but what can you do? Gotta get the mixture where it needs to be." Dr. King secured the crucible and extended the long iron holder across a set of rails such that the crucible crept slowly closer to the middle of the pool of water while Dr. King remained firmly on solid ground.

"And where does it need to be?" Matthew asked nervously. He had come here with the power, with the drive, with the need to protect Massachusetts from mercury poisoning originating in this town. Now he was cowering in fear of this odd doctor on a gloomy, smothering night beside a stinking green pond.

Dr. King didn't answer. To Matthew's eye, he seemed to be listening for something.

There was suddenly the smell of brimstone and Dr. King leapt into action. He turned the iron rod so that the crucible emptied into the pond and then began stacking large, flat rocks on top of the rod.

"Wanna be helpful? Throw a few rocks up here." Dr. King motioned to the metal apparatus with his shoulder as he heaved another boulder into place.

Trembling, Matthew stepped closer and hesitantly picked up a rock, trying to keep his eyes on the crucible and the pond. The scent of sulfur emanated from the pond, he was certain of it. The fog and the dimming light didn't let him see very well, but he thought that the surface of the water was beginning to boil.

"C'mon, toss that thing up here," Dr. King said. "We don't have long."

Matthew hoisted the rock onto the apparatus. "Wh-what's going on?"

"The saponification lets you know its about to breach and eat," said Dr. King as if that was a completely rational thing to say to Matthew, the Water Inspector who was not from Arkham and knew nothing of its workings.

As Matthew's shaking hands pried another rock from the algae-slick loam, the bubbles on the water's surface began to pop and sizzle, shooting spray onto the iron and quite near Matthew's feet.

"Don't let it get on you," Dr. King warned.

Matthew jumped back from the roiling pond and as he did, the rock he was holding slipped from his grasp. He took his eyes off the water to try to catch the rock and two things happened simultaneously. The rock Matthew had dropped smashed onto his forefoot at precisely the same time as something pulled the crucible at the end of the iron bar with such great force that it sent all the rocks Dr. King had placed upon it to fly into the air. Matthew yelped from the impact of the rock on his foot as he tried to cover his head from the flying stones. Fortunately, none hit him nor Dr. King; some landed in the pond itself.

By the time Matthew remembered he was supposed to be watching the water, the boiling had reduced to a simmer and solids in the water were separating into clumps and clusters.

"What…was that?"

"The process." Dr. King pointed to the clumps in the water. "Those are the waste solids, separating on their own. That creature's saponification agent is so powerful it does this mostly automatically." He sighed. "Damn shame about that crucible and rod though. Hate to have to reforge equipment."

Matthew stared at him, considering what impossibilities had just befallen him. He lost his mind to a delirious fugue.

"No. No!" Matthew was screaming. "This is... no! This is not how sewage treatment works! You... you just put mercury into the water. That...that doesn't even make...And a creature that..."

Dr. King wasn't engaging with the tantrum—he had rocks to pick up and an iron apparatus that needed mending before the next cinnabar and bloodletting contribution to Arkham's waste pond.

If someone else had been there at the water's edge that night, it would have been difficult for them to distinguish whether it was Dr. King's nonchalance or Matthew's sheer shock that was responsible for what happened next. Even Matthew didn't know—he wasn't in control of his own feelings.

"I'm shutting you down," Matthew said, his voice squeaking into higher registers as he backpedaled away from Dr. King and the sewage treatment pond next to the three-room office and electrical shack. "By the Massachusetts State Board of Health I declare..."

But Matthew couldn't finish his sentence. He tripped over a mossy log and when he came up, he was pointing angrily at Dr. King with one arm and scratching furiously at the back of his neck with the other. When his back bumped against his car, he scrambled to get in and turn the key, the motor slow to turn over, the exhaust loud and rough when it finally did. The whitewall tires of his Ford spun and were quickly coated in mud before he managed to make any headway.

Matthew kept his finger pointed at Dr. King as he sped away, a wild look in his eye, but no words coming from his wide open mouth.

Dr. King finished stacking his rocks in place and lamented the loss of his crucible. He stared off into the distance where Matthew had driven, having made note of the fervor with which he had been scratching his neck.

"He'll be back," Dr. King muttered to himself before heading back inside. It was going to be a late night getting started on a new crucible. He shuddered to think what would happen if enough offerings were not given to the pond creature. At least with Dr. King's efforts it no longer roamed the Miskatonic or the spring underneath the cemetery anymore. Dr. King hoped to keep it that way.

———

By the time Dr. King received the cease and desist letter from the Massachusetts State Board of Health, the crucible with Alabaster Danvers' bloodletting fermentation products was ready to be given to the creature. Dr. King had only seen incidental glimpses of the creature in all his years—he knew better than to look. And what he had seen, he dared not remember, much less write down where anyone else might find it and have their brains go to soup upon reading the description.

But the state's letter didn't have any teeth. Arkham had sewage waste somebody had to filter and nobody was going to do it if Dr. King didn't.

So he went about his businesses, saw his patients and swept free the solid bits of sewage. Everything was as it should be, or at least as the routine should go and had gone for generations in the King family.

That is until Dr. King's electricity went out. He didn't think much of it at first—power outages happened in Arkham. But after half a day without power, Dr. King had gone into town and found he was the only one in Arkham who normally had electricity that was without it.

When he returned to his three-room office and stagnant pond by the shore of the Miskatonic, he was greeted by a Ford with familiar whitewalled tires.

Dr. King glared at the empty car and walked into his office. The door was standing open.

"I told you I was going to shut you down," Matthew said when Dr. King walked in. The man was sitting in a chair in Dr. King's medical office, a weak ray of light partially illuminating him from the room's single high window.

"I see you ditched the jump suit," Dr. King said flatly.

Matthew huffed. "I only wear that when I'm planning to get dirty. No dirt in letter delivery." He raised his head and stared at Dr. King. In his hand was an envelope.

Dr. King ignored the letter, focusing instead on Matthew's face in the dim light, more specifically, the exposed portion of his neck.

"Matthew, you're not looking so good," Dr. King said, the concern in his voice genuine.

Matthew ignored him. "Read the letter doc. The results are in and the prognosis is bad. I'm afraid this little operation has permanently reached the end of its rope."

Dr. King pulled on two latex gloves, took the letter, and tossed it into the 'incinerate' bin. "I can cure that, you know," he said before Matthew could yell about him throwing away the letter.

"It's just a rash," Matthew said, dragging his nails across the ragged flesh of his neck, thick black fluid trailing in their wake.

"It started that night you first came here, didn't it?" Dr. King knew. Only people who'd been to Arkham ever got it, though Matthew was the first patient Dr. King had ever seen who wasn't an Arkham resident who'd been afflicted. "Must have spent too long by the riverbank looking for me."

Matthew's eyes twitched, his haughty façade softening ever so slightly. His fingers reflexively went to his neck and scratched again.

"You know, my great-great-great Uncle Thomas told me that that creature what lives in the pond used to live in the river," said Dr. King. "Said before we started feeding it it used to prowl the waters, boiling up the surface as it went. Good thing we got it contained now. It'd be a shame if it got back out there. Uncle Thomas said the only food it's got anymore is in people's necks and if we don't extract it from their necks for them..."

By the time Dr. King stopped with his implication-heavy speech, Matthew's fingernails were caked with sticky black grime and he was pacing the poorly lit room.

"Enough!" Matthew shouted, spittle flying from his lips. He stopped pacing and glared at Dr. King with bloodshot eyes. "I hope you rot beneath the sewage of this wretched place."

The door slammed behind Matthew and with it came the scent of sulfur. Dr. King stood abruptly and followed him.

"Matthew!" he called. He didn't particularly like the man who was shutting down his office, but he didn't want him to get eaten either.

Matthew didn't listen, stomping through the muck toward his whitewall-tired Ford. Dr. King stopped short, studying closely the area around them. The iron apparatus he used to position the crucibles had been uprooted. But this could not have been Matthew's doing—no man could tear that apart by himself.

In the pool, solid wastes had clumped together neatly and the saponification bubbling was just subsiding from a wide swath of water at the bank.

"Matthew!" Dr. King called again to no avail.

Dr. King looked toward his office, but knew he and Matthew were both in serious danger. He was too far away from the crucibles inside to retrieve one. Great-great-great Uncle Thomas had told Dr. King the creature could be extremely swift on land when it was hungry. Judging by the path of destruction leading out of the pond, the creature was quite hungry indeed. It did not like leaving the water, which meant it was not only hungry, but likely irritable and angry to be on dry land.

Dr. King followed the path of flattened grass with his eyes—it led directly behind Matthew's car.

Matthew turned toward Dr. King as he grabbed the car door handle. He opened his mouth to say something, but before he could a great, heaping mass launched itself over the roof of his car and grabbed Matthew by the neck.

Dr. King ran. The slippery, mud and twig covered behemoth writhed on top of Matthew's body. Dr. King knew to look away, knew that both his and Matthew's only hope of survival was to retrieve a crucible and feed it before the creature got what it needed from the sores on Matthew's neck.

When Dr. King returned with the festering crucible in his hands, the muck-covered creature was coiling around itself like a hagfish, squeezing to wrench off a meaty piece of flesh from Matthew's neck. The coils of its snake-like body wound well past Matthew's feet, the creatures primitive appendages lining the coils at irregular intervals. Dr. King stared in horror at it for a moment—he'd only caught glimpses of it before, never with it fully out of the water. He'd been a good keeper.

A choked moan from Matthew jolted Dr. King back to awareness of the task he needed to complete. The man was still alive. For now.

Dr. King approached the creature with the crucible in hand, the mixture from another young boy who'd gotten the neck rash after spending too long by the river. As he approached, he removed the lid from the crucible and the odor caused the creature to pause its writhing.

But only for a moment. It seemed live prey was its preference to Dr. King's concoction.

Dr. King edged closer and closer until the scent of decaying fish was nearly overwhelming and the crucible could be poured directly onto the creature's cranial section. Dr. King paused for a moment, considering the damage he might do to Matthew, but then realized there would be no Matthew left if he didn't do something.

Dr. King poured the contents of the crucible in one motion, splattering the chunky, dark fluid across the creature and Matthew's neck. The creature let out a terrible sucking noise, loud as the misfiring of a car engine directly in one's ear. Unable to resist the concentrated nutrition, it detached itself from Matthew's neck and began rooting around in the fluids Dr. King had emptied.

Working quickly, Dr. King dragged Matthew's limp body from beneath the hulking mass of flesh. The creature turned at the commotion he caused and bared down on Dr. King. He pulled another crucible from his large coat pocket, flung a few drops at the creature, and then threw the crucible toward the pond. The creature made the loud sucking noise again, raining saponifying fluid across Dr. King and Matthew, then took off in the direction of the pond.

Dr. King jumped to his feet, throwing off his white coat before the lye-like fluid soaked through to his skin. He did his best for Matthew, but wasn't quite in time to prevent all the liquid from getting to him. Matthew moaned in pain. Dr. King decided it was a good sign that he could still moan.

From his pants pocket, Dr. King produced another set of latex gloves and with them retrieved a piece of cinnabar from his smoking white coat. In the distance, the sound of the sewage pond boiling gave him a measure of relief—the creature was contained. For now.

Working quickly, Dr. King dug the cinnabar into Matthew's neck sores, sticky black muck coming to the surface with each gouge. Matthew groaned and his eyes rolled back in his head, but he didn't flinch away.

When he'd finished his task, Matthew was alive, but breathing shallowly. Dr. King hauled his body into the backseat of Matthew's car and ran inside to the telegram. He sent a message to Ajax Smith, the father of one of his patients who he knew often made a habit of giving people rides to the big city hospital outside of town when there was something that couldn't be handled in Arkham. Dr. King had to stay behind in case the creature decided to leave the pond again.

Ajax, it's Bob King. Come quick.

Dr. King telegrammed.

Urgent hospital transport required.

Dr. King walked outside to sit with Matthew while he waited for Ajax Smith to arrive. He studied the pond from a distance—it was quiescent, as it should be. Dr. King narrowed his eyes in thought and then began collecting the cinnabar and fluids he'd removed from Matthew. The pond creature was still going to need to eat and Dr. King didn't want anything to go to waste.

Two months after the night that Matthew had delivered the final cease and desist letter, Dr. King received another letter from the Massachusetts State Board of Health.

To Whom it May Concern:

Effective immediately, this letter reinstates the sewage treatment privileges of the Arkham enterprise operated by one Robert King.

-Massachusetts State Board of Health

Dr. King folded the letter and put it into his desk. What people outside of Arkham told people inside Arkham to do was of no consequence to him. He'd continued to operate the sewage treatment pond—he knew Matthew wouldn't protest and that after his incident, the Board wouldn't be sending anyone in person until they'd forgotten the tale of what had happened that night.

Ajax Smith had given another patient of Dr. King's a ride to the big city hospital the week before and had inquired about Matthew's condition. The doctor had reported a guarded prognosis. Matthew had been in intensive care for over a month before he'd moved to a regular medical floor. The doctors had been puzzled as to what ailed him, but he'd slowly recovered with no memory of what had transpired the night of his injuries. According to Ajax, Matthew was finally scheduled to be released to a rehabilitation home after having refused several facilities due to their proximity to bodies of water.

Dr. King prepared another crucible and made his way to the pond, where he'd rebuilt his iron apparatus. It was feeding night—he didn't want his business partner to go hungry.

HIS TIME IS NIGH

DANIEL POWELL

Innsmouth Township Police Department

Missing Persons/Report Form

Case Number: 0100024

Date: June 14, 2024

Reporting Officer: Deputy Sebastian Moss

Incident Details:

On fourteenth June, 2024, at approximately 1600 hrs, I received a call from dispatch alerting me to a possible missing-person case in the vicinity of Tookland's Saloon, 1641 High Street, Innsmouth, Mass. After arriving at Tookland's at 1630 hrs., I observed a pair of young Caucasian subjects arguing with a crowd of agitated bystanders in the parking lot outside of the establishment.

Upon arrival, I attempted to defuse what appeared to be a tense situation. Subjects Wayne Francis (DOB 01-12-2003) and Alison Garcia (DOB 05-15-2003) immediately requested assistance in locating a missing person—one Jared "Red" Francis (DOB 10-22-2005).

Subjects Francis and Garcia appeared frantic, disheveled, and distraught, with Garcia visibly crying. Students from the University of Maine (both furnished university identification upon request) on a road tour of New England, subjects claimed that they walked into Innsmouth after experiencing a flat tire near the northern end of town.

Subjects walked to Tookland's in search of assistance, where they subsequently engaged with local citizens at around 1400 hrs.

According to witnesses Jocelyn Marsh and Jed Tookland—proprietor of the saloon—Garcia and the Francis brothers ingested large amounts of alcohol while attempting to arrange for vehicular assistance. At shortly before 1600, subjects Garcia and Francis claim the local patrons of Tookland's saloon provoked J. Francis into exploring a storage area in the basement of Tookland's Saloon.

Witnesses Marsh and Tookland contend that they actually did the opposite—that they in fact warned J. Francis not to explore the area in question. Upon further investigation, the room in question was empty (with the exception of ordinary metal shelving stocked with supplies for the bar and restaurant above) and showed no signs of human occupancy or possible through transit. The room has only the single doorway leading in and out, and there were no signs of a disturbance.

Efforts to locate J. Francis remain ongoing, although his belongings are accounted for in subjects' impounded vehicle, a 2016 Honda CRV, gray. This vehicle was located approximately five miles outside of town on Old Jacob's Walk.

Subjects Francis and Garcia were taken to the Gilman Hotel pending the outcome of further investigation, and law enforcement and volunteers from the communities of Arkham, Innsmouth, and Newburyport conducted extensive searches of the buildings, creeks, and marshes surrounding Tookland's Saloon for approximately three days.

The disappearance of J. Francis remains an open investigation, albeit one still shrouded in mystery. Investigators remain puzzled while trying to ascertain the meaning behind Garcia's repeated, frantic plea upon first contact in the parking lot of Tookland's Saloon: "There's a room beneath the room."

I kept the report, of course, and with the benefit of hindsight and the passage of time, I can actually admit to a grudging admiration for Deputy Moss's precise, sensible prose. The chronology of events in the report is accurate and dutifully recorded, although there was nothing precise and sensible at all about the day that we lost my little brother Red.

I don't venture into Innsmouth anymore. Before her involuntary committal to Spring Harbor Hospital in Southern Maine, Alison and I made occasional trips to Innsmouth to search for my brother. Alas, I haven't been back in almost three years, and I have no plans to step foot in that godforsaken place in whatever days I have left ahead of me.

Not after what I saw the last time.

While I haven't suffered to the extent that Ali has, I am by no means okay. I am writing this account from a shabby desk in my shabby room in the bowels of a place called Divinity House in Bangor—a decrepit halfway house for alcoholics a step away from hospice and reformed criminals a step away from re-entering society. My time here is approaching an end, and I have no place else to go. My family no longer supports me, and whatever friends I had back at the University of Maine have exhausted their patience and moved on with their own lives.

I fear I'll be living on the streets soon (viewed by society as just another disposable person that couldn't navigate the world—*sigh*), so I want to document what happened while I still have a roof over my head and writing supplies at my disposal.

Innsmouth isn't on the map, and we never expected to get waylaid there. While I've never been the best with directions (Ali used to joke that Lewis and Clark never would have left Missouri if I'd been on the navigation team), I *do* know that we were on a road heading south when we had the problems with the tire.

It had been such a grand idea—a two-week tour of rural New England with my kid brother and a girl that I loved enough to begin putting money by for a ring. Ali and I had just finished our third year at UM, and we were trying to convince Red to consider enrolling for the fall after he'd spent a few years after graduation spinning his wheels as a sous-chef in Boothbay Harbor.

We thought we had it all planned out, of course, and after a delightful evening in Newburyport, we set off for Rowley and some afternoon hiking in Willowdale State Forest. It wasn't long before we found ourselves on a mysterious and winding dirt road cutting through a dense wilderness in which the branches smacked against the windshield of our SUV. The GPS was useless, and we had trouble getting a signal on our phones. Ali pleaded with me to turn around multiple times. While I had no idea where I was going, I had a gut feeling that we were heading south, damn it, and we just had to keep pushing forward.

I mean, all roads have to lead somewhere, right?

It was slow-going, and Red was getting anxious about missing out on our time on the trails in Willowdale when we hit the spike in the road. It popped the tire like we'd hit a grenade, shredding the rubber and leaving the Honda sagging on its rim. Red did some exploring and discovered that it was a part from of an old rusted tiller that had been abandoned in the brush on the side of the road—although any notion of a successful agricultural concern in that dense swath of forest was way beyond me.

We searched in vain for the absent spare tire for about twenty minutes before concluding that our only option was walking out. We took as much water as we could carry and kept heading south, a sour mood permeating what had been a happy and optimistic trip up to that point.

It was still early in the day, but the weather was cool and the forest smelled of saltwater and decaying marine life. The sun had been bright and hot in Newburyport, but it was overcast and gloomy in that tract of wilderness.

We walked for more than an hour until the woods gave way to meadows and then yielded to marshland. Soon—and this was around 2:00 p.m., although it felt much later—we found ourselves on the outskirts of Innsmouth. A decaying wooden sign proclaimed *The Sea is Her Virtue* in faded cursive script beneath the town's name. Right next to it was some strange, cryptic emblem.

How can one describe the place?

Well, I compare it to this old woman that lived on our street when we were kids growing up in Farmington. Her name was Penny Pilkington, but we called her Penny the Hen. She lived by herself in this rambling Victorian at the end of the street, and the house and the yard were slowly falling into serious disrepair.

Penny scared us. She looked to be about a hundred years old back then, and she always walked into town wearing too much makeup and too many clothes—coats on top of coats, regardless of the weather— and always some audacious hat. When she stopped for a word with us on the street, there was usually lipstick smeared across her yellowing teeth.

But there was *something* there. Even I could see it—even as just some clueless kid. My friends made up stories about her. They spun yarns that she was a witch, and that she'd trapped a boy in her cellar many years ago and fed him chicken scraps that she bought on the cheap from Sal's Butcher Shop.

But I never uttered a bad word about her, and it's because you could *see*—under all those clothes and all that makeup—that she'd truly been something in her youth. She had an air about her, and you could tell she'd once been a striking woman. I asked my dad about her once, and he told me she'd been a pretty prominent movie star in the 1960s.

Innsmouth was like that, with all manner of stately buildings and impressive architecture, but also some serious underpinnings of dread, sorrow, and neglect. The whole place looked like it was slowly sliding toward the harbor, and we walked past dozens of abandoned buildings before finally stumbling upon Tookland's Saloon.

The big difference in my comparison was that Penny Pilkington just seemed lonely, while Innsmouth gave the impression that it didn't want to be found.

There weren't any dogs or squirrels running about the yards, or even much in the way of birds. It was quiet as a mausoleum, and maybe that's just what it is—a collection place for the dead and dying. Museums can be that way too, of course, but Innsmouth is no place to learn about the past.

Anyway, Tookland's was the first establishment that showed any signs of human habitation. It's a ramshackle bar that looks like an old barn from one angle and a lapsed church from another. I had the impression that the townsfolk had been adding to it, somehow, over the years, although the seams between any alterations to the structure weren't readily apparent. It sprang up out of the ground like some ancient, blighted toadstool on a bluff overlooking the harbor. We could hear the waves crashing on the shore below, and the place was bordered to the rear by a copse of gently waving evergreens.

Does it sound like I'm rambling? I apologize if I'm out over my skis here, but the big takeaway is that the whole place just seemed *wrong*. Lichen-crusted cedar shakes comprised a steep roof over a long, wide porch upon which a few rusting tables and chairs dotted the dusty cement floor.

A half-dozen vehicles—mostly trucks, coated with primer and rust—that were decades past their prime were parked haphazardly in the gravel lot. A few leaning outbuildings bordered the main structure, and someone had actually hitched a horse to one corner of the porch railing. The poor swayback swished its tail at us between lazy mouthfuls of the brown grass sprouting there along the railing.

But a thin line of smoke lazed from a chimney, and an old neon sign blinked *OPEN* in the front window.

"I don't like this," Alison warned when Red expressed his excitement at discovering signs of civilization. "There has to be a police station or an auto shop further into town."

"We've been walking for miles," Red countered, and I could tell that he was excited to use his fake ID. It had been a recent thing, that ID, and while none of us were big drinkers, the idea of a beer at the end of that long walk didn't sound terrible.

"I think he's right," I told her. "Based on what we've seen so far, this might be it, honey."

Even though I could tell she was worried (scared wasn't the right word —not just then), I could also see that she was tired and more than a little relieved that we could get off our feet.

We crunched down that gravel drive and right into something that is hard to faithfully portray. Tookland's Saloon gives the impression of being large from the outside—a cavernous place with high ceilings. The opposite was true, however, and we opened the door and stepped into a foyer with a deserted hosting stand and low-slung, hardwood ceilings. There was about an inch of tobacco smoke hovering along the ceiling, and a little wooden sign with an arrow and the simple directive PROCEED hung on the stand with frayed twine.

And proceed we did—navigating a narrow hallway filled with all manner of black-and-white portraits of long-dead fisherman displaying their catches. There was an image of a gangly elderly woman with thick-framed glasses standing proudly next to dozens of the ugliest fish

I'd ever seen—fat, bulbous things dangling from a metal bar. Red grabbed my arm before we walked into the public house proper.

"Get a load of this," he whispered, gesturing at a sepia daguerreotype of a bug-eyed, balding man in a suit that had to date back to the Victorian Era.

The image gave me pause, and I felt a cool breath at the nape of my neck. In retrospect, that was our chance. That was the moment when I wish we'd just cut bait and retraced our steps down that long, narrow hallway.

And yet, I don't know if it would have made any difference. When I look back on that day, there's this ineffable notion of predestination that clouds my memory. Perhaps we could have simply turned and walked away, but something in my gut tells me they would have found us in the end.

When we stepped into the bar, it was like they were already expecting us. There were more than a dozen of them, all dressed up in the middle of June in thick peacoats and woolen vests. The women wore petticoats and the men sported brown and gray flat caps. It was like walking into a Depression-era soup kitchen, only these folks were smoking and drinking and staring at us with the kind of subtle intensity that would make the puppies squirm at your local pet store.

"Hi!" Alison said brightly in the sudden stillness of the room, and my heart broke a little in that moment, for I knew that her first response when she was frightened was to smile and deflect.

Her greeting had the desired effect, however, and the room broke out into raucous laughter.

"Hi yerself, missy!" an old woman cackled from the bar, sitting over two fingers of dark brown liquid in a highball glass. This was followed by a parroting, mocking chorus: "Hi!" "Hi!" "Hi!"

They were having a grand old time at our expense, except for one pale, lanky fellow in the corner who only stared at the ceiling. He simply didn't move, and I did a double-take when I thought I saw something squirming at the place where his shirt collar touched his neck.

"Come in, come in!" a gnarled old man said, stepping around from behind the bar. He made a beckoning motion with his hand. "We don't bite, young folks. Have a sit and rest a spell. Welcome to Tookland's."

His welcome seemed to put the place at ease, and they returned to their conversations. I traded glances with Red. Grinning, he gently nodded.

There were plenty of empty seats at the bar, and we stowed our packs beneath our stools and bellied up. The woman with the highball studied us with unblinking focus.

Her eyes seemed off. I know now that's what they call "the Innsmouth look," but it was my first real exposure to it and I couldn't help but think about all of those thyroid eye commercials that played on a loop during the Red Sox games we used to watch on NESN.

The conversational din was comforting, and I studied the place for the first time in greater detail. It was (surprise, surprise) dank and gloomy. There were windows, but they were crusted with salt and grime. A thin, gray light permeated the space, the tobacco smoke a hovering blue rim along the low ceilings.

The room was cool and a fire crackled in the hearth on the ocean-facing side of the room, summer be damned.

"What'll ye have?" he said while offering his hand. "Jed Tookland. This is my place, and my pappy's before me, and his pappy's before him."

We shook, and Red ordered a Guinness.

"Afraid we only have the local. Dark, ye want? Got some here."

"Dark beer would be great," Red replied, barely concealing his smirk. The awkward moment had passed, and I could see he was warming to the place. We ordered the same, and Tookland stepped behind the bar to pull our beers from an ivory tap. That struck me—none of the taps or the bottles on the shelves bore mainstream labels.

Ornate wooden carvings of monstrous creatures—some resembling leaping frogs, others like eels striding ominously on human legs—adorned the bar, and a meticulous wooden model of a large ship took pride of place inside of a dusty glass bottle.

The Sumatra Queen, read a plaque at the base of the model.

Tookland's is an odd place, to be sure, but the ale was delicious and we clinked glasses and huddled over our predicament.

"We can just ask Mr. Tookland," Ali said. "He seems to have his finger on the pulse of things. Maybe we can get back on the road before sundown."

"You saw that thing, Ali," Red replied. "We're not talking a simple repair here. And I can't imagine what it'll cost to get a tow truck up that road. We're going to need a new tire."

The reality that our budget was in serious trouble was enough of a downer to order another round immediately after we'd finished our beers. I was feeling warm in my stomach and chest, and the tips of my fingers tingled. The ale had bite, and we were pretty content to simply rest for a moment while we licked our proverbial wounds.

"Car trouble?" the old woman asked. She had thick, owlish eyebrows. "I don't mean to intrude, but I couldn't help overhearing your conference, there."

We'd barely spoken above a whisper.

"We had a flat tire a few miles north of here. Car's on the side of an old dirt road, deep in the woods," I replied.

"Old Jacob's Walk," she said, smiling and nodding. "It's a good thing that you got in when you did. Those woods are haunted, ayuh."

It was so matter of fact, we were too stunned to offer a reply. "Old Jacob Allen—son of Zadok hisself—haunts that place," she continued. "Ye did right coming here, children. Ye did damned right."

She spun in her chair to face the rest of the bar and loosed a shrill whistle. "Listen up! These kids threw a tire up Old Jacob's Walk. They need help."

This prompted a renewed murmur, and I remember chuckling to myself when a stout woman in a billowy dress buttoned to her neck tossed a pinch of salt over her shoulder. I'd heard of people doing that, but I'd surely never seen it in person.

A lanky fellow with an Adam's apple that looked like he'd swallowed a misshapen gourd sauntered over to the bar. "Got us a shop in Innsmouth. We can get you on your feet again, but might take some time. Daylight's wasting, and won't many go into those woods come nightfall."

"And if we left now?" Red said, his eyes shining with drink. My brother could handle his alcohol, but his cheeks were flushed, that flaming thatch of thick red hair of his making him seem all the more excited. "Could we turn it around in a few hours? It's still only a little after 3:00."

The man hemmed and hawed for a moment, and then the old lady sprang from her stool and offered a gnarled hand. "Where are our manners? I'm Jocelyn Marsh. This is Elliot Croom, and his uncle runs the shop. We aim to help those in need in our neck of the woods, ayuh. Course we do, but it gets late early here in Innsmouth, don't it Elly?"

This drew another round of laughter from the patrons seated around us, and it occurred to me then that they'd crept in on us. They were sitting closer—everyone except the loner staring at the ceiling. I remember looking to the barkeep in that moment, and Jed Tookland just studied us from behind the bar, his arms crossed over his chest like he was about to officiate a wrestling match.

"Maybe you can do us a favor, and we'll pay it back in kind?" Marsh said, a little smile there on her deeply wrinkled face. Her eyes were like a pair of big brown buttons behind those thick lenses. "A little *quid pro quo*, so to speak?"

"What do you need?" Red replied immediately. He was getting agitated, and Ali just watched us from behind that tankard of ale. She was still smiling, but there was no warmth in it.

"Just go down yonder to the cellar and fetch us some bottles," Tookland said, his deep voice cutting through the suddenly quiet room like the beam of a lighthouse through a midnight fog. "Won't take but five minutes."

This seemed to spark something in the locals, and they all pitched in with their agreement. Elliot's head bobbed, and he even slapped my brother on the shoulder, as if to say *Ain't nothing to it, bub. Just five minutes.*

"I don't think so," I replied. "Look, we don't kn—."

"Nonsense," the old woman cut in. "You can see I need a refill, and the young man looks capable. Strapping, even. Just tote a case of the Innsmouth Strong topside and we'll call Bert Croom on Jed's phone in the back. Have you back on yer way before nightfall."

"If it's all the same to you, we'd rather just pay our tab. There has to be a place here in town where we can stay the night, and we'll visit Mr. Croom's shop in the morning. Be plenty of time to make the repair," I said, fishing for my wallet.

"Why can't *you* do it?" Red said, nodding at Jed Tookland. "It's your bar. Why do you need me?"

"My back," the old barkeep replied immediately. He touched his lumbar and winced. "Hasn't been right in weeks. It's just an old root cellar, anyway. What…are you scared?"

And that's when our fate was sealed. My brother was a lot of things (intelligent, kind, and charismatic among them, which is why this has all been so particularly difficult), but afraid was never one of them. That was all it took to get his dander up, and I knew in that moment that Red was going to be doing an errand for these strange people in that strange place.

Tookland's cronies responded to his challenge with laughter and gentle chiding, and that's when Red asked the perfect question: "Should I be?"

A hush fell over the place, and Tookland's smile turned into a frown. "Well, it's dark," he admitted. "It's old and dark, and there might be some critters down there. Rats and such. Other than that, it's just a root cellar."

"Excuse me," Ali interjected. She motioned toward the man staring at the ceiling. "I have to ask—is he okay?"

If he'd moved in the hour we'd sat at the bar, I missed it. The room went quiet, and it was the first thing she'd said in a long time. "He— um…" she stuttered. "He's been like that for a while."

"Oh, that's just Ephram," Marsh replied, with a dismissive wave. "Don't worry about him. His time is nigh."

You could have heard a baby sigh, the room got so quiet. Red and Ali and I just sat and watched that curious man staring at the ceiling, and that's when my brother must have decided it was time to go. And if he had to do these folks a favor (and especially if they were questioning his courage) to make it happen, then that's just what he would do.

He slapped the bar. "Show me the way," he said, and a triumphant cry went up from the locals.

"Follow me," Tookland said, gesturing around the edge of the bar. We stood and walked over there, and he led us through a warren of narrow halls. The locals followed, keeping their distance.

We passed a great many more of those strange antiquated photographs, and then we went down some rickety old steps and found ourselves in a dim basement filled with all manner of furniture shrouded in dust covers. The three of us activated the flashlights on our phones (service remained nonexistent) and followed Tookland to a great wooden door hewn into the stone masonry of the place's foundation. It had thick iron hinges and was bolted with a fat padlock.

"You worried about thieves?" Red remarked as Tookland worked the lock from a keyring on a string connected to his pants loop.

"The Innsmouth Strong is mighty popular," he said, his voice hushed.

I stood nearest him, and for the first time I noticed that he had an odd smell about him. It was dank—musty. Upon reflection, I swear that what I smelled on the old man was fear.

He opened the door and took a step back, and we followed suit. All of us but Red, who was in his element. He grinned at me and Ali and tipped us a wink. *I got this*, that grin said. He'd said he wasn't scared, and damned if he didn't plunge straight ahead and into the darkness.

"Careful, now," Tookland called. "Be a few steps there. Boxes are along the back wall. One case will do, young man."

I couldn't see my brother, but from where I stood I could see his light bobbing down the stairs and briefly flashing about the room. "I don't see it," he called, and his voice echoed. I'll never forget that—it echoed, from not more than ten or twenty feet away.

"Just keep going," Tookland said, taking another step back. "There on the back wall…"

And that's when my brother screamed.

There was an audible thump—like a sack of flour dropped from a considerable height—and I heard him shouting in that murky place while a wet, fleshy sound swallowed his cries. It was like the sound a tenderizer makes when it hits a raw steak, and then my brother was silent.

"Red!" I screamed. "Red, are you okay?"

Ali was hysterical, and I saw her frantically trying to dial 911. I screamed again and again after my brother, and then Tookland—now noticeably relieved—stepped forward and looked into the cellar. "Young man?" he called, only it was all for show.

Red was gone. I know that now.

Ali and I forced our way past him and stood at the edge of the stairs, and that's when we saw it. It wasn't a cellar, but more of a dungeon—a dank stone room illuminated by some eerie green light that seemed to be emanating from the moss covering the walls. Something enormous slithered in the dark, and Ali screamed.

We called for him, but Red never responded. Ali screamed herself hoarse, and then she just seemed to shut down. She's never been the same since seeing the chamber beneath Tookland's Saloon, and I never will be either.

After a time, I insisted that we head upstairs to call the authorities. Tookland agreed, and we used the phone in his office. The rest? Well, the rest is in that police report.

But there *was* something else that was awfully peculiar. When we returned to the pub, the locals were gathered around that inexplicable, gawking man that had only looked to the ceiling since we'd made our entrance.

Ephram.

He'd recovered his wits some, and the townspeople crowded around him, slapping him on the back and talking to him like he'd survived triple-bypass surgery or something. He seemed like a new man.

And in the end, I guess that's just what he was.

You see, I mentioned that we'd returned to Innsmouth while looking for my brother. You remember that part, right? Well, on our last trip, we stumbled across old Ephram. When we'd first encountered him that day in Tookland's Saloon, he'd been sallow and gaunt, with nothing more than a few straggling, gray hairs falling from his bullet-shaped skull. His skin had bunched in piles of jowly flesh at the base of his neck. He'd seemed catatonic.

But on our last trip, we ran into him on High Street. He was making his way by foot to the same old pub where we'd lost our brother.

Only this time, he was hale and hearty, with a thick head of bright orange hair. That jowly neck was concealed beneath the layers of a woolen scarf, but he smiled at us and tipped his flat cap, a vaguely familiar twinkle in his eyes.

This happened years ago, and I'm no closer now to understanding the ways and rituals of that strange place and the people that call it home. I only know that Ali isn't speaking anymore, I'll soon be living on the streets, and my brother is gone.

But they have their ways, and they keep their secrets close to the vest. When we tried to show Deputy Moss the place where my brother disappeared, it was nothing more than a simple pantry, but I think Ali said it best—*There's a room beneath the room.*

And whatever lives there, it serves its sinful, curative purpose for the people of Innsmouth.

WHAT HAPPENED IN ROOM 201

WILLOW REDD

It was 3am when the call came through. Summer in Arkham was hot and muggy and Toma Kent's sleep was troubled even before she looked at the caller ID to see Arkham Hospital displayed. She was up and moving before the nurse told her why she was calling.

Nurse Richter hated working 3rd shift at the hospital. It was always the weirdos that came in this time of night. So far there was a whole cult in the burn unit after an accident with some anointed oil and a candle. Maybe next time they'd spend the extra money on real robes instead of cheap costumes that went up like flash paper. The ones that survived, anyway.

There was the self-inflicted stabbing currently in the operating room. The large ceremonial dagger the fool used on himself punctured a bile duct and caused the patient such pain that he started screaming. Responders who brought the guy in said the neighbors called it in. By the time they wheeled him in on their gurney, they'd pumped him full of morphine just to shut him up. He likely wouldn't survive the night. Lord knows what he was trying to do.

Then there was the patient in Room 201.

She'd come into the emergency room 4 hours ago complaining of abdominal pains and sweating buckets. At first, Dr. Merrick assumed the sweat was from the heat, but then he realized how cold and clammy she felt. She doubled over during his initial examination and released a guttural, otherworldly howl that resonated through the entire building and passed out. The usual hustle and bustle of the emergency room was silenced by that howl. She was admitted immediately. Dr. Merrick, his eyes wild, ordered Nurse Richter to stand watch and call him immediately if the patient's condition changed. He told her he had some research to do and rushed off.

The poor girl had returned to consciousness long enough to ask the nurse to call someone. "Toma," she breathed. "Call Toma," she fumbled her unlocked phone into Richter's hand with a name and phone number on it. After making sure the girl was comfortable in the bed, she made the call.

About twenty minutes later, a commotion up front was Nurse Richter's first inkling that Toma might have arrived.

"I said my name is Toma Kent and *you* called *me*! Where's Samantha? Why the hell won't any of you assholes tell me where she is?"

Nurse Richter approaches calmly and makes eye contact with Mary at the desk. The look said: "I got this."

"Miss Kent?"

"*What?*"

Richter put her hands up in an effort to calm the newcomer. "I'm Nurse Richter. I called you. Please come with me. I'll take you to Samantha."

Still flustered and breathing heavily, Toma's shoulders slump as she nods. Nurse Richter gently takes her arm and begins walking her to Room 201.

Once she sees her friend, Toma rushes to Samantha's side. She grabs the poor girl's hand and places her other on Samantha's forehead. Samantha's skin feels rubbery to the touch and has a bluish pallor.

"What's happened to her?" Toma asks Nurse Richter.

"We were hoping you could tell us. She's been mostly unconscious since she came in."

"I don't... what... I mean... she... she was spending a lot of time in the library. I... I think she was reading that book..."

"Which book?" Nurse Richter asked dreading the answer.

"*That* book," Toma replied as she made eye contact with the nurse.

"Shit." Nurse Richter immediately moves to a phone along the wall, punches in a number, and speaks to the whole hospital. Her voice echoes through the hall outside. "Code Damascus, Room 201. Repeat: Code Damascus, Room 201."

The already hectic activity in the emergency room rises to a frantic panic as people begin to rush around at Nurse Richter's words. Toma, already confused, is now trying to stave off a rising panic.

"What does that mean?" she almost screeches towards the nurse.

Richter puts a comforting hand on Toma's upper arm. "We've dealt with things like this before, dear. Just let us work." She gently pushes Toma to the side as she says this.

Almost on cue, Dr. Merrick comes running into the room trailed by two orderlies. He grabs a pair of gloves from a dispenser along the wall and quickly puts them on. "A Code Damascus, Nurse?"

"It appears so, Doctor."

"Shit." he walks up to Toma, looks her in the eye, and says, "Tell me exactly what she was trying to do."

Toma shrugs, her eyes wild. "I - I - I don't know. She's been distant since..." Her whole upper body slumps with sudden realization.

"Since?"

"Since she lost her sister three weeks ago."

"Dead?"

She nods. "Drunk driver."

Dr. Merrick puts his hand to his chin and strokes it in thought.

As he considers what to do next, a noise comes from Samantha, an inhuman, guttural sound not unlike a crocodile's growl. Everyone turns to her to see her sitting up in bed staring at them. Her face now has a bluish pallor and is twisted into a hideous snarl. The whites of her eyes have turned a sickly yellow.

She opens her mouth wide, wider than natural, and fires a stream of inky black ichor towards the doctor and her friend. Toma is able to get out of the way, but Dr. Merrick isn't quite so lucky. The spray hits him square in the chest, knocking him back against the wall.

Once the spray stops, Samantha falls back onto the bed, unconscious again. The blue, spotted appearance of her face remains and Toma notices a series of ring-like marks along the girl's arm.

Toma, trying her best to remain calm, asks Dr. Merrick, "What's happening to her, Doctor?"

He grabs a towel from the bathroom and tries to wipe the worst of the ichor from his coat and shirt and sighs. "If I had to guess, based on what you've told me, what we're seeing, and my previous dealings with these things...I'd say she was trying to bring her sister back."

"Is that even possible?"

"Not that I've ever seen, but the people who become obsessed with that book seem to think things like that are."

Toma tries to process this. "Okay...I guess that makes sense. They were exceptionally close and she was absolutely broken after the funeral. But that still doesn't explain..." she gestures to Samantha on the hospital bed, "*this!*"

The doctor sighs again as he gives up on removing the rest of the sticky ichor and drops the towel into a nearby medical waste bin along with the now filthy nitrile gloves he was wearing." I think she was partially successful. She brought *something* back, but it definitely wasn't her sister."

A creeping dread crawls up Toma's spine. From somewhere near the door, Nurse Richter speaks up. "So...what *did* she bring back?"

The doctor takes off his glasses and checks them for splatter. "I don't know, but it can't be good."

"No shit," Toma adds quietly fighting back a dark chuckle as she again looks at Samantha's arm. The marks look more prominent than before, a line of ring-like welts raising up all along it from wrist to shoulder.

An earth-shattering BOOM rocks the room. It seems to come from everywhere and rattles everything. It might have been mistaken for thunder and quickly forgotten if it hadn't been for what happened next.

Samantha's unconscious body begins to shudder as soon as the "thunder" hits, causing the entire bed to shake and rattle. Toma is so scared by this that she jumps and lets out a yelp, her hand raising to cover her mouth. She backs away.

Dr. Merrick jumps to action as the shuddering threatens to become more violent flailing.

"Nurse! The restraints!" He and Nurse Richter rush to the bed, one on each side, and begin to pull straps from along the corners of the bed frame. They secure Samantha's arms and legs to the bed using these restraints. Nurse Richter then reaches across the girl's head and pulls a single padded leather strap across it, keeping her from wrenching her neck while convulsing.

The moment the last strap is secured, Samantha stops shuddering and is again still. However, the guttural growl once more starts up very deep in the girl's throat. Nurse Richter puts her hand on Samantha's forehead only to be met with a sizzle as her hand is burned by an intense heat.

The nurse screams, peeling her hand away, but unfortunately leaving the skin of her palm behind. Dr. Merrick rushes to her side and calls for an orderly as he moves her to the door. One of the men waiting outside steps in, takes the nurse from Dr. Merrick, and rushes her out to care for her hand.

The smell of burning flesh hangs in the air as the skin sticking to Samantha's forehead continues to cook away from the intense heat.

Tom covers her nose as the smell begins to get to her. She feels the build up of saliva at the back of her throat as the urge to throw up increases.

"Oh God."

Dr. Merrick steps out to check on Nurse Richter, and not that he would ever tell Toma, but also in order to get some fresh air. Toma takes several gulps to keep the bile down as she stares at her friend. Her eyes grow wide as she sees Samantha's stomach begin to expand as it fills with...something. Within seconds, Samantha looks like she is nine month's pregnant... with twins.

"*Doctor!*" she screams, her voice scratchy and hoarse from the effort.

He returns at a run, pulled by the volume of Toma's cry. He looks to her, then follows her terrifyingly wide eyes and is stopped by the sudden, inexplicable change to his patient on the bed.

"Good heavens." After a long pause, he swallows heavily and makes his way to Samantha. He palpates the girl's belly, inhales sharply, and steps back.

Dr. Merrick moves to the wall-mounted phone. He punches in the same combination of numbers Nurse Richter and says, "Code Whateley, Room 201. I repeat, a Code Whateley in Room 201."

A silence hangs as he stands there staring at Samantha's rounded belly, phone in hand. An alarm sounds. Its shrill ring resonates throughout the whole building. Toma's hands cover her ears as the alarm blares. She crouches into the corner of the room.

Over the din, a voice screams out of the receiver hanging loosely in Dr. Merrick's hand. After a moment, he shakes his head and puts the phone back to his ear. "Say again," he says into the mouthpiece as he cups his other ear from the noise. Listening to what the person on the other end of the line says, he glances down at Toma, who now looks up at him confused and terrified. He turns from her and whispers, "Yes. Send a Burn Team to Room 201. Tell them to stay outside."

Toma starts to ask what the doctor is saying, knowing he is keeping something from her, when a horrible screeching sound comes from the direction of the hospital bed. She and Dr. Merrick turn towards Samantha. Her visage has turned from simply concerning to absolutely horrifying.

The thing on the bed is no longer the human form of Samantha. In her place is a large, bulging, rubbery blue orb where her belly was with a series of tentacles waving around it. They appear to be where the poor girl's limbs used to be. It flails there screeching nonstop.

Dr. Merrick turns back to the phone and screams, "Turn off that damned claxon now!"

A second later, the alarm dies. The screeching fades out soon after. Breathing hard, Dr. Merrick turns back to the bed, unclear exactly what he will see. The form on the bed has returned to its human shape. Mostly.

The blue, rubbery texture has now covered every inch of her visible skin. Her belly is still very large and much extended. Her arms and legs are back to being arms and legs, but her right arm now comes to a point more like a tentacle. There is no longer a hand to speak of.

Turning to check on Toma, the doctor sees her rocking back and forth on the floor, her knees tucked under her chin, her eyes as wide as saucers. It is hard to hear, but she is murmuring something low under her breath. As he leans in to check on her, he can just make out, "This isn't real. This isn't real. This isn't real. Thisisntreal. Thisisntreal..." it fades out into a indecipherable muttering.

Nurse Richter returns to the room with her hand bandaged, looking a little more disheveled than she was before. The orderly who took her away is with her. She pats him on the arm and tells him to stay by the door. The doctor motions for the nurse to help him with Toma. She joins him and kneels beside him on the floor before the traumatized girl.

Nurse Richter sticks her unbandaged hand out towards Toma. "Come along, dear. Let's go get you some air." Now completely out of it, Toma automatically begins to take the nurse's hand when a hoarse voice calls to her from the bed.

"Toma? Toma, are you there?"

All three turn towards Samantha. Toma snaps out of her daze and rushes past the doctor and the nurse to be at her friend's side.

"Sam? How are you feeling?" Toma reaches for Samantha's hand only to be met with a rubbery tentacle. She tries with all her might not to recoil as the end of the tentacle wraps tightly around her hand.

"I feel like shit," she says through a hoarse chuckle that turns into a cough.

Toma puts her free hand on Samantha's forehead, completely forgetting what happened to Nurse Richter's hand just moments ago. It is ice cold. She smiles awkwardly at her friend and tells her, "That's okay. You look like shit, too."

Samantha tries to laugh, but can only cough instead. After it passes, she looks up at her friend. "I'm so sorry, Toma. I should have listened to you."

A tear forms in Toma's eye as she fights to keep the smile on her face. "Yeah," her voice catches. "You really should have."

"Jerk," Samantha coughs out.

"Asshole," Toma returns, the tears now falling freely down her cheek.

The tentacle grips Toma's hand tighter. "It's coming, Toma. It's coming." Samantha coughs a few more times, then the coughing becomes a sigh, then a rattle. With a final breath, she's gone.

Toma weeps openly, still holding on to Samantha's tentacle. After a moment, it begins to tighten even more around her hand, crushing it. Then, the crocodilian growl returns. She tries to pull her hand out of the tentacle's grasp.

Nurse Richter, seeing what is happening; rushes to the girl's side and tries to help her free her trapped hand. It takes a great deal of effort for both of them, but they eventually break Toma's hand free.

Looking at the hand, the nurse immediately knows it is broken. There is also a red sucker mark along the back of it. She tucks it against Toma's body and asks her to hold it there. Nurse Richter escorts Toma from the room to see to her had when the screeching comes from the thing in the bed once more. Toma freezes in place and, though a part of her wants only to flee, turns back to the body of her friend.

What she sees will stay with her for the rest of her days. What was her friend Samantha's belly has swelled to an even greater size, raising above every head in the room. Her former limbs are now all tentacles, and several more have appeared around the bulbous mass, all flailing wildly. The screeching continues even though there is no longer a discernible mouth.

On instinct, Nurse Richter steps between Toma and the wild, flailing thing on the bed. She stares at it in absolute horror, noticing a tear beginning to form down the center of its mass. Seeing this, she turns back to Toma and starts to push her from the room. Toma remains frozen for a moment, eyes wide in terror, until she hears Richter screaming, 'Move, girl! Move!"

Dr. Merrick, also transfixed by this final inhuman transformation, is brought back to his senses by Nurse Richter's screams. He to sees the widening tear, a hideous gaping maw, and joins her in pushing Toma out of the room to safety. "Get her out of here. Now!"

Once in the hallway, Merrick pushes the nurse and Toma to one side, turns to the Burn Team currently standing against the wall, and says, "Now! Inside! Do it now!" before jumping out of their way to allow entrance to the room.

The Burn Team, a group of four men in flame resistant suits, two with flamethrowers and two with fire extinguishers, rush into Room 201. They see the thing on the bed and pause at the sight. The widening maw still growing and something beginning to move within it. Dr. Merrick pokes his head in, sees their fear, and screams again, "Now! Burn it!"

This spurs the men to action and the two wielding flamethrowers step forth and begin to burn the thing in the bed. The two men with fire extinguishers move around the bed, focusing on any flames that catch beyond it. The screeching raises to a horrifying pitch. The smell is horrible.

Meanwhile, Nurse Richter moves through the people milling around in curiosity and fear around Room 201. She maneuvers Toma into a quiet corner and sits her down in a chair. She slumps down next to the girl and exhales the breath she has been holding.

After a moment's pause in which she stares blankly ahead, Toma leans forward, puts her head in her hands, and begins to cry in earnest. The tension and horror of the night finally easing enough for her to truly feel everything that has been bubbling up inside her.

Nurse Richter absently puts her hand on Toma's back and begins to rub. It is a gesture of comfort that she doesn't even have to think about anymore, it just comes to her naturally. She sits back in her chair and again thinks about how much she hates working 3rd shift at Arkham Hospital as the roar of flamethrowers and hiss of extinguishers continue around the corner in Room 201.

MIDNIGHT AT THE DEPARTMENT OF HORRORS

TIM O'NEAL

B *lerrp. Blerrp.*

I answer the ringing office phone in the saccharine voice I've used for the past thirty-five years. "Hello and thank you for calling the Arkham County Department of Horrors, Susan speaking. How may I help you?"

"Hi, yes. I have a problem," the woman caller said.

Yeah? I bet…

"What can I do for you, ma'am?"

"Uh, there's a headless tiger in dirty pink pajamas stalking around my house." The caller sobbed. "And I think it just ate my cat, Sprinkles."

I suppress a chuckle. Working here has given me a dark sense of humor.

I slurp my Diet Pepsi. "Mm-hmm. I see. That's too bad."

"Guh, can you hurry? The tiger-thing won't let me leave for work."

I swallow another rogue chuckle at this visual. "That sounds quite alarming, ma'am. Unfortunately, I'm afraid all our responders are busy, but I'll send help once they're available."

I pause and wait, because this is where, after thirty-plus years of experience, I've learned the callers will say something mean. Sure enough, upon learning that she wasn't my highest priority, the women's tone becomes waspish.

"Well, can you step on it?" she whines. "I know you County workers sit on your asses all day and never do anything. You're a living waste of tax dollars, you, you high school flunky!"

I smirk. Since the callers already believe that myth, I do my best to perpetuate the stereotype for them.

It seems only fair.

With years of practice, I keep my tone professional. "I understand your feelings, ma'am. I'll let the responders know as soon as they're available. Have yourself a nice day."

Without waiting for her curt reply, I note the caller's address and replace the old-fashioned phone with its long curled gray cord back into its cradle. It's a relic from the early Eighties. A lot of the stuff in my office is from previous eras. I lean back in my threadbare chair. It's not comfortable, but it might've once been ergonomic during the Nixon Administration.

My hands fold over my ample belly and I kick my feet up for a nap.

I'm not in a hurry to help the rude caller. Why should I? Today's my last day of work. I'm the only night dispatcher for the Department. Anytime someone calls to report a loose Horror they need removed, they speak to me. Thus, I get *all* the crazies, all the time.

At the prospect of finishing with them—forever—something flaps its dark wings within my belly. My pencil eraser jitters against the desk, partly in excitement for my retirement, and partly because tonight I have a Big Decision to make.

I've been under-appreciated my entire career. No promotion, no bonus, no plastic award for exemplary service.

Nothing

I promised myself I'd give the County until midnight on my last day to recognize my contributions. And if they don't, well, let's just say I have a cosmically dreadful surprise planned.

———

L onely seconds pass. The final hours of my employment creep by.

I sit alone in my gray cubicle in a gray building with stained gray carpet and gray cinderblock walls. Soulless fluorescent lighting spills down on me as it has for decades. The stale air smells of paper, burnt coffee, and the moldy water-stained ceiling tiles. Oh, and the droppings of all the immortal Horrors, living in their cages.

Ah, yes. My sweet little charges. They encompass all manner of nightmares. I have glaring orb-eyed six-armed toads, growling shadow monsters, babbling ragdolls with mismatched eyes. A few years back, technicians bagged Dagon and we now keep him in a giant steel-meshed aquarium. Yes, my menagerie of monsters contains thousands of others that the DoH has recaptured over the hundred years of its existence.

All the Horrors that fill the cages form a living labyrinth in the warehouse extending beyond my lonely cubicle. I hear them constantly —*have* heard them for the past thirty-five years. They moan, wail, cry, shriek, curse, groan, rattle, cluck, bleat, and click without ceasing. That cacophony of imprisoned Horrors colors my every working night and continues into my sleep. But County management won't let me play the radio to drown them out, arguing that I need to be attentive in case anything should happen.

"Situational awareness, Susan," Jenny in HR will say after dismissing my request. Again. "Do you need to rewatch the County Safety training video, hon?"

To maximize my workplace discomfort, there're no windows in the whole building—some policy about not wanting the public to see the Horrors we keep here. A memorandum when I started explained it would frighten civilians too much. It's the same reason the government don't allow tourists in Area 51.

Who-ee! If John Q Public could see the eldritch critters I have here…

I get the no-windows rule, but I'm also not allowed to keep photos or personal effects about my gunmetal gray desk. My cubicle is as austere as a prison cell because the Horrors might get ideas. Thirty-five years and I still have a desk as bare as the day I began.

Instead, to pass the time, I started conversing with the Horrors. Getting to know them. It was the start of my defiance toward my employer since the only splash of color they allowed me to brighten my cubicle was a calendar of tropical places. Places without extraditions treaties.

Like an unexpected belch, a stray giggle escapes my lips. I cover my mouth with my hand and glance around.

Did anyone hear that? Can't risk getting caught now, can I?

I'm so close, so very close…

But there's no one around. It's almost midnight. Just me and all my caged Horrors. I still have my Big Decision to make, after all. I check my county email for any sign of appreciation or acknowledgement.

Still nothing.

I shrug. Oh well. It doesn't surprise me. Arkham County has a long habit of mistreating and ignoring its 'highly valued' employees.

Yes, year after endless year, I've sat alone in this great warehouse and, other than the immortal Horrors, it's just me and the rows of gray metal filing cabinets that document the thousands of recaptures since I took over this department from my predecessor Arthur Goodwin.

Now, is that a diehard county employee name or what?

Arthur was a buck-toothed comb-over sort of a man whose fashion choices leaned toward horned-rim glasses, tweed, and suspenders. I suspect he *relished* playing up the stereotype of frumpy county employee. A vomit-inducing do-gooder, he never missed work and could inflame one's nerves even in total silence. I met him once and that meeting colored my thirty-five-year dislike for the man. Naturally, for the duration of my career, county Admin have compared me to him.

They'll throw jabs like "Well, Arthur never did it *that* way."

Or, "Can you do it *this* way? Arthur used to always do it *this* way when he was here."

It drives me nuts, sure, but this isn't the kind of job I could easily leave. I signed a lifetime contract and I'm expected to be at my desk every work-day except Christmas and Fourth of July. Sure, I accrue sick time that I can only use when I'm deathly ill. And even then, Jenny in HR puts snide notes in my permanent employee file.

Thirty-five years without a single vacation has been terrific for my mental health.

I turn back to my computer. It's an enormous and ancient Windows '98 processor. The monitor is a beige plastic monster propped up beside the equally huge tower. It's so clunky, it doesn't even have solitaire installed. It barely has a dial-up internet connection, allowing me enough connectivity to access our informatics program, DHRMIS, the Department of Horror Messaging & Information System, and nothing else.

The joke goes: you gotta have a thick ol' DHRMIS to work for the public of Arkham County.

Har har har.

Isn't that just hilarious?

This software is where I document each caller's complaint. It interfaces with the overworked responders who go and mop up the rogue Horrors. DHRMIS is a pre-DOS dinosaur that employs a black backdrop and chunky, pixelated, bright-green letters. They're absolute murder on the eyes after a quarter hour.

Imagine looking at it for ten hours a day for thirty-five years...

The program's glowing green cursor blinks at me like a black cat's eye. Tapping F-11 advances the system through its black-and-green menu. I can't go backward, so if I miss my choice the first time, I've gotta go back through the hundreds of pages again.

Believe me, atop the acerbic customer complaints, this software has played no small part in my overall job dissatisfaction. It often makes me want to hurt someone. Or several someone's. It's like the technological form of Y'Golonac, God of Depravity and Perversion—existing solely to cause humans misery and pain.

But over the years, I've had ample time to explore all those menu pathways. I know them as well as I know the federal statutes for murder in the first degree or the milage to the closest country without extradition. Within that labyrinth of DHRMIS pages, there are options to create new reports, view archived files, or read notes from my counterparts in counties across New England who also use the program. Almost all the comments are commiserations about experiences with rude callers.

A few DHRMIS users respond to these with jest, but I stopped replying since they didn't understand *my* kind of humor. I guess they can't appreciate jokes about chaos and murder. Nope, I learned that one the hard way back in the Nineties. Ever since, I've retreated into my own mind and keep my dark quips to myself.

It's safer that way.

Most of DHRMIS is meaningless crap that should've got an overhaul twenty-plus years ago. However, tucked away in the mind-numbing pages, there is one selection that does interest me. It's buried under a previous heading called "VIEW FINANCIAL" which leads to another tab called "TAX FORMS."

See, twenty years ago, around Christmas—a time when callers tend to rediscover their family drama and temporarily lose interest in harassing county employees—I was going through the layers of DHRMIS, dissecting its dark secrets, when I made a discovery. Under the file titled "1972 TAX INFO," I expected the usual list of mundane expenses that would make an auditor salivate (staples, $5.00; toner, $3.00; paper clips, $0.55…), but embedded in the list of office supplies was an option which read "RELEASE ALL."

In neon green all-caps, of course.

I blinked a couple times until I realized what it meant. I glanced over my shoulder to make sure my mysterious and rarely-seen Shoggoth-esque supervisor wasn't lurking nearby, waiting to see what I was looking up on a county computer that could barely connect to the internet.

I placed my cursor beside the 'release option' and pressed F-11, the black-and-green page shifted to a screen which read: "ENTER AUTHORIZATION."

I rifled through my desk drawer, seeking the steno pad upon which I'd written the last ten years' worth of nonsensical password. There it was, stained in coffee and sticky with crumbs, the code: Az@th0th$55. Ah, Azathoth, right. The Outer God sleeping at the center of our department's record-keeping software.

I snorted.

Clearly some undersexed IT nerd had dreamed that one up.

I typed in the arcane password and hit F-11. The screen blinked. "AUTHORIZATION APPROVED."

The next page had one line of green text. It read: "RELEASE ALL. CERTIFY? Y/N," followed by an underscore in which the user could enter their choice and confirm.

Or chicken out.

When I discovered this secret, I poured myself some hard eggnog and vowed that on my last day of work, if I still hadn't received the acknowledgement I deserved, I'd select 'YES' and see what happened. Because once I was retired, the outcome would no longer be my problem.

So, I waited.

Now, it's nearly midnight, twenty years later. Time's up. My last midnight working for the county and still no signed card, no gold wristwatch, not even a phone call to congratulate me on a career well-spent.

Nothing.

Well, it appears the higher-ups have made my Big Decision for me.

My fingers tremble as I begin the keystrokes through the DHRMIS menus. I suppose it's criminal how eager I am to release hell on the denizens of this shitty county and the even shittier public who've made *my* life hell. A film of sweat makes my rayon blouse cling to my skin. My breath quickens like it does before a solo orgasm. (Oh, believe me, I have a lot of experience in *that* department because of this job's graveyard shift hours).

When I reach the list of tax forms, I'm practically panting with anticipation. I'm just about to select the one for 1972, when my gray plastic phone rings, stopping me short.

Blerrp. Blerrp. A red-light strobes along with the bleating tone. *Blerrp. Blerrp.*

I grimace. *Do I* really *have to answer that?*

I've less than ten minutes of employment, and I have a couple hundred monsters to unleash.

What the hell, I figure, *it could be my last ever call with the Department of Horrors.*

A combination of habit and sentiment forces me to answer on the last ring. Who knows? Maybe it's the *coup de grace* from HR, giving me some token validation for all my years of service.

Or something.

I adopt my most ingratiating tone and start to say, "Hello and thank you for calling the—"

"Took you long enough to answer," a man snarls. "Don't know why my taxes pay for *your* job. You county slobs don't do shit."

"Sir, please do not address me like—"

"Bitch, quit whining. I got a real problem here. There's a scary-assed monster running around my street. It's got all kinds of tentacles and suckers and shit."

I sigh. "I see. How may I—"

"For starters, you can shut up and do your job. Get your fat-ass down here ASAP and clean this shit up." The caller rattles off an address, without bothering to confirm it. "And step on it, Fatty."

The line goes dead.

I smile to myself as I replace the buzzing phone in its cradle.

Yup, should've let that one go to voicemail.

I glance at the old black-and-white analog clock that has swallowed up seventy-thousand hours of my life. Seven more minutes until I'm done with this place. Forever.

A sudden jubilance lifts my flabby spirits. For thirty-five years I've dealt with similar callers: cruel, impatient, demeaning, and rude. For thirty-five years I've endured the talking down, the attitude, the entitlement, the superiority.

I'm done with that crap.

I guess this is what happens after spending too many nights speaking with the caged Nyarlathotep; that would do weird things to anyone's mind.

I don't bother logging the angry caller's complaint. Let my replacement, Alanna, handle it on Monday—along with all the other monsters about to flood the streets. In a couple minutes, it won't matter. I'm headed straight to the Arkham County Airport after this. My packed suitcase waits for me in my modest '82 Chevy Spectrum.

I couldn't ever afford a new car. Couldn't afford much of anything on my county-employee salary as a dispatcher for the Department of Horrors. All work and no play, makes Susan one crazy lady.

Har har har.

I login to DHRMIS and follow the keystrokes to the RELEASE page. I enter a Y in the last blinking underscore and gleefully strike F-11. Instead of all the blaring alarms and flashing lights I'd expected, a note pops up on screen. It has Arthur Goodwin's County tagline: agood13 and it's dated a day before I began working for the county back in 'eighty-six.

Congrats on your retirement, Susan. At least, I presume you're ready to retire since you've opted to activate the release option. I knew you'd find it eventually. I know this seems tempting, but I beg you not to. I never did and I urge you not to throw away our combined century of service with the county. Think of the innocent public we serve. I trust you'll make the right decision.

Professionally your,

Arthur K. Goodwin.

Curious, I push up my thick glasses and, leaning in, read:
Jesus Christ, what a fastidious little prick!

What innocents did Arthur ever interact with? Had we even *worked* for the same department?

That prissy note heightens my annoyance. Just because Arthur didn't have the balls to do this release because he was a rule-following, goody two-shoes, model employee, doesn't mean I have to follow his perfect example, with which I've struggled for the past thirty-five goddam years!

No, I've put in too many long years of belittlement and shit-taking from the same precious 'innocent public' that Arthur adored. His simpering note only stokes my desire for revenge. I decide to continue and satisfaction at defying Arthur swells in me since that twat represented the entire county's superficial veneer and all that I hate about working here.

My finger jabs F-11, forcing my way past Arthur's note. The green-and-black screen reads, "FINAL RELEASE Y/N?"

I grin, hit Y and F-11 one last time.

"CONFIRMED" the screen announces in blocky green all-caps.

A half-second later, all the alarms in the squat concrete building start blaring and whooping, augmenting the gleeful cacophony of liberated Horrors now flooding the hallways, stampeding toward the exits. I smile, savoring the symphony of hisses, clicks and clucks, whispers, snarls, and buzzes. Their combined cries rise in a clamoring crescendo as the twisted, nightmarish, slimy, ghoulish, winged, and tentacled tenants find themselves free to cause all manner of malfeasance.

Absurd pleasure floods through me to hear the combined voices of all the monsters, horrors, and minor eldritch gods I've spent decades getting to know. I realize, over my career, I've probably spent more time with the Horrors than with other people.

Oh well.

Naturally, all DoH employees have drilled for an incident like this— maybe a dozen times over the decades. I know all the "safe" escape routes. Despite the affection I've gained for the Horrors over our decades-long co-residence in this office, I've no intention of meeting my captives face-to-face.

Prisoners never take kindly to their jailers.

No, I'd rather let them have their fun with Arkham County while I enjoy my retirement.

It seems only fair.

I wait at my desk until their cacophony dwindles. Once I'm sure I'm alone in the DoH building, I calmly log out of my computer and unclip my County ID Badge, leaving it on the keyboard. I don't bother clocking out. I'm *way* past caring what Jenny in HR thinks of me. Besides, it's not like I expect to get paid for today.

I am retired. And now I'm part of the mythos.

Swinging my purse over my shoulder, I stride down the eerily quiet hallway, past all the empty cages. Every single Horror, collected over the decades, is loose on the charming streets of Arkham.

I can almost hear the screams, the ensuing chaos.

The thought warms my dead heart.

Already, behind me, my phone starts ringing. *Blerrp. Blerrp.*

I sneer and keep walking toward the parking lot. Let Alanna, my replacement—that bright-eyed teenager—deal with the mess when she starts work on Monday.

I snicker to think of the decades of drudgery ahead of her. No more perky smiles for you, hon.

Welcome to the Department of Horrors.

ACKNOWLEDGMENTS

Dragon's Roost Press would like to extend our deepest gratitude to the following:

Thank you to all of the authors who submitted your work. We've said it many times: the best part about putting together an anthology is getting to read amazing stories and then share them with the world.

Thank you to the friends and family of our authors who gave them the time and support needed to allow their creativity to manifest.

Thank you to K.H. Koehler for another incredible cover. We are deeply indebted.

Thank you to all of you who support the Kickstarter Campaign associated with this publication, including:

Maggie B

Traci Belanger

Nick Botic

Brian Burgoyne

Bret Burks

Sal Cottrell

Croik

C & C Dauvin

Lekden Davis

Dead Fish Books

Eileen

Jessie Van Esselstyn

Colleen Feeney

Caroline Flore

Mark R. Froom

Dave Gonzalez

Damon Griffin

Peter F. Guenther

M. T. Hall

Nathan Harris

Chris Jarocha-Ernst

Anna & Josh Kaput

Walter Koegel

Ethan L

Phillip A. Leavenworth

Casey Letendre

Tim Lonegan

Sven & Carolyn Lugar

Andy McAllister

Daniel McCullough

Dylan Mooney

Richard O'Shea

Ruth Ann Orlansky

Karen Ovér

Owens

Matthew Plank

Radar's Game Room

Jason Ramer

Solomon Stone Romney

Casey J Rudkin

Will Sampson

Sarah Schadegg

D Scheirer

Sean

Settle

Mason Settle

Alissa Sharp

The Steiners

Nicholas Stephenson

Quinn Swain-Nisbet

Patrick Toner

Trip Space-Parasite

Bryan Tyner

Hailee Vandale

Charli Widynowski

Dr. Carl Willis-Ford

ABOUT THE AUTHORS

Alexandr Bond (One Night in Arkham) has been writing since he was nine years old, often writing down stories rather than taking notes in school. He has a love for all kinds of horror and his work has been published by *Cosmic Horror Monthly, Sinister Smile Press*, and *Horrorsmith Publishing*. More can be found at https://alexandrbond. wordpress.com and on his X: @A_Bond_Author

He is legally blind and albino and has received his BA in English/Creative Writing from Southern New Hampshire University. When not writing, he spends his time reading and learning and has traveled throughout the continental United States but currently resides in North Carolina with his family, including six lazy cats, a sixteen year old dog, and a new puppy.

Willard Brannen (he/him) (What Our Fathers Wrought) is a bisexual author who lives with his partner in Salt Lake City, UT. Born in Florida, his love of reading and writing started young and was fostered by his parents throughout his teenage years. His mother still keeps a collection of stories he wrote as a child.

His love of storytelling has led to creating a world of his own to run TTRPG campaigns in, where he likes to tackle difficult subjects with friends, and believes in role play as a form of therapy. His love of horror began as a teenager and has only grown in adulthood.

Jason P. Burnham (The Sewage Treatment Pond) loves to spend time with his wife, children, and dog. He's never had a neck rash after spending time by the river.

Mia Dalia (Books of the Dead) is an internationally published, CWA-nominated author of all things fantastic, thrilling, scary, and strange.

Short fiction credits: online in *Night Terror Novels, 50-word stories, Flash Fiction Magazine, Pyre Magazine, Tales from the Moonlit Path, carte blanche magazine* and in print anthologies by Sunbury Press, HellBound Press, Black Ink Fiction, Dragon Roost Press, Unsettling Reads, Moon, Anthology of Lunar Horror, Phobica Books, PsychoToxin Press, Wandering Wave Press, Bullet Points vol. 3, Critical Blast, Sinister Smile Press, DraculaBeyondStoker Magazine, Mystery Magazine, Exploding Head Press, Headshot Press, Zoetic Press' Alphanumeric, Off-Topic Publishing, RebellionLIT Press, Nightshade Press. Her story, "Dig" was selected as one of Tales to Terrify ten best tales of 2023. Her story, "The Last Best Thing" was shortlisted for the 2024 Crime Writers Association's Daggers Award.

Upcoming short fiction publication in anthologies by Grendel Press, Crystal Lake Entertainment, Jaded Ibis Press, and more.

Novellas: *Tell Me a Story* and *Discordant* (PTP, reprinted by Anuci Press); *Arrokoth* (Spaceboy Books)

Upcoming: *Do You Know The Muffin Man?* (Spaceboy Books)

Novels: *Estate Sale* (Black Ink Fiction); *Haven* (CamCat Books)

Collections: *Smile So Red and Other Tales of Madness* (Anuci Press)

Find her at:

Official website: https://daliaverse.wixsite.com/author

Twitter: @ Dalia_Verse

FB: DaliaVerse

Instagram: daliaverse

https://linktr.ee/daliaverse

E. N. Dauvin (One More Bite) lives in rural Saskatchewan with her husband, cats and horses. When not writing, she is studying for her horticulture certificate, working in the garden, and trying to keep up with too many hobbies. She writes short stories and is trying to focus on novels, when the weeds aren't growing faster than her pumpkins. Her work has appeared in *Things With Feathers: Stories of Hope*, and *Creepy Podcast Patreon*.

Jonathan Louis Duckworth (Aquamarine Alert) is a completely normal, entirely human person with the right number of heads and everything. He received his MFA from Florida International University and his PhD from University of North Texas. He is the author of *Have You Seen the Moon Tonight? & Other Rumors* (JournalStone Publishing) and his work appears in *Best American Science Fiction & Fantasy*, *Vastarien, Pseudopod, Fantasy & Science Fiction, Beneath Ceaseless Skies*, and elsewhere. He is an active HWA member.

Asher Ellis (Adjustments) is a screenwriter, educator, and author of the novels *The Remedy, PET, Curse of the Pigman, Cracker Jack*, and *The Therapy*. He has written multiple award-winning short films, including *My Name Is Art*, which was featured in Amazon.com's first annual All Voices Film Festival, celebrating underrepresented communities. His short fiction includes the story, "Expertise," which was among the award winners in the Writer's Digest Thriller Competition, judged by the best-selling author of *First Blood* and creator of Rambo, David Morrell. Asher currently lives near the Connecticut River, residing in Vermont and working in New Hampshire as the Library Director at an independent boarding school.

Lucas Franki (The Cat Whisperer in Darkness) is a freelance science writer/editor living in southern Pennsylvania. He has a BA in English from Penn State University and is an Eagle Scout. He's had short stories published in *The Helix* magazine as well as in the anthologies *Burning Down The House: Crime Fiction Incited by the Songs of the Talking Head*s published in April 2024 by Shotgun Honey and *LOLcraft: A Compendium of Eldritch Humor* published by Dragon's Roost Press.

David Gonzalez (No Questions Asked) is a high school dropout, lifelong blue collar technician, and truck driver, also somewhat successful, patent holding inventor, currently working in the movie industry as a Key Grip. He lives near Los Angeles with a lovely and very patient fiancee and two small dogs of a significantly less patient demeanor. Hobbies include medieval fighting, post-apocalyptic camping, and ski-biking. He is currently (temporarily?) unpublished.

Sarah Hans (U.S. Fish and Wildlife Service Inspection Report No. IF-32651) is an award-winning writer, editor, artist, and teacher whose stories have appeared in more than 40 publications, including *Apex Magazine* and *Pseudopod*. Her most recent project is the cat-filled horror novella *Asylum*; she previously published the bug-filled horror novel *Entomophobia*, the demonic dark fantasy novella *An Ideal Vessel*, and two short fiction collections, *Dead Girls Don't Love* and *Chorus of Whispers*. She lives in Ohio with her partner, an amazing kid, more pets than she can afford, and enough craft supplies to keep her busy for the next 200 years.

Sam Harris (The Old Gods' Banker) is a writer, teacher, and sometime archaeologist currently living in the Midwest with his wife, two children, and many books. His other work has appeared or is forthcoming in *Strange Horizons, Pseudopod, Apex, Lightspeed*, and elsewhere.

Henry Herz's (Billington's Wood Befouled) stories will/have appear(ed) in *Daily Science Fiction, Weird Tales, Pseudopod, Metastellar,*

Titan Books, Highlights for Children, Ladybug Magazine, and anthologies from Albert Whitman & Co., Blackstone Publishing, Brigids Gate Press, Air and Nothingness Press, Baen Books, and elsewhere. He's edited seven anthologies and written twelve picture books. www.henryherz.com.

Liam Hogan (Colour Out of Nothing) is an award-winning short story writer, with stories in *Best of British Science Fiction* and in *Best of British Fantasy* (NewCon Press). He helps host the live literary event Liars' League and volunteers at the creative writing charity Ministry of Stories. More details at http://happyendingnotguaranteed.blogspot.co.uk

Emily Lowery (Arkham Music Hall) is a 26 year old born and raised in Phoenix, Arizona. She currently works as a full time surgical nurse and is an author focusing on the fantasy and horror genres. Sharing stories with her friends and family has always been a beloved pastime whether it be movies, television shows, or books. She lives with her husband and two french bulldogs, who are her greatest loves. When she isn't absorbing the fictional stories of others, she is traveling to see as much of the world as she can and make some true stories of her own.

D. Marmara (she/her) (Licensing) was born and reared in Midwestern USA and now lives in southern California. She has an affinity for science, horror, and the macabre. A former researcher, she now works in laboratory safety. Her work can be found in *Xanax Hamster* and *Cosmic Horror Monthly*.

Jake Matthews (The Pupils of Dr Vogt) lives under a bridge in Michigan, surrounded by old bones and neon skulls. In his free time, he enjoys fossil hunting, cryptid hunting, and the occasional stout. He is previously unpublished, but he has been annoying his imaginary friends with stories for the last three decades.

K.G. McAbee (Eldritch Edge Promotions) writes fantasy, horror, science fiction, mystery, Westerns, steampunk and pulp. She's had short stories in more than a dozen anthologies, including Broken Eye Books' *Welcome to Miskatonic University*, Moonstone Books' *Chicks in Capes*, Bloodbound Books' *Unspeakable*, and Rogue Planet Press' *Of Poets, Spies, and Unearthliness*. She's currently writing the Cyborg Squad series for Raven Tale Press, and the Jake Lazarus series for Dusty Saddle Press. She's won several awards for her writing, including the Dream Realm for fantasy and the Black Orchid for mystery. She lives in a 200-year-old log cabin full of books in the middle of the woods in upstate SC, on property haunted by the ghost of a young woman killed in the Revolutionary War. She really hates writing about herself in 1st person but hates 3rd person even more. Check out her work at https://linktr.ee/kgmwriter.

Elizabeth McEntee (Damp Envelopes) is a writer, musician, artist, and puppeteer currently based in Albany, NY. She loves to write about characters who have idiosyncratic views of the world. She is currently writing her first novel.

Clancy Nacht (Light & Power) is a bisexual genderqueer person who lives in Austin. Clancy has published several bestselling romantic suspense novels. Many of her books have been honored with Rainbow Awards; *Le Jazz Hot* won for Best Bisexual/Transgender Romance & Erotic Romance. In 2015, *Gemini* won an Honorable Mention for Gay Romantic Suspense and in 2016, *Strange Times* won an Honorable Mention for Science Fiction. *Wyatt's Recipes for Wooing Rock Stars* was a finalist in the highly competitive William Neale Award for Best Gay Contemporary Romance. *The Phisher King* won second place in the Rainbow Award for Romantic Suspense, 16th for Gay Book of the Year.

Tim O'Neal (Midnight at the Department of Horrors) is an Associate Member of the SFWA. He has sold over 20 short stories to various indie horror publications. Recent markets include: the British Science Fiction Association's *Fission #2 vol 1*, D&T Publishing via *Godless*, and

Planet Bizarro Press. His story "Face Thieves" won first place in *Page Turner Magazine*'s 2021 writing contest. Tim has held his share of dreadful jobs. As a dietitian, he spent several years working for a county Public Health Department, much like the one depicted in this story. Currently, he's working on a PhD in Exercise and Nutrition Science in Washington, DC.

Here's a link to Tim's Amazon Author Page: https://www.amazon.com/stores/Tim-ONeal/author/B07RN9JSQ3.

Jacob Henry Orloff (Something's In The Water) writes predominantly in the horror genre and is currently working on a collection of short fiction to be released in the near future. He resides in South Carolina with his wife and six cats.

Karen Ovér (The Green Act) is back in Texas after more than a decade in New York City. Her latest works appear in the anthologies *Bubble Off-Plumb*, *From a Cat's View Volumes I* and *II*, *The Book of Carnacki*, *Two Thousand Word Terrors*, and *The Legion Press*. Visit her author pages at: balletsandbogeys.weebly.com/golemwerks and https://www.facebook.com/KarenOverAuthor/

When not in the midst of wrestling the cat for the keyboard, (and dealing with persistent feline editing) she can sometimes be found clinging to a ballet barre, attempting to realign the vertebrae sent in all directions by hours of maniacal word processing.

Daniel Powell (His Time Is Nigh) teaches a variety of writing courses at Florida State College at Jacksonville, where he lives with his wife and children near Florida's Intracoastal Waterway. His stories have appeared in *Redstone Science Fiction*, *Buzzy Mag*, *Something Wicked Magazine*, *Dead but Dreaming 2*, and *Brain Harvest*, among other publications.

Willow Redd (What Happened in Room 201) is a filmmaker, paranormal investigator, and writer from Eastern North Carolina. She has been writing and creating all her life and can best be described as "terminally online." Willow lives with her cat, a tortie with an attitude problem, and when not writing she can usually be found watching horror films or RPG liveplays.

You can find Willow online in most places @warriorwitchwillow

Patrick Rutigliano (Tailor-made) resides in Indiana with his wife and a medically challenged cat. His collection *Wind Chill* was published by Crystal Lake Publishing in 2016. Patrick's most recent book, *The Last Look*, was published by Bleeding Edge Books in 2023.

Chris Settle (Wasted) is an author from Oklahoma. He studied at Oklahoma State University, and has since written in a variety of genres, including creative non-fiction and poetry. However, horror will always be his favorite, ever since he first stumbled on to *At the Mountains of Madness*. He hopes to expand the genre of Lovecraftian horror to include climate fiction and awareness.

DRAGON'S ROOST PRESS

Dragon's Roost Press is the fever dream brainchild of dark speculative fiction author Michael Cieslak. Since 2014, their goal has been to find the best speculative fiction authors and share their work with the public. For more information about Dragon's Roost Press and their publications, please visit:

http://www.thedragonsroost.biz

LAST DAY DOG RESCUE

Last Day is more than just a name, it's the situation all the dogs were faced with. Because of LDDR these wonderful dogs get another chance at life. All dogs coming into their rescue were saved from high-kill animal shelters or being sold for research.

A Little About LDDR:

Last Day Dog Rescue is an ALL volunteer based organization. They do not have a physical location; all of their dogs are placed in the care of foster homes until they are adopted.

The group focuses on rescuing dogs from the "Urgent" list in shelters and pounds across lower Michigan and parts of Ohio with an emphasis on those shelters who euthanize by gas or those shelters who sell the dogs in their care to research labs where they are used for barbaric and most times painful testing and experiments. They hold a special place in their hearts for the big and black dogs, even 'ugly' dogs (whom they don't find ugly at all!) and the special senior dogs. These dogs most often get overlooked and passed up in shelters and pounds everywhere for puppies, small breeds, and the "prettier," lighter colored dogs.

Dogs found in shelters are there for many reasons; some are owner surrenders, strays, cruelty or abuse cases, and some dogs are found abandoned, left to fend for themselves in vacant homes, fields, ditches, and some have even been tied out in the woods and left to starve. Last Day Dog Rescue does not discriminate and feels that each of these dogs, no matter their size, age, color, or the reason they are there, deserve a second chance at life...they help all those they can.

Donations via check and money orders:

Last Day Dog Rescue

P.O. Box 51935

Livonia, MI 48151-5935

Donations also accepted via PayPal:

http://www.lastdaydogrescue.org/info/

www.ingramcontent.com/pod-product-compliance
Lightning Source LLC
Chambersburg PA
CBHW072339020726
47506CB00004B/937